The Haunters & The Haunted

by

Ed. Ernest Rhys

Double 9
BOOKS

The Haunters & The Haunted
by Ed. Ernest Rhys

ISBN: 978-93-69072-60-6

Published by

DOUBLE 9 BOOKS
2/13-B, Ansari Road
Daryaganj, New Delhi – 110002
info@double9books.com
www.double9books.com
Tel. 011-40042856

ABOUT THE EDITOR

Ernest Percival Rhys was a Welsh-English writer, renowned for his contribution to literature as the founding editor of the Everyman's Library series, which made classic works of literature more accessible. Born on July 17, 1859, in Islington, London, he had a diverse literary career that spanned essays, stories, poetry, novels, and plays. Rhys was deeply involved in the literary culture of his time, offering both original works and edited collections that brought together various voices in literature. His most notable achievement was the creation of the Everyman's Library series, which became highly influential by making high-quality literary works available to a broader audience. Rhys also contributed to the genre of ghost stories and supernatural fiction, with "The Haunters & The Haunted" being one of his key works in this area. He was married to Edith Rhys, and they had a daughter, Megan Rhys. Rhys's literary legacy endures through his editing work and his contributions to a wide range of genres. He passed away on May 25, 1946, in London at the age of 86.

CONTENTS

II GHOST STORIES FROM LOCAL RECORDS, FOLK LORE AND LEGEND

III OMENS AND PHANTASMS

INTRODUCTION

In this Ghost Book, M. Larigot, himself a writer of supernatural tales, has collected a remarkable batch of documents, fictive or real, describing the one human experience that is hardest to make good. Perhaps the very difficulty of it has rendered it more tempting to the writers who have dealt with the subject. His collection, notably varied and artfully chosen as it is, yet by no means exhausts the literature, which fills a place apart with its own recognised classics, magic masters, and dealers in the occult. Their testimony serves to show that the forms by which men and women are haunted are far more diverse and subtle than we knew. So much so, that one begins to wonder at last if every person is not liable to be "possessed." For, lurking under the seeming identity of these visitations, the dramatic differences of their entrances and appearances, night and day, are so marked as to suggest that the experience is, given the fit temperament and occasion, inevitable.

One would even be disposed, accepting this idea, to bring into the account, as valid, stories and pieces of literature not usually accounted part of the ghostly canon. There are the novels and tales whose argument is the tragedy of a haunted mind. Such are Dickens' *Haunted Man*, in which the ghost is memory; Hawthorne's *Scarlet Letter*, in which the ghost is cruel conscience; and Balzac's *Quest of the Absolute*, in which the old Flemish house of Balthasar Claes, in the Rue de Paris at Douai, is haunted by a dæmon more potent than that of Canidia. One might add some of Balzac's shorter stories, among them "The Elixir"; and some of Hawthorne's *Twice-Told Tales*, including "Edward Randolph's Portrait." On the French side we might note too that terrible graveyard tale of Guy de Maupassant, *La Morte*, in which the lover who has lost his beloved keeps vigil at her grave by night in his despair, and sees—dreadful resurrection—"que toutes les tombes étaient ouvertes, et tous les cadavres en étaient sortis." And why? That they might efface the lying legends inscribed on their tombs, and replace them with the actual truth. Villiers de l'Isle Adam has in his *Contes Cruels* given us the strange story of Véra, which may be read as a companion study to *La Morte*, with another recall from the dead to end a lover's obsession. Nature and supernature cross in de l'Isle Adam's mystical drama *Axël* a play which will never hold the stage, masterly attempt as it is to dramatise the inexplainable mystery.

Among later tales ought to be reckoned Edith Wharton's *Tales of Men and Ghosts*, and Henry James's *The Two Magics*, whose "Turn of the Screw" gives us new instances of the evil genii that haunt mortals, in this case two innocent children. One remembers sundry folk-tales with the same motive—of children bewitched or forespoken—inspiring them. And an old charm in Orkney which used to run:

> "Father, Son, Holy Ghost!
> Bitten sall they be,
> Bairn, wha have bitten thee!
> Care to their black vein,
> Till thou hast thy health again!
> Mend thou in God's name!"

John Aubrey in his *Miscellanies* has many naïve evidences of the twilight region of consciousness, like that between wake and sleep, which tends to fade when we are wideawake; so much so, that we call it visionary. Yet it is very real to the haunted folk, to Aubrey's correspondent, the Rector of Chedzoy, or to the false love of the Demon Lover, or that Mr Bourne of whom Glanvil tells in *The Iron Chest of Durley*, or the Bishop Evodius who was St Augustine's friend, or for that matter the son of Monica himself. The reality of these visitations may seem dim, but the most sceptical of us cannot doubt that, whether from some quickened fear of death or impending disaster, from evil conscience or swift intensification of vision; whether in the forms of beloved sons lost at sea or of other revenants who were held indispensably dear in life, the haunters have appeared, to the absolute belief of those who saw them or their simulacra.

"It poseth me," said Richard Baxter, "to think of what kind these visitants are. Do good spirits dwell then so near us, or are they sent on such messages?" The question, indeed, poseth most of us, but we cannot leave the inquiry alone. M. Larigot, realising this preoccupation, has in the course of his investigations, during many years, arrived at the conclusion that there is an Art of the Supernatural, apart from the difficult science of psychical research, worth cultivating for its own sake. So he has gone to Glanvil and Arise Evans and the credulous old books—to Edgar Poe and Lord Lytton and the modern writers who tell supernatural tales. He gives us their material without positing its unquestionable effect as police-court evidence, and if we recognise its artistic interest, he does not mind much if we say at last with one great visionary, "Hoc est illusionum." But into those realms of illusion we ought not, if he is right, to enter lightly. Those who do enter there are warned that, having done so, they will not remain the same; they become aware of what Eugenius meant, who said:

"I am unbody'd by thy Books, and Thee,
And in thy papers find my Extasie;
Or if I please but to descend a strain,
Thy Elements do screen my Soul again.

I can undress myself by thy bright Glass,
And then resume th' Inclosure, as I was.
Now I am Earth, and now a Star, and then
A Spirit: now a Star, and earth again ..."

We see that there is another aspect to the occultation of Orion, and a very ominous one. Aurelius appeared to St. Augustine and made clear a dark passage to him in his reading, and that great Divine and Father of the Church knew it to be an enlightenment from above. But what of the other visitants from regions that are unblessed? Paracelsus has taught us to be careful in our dealings with the realities and the phantasies, as he would conceive them, of the other world; for "under the Earth do wander half-men." And there are other and worse manifestations due to Black Magic or Nigromancy, and to the black witches and white and the false sorcerers who have violently intruded into the true mystery—"like swine broken into a delicate Garden." Against these subtle and powerful magicians no weapons, coats of mail, or brigandines will help, no shutting of doors or locks; for they penetrate through all things, and all things are open to them.

Writing as a physician, Paracelsus sought to anticipate by his *Celestial Medicine* and his *Twelve Signs* the whole mystery of healing, and the cure of the troubled souls and bodies of men and women, which are not accorded but at odds with nature and supernature. The spirits of discord are indeed always with us; and whether you see them as witches, disguised in the living human form, or as monstrous and terrifying dream-figures, or as floating impalpable atmospheres, they are vigilantly to be guarded against. We know

"Vervain and dill
Hinders witches from their will!"

in the old herbals; but we need new drugs. As for that witch which hath haunted all of us, "Maladicta," Lilly in his *Astrology* has a remedy. "Take unguentum populeum, and Vervain and Hypericon, and put a red-hot iron into it: You must anoint the back-bone, or wear it in your breast."

The haunting apparitions are not all of earth. Cornelius Agrippa, in his book of the Secret Doctrine, shows that they are astral too. The familiar spirits of Mars, in his account, are no lovelier than Macbeth's witches:—
"They appear in a tall body, cholerick, a filthy countenance, of colour brown,

swarthy or red, having horns, like Harts' Horns, and gryphon's claws, and bellowing like wild Bulls."

But the spirits of Mercury are delightful. They indeed are "of colour clear and bright, like unto a knight armed, — and the motion of them is as it were silver-coloured clouds." So, if Mars has troubled the world, as in the unhappy history of our own time, we must hope for the brighter forms, and the remedial and aerial messengers of Mercury.

We may seem to have strayed from the proper boundaries in going so far. But it is one of the offices of this book to widen the area of research, and relate the ghost-story anew to the whole literature of wonder and imagination. Such sagas as that which Dr Douglas Hyde has translated with consummate art from the Irish, "Teig O'Kane and the Corpse," which Mr W.B. Yeats called a little masterpiece; or Boccaccio's story of the spectre-hounds that pulled down the daughter of Anastasio, or Scott's "Wandering Willie's Tale," or Hawker's "Cruel Coppinger," or Edgar Poe's "Fall of the House of Usher," are of their kind not to be beaten. And in their own way some of the later records are as telling. One can take the book as a text-book of the supernatural, or as a story-book of that middle world which has given us the ghosts that Homer and Shakespeare conjured up.

ERNEST RHYS.

I
GHOST STORIES FROM LITERARY SOURCES

I
THE FALL OF THE HOUSE OF USHER

By Edgar Allan Poe

Son cœur est un luth suspendu;
Sitôt qu'on le touche il résonne.

De Beranger.

During the whole of a dull, dark, and soundless day in the autumn of the year, when the clouds hung oppressively low in the heavens, I had been passing alone, on horseback, through a singularly dreary tract of country; and at length found myself, as the shades of the evening drew on, within view of the melancholy House of Usher. I know not how it was—but, with the first glimpse of the building, a sense of insufferable gloom pervaded my spirit. I say insufferable; for the feeling was unrelieved by any of that half-pleasurable, because poetic, sentiment with which the mind usually receives even the sternest natural images of the desolate or terrible. I looked upon the scene before me—upon the mere house, and the simple landscape features of the domain—upon the bleak walls—upon the vacant eye-like windows—upon a few rank sedges—and upon a few white trunks of decayed trees—with an utter depression of soul which I can compare to no earthly sensation more properly than to the after-dream of the reveller upon opium—the bitter lapse into everyday life—the hideous dropping off of the veil. There was an iciness, a sinking, a sickening of the heart—an unredeemed dreariness of thought which no goading of the imagination could torture into aught of the sublime. What was it—I paused to think—what was it that so unnerved me in the contemplation of the House of Usher? It was a mystery all insoluble; nor could I grapple with the shadowy fancies that crowded upon me as I pondered. I was forced to fall back upon the unsatisfactory conclusion, that while, beyond doubt, there *are* combinations of very simple natural objects which have the power of thus affecting us, still the analysis of this power lies among considerations beyond our depth. It was possible, I reflected, that a mere different arrangement of the particulars of the scene, of the details of the picture, would be sufficient to modify, or perhaps to annihilate its capacity for sorrowful impression; and, acting upon this idea, I reined my horse to the precipitous brink of a black and lurid tarn that lay in unruffled lustre by the dwelling, and gazed down—but with a shudder even more thrilling than before—upon the remodelled and inverted images of the grey sedge, and the ghastly tree-stems, and the vacant and eye-like windows.

Nevertheless, in this mansion of gloom I now proposed to myself a sojourn of some weeks. Its proprietor, Roderick Usher, had been one of my boon companions in boyhood; but many years had elapsed since our last meeting. A letter, however, had lately reached me in a distant part of the country—a letter from him—which, in its wildly importunate nature, had admitted of no other than a personal reply. The MS. gave evidence of nervous agitation. The writer spoke of acute bodily illness—of a mental disorder which oppressed him—and of an earnest desire to see me, as his best, and indeed his only personal friend, with a view of attempting, by the cheerfulness of my society, some alleviation of his malady. It was the manner in which all this, and much more, was said—it was the apparent *heart* that went with his request—which allowed me no room for hesitation; and I accordingly obeyed forthwith what I still considered a very singular summons.

Although, as boys, we had been even intimate associates, yet I really knew little of my friend. His reserve had been always excessive and habitual. I was aware, however, that his very ancient family had been noted, time out of mind, for a peculiar sensibility of temperament, displaying itself, through long ages, in many works of exalted art, and manifested, of late, in repeated deeds of munificent yet unobtrusive charity, as well as in a passionate devotion to the intricacies, perhaps even more than to the orthodox and easily recognisable beauties, of musical science. I had learned, too, the very remarkable fact, that the stem of the Usher race, all time-honoured as it was, had put forth, at no period, any enduring branch; in other words, that the entire family lay in the direct line of descent, and had always, with very trifling and very temporary variation, so lain. It was this deficiency, I considered, while running over in thought the perfect keeping of the character of the premises with the accredited character of the people, and while speculating upon the possible influence which the one, in the long lapse of centuries, might have exercised upon the other—it was this deficiency, perhaps, of collateral issue, and the consequent undeviating transmission, from sire to son, of the patrimony with the name, which had, at length, so identified the two as to merge the original title of the estate in the quaint and equivocal appellation of the "House of Usher"—an appellation which seemed to include, in the minds of the peasantry who used it, both the family and the family mansion.

I have said that the sole effect of my somewhat childish experiment— that of looking down within the tarn—had been to deepen the first singular impression. There can be no doubt that the consciousness of the rapid increase of my superstition—for why should I not so term it?—served mainly to accelerate the increase itself. Such, I have long known, is the paradoxical law of all sentiments having terror as a basis. And it might have been for this reason only, that, when I again uplifted my eyes to the house itself, from its image in the pool, there grew in my mind a strange fancy—a fancy so ridiculous, indeed, that I but mention it to show the vivid force of the sensations which oppressed me. I had so worked upon my imagination as really to believe that about the whole mansion and domain there hung an atmosphere peculiar to themselves and their immediate vicinity—an atmosphere which had no affinity with the air of heaven, but which had reeked up from the decayed trees, and the grey wall, and the silent tarn—a pestilent and mystic vapour, dull, sluggish, faintly discernible, and leaden-hued.

Shaking off from my spirit what *must* have been a dream, I scanned more narrowly the real aspect of the building. Its principal feature seemed to be that of an excessive antiquity. The discoloration of ages had been great. Minute *fungi* overspread the whole exterior, hanging in a fine tangled web-work from the eaves. Yet all this was apart from any extraordinary dilapidation. No portion of the masonry had fallen; and there appeared to be a wild inconsistency between its still perfect adaptation of parts, and the crumbling condition of the individual stones. In this there was much that reminded me of the specious totality of old woodwork which has rotted for long years in some neglected vault, with no disturbance from the breath of the external air. Beyond this indication of extensive decay, however, the fabric gave little token of instability. Perhaps the eye of a scrutinising observer might have discovered a barely perceptible fissure, which, extending from the roof of the building in front, made its way down the wall in a zigzag direction, until it became lost in the sullen waters of the tarn.

Noticing these things, I rode over a short causeway to the house. A servant in waiting took my horse, and I entered the Gothic archway of the hall. A valet, of stealthy step, thence conducted me, in silence, through many dark and intricate passages in my progress to the *studio* of his master. Much that I encountered on the way contributed, I know not how, to heighten the vague sentiments of which I have already spoken. While the objects around me—while the carvings of the ceilings, the sombre tapestries of the walls, the ebon blackness of the floors, and the phantasmagoric armorial trophies which rattled as I strode, were but matters to which, or to such as which, I had been accustomed from my infancy—while I hesitated not to acknowledge how familiar was all this—I still wondered to find how unfamiliar were the fancies which ordinary images were stirring up. On one of the staircases, I met the physician of the family. His countenance, I thought, wore a mingled expression of low cunning and perplexity. He accosted me with trepidation and passed on. The valet now threw open a door and ushered me into the presence of his master.

The room in which I found myself was very large and lofty. The windows were long, narrow, and pointed, and at so vast a distance from the black oaken floor as to be altogether inaccessible from within. Feeble gleams of encrimsoned light made their way through the trellised panes, and served to render sufficiently distinct the more prominent objects around; the eye, however, struggled in vain to reach the remoter angles of the chamber, or the recesses of the vaulted and fretted ceiling. Dark draperies hung upon the walls. The general furniture was profuse, comfortless, antique, and tattered. Many books and musical instruments lay scattered about, but failed to give any vitality to the scene. I felt that I breathed an atmosphere of sorrow. An air of stern, deep, and irredeemable gloom hung over and pervaded all.

Upon my entrance, Usher arose from a sofa on which he had been lying at full length, and greeted me with a vivacious warmth which had much in it, I at first thought, of an overdone cordiality—of the constrained effort of the *ennuyé* man of the world. A glance, however, at his countenance, convinced me of his perfect sincerity. We sat down; and for some moments, while he spoke not, I gazed upon him with a feeling half of pity, half of awe. Surely, man had never before so terribly altered, in so brief a period, as had Roderick Usher! It was with difficulty that I could bring myself to admit the identity of the wan being before me with the companion of my early boyhood. Yet the character of his face had been at all times remarkable. A cadaverousness of complexion; an eye large, liquid, and luminous beyond comparison; lips somewhat thin and very pallid, but of a surpassingly beautiful curve; a nose of a delicate Hebrew model, but with a breadth of nostril, unusual in similar formations; a finely moulded chin, speaking, in its want of prominence, of a want of moral energy; hair of a more than web-like softness and tenuity; these features, with an inordinate expansion above the regions of the temple, made up altogether a countenance not easily to be forgotten. And now in the mere exaggeration of the prevailing character of these features, and of the expression they were wont to convey, lay so much of change that I doubted to whom I spoke. The now ghastly pallor of the skin, and the now miraculous lustre of the eye, above all things startled and even awed me. The silken hair, too, had been suffered to grow all unheeded, and as, in its wild gossamer texture, it floated rather than fell about the face, I could not, even with effort, connect its arabesque expression with any idea of simple humanity.

In the manner of my friend I was at once struck with an incoherence—an inconsistency; and I soon found this to arise from a series of feeble and futile struggles to overcome an habitual trepidancy—an excessive nervous agitation. For something of this nature I had indeed been prepared, no less by his letter, than by reminiscences of certain boyish traits, and by conclusions deduced from his peculiar physical conformation and temperament. His action was alternately vivacious and sullen. His voice varied rapidly from a tremulous indecision (when the animal spirits seemed utterly in abeyance) to that species of energetic concision—that abrupt, weighty, unhurried, and hollow-sounding enunciation—that leaden, self-balanced and perfectly modulated guttural utterance, which may be observed in the lost drunkard, or the irreclaimable eater of opium, during the periods of his most intense excitement.

It was thus that he spoke of the object of my visit, of his earnest desire to see me, and of the solace he expected me to afford him. He entered, at some length, into what he conceived to be the nature of his malady. It was, he said, a constitutional and a family evil, and one for which he despaired to find a remedy—a mere nervous affection, he immediately added, which would undoubtedly soon pass on. It displayed itself in a host of unnatural sensations. Some of these, as he detailed them, interested and bewildered me; although, perhaps, the terms, and the general manner of the narration had their weight. He suffered much from a morbid acuteness of the senses; the most insipid food was alone endurable; he could wear only garments of certain texture; the odours of all flowers were oppressive; his eyes were tortured by even a faint light; and there were but peculiar sounds, and these from stringed instruments, which did not inspire him with horror.

To an anomalous species of terror I found him a bounden slave. "I shall perish," said he, "I *must* perish in this deplorable folly. Thus, thus, and not otherwise, shall I be lost. I dread the events of the future, not in themselves, but in their results. I shudder at the thought of any, even the most trivial, incident, which may operate upon this intolerable agitation of soul. I have, indeed, no abhorrence of danger, except in its absolute effect—in terror. In this unnerved—in this pitiable condition—I feel that the period will sooner or later arrive when I must abandon life and reason together, in some struggle with the grim phantasm, Fear."

I learned, moreover, at intervals, and through broken and equivocal hints, another singular feature of his mental condition. He was enchained by certain superstitious impressions in regard to the dwelling which he tenanted, and whence, for many years, he had never ventured forth—in regard to an influence whose supposititious force was conveyed in terms too shadowy here to be re-stated—an influence which some peculiarities in the mere form and substance of his family mansion, had, by dint of long sufferance, he said, obtained over his spirit—an effect which the *physique* of the grey walls and turrets, and of the dim tarn into which they all looked down, had, at length, brought about upon the *morale* of his existence.

He admitted, however, although with hesitation, that much of the peculiar gloom which thus afflicted him could be traced to a more natural and far more palpable origin—to the severe and long-continued illness—indeed to the evidently approaching dissolution—of a tenderly beloved sister—his sole companion for long years—his last and only relative on earth. "Her decease," he said, with a bitterness which I can never forget, "would leave him (him the hopeless and the frail) the last of the ancient race of the Ushers." While he spoke, the Lady Madeline (for so was she called) passed slowly through a remote portion of the apartment, and, without having noticed my presence, disappeared. I regarded her with an utter astonishment not unmingled with dread—and yet I found it impossible to account for such feelings. A sensation of stupor oppressed me, as my eyes followed her retreating steps. When a door, at length, closed upon her, my glance sought instinctively and eagerly the countenance of the brother—but he had buried his face in his hands, and I could only perceive that a far more than ordinary wanness had overspread the emaciated fingers through which trickled many passionate tears.

The disease of the Lady Madeline had long baffled the skill of her physicians. A settled apathy, a gradual wasting away of the person, and frequent although transient affections of a partially cataleptical character, were the unusual diagnosis. Hitherto she had steadily borne up against the pressure of her malady, and had not betaken herself finally to bed; but, on the closing in of the evening of my arrival at the house, she succumbed (as her brother told me at night with inexpressible agitation) to the prostrating power of the destroyer; and I learned that the glimpse I had obtained of her person would thus probably be the last I should obtain—that the lady, at least while living, would be seen by me no more.

For several days ensuing, her name was unmentioned by either Usher or myself: and during this period I was busied in earnest endeavours to alleviate the melancholy of my friend. We painted and read together; or I listened, as if in a dream, to the wild improvisations of his speaking guitar. And thus, as a closer and still closer intimacy admitted me more unreservedly into the recesses of his spirit, the more bitterly did I perceive the futility of all attempt at cheering a mind from which darkness, as if an inherent positive quality, poured forth upon all objects of the moral and physical universe, in one unceasing radiation of gloom.

I shall ever bear about me a memory of the many solemn hours I thus spent alone with the master of the House of Usher. Yet I should fail in any attempt to convey an idea of the exact character of the studies, or of the occupations, in which he involved me, or led me the way. An excited and highly distempered ideality threw a sulphureous lustre over all. His long improvised dirges will ring for ever in my ears. Among other things, I hold painfully in mind a certain singular perversion and amplification of the wild air of the last waltz of Von Weber. From the paintings over which his elaborate fancy brooded and which grew, touch by touch, into vagueness at which I shuddered the more thrillingly, because I shuddered knowing not why;—from these paintings (vivid as their images now are before me) I would in vain endeavour to educe more than a small portion which should lie within the compass of merely written words. By the utter simplicity, by the nakedness of his designs, he arrested and overawed attention. If ever mortal painted an idea, that mortal was Roderick Usher. For me at least— in the circumstances then surrounding me—there arose out of the pure abstractions which the hypochondriac contrived to throw upon his canvas, an intensity of intolerable awe, no shadow of which felt I ever yet in the contemplation of the certainly glowing yet too concrete reveries of Fuseli.

One of the phantasmagoric conceptions of my friend, partaking not so rigidly of the spirit of abstraction, may be shadowed forth, although feebly, in words. A small picture presented the interior of an immensely long and rectangular vault or tunnel, with low walls, smooth, white, and without interruption or device. Certain accessory points of the design served well to convey the idea that this excavation lay at an exceeding depth below the surface of the earth. No outlet was observed in any portion of its vast extent, and no torch, or other artificial source of light, was discernible; yet a flood of intense rays rolled throughout, and bathed the whole in a ghastly and inappropriate splendour.

I have just spoken of that morbid condition of the auditory nerve which rendered all music intolerable to the sufferer, with the exception of certain effects of stringed instruments. It was, perhaps, the narrow limits to which he thus confined himself upon the guitar, which gave birth, in great measure, to the fantastic character of his performances. But the fervid *facility* of his *impromptus* could not be so accounted for. They must have been, and were, in the notes, as well as in the words of his wild fantasias (for he not unfrequently accompanied himself with rhymed verbal improvisations), the result of that intense mental collectedness and concentration to which I have previously alluded as observable only in particular moments of the highest artificial excitement. The words of one of these rhapsodies I have easily remembered. I was, perhaps, the more forcibly impressed with it, as he gave it, because, in the under or mystic current of its meaning, I fancied that I perceived, and for the first time, a full consciousness on the part of Usher, of the tottering of his lofty reason upon her throne. The verses, which were entitled "The Haunted Palace," ran very nearly, if not accurately, thus:

I

In the greenest of our valleys,
By good angels tenanted
Once a fair and stately palace—
Radiant palace—reared its head.
In the monarch Thought's dominion—
It stood there!
Never seraph spread a pinion
Over fabric half so fair.

II

Banners yellow, glorious, golden,
On its roof did float and flow;
(This—all this—was in the olden
Time long ago)
And every gentle air that dallied,
In that sweet day,
Along the ramparts plumed and pallid,
A winged odour went away.

III

Wanderers in that happy valley
Through two luminous windows saw
Spirits moving musically
To a lute's well tunèd law,
Round about a throne, where sitting
(Porphyrogene!)
In state his glory well befitting,
The ruler of the realm was seen.

IV

And all with pearl and ruby glowing
Was the fair palace door,
Through which came flowing, flowing, flowing
And sparkling evermore,
A troop of Echoes whose sweet duty
Was but to sing,
In voices of surpassing beauty,
The wit and wisdom of their king.

V

But evil things, in robes of sorrow,
Assailed the monarch's high estate;
(Ah, let us mourn, for never morrow
Shall dawn upon him, desolate!)
And, round about his home, the glory
That blushed and bloomed
Is but a dim-remembered story
Of the old time entombed.

VI

And travellers now within that valley,
Through the red-litten windows, see
Vast forms that move fantastically
To a discordant melody;
While, like a rapid ghastly river,
Through the pale door,
A hideous throng rush out forever,
And laugh—but smile no more.

I well remember that suggestions arising from this ballad, led us into a train of thought wherein there became manifest an opinion of Usher's which I mention not so much on account of its novelty (for other men[1] have thought thus), as on account of the pertinacity with which he maintained it. This opinion, in its general form, was that of the sentience of all vegetable things. But, in his disordered fancy, the idea had assumed a more daring character, and trespassed, under certain conditions, upon the kingdom of inorganisation. I lack words to express the full extent, or the earnest *abandon* of his persuasion. The belief, however, was connected (as I have previously hinted) with the grey stones of the home of his forefathers. The conditions of the sentience had been here, he imagined, fulfilled in the method of collocation of these stones—in the order of their arrangement, as well as in that of the many *fungi* which overspread them, and of the decayed trees which stood around—above all, in the long undisturbed endurance of this arrangement, and in its reduplication in the still waters of the tarn. Its evidence—the evidence of the sentience—was to be seen, he said (and I here started as he spoke), in the gradual yet certain condensation of an atmosphere of their own about the waters and the walls. The result was discoverable, he added, in that silent, yet importunate and terrible influence which for centuries had moulded the destinies of his family, and which made *him* what I now saw him—what he was. Such opinions need no comment, and I will make none.

Our books—the books which, for years, had formed no small portion of the mental existence of the invalid—were, as might be supposed, in strict keeping with this character of phantasm. We pored together over such works as the *Ververt et Chartreuse* of Gresset; the *Belphegor* of Machiavelli; the *Heaven and Hell* of Swedenborg; the *Subterranean Voyage of Nicholas Klimm* by Holberg; the *Chiromancy* of Robert Flud, of Jean D'Indaginé, and of De la Chambre; the *Journey into the Blue Distance* of Tieck; and the *City of the Sun* of Campanella. One favourite volume was a small octavo edition of the *Directorium Inquisitorum*, by the Dominican Eymeric de Gironne; and there were passages in *Pomponius Mela*, about the old African Satyrs and Ægipans, over which Usher would sit dreaming for hours. His chief delight, however, was found in the perusal of an exceedingly rare and curious book in quarto Gothic—the manual of a forgotten church—the *Vigiliæ Mortuorum Chorum Ecclesiæ Maguntinæ*.

I could not help thinking of the wild ritual of this work, and of its probable influence upon the hypochondriac, when, one evening, having informed me abruptly that the Lady Madeline was no more, he stated his intention of preserving her corpse for a fortnight (previously to its final interment), in one of the numerous vaults within the main walls of the building. The worldly reason, however, assigned for this singular proceeding, was one which I did not feel at liberty to dispute. The brother had been led to his resolution (so he told me) by consideration of the unusual character of the malady of the deceased, of certain obtrusive and eager inquiries on the part of her medical men, and of the remote and exposed situation of the burial-ground of the family. I will not deny that when I called to mind the sinister countenance of the person whom I met upon the staircase, on the day of my arrival at the house, I had no desire to oppose what I regarded as at best but a harmless, and by no means an unnatural, precaution.

At the request of Usher, I personally aided him in the arrangements for the temporary entombment. The body having been encoffined, we two alone bore it to its rest. The vault in which we placed it (and which had been so long unopened that our torches, half smothered in its oppressive atmosphere, gave us little opportunity for investigation) was small, damp, and entirely without means of admission for light; lying, at great depth, immediately beneath that portion of the building in which was my own sleeping apartment. It had been used, apparently, in remote feudal times, for the worst purpose of a donjon-keep, and, in later days, as a place of deposit for powder, or some other highly combustible substance, as a portion of its floor, and the whole interior of a long archway through which we reached it, were carefully sheathed with copper. The door, of massive iron, had been, also, similarly protected. Its immense weight caused an unusually sharp grating sound as it moved upon its hinges.

Having deposited our mournful burden upon tressels within this region of horror, we partially turned aside the yet unscrewed lid of the coffin, and looked upon the face of the tenant. A striking similitude between the brother and sister now first arrested my attention; and Usher, divining, perhaps, my thoughts, murmured out some few words from which I learned that the deceased and himself had been twins, and that sympathies of a scarcely intelligible nature had always existed between them. Our glances, however, rested not long upon the dead—for we could not regard her unawed. The disease which had thus entombed the lady in the maturity of youth, had left, as usual in all maladies of a strictly cataleptical character, the mockery of a faint blush upon the bosom and the face, and that suspiciously lingering smile upon the lip which is so terrible in death. We replaced and screwed down the lid, and, having secured the door of iron, made our way, with toil, into the scarcely less gloomy apartments of the upper portion of the house.

And now, some days of bitter grief having elapsed, an observable change came over the features of the mental disorder of my friend. His ordinary manner had vanished. His ordinary occupations were neglected or forgotten. He roamed from chamber to chamber with hurried, unequal, and objectless step. The pallor of his countenance had assumed, if possible, a more ghastly hue—but the luminousness of his eye had utterly gone out. The once occasional huskiness of his tone was heard no more; and a tremulous quaver, as if of extreme terror, habitually characterised his utterance. There were times, indeed, when I thought his unceasingly agitated mind was labouring with some oppressive secret, to divulge which he struggled for the necessary courage. At times, again, I was obliged to resolve all into the mere inexplicable vagaries of madness, for I beheld him gazing upon vacancy for long hours, in an attitude of the profoundest attention, as if listening to some imaginary sound. It was no wonder that his condition terrified—that it infected me. I felt creeping upon me, by slow yet certain degrees, the wild influences of his own fantastic yet impressive superstitions.

It was, especially, upon retiring to bed late in the night of the seventh or eighth day after the placing of the Lady Madeline within the donjon, that I experienced the full power of such feelings. Sleep came not near my couch—while the hours waned and waned away. I struggled to reason off the nervousness which had dominion over me. I endeavoured to believe that much, if not all of what I felt, was due to the bewildering influence of the gloomy furniture of the room—of the dark and tattered draperies, which, tortured into motion by the breath of a rising tempest, swayed fitfully to and fro upon the walls, and rustled uneasily about the decorations of the bed. But my efforts were fruitless. An irrepressible tremor gradually pervaded my frame; and, at length, there sat upon my very heart an incubus of utterly causeless alarm. Shaking this off with a gasp and a struggle, I uplifted myself upon the pillows, and, peering earnestly within the intense darkness of the chamber, hearkened—I know not why, except that an instinctive spirit prompted me—to certain low and indefinite sounds which came, through the pauses of the storm, at long intervals, I knew not whence. Overpowered by an intense sentiment of horror, unaccountable yet unendurable, I threw on my clothes with haste (for I felt that I should sleep no more during the night), and endeavoured to arouse myself from the pitiable condition into which I had fallen, by pacing rapidly to and fro through the apartment.

I had taken but a few turns in this manner, when a light step on an adjoining staircase arrested my attention. I presently recognised it as that of Usher. In an instant afterward he rapped, with a gentle touch, at my door, and entered, bearing a lamp. His countenance was, as usual, cadaverously wan—but, moreover, there was a species of mad hilarity in his eyes—an evidently restrained *hysteria* in his whole demeanour. His air appalled me— but anything was preferable to the solitude which I had so long endured, and I even welcomed his presence as a relief.

"And you have not seen it?" he said abruptly, after having stared about him for some moments in silence—"you have not then seen it?—but, stay! you shall." Thus speaking, and having carefully shaded his lamp, he hurried to one of the casements, and threw it freely open to the storm.

The impetuous fury of the entering gust nearly lifted us from our feet. It was, indeed, a tempestuous yet sternly beautiful night, and one wildly singular in its terror and its beauty. A whirlwind had apparently collected its force in our vicinity; for there were frequent and violent alterations in the direction of the wind; and the exceeding density of the clouds (which hung so low as to press upon the turrets of the house) did not prevent our perceiving the lifelike velocity with which they flew careering from all points against each other, without passing away into the distance. I say that even their exceeding density did not prevent our perceiving this—yet we had no glimpse of the moon or stars—nor was there any flashing forth of the lightning. But the under surfaces of the huge masses of agitated vapour, as well as all terrestrial objects immediately around us, were glowing in the unnatural light of a faintly luminous and distinctly visible gaseous exhalation which hung about and enshrouded the mansion.

"You must not—you shall not behold this!" said I, shudderingly, to Usher, as I led him, with a gentle violence, from the window to a seat. "These appearances, which bewilder you, are merely electrical phenomena not uncommon—or it may be that they have their ghastly origin in the rank miasma of the tarn. Let us close this casement;—the air is chilling and dangerous to your frame. Here is one of your favourite romances. I will read, and you shall listen;—and so we will pass away this terrible night together."

The antique volume which I had taken up was the *Mad Trist* of Sir Launcelot Canning; but I had called it a favourite of Usher's more in sad jest than in earnest; for, in truth, there is little in its uncouth and unimaginative prolixity which could have had interest for the lofty and spiritual ideality of my friend. It was, however, the only book immediately at hand; and I indulged a vague hope that the excitement which now agitated the hypochondriac, might find relief (for the history of mental disorder is full of similar anomalies) even in the extremeness of the folly which I should read. Could I have judged, indeed, by the wild overstrained air of vivacity with which he hearkened, or apparently hearkened, to the words of the tale, I might well have congratulated myself upon the success of my design.

I had arrived at that well-known portion of the story where Ethelred, the hero of the Trist, having sought in vain for peaceable admission into the dwelling of the hermit, proceeds to make good an entrance by force. Here, it will be remembered, the words of the narrative run thus:

"And Ethelred, who was by nature of a doughty heart, and who was now mighty withal, on account of the powerfulness of the wine which he had drunken, waited no longer to hold parley with the hermit, who, in sooth, was of an obstinate and maliceful turn, but, feeling the rain upon his shoulders, and fearing the rising of the tempest, uplifted his mace outright, and, with blows, made quickly room in the plankings of the door for his gauntleted hand; and now pulling therewith sturdily, he so cracked and ripped, and tore all asunder, that the noise of the dry and hollow-sounding wood alarmed and reverberated throughout the forest."

At the termination of this sentence I started, and, for a moment, paused; for it appeared to me (although I at once concluded that my excited fancy had deceived me)—it appeared to me that, from some very remote portion of the mansion, there came, indistinctly, to my ears, what might have been, in its exact similarity of character, the echo (but a stifled and dull one certainly) of the very cracking and ripping sound which Sir Launcelot had so particularly described. It was, beyond doubt, the coincidence alone which had arrested my attention; for, amid the rattling of the sashes of the casements, and the ordinary commingled noises of the still increasing storm, the sound, in itself, had nothing, surely, which should have interested or disturbed me. I continued the story:

"But the good champion Ethelred, now entering within the door, was sore enraged and amazed to perceive no signal of the maliceful hermit; but, in the stead thereof, a dragon of a scaly and prodigious demeanour, and of a fiery tongue, which sate in guard before a palace of gold, with a floor of silver; and upon the wall there hung a shield of shining brass with this legend enwritten—

Who entereth herein, a conqueror hath bin;
Who slayeth the dragon, the shield he shall win;

and Ethelred uplifted his mace, and struck upon the head of the dragon, which fell before him, and gave up his pesty breath, with a shriek so horrid and harsh, and withal so piercing, that Ethelred had fain to close his ears with his hands against the dreadful noise of it, the like whereof was never before heard."

Here again I paused abruptly, and now with a feeling of wild amazement—for there could be no doubt whatever that, in this instance, I did actually hear (although from what direction it proceeded I found it impossible to say) a low and apparently distant, but harsh, protracted, and most unusual screaming or grating sound—the exact counterpart of what my fancy had already conjured up for the dragon's unnatural shriek as described by the romancer.

Oppressed, as I certainly was, upon the occurrence of the second and most extraordinary coincidence, by a thousand conflicting sensations, in which wonder and extreme terror were predominant, I still retained sufficient presence of mind to avoid exciting, by any observation, the sensitive nervousness of my companion. I was by no means certain that he had noticed the sounds in question; although, assuredly, a strange alteration had, during the last few minutes, taken place in his demeanour. From a position fronting my own, he had gradually brought round his chair, so as to sit with his face to the door of the chamber; and thus I could but partially perceive his features, although I saw that his lips trembled as if he were murmuring inaudibly. His head had dropped upon his breast—yet I knew that he was not asleep, from the wide and rigid opening of the eye as I caught a glance of it in profile. The motion of his body, too, was at variance with this idea—for he rocked from side to side with a gentle yet constant and uniform sway. Having rapidly taken notice of all this, I resumed the narrative of Sir Launcelot, which thus proceeded:

"And now, the champion, having escaped from the terrible fury of the dragon, bethinking himself of the brazen shield, and of the breaking up of the enchantment which was upon it, removed the carcass from out of the way before him, and approached valorously over the silver pavement of the castle to where the shield was upon the wall; which in sooth tarried not for his full coming, but fell down at his feet upon the silver floor, with a mighty great and terrible ringing sound."

No sooner had these syllables passed my lips, than—as if a shield of brass had indeed, at the moment, fallen heavily upon a floor of silver—I became aware of a distinct, hollow, metallic, and clangorous, yet apparently muffled reverberation. Completely unnerved, I leaped to my feet; but the measured rocking movement of Usher was undisturbed. I rushed to the chair on which he sat. His eyes were bent fixedly before him, and throughout his whole countenance there reigned a stony rigidity. But, as I placed my hand upon his shoulder, there came a strong shudder over his whole person; a sickly smile quivered about his lips; and I saw that he spoke in a low, hurried, and gibbering murmur, as if unconscious of my presence. Bending closely over him, I at length drank in the hideous import of his words.

"Not hear it?—yes, I hear it, and *have* heard it. Long—long—long— many minutes, many hours, many days, have I heard it—yet I dared not—- oh, pity me, miserable wretch that I am!—I dared not—I *dared* not speak! *We have put her living in the tomb!* Said I not that my senses were acute? I *now* tell you that I heard her first feeble movements in the hollow coffin. I heard them—many, many days ago—yet I dared not—*I dared not speak!* And now—to-night—Ethelred—ha! ha!—the breaking of the hermit's door, and the death-cry of the dragon, and the clangour of the shield!—say, rather, the rending of her coffin, and the grating of the iron hinges of her prison, and her struggles within the coppered archway of the vault! Oh whither shall I fly? Will she not be here anon? Is she not hurrying to upbraid me for my haste? Have I not heard her footstep on the stair? Do I not distinguish that heavy and horrible beating of her heart? Madman!" here he sprang furiously to his feet, and shrieked out his syllables, as if in the effort he were giving up his soul—"Madman! I tell you that she now stands without the door!"

As if in the superhuman energy of his utterance there had been found the potency of a spell—the huge antique panels to which the speaker pointed, threw slowly back, upon the instant, their ponderous and ebony jaws. It was the work of the rushing gust—but then without those doors there did stand the lofty and enshrouded figure of the Lady Madeline of Usher. There was blood upon her white robes, and the evidence of some bitter struggle upon every portion of her emaciated frame. For a moment she remained trembling and reeling to and fro upon the threshold, then, with a low moaning cry, fell heavily inward upon the person of her brother, and in her violent and now final death-agonies, bore him to the floor a corpse, and a victim to the terrors he had anticipated.

From that chamber, and from that mansion, I fled aghast. The storm was still abroad in all its wrath as I found myself crossing the old causeway. Suddenly there shot along the path a wild light, and I turned to see whence a gleam so unusual could have issued; for the vast house and its shadows were alone behind me. The radiance was that of the full, setting, and blood-red moon which now shone vividly through that once barely discernible fissure of which I have before spoken as extending from the roof of the building, in a zigzag direction, to the base. While I gazed, this fissure rapidly widened—there came a fierce breath of the whirlwind—the entire orb of the satellite burst at once upon my sight—my brain reeled as I saw the mighty walls rushing asunder—there was a long tumultuous shouting sound like the voice of a thousand waters—and the deep and dank tarn at my feet closed sullenly and silently over the fragments of the "House of Usher."

FOOTNOTES

[1] Watson, Dr Percival, Spallanzani, and especially the Bishop of Landaff.

II
THE OLD NURSE'S STORY

From "The Portent"

By George MacDonald

I set out one evening for the cottage of my old nurse, to bid her good-bye for many months, probably years. I was to leave the next day for Edinburgh, on my way to London, whence I had to repair by coach to my new abode— almost to me like the land beyond the grave, so little did I know about it, and so wide was the separation between it and my home. The evening was sultry when I began my walk, and before I arrived at its end, the clouds rising from all quarters of the horizon, and especially gathering around the peaks of the mountain, betokened the near approach of a thunderstorm. This was a great delight to me. Gladly would I take leave of my home with the memory of a last night of tumultuous magnificence; followed, probably, by a day of weeping rain, well suited to the mood of my own heart in bidding farewell to the best of parents and the dearest of homes. Besides, in common with most Scotchmen who are young and hardy enough to be unable to realise the existence of coughs and rheumatic fevers, it was a positive pleasure to me to be out in rain, hail, or snow.

"I am come to bid you good-bye, Margaret, and to hear the story which you promised to tell me before I left home: I go to-morrow."

"Do you go so soon, my darling? Well, it will be an awful night to tell it in; but, as I promised, I suppose I must."

At the moment, two or three great drops of rain, the first of the storm, fell down the wide chimney, exploding in the clear turf-fire.

"Yes, indeed you must," I replied.

After a short pause, she commenced. Of course she spoke in Gaelic; and I translate from my recollection of the Gaelic; but rather from the impression left upon my mind, than from any recollection of words. She drew her chair near the fire, which we had reason to fear would soon be put out by the falling rain, and began.

"How old the story is, I do not know. It has come down through many generations. My grandmother told it to me as I tell it to you; and her mother and my mother sat beside, never interrupting, but nodding their heads at every turn. Almost it ought to begin like the fairy tales, *Once upon a time,*—it took place so long ago; but it is too dreadful and too true to tell like a fairy tale.—There were two brothers, sons of the chief of our clan, but as different in appearance and disposition as two men could be. The elder was fair-haired and strong, much given to hunting and fishing; fighting too, upon occasion, I daresay, when they made a foray upon the Saxon, to get back a mouthful of their own. But he was gentleness itself to everyone about him, and the very soul of honour in all his doings. The younger was very dark in complexion, and tall and slender compared to his brother. He was very fond of book-learning, which, they say, was an uncommon taste in those times. He did not care for any sports or bodily exercises but one; and that, too, was unusual in these parts. It was horsemanship. He was a fierce rider, and as much at home in the saddle as in his study-chair. You may think that, so long ago, there was not much fit room for riding hereabouts; but, fit or not fit, he rode. From his reading and riding, the neighbours looked doubtfully upon him, and whispered about the black art. He usually bestrode a great powerful black horse, without a white hair on him; and people said it was either the devil himself, or a demon-horse from the devil's own stud. What favoured this notion was that in or out of the stable, the brute would let no other than his master go near him. Indeed, no one would venture, after he had killed two men, and grievously maimed a third, tearing him with his teeth and hoofs like a wild beast. But to his master he was obedient as a hound, and would even tremble in his presence sometimes.

"The youth's temper corresponded to his habits. He was both gloomy and passionate. Prone to anger, he had never been known to forgive. Debarred from anything on which he had set his heart, he would have gone mad with longing if he had not gone mad with rage. His soul was like the night around us now, dark, and sultry, and silent, but lighted up by the red levin of wrath, and torn by the bellowings of thunder-passion. He must have his will: hell might have his soul. Imagine, then, the rage and malice in his heart, when he suddenly became aware that an orphan girl, distantly related to them, who had lived with them for nearly two years, and whom he had loved for almost all that period, was loved by his elder brother, and loved him in return. He flung his right hand above his head, and swore a terrible oath that if he might not, his brother should not, rushed out of the house, and galloped off among the hills.

"The orphan was a beautiful girl, tall, pale, and slender, with plentiful dark hair, which, when released from the snood, rippled down below her knees. Her appearance formed a strong contrast with that of her favoured lover, while there was some resemblance between her and the younger brother. This fact seemed, to his fierce selfishness, ground for a prior claim.

"It may appear strange that a man like him should not have had instant recourse to his superior and hidden knowledge, by means of which he might have got rid of his rival with far more of certainty and less of risk; but I presume that, for the moment, his passion overwhelmed his consciousness of skill. Yet I do not suppose that he foresaw the mode in which his hatred was about to operate. At the moment when he learned their mutual attachment, probably through a domestic, the lady was on her way to meet her lover as he returned from the day's sport. The appointed place was on the edge of a deep, rocky ravine, down in whose dark bosom brawled and foamed a little mountain torrent. You know the place, Duncan, my dear, I daresay."

(Here she gave me a minute description of the spot, with directions how to find it.)

"Whether any one saw what I am about to relate, or whether it was put together afterwards, I cannot tell. The story is like an old tree—so old that it has lost the marks of its growth. But this is how my grandmother told it to me. An evil chance led him in the right direction. The lovers, startled by the sound of the approaching horse, parted in opposite directions along a narrow mountain-path on the edge of the ravine. Into this path he struck at a point near where the lovers had met, but to opposite sides of which they had now receded; so that he was between them on the path. Turning his horse up the course of the stream, he soon came in sight of his brother on the ledge before him. With a suppressed scream of rage, he rode headlong at him, and, ere he had time to make the least defence, hurled him over the precipice. The helplessness of the strong man was uttered in one single despairing cry as he shot into the abyss. Then all was still. The sound of his fall could not reach the edge of the gulf. Divining in a moment that the lady, whose name was Elsie, must have fled in the opposite direction, he reined his steed on his haunches. He could touch the precipice with his bridle-hand half outstretched; his sword-hand half outstretched would have dropped a stone to the bottom of the ravine. There was no room to wheel. One desperate practibility alone remained. Turning his horse's head towards the edge, he compelled him, by means of the powerful bit, to rear till he stood almost erect; and so, his body swaying over the gulf, with quivering and straining muscles, to turn on his hind legs. Having completed the half-circle, he let him drop, and urged him furiously in the opposite direction. It must have been by the devil's own care that he was able to continue his gallop along that ledge of rock.

"He soon caught sight of the maiden. She was leaning, half fainting, against the precipice. She had beard her lover's last cry, and, although it had conveyed no suggestion of his voice to her ear, she trembled from head to foot, and her limbs would bear her no farther. He checked his speed, rode gently up to her, lifted her unresisting, laid her across the shoulders of his horse, and, riding carefully till he reached a more open path, dashed again wildly along the mountain side. The lady's long hair was shaken loose, and dropped, trailing on the ground. The horse trampled upon it, and stumbled, half dragging her from the saddle-bow. He caught her, lifted her up, and looked at her face. She was dead. I suppose he went mad. He laid her again across the saddle before him, and rode on, reckless whither. Horse, and man, and maiden were found the next day, lying at the foot of a cliff, dashed to pieces. It was observed that a hind shoe of the horse was loose and broken. Whether this had been the cause of his fall, could not be told; but ever when he races, as race he will, till the day of doom, along that mountain side, his gallop is mingled with the clank of the loose and broken shoe. For, like the sin, the punishment is awful; he shall carry about for ages the phantom-body of the girl, knowing that her soul is away, sitting with the soul of his brother, down in the deep ravine, or scaling with him the topmost crags of the towering mountain peaks. There are some who, from time to time, see the doomed man careering along the face of the mountain, with the lady hanging across the steed; and they say it always betokens a storm, such as this which is now raving about us."

I had not noticed till now, so absorbed had I been in her tale, that the storm had risen to a very ecstasy of fury.

"They say, likewise, that the lady's hair is still growing; for, every time they see her, it is longer than before; and that now such is its length and the headlong speed of the horse, that it floats and streams out behind, like one of those curved clouds, like a comet's tail, far up in the sky; only the cloud is white, and the hair dark as night. And they say it will go on growing until the Last Day, when the horse will falter, and her hair will gather in; and the horse will fall, and the hair will twist, and twine, and wreathe itself like a mist of threads about him, and blind him to everything but her. Then the body will rise up within it, face to face with him, animated by a fiend, who, twining *her* arms around him, will drag him down to the bottomless pit."

I may mention something which now occurred, and which had a strange effect on my old nurse. It illustrates the assertion that we see around us only what is within us; marvellous things enough will show themselves to the marvellous mood. During a short lull in the storm, just as she had finished her story, we heard the sound of iron-shod hoofs approaching the cottage. There was no bridle-way into the glen. A knock came to the door, and, on opening it, we saw an old man seated on a horse, with a long, slenderly-filled sack lying across the saddle before him. He said he had lost the path in the storm, and, seeing the light, had scrambled down to inquire his way. I perceived at once, from the scared and mysterious look of the old woman's eyes, that she was persuaded that this appearance had more than a little to do with the awful rider, the terrific storm, and myself who had heard the sound of the phantom hoofs. As he ascended the hill, she looked after him, with wide and pale but unshrinking eyes; then turning in, shut and locked the door behind her, as by a natural instinct. After two or three of her significant nods, accompanied by the compression of her lips, she said:—

"He need not think to take me in, wizard as he is, with his disguises. I can see him through them all. Duncan, my dear, when you suspect anything, do not be too incredulous. This human demon is, of course, a wizard still, and knows how to make himself, as well as anything he touches, take a quite different appearance from the real one; only every appearance must bear some resemblance, however distant, to the natural form. That man you saw at the door, was the phantom of which I have been telling you. What he is after now, of course, I cannot tell; but you must keep a bold heart, and a firm and wary foot, as you go home to-night."

I showed some surprise, I do not doubt, and, perhaps, some fear as well; but I only said: "How do you know him, Margaret?"

"I can hardly tell you," she replied; "but I do know him. I think he hates me. Often, of a wild night, when there is moonlight enough by fits, I see him tearing round this little valley, just on the top edge—all round; the lady's hair and the horse's mane and tail driving far behind, and mingling, vaporous, with the stormy clouds. About he goes, in wild careering gallop; now lost as the moon goes in, then visible far round when she looks out again—an airy, pale-grey spectre, which few eyes but mine could see; for, as far as I am aware, no one of the family but myself has ever possessed the double gift of seeing and hearing both. In this case I hear no sound, except now and then a clank from the broken shoe. But I did not mean to tell you that I had ever seen him. I am not a bit afraid of him. He cannot do more than he may. His power is limited; else ill enough would he work, the miscreant."

"But," said I, "what has all this, terrible as it is, to do with the fright you took at my telling you that I had heard the sound of the broken shoe? Surely you are not afraid of only a storm?"

"No, my boy; I fear no storm. But the fact is, that that sound is seldom heard, and never, as far as I know, by any of the blood of that wicked man, without betokening some ill to one of the family, and most probably to the one who hears it—but I am not quite sure about that. Only some evil it does portend, although a long time may elapse before it shows itself; and I have a hope it may mean some one else than you."

"Do not wish that," I replied. "I know no one better able to bear it than I am; and I hope, whatever it may be, that I only shall have to meet it. It must surely be something serious to be so foretold—it can hardly be connected with my disappointment in being compelled to be a pedagogue instead of a soldier."

"Do not trouble yourself about that, Duncan," replied she. "A soldier you must be. The same day you told me of the clank of the broken horseshoe, I saw you return wounded from battle, and fall fainting from your horse in the street of a great city—only fainting, thank God. But I have particular reasons for being uneasy at *your* hearing that boding sound. Can you tell me the day and hour of your birth?"

"No," I replied. "It seems very odd when I think of it, but I really do not know even the day."

"Nor any one else, which is stranger still," she answered.

"How does that happen, nurse?"

"We were in terrible anxiety about your mother at the time. So ill was she, after you were just born, in a strange, unaccountable way, that you lay almost neglected for more than an hour. In the very act of giving birth to you, she seemed to the rest around her to be out of her mind, so wildly did she talk; but I knew better. I knew that she was fighting some evil power; and what power it was, I knew full well; for twice, during her pains, I heard the click of the horseshoe. But no one could help her. After her delivery, she lay as if in a trance, neither dead, nor at rest, but as if frozen to ice, and conscious of it all the while. Once more I heard the terrible sound of iron; and, at the moment your mother started from her trance, screaming, 'My child! my child!' We suddenly became aware that no one had attended to the child, and rushed to the place where he lay wrapped in a blanket. Uncovering him, we found him black in the face, and spotted with dark spots upon the throat. I thought he was dead; but, with great and almost hopeless pains, we succeeded in making him breathe, and he gradually recovered. But his mother continued dreadfully exhausted. It seemed as if she had spent her life for her child's defence and birth. That was you, Duncan, my dear.

"I was in constant attendance upon her. About a week after your birth, as near as I can guess, just in the gloaming, I heard yet again the awful clank—only once. Nothing followed till about midnight. Your mother slept, and you lay asleep beside her. I sat by the bedside. A horror fell upon me suddenly, though I neither saw nor heard anything. Your mother started from her sleep with a cry, which sounded as if it came from far away, out of a dream, and did not belong to this world. My blood curdled with fear. She sat up in bed, with wide staring eyes, and half-open rigid lips, and, feeble as she was, thrust her arms straight out before her with great force, her hands open and lifted up, with the palms outwards. The whole action was of one violently repelling another. She began to talk wildly as she had done before you were born, but, though I seemed to hear and understand it all at the time, I could not recall a word of it afterwards. It was as if I had listened to it when half asleep. I attempted to soothe her, putting my arms round her, but she seemed quite unconscious of my presence, and my arms seemed powerless upon the fixed muscles of hers. Not that I tried to constrain her, for I knew that a battle was going on of some kind or other, and my interference might do awful mischief. I only tried to comfort and encourage her. All the time, I was in a state of indescribable cold and suffering, whether more bodily or mental I could not tell. But at length I heard yet again the clank of the shoe. A sudden peace seemed to fall upon my mind—or was it a warm, odorous wind that filled the room? Your mother dropped her arms, and turned feebly towards her baby. She saw that he slept a blessed sleep. She smiled like a glorified spirit, and fell back exhausted on the pillow. I went to the other side of the room to get a cordial. When I returned to the bedside, I saw at once that she was dead. Her face smiled still, with an expression of the uttermost bliss."

Nurse ceased, trembling as overcome by the recollection; and I was too much moved and awed to speak. At length, resuming the conversation, she said: "You see it is no wonder, Duncan, my dear, if, after all this, I should find, when I wanted to fix the date of your birth, that I could not determine the day or the hour when it took place. All was confusion in my poor brain. But it was strange that no one else could, any more than I. One thing only I can tell you about it. As I carried you across the room to lay you down—for I assisted at your birth—I happened to look up to the window. Then I saw what I did not forget, although I did not think of it again till many days after—a bright star was shining on the very tip of the thin crescent moon."

"Oh, then," said I, "it is possible to determine the day and the very hour when my birth took place."

"See the good of book-learning!" replied she. "When you work it out, just let me know, my dear, that I may remember it."

"That I will."

A silence of some moments followed. Margaret resumed:

"I am afraid you will laugh at my foolish fancies, Duncan; but in thinking over all these things, as you may suppose I often do, lying awake in my lonely bed, the notion sometimes comes to me: What if my Duncan be the youth whom his wicked brother hurled into the ravine, come again in a new body, to live out his life, cut short by his brother's hatred? If so, his persecution of you, and of your mother for your sake, is easy to understand. And if so, you will never be able to rest till you find your fere, wherever she may have been born on the face of the earth. For born she must be, long ere now, for you to find. I misdoubt me much, however, if you will find her without great conflict and suffering between, for the Powers of Darkness will be against you; though I have good hope that you will overcome at last. You must forgive the fancies of a foolish old woman, my dear."

I will not try to describe the strange feelings, almost sensations, that arose in me while listening to these extraordinary utterances, lest it should be supposed I was ready to believe all that Margaret narrated or concluded. I could not help doubting her sanity; but no more could I help feeling peculiarly moved by her narrative.

Few more words were spoken on either side, but, after receiving renewed exhortations to carefulness on the way home, I said good-bye to dear old nurse, considerably comforted, I must confess, that I was not doomed to be a tutor all my days; for I never questioned the truth of that vision and its consequent prophecy.

I went out into the midst of the storm, into the alternating throbs of blackness and radiance; now the possessor of no more room than what my body filled, and now isolated in world-wide space. And the thunder seemed to follow me, bellowing after me as I went.

Absorbed in the story I had heard, I took my way, as I thought, homewards. The whole country was well known to me. I should have said, before that night, that I could have gone home blindfold. Whether the lightning bewildered me and made me take a false turn, I cannot tell, for the hardest thing to understand, in intellectual as well as moral mistakes, is how we came to go wrong. But after wandering for some time, plunged in meditation, and with no warning whatever of the presence of inimical powers, a brilliant lightning-flash showed me that at least I was not near home. The light was prolonged for a second or two by a slight electric pulsation; and by that I distinguished a wide space of blackness on the ground in front of me. Once more wrapt in the folds of a thick darkness, I dared not move. Suddenly it occurred to me what the blackness was, and whither I had wandered. It was a huge quarry, of great depth, long disused, and half filled with water. I knew the place perfectly. A few more steps would have carried me over the brink. I stood still, waiting for the next flash, that I might be quite sure of the way I was about to take before I ventured to move. While I stood, I fancied I heard a single hollow plunge in the black water far below. When the lightning came, I turned, and took my path in another direction. After walking for some time across the heath, I fell. The fall became a roll, and down a steep declivity I went, over and over, arriving at the bottom uninjured.

Another flash soon showed me where I was—in the hollow valley, within a couple of hundred yards from nurse's cottage. I made my way towards it. There was no light in it, except the feeblest glow from the embers of her peat fire. "She is in bed," I said to myself, "and I will not disturb her." Yet something drew me towards the little window. I looked in. At first I could see nothing. At length, as I kept gazing, I saw something, indistinct in the darkness, like an outstretched human form.

By this time the storm had lulled. The moon had been up for some time, but had been quite concealed by tempestuous clouds. Now, however, these had begun to break up; and, while I stood looking into the cottage, they scattered away from the face of the moon, and a faint, vapoury gleam of her light, entering the cottage through a window opposite that at which I stood, fell directly on the face of my old nurse, as she lay on her back outstretched upon chairs, pale as death, and with her eyes closed. The light fell nowhere but on her face. A stranger to her habits would have thought that she was dead; but she had so much of the appearance she had had on a former occasion, that I concluded at once she was in one of her trances. But having often heard that persons in such a condition ought not to be disturbed, and feeling quite sure she knew best how to manage herself, I turned, though reluctantly, and left the lone cottage behind me in the night, with the death-like woman lying motionless in the midst of it.

I found my way home without any further difficulty, and went to bed, where I soon fell asleep, thoroughly wearied, more by the mental excitement I had been experiencing, than by the amount of bodily exercise I had gone through.

My sleep was tormented with awful dreams; yet, strange to say, I awoke in the morning refreshed and fearless. The sun was shining through the chinks in my shutters, which had been closed because of the storm, and was making streaks and bands of golden brilliancy upon the wall. I had dressed and completed my preparations long before I heard the steps of the servant who came to call me.

What a wonderful thing waking is! The time of the ghostly moonshine passes by, and the great positive sunlight comes. A man who dreams, and knows that he is dreaming, thinks he knows what waking is; but knows it so little that he mistakes, one after another, many a vague and dim change in his dream for an awaking. When the true waking comes at last, he is filled and overflowed with the power of its reality. So, likewise, one who, in the darkness, lies waiting for the light about to be struck, and trying to conceive, with all the force of his imagination, what the light will be like, is yet, when the reality flames up before him, seized as by a new and unexpected thing, different from and beyond all his imagining. He feels as if the darkness were cast to an infinite distance behind him. So shall it be with us when we wake from this dream of life into the truer life beyond, and find all our present notions of being thrown back as into a dim vapoury region of dreamland, where yet we thought we knew, and whence we looked forward into the present. This must be what Novalis means when he says: "Our life is not a dream; but it may become a dream, and perhaps ought to become one."

And so I look back upon the strange history of my past, sometimes asking myself: "Can it be that all this has really happened to the same *me*, who am now thinking about it in doubt and wonderment?"

III
THE SUPERSTITIOUS MAN'S STORY

By Thomas Hardy

"There was something very strange about William's death—very strange indeed!" sighed a melancholy man in the back of the van. It was the seedman's father, who had hitherto kept silence.

"And what might that have been?" asked Mr Lackland.

"William, as you may know, was a curious, silent man; you could feel when he came near 'ee; and if he was in the house or anywhere behind you without your seeing him, there seemed to be something clammy in the air, as if a cellar door opened close by your elbow. Well, one Sunday, at a time that William was in very good health to all appearance, the bell that was ringing for church went very heavy all of a sudden; the sexton, who told me o't, said he had not known the bell go so heavy in his hand for years—it was just as if the gudgeons wanted oiling. That was on the Sunday, as I say.

"During the week after, it chanced that William's wife was staying up late one night to finish her ironing, she doing the washing for Mr and Mrs Hardcome. Her husband had finished his supper, and gone to bed as usual some hour or two before. While she ironed she heard him coming downstairs; he stopped to put on his boots at the stair-foot, where he always left them, and then came on into the living-room where she was ironing, passing through it towards the door, this being the only way from the staircase to the outside of the house. No word was said on either side, William not being a man given to much speaking, and his wife being occupied with her work. He went out and closed the door behind him. As her husband had now and then gone out in this way at night before when unwell, or unable to sleep for want of a pipe, she took no particular notice, and continued at her ironing. This she finished shortly after, and, as he had not come in, she waited awhile for him, putting away the irons and things, and preparing the table for his breakfast in the morning. Still he did not return, but supposing him not far off, and wanting to go to bed herself, tired as she was, she left the door unbarred and went to the stairs, after writing on the back of the door with chalk: *Mind and do the door* (because he was a forgetful man).

"To her great surprise, and I might say alarm, on reaching the foot of the stairs his boots were standing there as they always stood when he had gone to rest. Going up to their chamber, she found him in bed sleeping as sound as a rock. How he could have got back again without her seeing or hearing him was beyond her comprehension. It could only have been by passing behind her very quietly while she was bumping with the iron. But this notion did not satisfy her: it was surely impossible that she should not have seen him come in through a room so small. She could not unravel the mystery, and felt very queer and uncomfortable about it. However, she would not disturb him to question him then, and went to bed herself.

"He rose and left for his work very early the next morning, before she was awake, and she waited his return to breakfast with much anxiety for an explanation, for thinking over the matter by daylight made it seem only the more startling. When he came in to the meal he said, before she could put her question, 'What's the meaning of them words chalked on the door?'

"She told him, and asked him about his going out the night before. William declared that he had never left the bedroom after entering it, having in fact undressed, lain down, and fallen asleep directly, never once waking till the clock struck five, and he rose up to go to his labour.

"Betty Privett was as certain in her own mind that he did go out as she was of her own existence, and was little less certain that he did not return. She felt too disturbed to argue with him, and let the subject drop as though she must have been mistaken. When she was walking down Longpuddle Street later in the day she met Jim Weedle's daughter Nancy, and said: 'Well Nancy, you do look sleepy to-day!'

"'Yes, Mrs Privett,' said Nancy. 'Now, don't tell anybody, but I don't mind letting you know what the reason o't is. Last night, being Old Midsummer Eve, some of us church porch, and didn't get home till near one.'

"'Did ye?' says Mrs Privett. 'Old Midsummer yesterday was it? Faith, I didn't think whe'r 'twas Midsummer or Michaelmas; I'd too much work to do.'

"'Yes. And we were frightened enough, I can tell 'ee by what we saw.'

"'What did ye see?'

"(You may not remember, sir, having gone off to foreign parts so young, that on Midsummer Night it is believed hereabout that the faint shapes of all the folk in the parish who are going to be at death's door within the year can be seen entering the church. Those who get over their illness come out again after awhile; those that are doomed to die do not return.)

"'What did you see?' asked William's wife.

"'Well,' says Nancy, backwardly—'we needn't tell what we saw or who we saw.'

"'You saw my husband,' said Betty Privett in a quiet way.

"'Well, since you put it so,' says Nancy, hanging fire, 'we—thought we did see him; but it was darkish and we was frightened, and of course it might not have been he.'

"'Nancy, you needn't mind letting it out, though 'tis kept back in kindness. And he didn't come out of the church again: I know it as well as you.'

"Nancy did not answer yes or no to that, and no more was said. But three days after, William Privett was mowing with John Chiles in Mr Hardcome's meadow, and in the heat of the day they sat down to their bit o' nunch under a tree, and empty their flagon. Afterwards both of 'em fell asleep as they sat. John Chiles was the first to wake, and, as he looked towards his fellow-mower, he saw one of those great white miller's-souls as we call 'em—that is to say, a miller moth—come from William's open mouth while he slept and fly straight away. John thought it odd enough, as William had worked in a mill for several years when he was a boy. He then looked at the sun, and found by the place o't that they had slept a long while, and, as William did not wake, John called to him and said it was high time to begin work again. He took no notice, and then John went up and shook him and found he was dead.

"Now on that very day old Philip Hookhorn was down at Longpuddle Spring, dipping up a pitcher of water; and, as he turned away, who should he see coming down to the spring on the other side but William, looking very pale and old? This surprised Philip Hookhorn very much, for years before that time William's little son—his only child—had been drowned in that spring while at play there, and this had so preyed upon William's mind that he'd never been seen near the spring afterwards, and had been known to go half a mile out of his way to avoid the place. On enquiry, it was found that William in body could not have stood by the spring, being in the mead two miles off; and it also came out that at the time at which he was seen at the spring was the very time when he died."

"A rather melancholy story," observed the emigrant, after a minute's silence.

"Yes, yes. Well, we must take ups and downs together," said the seedman's father.

IV
A STORY OF RAVENNA

By Boccaccio

Ravenna being a very ancient city in Romagna, there dwelt sometime a great number of worthy gentlemen, among whom I am to speak of one more especially, named Anastasio, descended from the family of Onesti, who by the death of his father, and an uncle of his, was left extraordinarily abounding in riches and growing to years fitting for marriage. As young gallants are easily apt enough to do, he became enamoured of a very beautiful gentlewoman, who was daughter of Messer Paolo Traversario, one of the most ancient and noble families in all the country. Nor made he any doubt, by his means and industrious endeavour, to derive affection from her again, for he carried himself like a braveminded gentleman, liberal in his expenses, honest and affable in all his actions, which commonly are the true notes of a good nature, and highly to be commended in any man. But, howsoever, fortune became his enemy; these laudable parts of manhood did not any way friend him, but rather appeared hurtful to himself, so cruel, unkind, and almost merely savage did she show herself to him, perhaps in pride of her singular beauty or presuming on her nobility by birth, both which are rather blemishes than ornaments in a woman when they be especially abused. The harsh and uncivil usage in her grew very distasteful to Anastasio, and so insufferable that after a long time of fruitless service, requited still with nothing but coy disdain, desperate resolutions entered into his brain, and often he was minded to kill himself. But better thoughts supplanting those furious passions, he abstained from such a violent act, and governed by mere manly consideration, determined that as she hated him, he would requite her with the like, if he could, wherein he became altogether deceived, because as his hopes grew to a daily decaying, yet his love enlarged itself more and more.

Thus Anastasio persevering still in his bootless affection, and his expenses not limited within any compass, it appeared in the judgment of his kindred and friends that he was fallen into a mighty consumption, both of his body and means. In which respects many times they advised him to leave the city of Ravenna, and live in some other place for such a while as might set a more moderate stint upon his spendings, and bridle the indiscreet course of his love, the only fuel which fed his furious fire.

Anastasio held out thus a long time, without lending an ear to such friendly counsel; but in the end he was so closely followed by them, as being no longer able to deny them, he promised to accomplish their request. Whereupon making such extraordinary preparation as if he were to set out thence for France or Spain, or else into some further country, he mounted on horseback, and accompanied with some few of his familiar friends, departed from Ravenna, and rode to a country dwelling-house of his own, about three or four miles distant from the city, at a place called Chiassi; and there upon a very good green erecting divers tents and pavilions, such as great persons make use of in the time of progress, he said to his friends which came with him thither that there he determined to make his abiding, they all returning back unto Ravenna, and coming to visit him again so often as they pleased.

Now it came to pass that about the beginning of May, it being then a very mild and serene season, and he leading there a much more magnificent life than ever he had done before, inviting divers to dine with him this day and as many to-morrow, and not to leave him till after supper, upon a sudden falling into remembrance of his cruel mistress, he commanded all his servants to forbear his company, and suffer him to walk alone by himself a while, because he had occasion of private meditations, wherein he would not by any means be troubled. It was then about the ninth hour of the day, and he walking on solitary all alone, having gone some half a mile distance from the tents, entered into a grove of pine-trees, never minding dinner-time or anything else, but only the unkind requital of his love.

Suddenly he heard the voice of a woman seeming to make most mournful complaints, which breaking off his silent considerations, made him to lift up his head to know the reason of this noise. When he saw himself so far entered into the grove before he could imagine where he was, he looked amazedly round about him, and out of a little thicket of bushes and briars round engirt with spreading trees, he espied a young damsel come running towards him, naked from the middle upward, her hair lying on her shoulders, and her fair skin rent and torn with the briars and brambles, so that the blood ran trickling down mainly, she weeping, wringing her hands, and crying out for mercy so loud as she could. Two fierce bloodhounds also followed swiftly after, and where their teeth took hold did most cruelly bite her. Last of all, mounted on a lusty black courser, came galloping a knight, with a very stern and angry countenance, holding a drawn short sword in his hand, giving her very dreadful speeches, and threatening every minute to kill her.

This strange and uncouth sight bred in him no mean admiration, as also kind compassion to the unfortunate woman, out of which compassion sprung an earnest desire to deliver her, if he could, from a death so full of anguish and horror; but seeing himself to be without arms, he ran and plucked up the plant of a tree, which handling as if it had been a staff, he opposed himself against the dogs and the knight, who seeing him coming, cried out in this manner to him: "Anastasio, put not thyself in any opposition, but refer to my hounds and me to punish this wicked woman as she hath justly deserved." And in speaking these words, the hounds took fast hold on her body, so staying her until the knight was come nearer to her, and alighted from his horse, when Anastasio, after some other angry speeches, spake thus to him: "I cannot tell what or who thou art, albeit thou takest such knowledge of me, yet I must say it is mere cowardice in a knight, being armed as thou art, to offer to kill a naked woman, and make thy dogs thus to seize on her, as if she were a savage beast; therefore, believe me, I will defend her so far as I am able."

"Anastasio," answered the knight, "I am of the same city as thou art, and do well remember that thou wast a little lad when I, who was then named Guido Anastasio, and thine uncle, became as entirely in love with this woman as now thou art with Paolo Traversario's daughter. But through her coy disdain and cruelty, such was my heavy fate that desperately I slew myself with this short sword which thou beholdest in mine hand; for which rash sinful deed I was and am condemned to eternal punishment. This wicked woman, rejoicing immeasurably in mine unhappy death, remained no long time alive after me, and for her merciless sin of cruelty, and taking pleasure in my oppressing torments, dying unrepentant, and in pride of her scorn, she had the like sentence of condemnation pronounced on her, and was sent to the same place where I was condemned.

"There the three impartial judges imposed this further infliction on us both—namely, that she should fly in this manner before me, and I, who loved her so dearly while I lived, must pursue her as my deadly enemy, not like a woman that had a taste of love in her. And so often as I can overtake her, I am to kill her with this sword, the same weapon wherewith I slew myself. Then am I enjoined therewith to open her accursed body, and tear out her heart, with her other inwards, as now thou seest me do, which I give to my hounds to feed on. Afterward—such is the appointment of the supreme powers—that she re-assumeth life again, even as if she had not been dead at all, and falling to the same kind of flight, I with my hounds am still to follow her, without any respite or intermission. Every Friday, and just at this hour, our course is this way, where she suffereth the just punishment inflicted on her. Nor do we rest any of the other days, but are appointed unto other places, where she cruelly executed her malice against me, who am now, of her dear affectionate friend, ordained to be her endless enemy, and to pursue her in this manner for so many years as she exercised months of cruelty towards me. Hinder me not, then, in being the executioner of Divine justice, for all thy interposition is but in vain in seeking to cross the appointment of supreme powers."

Anastasio having heard all this discourse, his hair stood upright, like porcupines' quills, and his soul was so shaken with the terror, that he stepped back to suffer the knight to do what he was enjoined, looking yet with mild commiseration on the poor woman, who kneeling most humbly before the knight, and sternly seized on by the two bloodhounds, he opened her breast with his weapon, drawing forth her heart and bowels, which instantly he threw to the dogs, and they devoured them very greedily. Soon after the damsel, as if none of this punishment had been inflicted on her, started up suddenly, running amain towards the seashore, and the hounds swiftly following her, as the knight did the like, after he had taken his sword and was mounted on horseback, so that Anastasio had soon lost all sight of them, and could not guess what could become of them.

After he had heard and observed all these things, he stood a while as confounded with fear and pity, like a simple silly man, hoodwinked with his own passions, not knowing the subtle enemy's cunning illusions in offering false suggestions to the sight, to work his own ends thereby, and increase the number of his deceived servants. Forthwith he persuaded himself that he might make good use of this woman's tormenting, so justly imposed on the knight to prosecute, if thus it should continue still every Friday. Wherefore setting a good note or mark upon the place, he returned back to his own people, and at such times as he thought convenient, sent for divers of his kindred and friends from Ravenna, who being present with him, thus he spake to them:

"Dear kinsmen and friends, ye have long while importuned me to discontinue my over-doating love to her whom you all think, and I find to be my mortal enemy; as also to give over my lavish expenses, wherein I confess myself too prodigal; both which requests of yours I will condescend to, provided that you will perform one gracious favour for me—namely, that on Friday next, Messer Paolo Traversario, his wife, daughter, with all other women linked in lineage to them, and such beside only as you shall please to appoint, will vouchsafe to accept a dinner here with me. As for the reason thereto moving me, you shall then more at large be acquainted withal." This appeared no difficult matter for them to accomplish. Wherefore being returned to Ravenna, and as they found the time answerable to their purpose, they invited such as Anastasio had appointed them. And although they found it somewhat a hard matter to gain her company whom he had so dearly affected, yet notwithstanding, the other women won her along with them.

A most magnificent dinner had Anastasio provided, and the tables were covered under the pine-trees, where he saw the cruel lady so pursued and slain; directing the guests so in their seating that the young gentlewoman, his unkind mistress, sate with her face opposite unto the place where the dismal spectacle was to be seen. About the closing up of dinner, they began to hear the noise of the poor persecuted woman, which drove them all to much admiration, desiring to know what it was, and no one resolving them they rose from the tables, and looking directly as the noise came to them, they espied the woful woman, the dogs eagerly pursuing her; the knight galloping after them with his drawn weapon, and came very near unto the company, who cried out with loud exclaims against the dogs, and the knights stepped forth in assistance of the injured woman.

The knight spake unto them as formerly he had done to Anastasio, which made them draw back possessed with fear and admiration, while he acted the same cruelty as he did the Friday before, not differing in the least degree. Most of the gentlewomen there present, being near allied to the unfortunate woman, and likewise to the knight, remembering well both his love and death, did shed tears as plentifully as if it had been to the very persons themselves in usual performance of the action indeed. Which tragical scene being passed over, and the woman and knight gone out of their sight, all that had seen this strange accident fell into diversity of confused opinions, yet not daring to disclose them, as doubting some further danger to ensue thereon.

But beyond all the rest, none could compare in fear and astonishment with the cruel young maid affected by Anastasio, who both saw and observed all with a more inward apprehension, knowing very well that the moral of this dismal spectacle carried a much nearer application to her than any other in the company. For now she could call to mind how unkind and cruel she had shown herself to Anastasio, even as the other gentlewoman formerly did to her lover, still flying from him in great contempt and scorn, for which she thought the bloodhounds also pursued her at the heels already, and a sword of vengeance to mangle her body. This fear grew so powerful upon her, that to prevent the like heavy doom from falling on her, she studied, and therein bestowed all the night season, how to change her hatred into kind love, which at the length she fully obtained, and then purposed to procure in this manner: Secretly she sent a faithful chambermaid of her own to greet Anastasio on her behalf, humbly entreating him to come see her, because now she was absolutely determined to give him satisfaction in all which, with honour, he could request of her. Whereto Anastasio answered that he accepted her message thankfully, and desired no other favour at her hand but that which stood with her own offer, namely, to be his wife in honourable marriage. The maid knowing sufficiently that he could not be more desirous of the match than her mistress showed herself to be, made answer in her name that this motion would be most welcome to her.

Hereupon the gentlewoman herself became the solicitor to her father and mother, telling them plainly that she was willing to be the wife of Anastasio; which news did so highly content them, that upon the Sunday next following the marriage was very worthily solemnised, and they lived and loved together very kindly. Thus the Divine bounty, out of the malignant enemy's secret machinations, can cause good effects to arise and succeed. For from this conceit of fearful imagination in her, not only happened this long-desired conversion of a maid so obstinately scornful and proud, but likewise all the women of Ravenna, being admonished by her example, grew afterward more tractable to men's honest motions than ever they showed themselves before. And let me make some use hereof, fair ladies, to you not to stand over-nicely conceited of your beauty and good parts when men solicit you with their best services. Remember then this disdainful gentlewoman, but more especially her, who being the death of so kind a lover was therefore condemned to perpetual punishment, and he made the minister thereof whom she had cast off with coy disdain, from which I wish your minds to be free, as mine is ready to do you any acceptable service.

V

TEIG O'KANE AND THE CORPSE

[*Translated from the Irish*]

By Dr Douglas Hyde

There was once a grown-up lad in the County Leitrim, and he was strong and lively, and the son of a rich farmer. His father had plenty of money, and he did not spare it on the son. Accordingly, when the boy grew up he liked sport better than work, and, as his father had no other children, he loved this one so much that he allowed him to do in everything just as it pleased himself. He was very extravagant, and he used to scatter the gold money as another person would scatter the white. He was seldom to be found at home, but if there was a fair, or a race, or a gathering within ten miles of him, you were dead certain to find him there. And he seldom spent a night in his father's house, but he used to be always out rambling, and, like Shawn Bwee long ago, there was

"grádh gach cailin i mbrollach a léine,"

"the love of every girl in the breast of his shirt," and it's many's the kiss he got and he gave, for he was very handsome, and there wasn't a girl in the country but would fall in love with him, only for him to fasten his two eyes on her, and it was for that someone made this *rann* on him—

"Look at the rogue, it's for kisses he's rambling,
It isn't much wonder, for that was his way;
He's like an old hedgehog, at night he'll be scrambling
From this place to that, but he'll sleep in the day."

At last he became very wild and unruly. He wasn't to be seen day or night in his father's house, but always rambling or going on his *kailee* (night visit) from place to place and from house to house, so that the old people used to shake their heads and say to one another, "It's easy seen what will happen to the land when the old man dies; his son will run through it in a year, and it won't stand him that long itself."

He used to be always gambling and card-playing and drinking, but his father never minded his bad habits, and never punished him. But it happened one day that the old man was told that the son had ruined the character of a girl in the neighbourhood, and he was greatly angry, and he called the son to him, and said to him, quietly and sensibly—"Avic," says he, "you know I loved you greatly up to this, and I never stopped you from doing your choice thing whatever it was, and I kept plenty of money with you, and I always hoped to leave you the house and land, and all I had after myself would be gone; but I heard a story of you to-day that has disgusted me with you. I cannot tell you the grief that I felt when I heard such a thing of you, and I tell you now plainly that unless you marry that girl I'll leave house and land and everything to my brother's son. I never could leave it to anyone who would make so bad a use of it as you do yourself, deceiving women and coaxing girls. Settle with yourself now whether you'll marry that girl and get my land as a fortune with her, or refuse to marry her and give up all that was coming to you; and tell me in the morning which of the two things you have chosen."

"Och! *Domnoo Sheery!* father, you wouldn't say that to me, and I such a good son as I am. Who told you I wouldn't marry the girl?" says he.

But his father was gone, and the lad knew well enough that he would keep his word too; and he was greatly troubled in his mind, for as quiet and as kind as the father was, he never went back of a word that he had once said, and there wasn't another man in the country who was harder to bend than he was.

The boy did not know rightly what to do. He was in love with the girl indeed, and he hoped to marry her sometime or other, but he would much sooner have remained another while as he was, and follow on at his old tricks—drinking, sporting, and playing cards; and, along with that, he was angry that his father should order him to marry, and should threaten him if he did not do it.

"Isn't my father a great fool," says he to himself. "I was ready enough, and only too anxious, to marry Mary; and now since he threatened me, faith I've a great mind to let it go another while."

His mind was so much excited that he remained between two notions as to what he should do. He walked out into the night at last to cool his heated blood, and went on to the road. He lit a pipe, and as the night was fine he walked and walked on, until the quick pace made him begin to forget his trouble. The night was bright, and the moon half full. There was not a breath of wind blowing, and the air was calm and mild. He walked on for nearly three hours, when he suddenly remembered that it was late in the night, and time for him to turn. "Musha! I think I forgot myself," says he; "it must be near twelve o'clock now."

The word was hardly out of his mouth, when he heard the sound of many voices, and the trampling of feet on the road before him. "I don't know who can be out so late at night as this, and on such a lonely road," said he to himself.

He stood listening, and he heard the voices of many people talking through other, but he could not understand what they were saying. "Oh, wirra!" says he, "I'm afraid. It's not Irish or English they have; it can't be they're Frenchmen!" He went on a couple of yards further, and he saw well enough by the light of the moon a band of little people coming towards him, and they were carrying something big and heavy with them. "Oh, murder!" says he to himself, "sure it can't be that they're the good people that's in it!" Every *rib* of hair that was on his head stood up, and there fell a shaking on his bones, for he saw that they were coming to him fast.

He looked at them again, and perceived that there were about twenty little men in it, and there was not a man at all of them higher than about three feet or three feet and a half, and some of them were grey, and seemed very old. He looked again, but he could not make out what was the heavy thing they were carrying until they came up to him, and then they all stood round about him. They threw the heavy thing down on the road, and he saw on the spot that it was a dead body.

He became as cold as the Death, and there was not a drop of blood running in his veins when an old little grey *maneen* came up to him and said, "Isn't it lucky we met you, Teig O'Kane?"

Poor Teig could not bring out a word at all, nor open his lips, if he were to get the world for it, and so he gave no answer.

"Teig O'Kane," said the little grey man again, "isn't it timely you met us?"

Teig could not answer him.

"Teig O'Kane," says he, "the third time, isn't it lucky and timely that we met you?"

But Teig remained silent, for he was afraid to return an answer, and his tongue was as if it was tied to the roof of his mouth.

The little grey man turned to his companions, and there was joy in his bright little eye. "And now," says he, "Teig O'Kane hasn't a word, we can do with him what we please. Teig, Teig," says he, "you're living a bad life, and we can make a slave of you now, and you cannot withstand us, for there's no use in trying to go against us. Lift that corpse."

Teig was so frightened that he was only able to utter the two words, "I won't"; for as frightened as he was he was obstinate and stiff, the same as ever.

"Teig O'Kane won't lift the corpse," said the little *maneen*, with a wicked little laugh, for all the world like the breaking of a *lock* of dry *kippeens*, and with a little harsh voice like the striking of a cracked bell. "Teig O'Kane won't lift the corpse—make him lift it"; and before the word was out of his mouth they had all gathered round poor Teig, and they all talking and laughing through other.

Teig tried to run from them, but they followed him, and a man of them stretched out his foot before him as he ran, so that Teig was thrown in a heap on the road. Then before he could rise up the fairies caught him, some by the hands and some by the feet, and they held him tight, in a way that he could not stir, with his face against the ground. Six or seven of them raised the body then, and pulled it over to him, and left it down on his back. The breast of the corpse was squeezed against Teig's back and shoulders, and the arms of the corpse were thrown around Teig's neck. Then they stood back from him a couple of yards, and let him get up. He rose, foaming at the mouth and cursing, and he shook himself, thinking to throw the corpse off his back. But his fear and his wonder were great when he found that the two arms had a tight hold round his own neck, and that the two legs were squeezing his hips firmly, and that, however strongly he tried, he could not throw it off, any more than a horse can throw off its saddle. He was terribly frightened then, and he thought he was lost. "Ochone! for ever," said he to himself, "it's the bad life I'm leading that has given the good people this power over me. I promise to God and Mary, Peter and Paul, Patrick and Bridget, that I'll mend my ways for as long as I have to live, if I come clear out of this danger—and I'll marry the girl."

The little grey man came up to him again, and said he to him, "Now, Teig*een*," says he, "you didn't lift the body when I told you to lift it, and see how you were made to lift it; perhaps when I tell you to bury it, you won't bury it until you're made to bury it!"

"Anything at all that I can do for your honour," said Teig, "I'll do it," for he was getting sense already, and if it had not been for the great fear that was on him, he never would have let that civil word slip out of his mouth.

The little man laughed a sort of laugh again. "You're getting quiet now, Teig," says he. "I'll go bail but you'll be quiet enough before I'm done with you. Listen to me now, Teig O'Kane, and if you don't obey me in all I'm telling you to do, you'll repent it. You must carry with you this corpse that is on your back to Teampoll-Démus, and you must bring it into the church with you, and make a grave for it in the very middle of the church, and you must raise up the flags and put them down again the very same way, and you must carry the clay out of the church and leave the place as it was when you came, so that no one could know that there had been anything changed. But that's not all. Maybe that the body won't be allowed to be buried in that church; perhaps some other man has the bed, and, if so, it's likely he won't share it with this one. If you don't get leave to bury it in Teampoll-Démus, you must carry it to Carrick-fhad-vic-Orus, and bury it in the churchyard there; and if you don't get it into that place, take it with you to Teampoll-Ronan; and if that churchyard is closed on you, take it to Imlogue-Fada; and if you're not able to bury it there, you've no more to do than to take it to Kill-Breedya, and you can bury it there without hindrance. I cannot tell you what one of those churches is the one where you will have leave to bury that corpse under the clay, but I know that it will be allowed you to bury him at some church or other of them. If you do this work rightly, we will be thankful to you, and you will have no cause to grieve; but if you are slow or lazy, believe me we shall take satisfaction of you."

When the grey little man had done speaking, his comrades laughed and clapped their hands together. "Glic! Glic! Hwee! Hwee!" they all cried; "go on, go on, you have eight hours before you till daybreak, and if you haven't this man buried before the sun rises, you're lost." They struck a fist and a foot behind on him, and drove him on in the road. He was obliged to walk, and to walk fast, for they gave him no rest.

He thought himself that there was not a wet path, or a dirty *boreen*, or a crooked contrary road in the whole county, that he had not walked that night. The night was at times very dark, and whenever there would come a cloud across the moon he could see nothing, and then he used often to fall. Sometimes he was hurt, and sometimes he escaped, but he was obliged always to rise on the moment and to hurry on. Sometimes the moon would break out clearly, and then he would look behind him and see the little people following at his back. And he heard them speaking amongst themselves, talking and crying out, and screaming like a flock of sea-gulls; and if he was to save his soul he never understood as much as one word of what they were saying.

He did not know how far he had walked, when at last one of them cried out to him, "Stop here!" He stood, and they all gathered round him.

"Do you see those withered trees over there?" says the old boy to him again. "Teampoll-Démus is among those trees, and you must go in there by yourself, for we cannot follow you or go with you. We must remain here. Go on boldly."

Teig looked from him, and he saw a high wall that was in places half broken down, and an old grey church on the inside of the wall, and about a dozen withered old trees scattered here and there round it. There was neither leaf nor twig on any of them, but their bare crooked branches were stretched out like the arms of an angry man when he threatens. He had no help for it, but was obliged to go forward. He was a couple of hundred yards from the church, but he walked on, and never looked behind him until he came to the gate of the churchyard. The old gate was thrown down, and he had no difficulty in entering. He turned then to see if any of the little people were following him, but there came a cloud over the moon, and the night became so dark that he could see nothing. He went into the churchyard, and he walked up the old grassy pathway leading to the church. When he reached the door, he found it locked. The door was large and strong, and he did not know what to do. At last he drew out his knife with difficulty, and stuck it in the wood to try if it were not rotten, but it was not.

"Now," said he to himself, "I have no more to do; the door is shut, and I can't open it."

Before the words were rightly shaped in his own mind, a voice in his ear said to him, "Search for the key on the top of the door, or on the wall."

He started. "Who is that speaking to me?" he cried, turning round; but he saw no one. The voice said in his ear again, "Search for the key on the top of the door, or on the wall."

"What's that?" said he, and the sweat running from his forehead; "who spoke to me?"

"It's I, the corpse, that spoke to you!" said the voice.

"Can you talk?" said Teig.

"Now and again," said the corpse.

Teig searched for the key, and he found it on the top of the wall. He was too much frightened to say any more, but he opened the door wide, and as quickly as he could, and he went in, with the corpse on his back. It was as dark as pitch inside, and poor Teig began to shake and tremble.

"Light the candle," said the corpse.

Teig put his hand in his pocket, as well as he was able, and drew out a flint and steel. He struck a spark out of it, and lit a burnt rag he had in his pocket. He blew it until it made a flame, and he looked round him. The church was very ancient, and part of the wall was broken down. The windows were blown in or cracked, and the timber of the seats were rotten. There were six or seven old iron candlesticks left there still, and in one of these candlesticks Teig found the stump of an old candle, and he lit it. He was still looking round him on the strange and horrid place in which he found himself, when the cold corpse whispered in his ear, "Bury me now, bury me now; there is a spade and turn the ground." Teig looked from him, and he saw a spade lying beside the altar. He took it up, and he placed the blade under a flag that was in the middle of the aisle, and leaning all his weight on the handle of the spade, he raised it. When the first flag was raised it was not hard to raise the others near it, and he moved three or four of them out of their places. The clay that was under them was soft and easy to dig, but he had not thrown up more than three or four shovelfuls when he felt the iron touch something soft like flesh. He threw up three or four more shovelfuls from around it, and then he saw that it was another body that was buried in the same place.

"I am afraid I'll never be allowed to bury the two bodies in the same hole," said Teig, in his own mind. "You corpse, there on my back," says he, "will you be satisfied if I bury you down here?" But the corpse never answered him a word.

"That's a good sign," said Teig to himself. "Maybe he's getting quiet," and he thrust the spade down in the earth again. Perhaps he hurt the flesh of the other body, for the dead man that was buried there stood up in the grave, and shouted an awful shout. "Hoo! hoo!! hoo!!! Go! go!! go!!! or you're a dead, dead, dead man!" And then he fell back in the grave again. Teig said afterwards, that of all the wonderful things he saw that night, that was the most awful to him. His hair stood upright on his head like the bristles of a pig, the cold sweat ran off his face, and then came a tremour over all his bones, until he thought that he must fall.

But after a while he became bolder, when he saw that the second corpse remained lying quietly there, and he threw in the clay on it again, and he smoothed it overhead, and he laid down the flags carefully as they had been before. "It can't be that he'll rise up any more," said he.

He went down the aisle a little further, and drew near to the door, and began raising the flags again, looking for another bed for the corpse on his back. He took up three or four flags and put them aside, and then he dug the clay. He was not long digging until he laid bare an old woman without a thread upon her but her shirt. She was more lively than the first corpse, for he had scarcely taken any of the clay away from about her, when she sat up and began to cry, "Ho, you *bodach* (clown)! Ha, you *bodach*! Where has he been that he got no bed?"

Poor Teig drew back, and when she found that she was getting no answer, she closed her eyes gently, lost her vigour, and fell back quietly and slowly under the clay. Teig did to her as he had done to the man—he threw the clay back on her, and left the flags down overhead.

He began digging again near the door, but before he had thrown up more than a couple of shovelfuls, he noticed a man's hand laid bare by the spade. "By my soul, I'll go no further, then," said he to himself; "what use is it for me?" And he threw the clay in again on it, and settled the flags as they had been before.

He left the church then, and his heart was heavy enough, but he shut the door and locked it, and left the key where he found it. He sat down on a tombstone that was near the door, and began thinking. He was in great doubt what he should do. He laid his face between his two hands, and cried for grief and fatigue, since he was dead certain at this time that he never would come home alive. He made another attempt to loosen the hands of the corpse that were squeezed round his neck, but they were as tight as if they were clamped; and the more he tried to loosen them, the tighter they squeezed him. He was going to sit down once more, when the cold, horrid lips of the dead man said to him, "Carrick-fhad-vic-Orus," and he remembered the command of the good people to bring the corpse with him to that place if he should be unable to bury it where he had been.

He rose up, and looked about him. "I don't know the way," he said.

As soon as he had uttered the word, the corpse stretched out suddenly its left hand that had been tightened round his neck, and kept it pointing out, showing him the road he ought to follow. Teig went in the direction that the fingers were stretched, and passed out of the churchyard. He found himself on an old rutty, stony road, and he stood still again, not knowing where to turn. The corpse stretched out its bony hand a second time, and pointed out to him another road—not the road by which he had come when approaching the old church. Teig followed that road, and whenever he came to a path or road meeting it, the corpse always stretched out its hand and pointed with its fingers, showing him the way he was to take.

Many was the cross-road he turned down, and many was the crooked *boreen* he walked, until he saw from him an old burying-ground at last, beside the road, but there was neither church nor chapel nor any other building in it. The corpse squeezed him tightly, and he stood. "Bury me, bury me in the burying-ground," said the voice.

Teig drew over towards the old burying-place, and he was not more than about twenty yards from it, when, raising his eyes, he saw hundreds and hundreds of ghosts—men, women, and children—sitting on the top of the wall round about, or standing on the inside of it, or running backwards and forwards, and pointing at him, while he could see their mouths opening and shutting as if they were speaking, though he heard no word, nor any sound amongst them at all.

He was afraid to go forward, so he stood where he was, and the moment he stood, all the ghosts became quiet, and ceased moving. Then Teig understood that it was trying to keep him from going in, that they were. He walked a couple of yards forwards, and immediately the whole crowd rushed together towards the spot to which he was moving, and they stood so thickly together that it seemed to him that he never could break through them, even though he had a mind to try. But he had no mind to try it. He went back broken and dispirited, and when he had gone a couple of hundred yards from the burying-ground, he stood again, for he did not know what way he was to go. He heard the voice of the corpse in his ear, saying, "Teampoll-Ronan," and the skinny hand was stretched out again, pointing him out the road.

As tired as he was, he had to walk, and the road was neither short nor even. The night was darker than ever, and it was difficult to make his way. Many was the toss he got, and many a bruise they left on his body. At last he saw Teampoll-Ronan from him in the distance, standing in the middle of the burying-ground. He moved over towards it, and thought he was all right and safe, when he saw no ghosts nor anything else on the wall, and he thought he would never be hindered now from leaving his load off him at last. He moved over to the gate, but as he was passing in, he tripped on the threshold. Before he could recover himself, something that he could not see seized him by the neck, by the hands, and by the feet, and bruised him, and shook him, and choked him, until he was nearly dead; and at last he was lifted up, and carried more than a hundred yards from that place, and then thrown down in an old dyke, with the corpse still clinging to him.

He rose up, bruised and sore, but feared to go near the place again, for he had seen nothing the time he was thrown down and carried away.

"You corpse, up on my back?" said he, "shall I go over again to the churchyard?"—but the corpse never answered him. "That's a sign you don't wish me to try it again," said Teig.

He was now in great doubt as to what he ought to do, when the corpse spoke in his ear, and said, "Imlogue-Fada."

"Oh, murder!" said Teig, "must I bring you there? If you keep me long walking like this, I tell you I'll fall under you."

He went on, however, in the direction the corpse pointed out to him. He could not have told, himself, how long he had been going, when the dead man behind suddenly squeezed him, and said, "There!"

Teig looked from him, and he saw a little low wall, that was so broken down in places that it was no wall at all. It was in a great wide field, in from the road; and only for three or four great stones at the corners, that were more like rocks than stones, there was nothing to show that there was either graveyard or burying-ground there.

"Is this Imlogue-Fada? Shall I bury you here?" said Teig.

"Yes," said the voice.

"But I see no grave or gravestone, only this pile of stones," said Teig.

The corpse did not answer, but stretched out its long fleshless hand to show Teig the direction in which he was to go. Teig went on accordingly, but he was greatly terrified, for he remembered what had happened to him at the last place. He went on, "with his heart in his mouth," as he said himself afterwards; but when he came to within fifteen or twenty yards of the little low square wall, there broke out a flash of lightning, bright yellow and red, with blue streaks in it, and went round about the wall in one course, and it swept by as fast as the swallow in the clouds, and the longer Teig remained looking at it the faster it went, till at last it became like a bright ring of flame round the old graveyard, which no one could pass without being burnt by it. Teig never saw, from the time he was born, and never saw afterwards, so wonderful or so splendid a sight as that was. Round went the flame, white and yellow and blue sparks leaping out from it as it went, and although at first it had been no more than a thin, narrow line, it increased slowly until it was at last a great broad band, and it was continually getting broader and higher, and throwing out more brilliant sparks, till there was never a colour on the ridge of the earth that was not to be seen in that fire; and lightning never shone and flame never flamed that was so shining and so bright as that.

Teig was amazed; he was half dead with fatigue, and he had no courage left to approach the wall. There fell a mist over his eyes, and there came a *soorawn* in his head, and he was obliged to sit down upon a great stone to recover himself. He could see nothing but the light, and he could hear nothing but the whirr of it as it shot round the paddock faster than a flash of lightning.

As he sat there on the stone, the voice whispered once more in his ear, "Kill-Breedya"; and the dead man squeezed him so tightly that he cried out. He rose again, sick, tired, and trembling, and went forward as he was directed. The wind was cold, and the road was bad, and the load upon his back was heavy, and the night was dark, and he himself was nearly worn out, and if he had had very much farther to go he must have fallen dead under his burden.

The Haunters & The Haunted | 57

At last the corpse stretched out its hand, and said to him, "Bury me there."

"This is the last burying-place," said Teig in his own mind; "and the little grey man said I'd be allowed to bury him in some of them, so it must be this; it can't be but they'll let him in here."

The first, faint streak of the *ring of day* was appearing in the east, and the clouds were beginning to catch fire, but it was darker than ever, for the moon was set, and there were no stars.

"Make haste, make haste!" said the corpse; and Teig hurried forward as well as he could to the graveyard, which was a little place on a bare hill, with only a few graves in it. He walked boldly in through the open gate, and nothing touched him, nor did he either hear or see anything. He came to the middle of the ground, and then stood up and looked round him for a spade or shovel to make a grave. As he was turning round and searching, he suddenly perceived what startled him greatly—a newly-dug grave right before him. He moved over to it, and looked down, and there at the bottom he saw a black coffin. He clambered down into the hole and lifted the lid, and found that (as he thought it would be) the coffin was empty. He had hardly mounted up out of the hole, and was standing on the brink, when the corpse, which had clung to him for more than eight hours, suddenly relaxed its hold of his neck, and loosened its shins from round his hips, and sank down with a *plop* into the open coffin.

Teig fell down on his two knees at the brink of the grave, and gave thanks to God. He made no delay then, but pressed down the coffin lid in its place, and threw in the clay over it with his two hands, and when the grave was filled up, he stamped and leaped on it with his feet, until it was firm and hard, and then he left the place.

The sun was fast rising as he finished his work, and the first thing he did was to return to the road, and look out for a house to rest himself in. He found an inn at last; and lay down upon a bed there, and slept till night. Then he rose up and ate a little, and fell asleep again till morning. When he awoke in the morning he hired a horse and rode home. He was more than twenty-six miles from home where he was, and he had come all that way with the dead body on his back in one night.

All the people at his own home thought that he must have left the country, and they rejoiced greatly when they saw him come back. Everyone began asking him where he had been, but he would not tell anyone except his father.

He was a changed man from that day. He never drank too much; he never lost his money over cards; and especially he would not take the world and be out late by himself of a dark night.

He was not a fortnight at home until he married Mary, the girl he had been in love with, and it's at their wedding the sport was, and it's he was the happy man from that day forward, and it's all I wish that we may be as happy as he was.

Glossary. — *Rann*, a stanza; *kailee* (*céilidhe*), a visit in the evening; *wirra* (*a mhuire*), "Oh, Mary!" an exclamation like the French *dame*; *rib*, a single hair (in Irish, *ribe*); *a lock* (*glac*), a bundle or wisp, or a little share of anything; *kippeen* (*cipín*), a rod or twig; *boreen* (*bóithrín*), a lane; *bodach*, a clown; *soorawn* (*suarán*), vertigo. *Avic* (*a Mhic*)=my son, or rather, Oh, son. Mic is the vocative of Mac.

VI
THE HAUNTED AND THE HAUNTERS: OR THE HOUSE AND THE BRAIN

By Sir Edward Bulwer-Lytton

A friend of mine, who is a man of letters and a philosopher, said to me one day, as if between jest and earnest—"Fancy! since we last met, I have discovered a haunted house in the midst of London."

"Really haunted?—and by what?—ghosts?"

"Well, I can't answer these questions—all I know is this—six weeks ago I and my wife were in search of a furnished apartment. Passing a quiet street, we saw on the window of one of the houses a bill, 'Apartments Furnished.' The situation suited us: we entered the house—liked the rooms—engaged them by the week—and left them the third day. No power on earth could have reconciled my wife to stay longer, and I don't wonder at it."

"What did you see?"

"Excuse me—I have no desire to be ridiculed as a superstitious dreamer—nor, on the other hand, could I ask you to accept on my affirmation what you would hold to be incredible without the evidence of your own senses. Let me only say this, it was not so much what we saw or heard (in which you might fairly suppose that we were the dupes of our own excited fancy, or the victims of imposture in others) that drove us away, as it was an undefinable terror which seized both of us whenever we passed by the door of a certain unfurnished room, in which we neither saw nor heard anything. And the strangest marvel of all was, that for once in my life I agreed with my wife—silly woman though she be—and allowed, after the third night, that it was impossible to stay a fourth in that house. Accordingly, on the fourth morning, I summoned the woman who kept the house and attended on us, and told her that the rooms did not quite suit us, and we would not stay out our week. She said, dryly: 'I know why; you have stayed longer than any other lodger; few ever stayed a second night; none before you, a third. But I take it they have been very kind to you.'

"'They—who?' I asked, affecting a smile.

"'Why, they who haunt the house, whoever they are. I don't mind them; I remember them many years ago, when I lived in this house, not as a servant; but I know they will be the death of me some day. I don't care—I'm old, and must die soon, anyhow; and then I shall be with them, and in this house still.' The woman spoke with so dreary a calmness, that really it was a sort of awe that prevented my conversing with her farther. I paid for my week, and too happy were I and my wife to get off so cheaply."

"You excite my curiosity," said I; "nothing I should like better than to sleep in a haunted house. Pray give me the address of the one which you left so ignominiously."

My friend gave me the address; and when we parted, I walked straight towards the house thus indicated.

It is situated on the north side of Oxford Street, in a dull but respectable thoroughfare. I found the house shut up—no bill at the window, and no response to my knock. As I was turning away, a beer-boy, collecting pewter pots at the neighbouring areas, said to me, "Do you want anyone in that house, sir?"

"Yes, I heard it was to let."

"Let!—why, the woman who kept it is dead—has been dead these three weeks, and no one can be found to stay there, though Mr J— — offered ever so much. He offered mother, who chars for him, £1 a week just to open and shut the windows, and she would not."

"Would not!—and why?"

"The house is haunted; and the old woman who kept it was found dead in her bed, with her eyes wide open. They say the devil strangled her."

"Pooh!—you speak of Mr J— —. Is he the owner of the house?"

"Yes."

"Where does he live?"

"In G— — Street, No. — —."

"What is he?—in any business?"

"No, sir—nothing particular; a single gentleman."

I gave the pot-boy the gratuity earned by his liberal information, and proceeded to Mr J— —, in G— —Street, which was close by the street that boasted the haunted house. I was lucky enough to find Mr J— — at home—an elderly man, with intelligent countenance and prepossessing manners.

I communicated my name and my business frankly. I said I heard the house was considered to be haunted—that I had a strong desire to examine a house with so equivocal a reputation—that I should be greatly obliged if he would allow me to hire it, though only for a night. I was willing to pay for that privilege whatever he might be inclined to ask. "Sir," said Mr J— —, with great courtesy, "the house is at your service, for as short or as long a time as you please. Rent is out of the question—the obligation will be on my side should you be able to discover the cause of the strange phenomena which at present deprive it of all value. I cannot let it, for I cannot even get a servant to keep it in order or answer the door. Unluckily the house is haunted, if I may use that expression, not only by night, but by day; though at night the disturbances are of a more unpleasant and sometimes of a more alarming character.

"The poor old woman who died in it three weeks ago was a pauper whom I took out of a workhouse, for in her childhood she had been known to some of my family, and had once been in such good circumstances that she had rented that house of my uncle. She was a woman of superior education and strong mind, and was the only person I could ever induce to remain in the house. Indeed, since her death, which was sudden, and the coroner's inquest, which gave it a notoriety in the neighbourhood, I have so despaired of finding any person to take charge of it, much more a tenant, that I would willingly let it rent free for a year to anyone who would pay its rates and taxes."

"How long is it since the house acquired this sinister character?"

"That I can scarcely tell you, but very many years since. The old woman I spoke of said it was haunted when she rented it between thirty and forty years ago. The fact is that my life has been spent in the East Indies and in the civil service of the Company. I returned to England last year on inheriting the fortune of an uncle, amongst whose possessions was the house in question. I found it shut up and uninhabited. I was told that it was haunted, that no one would inhabit it. I smiled at what seemed to me so idle a story. I spent some money in repainting and roofing it—added to its old-fashioned furniture a few modern articles—advertised it, and obtained a lodger for a year. He was a colonel retired on half-pay. He came in with his family, a son and a daughter, and four or five servants: they all left the house the next day, and although they deponed that they had all seen something different, that something was equally terrible to all. I really could not in conscience sue, or even blame, the colonel for breach of agreement.

"Then I put in the old woman I have spoken of, and she was empowered to let the house in apartments. I never had one lodger who stayed more than three days. I do not tell you their stories—to no two lodgers have there been exactly the same phenomena repeated. It is better that you should judge for yourself, than enter the house with an imagination influenced by previous narratives; only be prepared to see and to hear something or other, and take whatever precautions you yourself please."

"Have you never had a curiosity yourself to pass a night in that house?"

"Yes. I passed not a night, but three hours in broad daylight alone in that house. My curiosity is not satisfied, but it is quenched. I have no desire to renew the experiment. You cannot complain, you see, sir, that I am not sufficiently candid; and unless your interest be exceedingly eager and your nerves unusually strong, I honestly add that I advise you *not* to pass a night in that house."

"My interest *is* exceedingly keen," said I, "and though only a coward will boast of his nerves in situations wholly unfamiliar to him, yet my nerves have been seasoned in such variety of danger that I have the right to rely on them—even in a haunted house."

Mr J—— said very little more; he took the keys of the house out of his bureau, gave them to me,—and thanking him cordially for his frankness, and his urbane concession to my wish, I carried off my prize.

Impatient for the experiment, as soon as I reached home I summoned my confidential servant,—a young man of gay spirits, fearless temper, and as free from superstitious prejudice as anyone I could think of.

"F——," said I, "you remember in Germany how disappointed we were at not finding a ghost in that old castle, which was said to be haunted by a headless apparition? Well, I have heard of a house in London which, I have reason to hope, is decidedly haunted. I mean to sleep there to-night. From what I hear, there is no doubt that something will allow itself to be seen or to be heard—something, perhaps, excessively horrible. Do you think, if I take you with me, I may rely on your presence of mind, whatever may happen?"

"Oh, sir! pray trust me," answered F——, grinning with delight.

"Very well—then here are the keys of the house—this is the address. Go now—select for me any bedroom you please; and since the house has not been inhabited for weeks, make up a good fire—air the bed well—see, of course, that there are candles as well as fuel. Take with you my revolver and my dagger—so much for my weapons—arm yourself equally well; and if we are not a match for a dozen ghosts, we shall be but a sorry couple of Englishmen."

I was engaged for the rest of the day on business so urgent that I had not leisure to think much on the nocturnal adventure to which I had plighted my honour. I dined alone, and very late, and while dining, read, as is my habit. The volume I selected was one of Macaulay's Essays. I thought to myself that I would take the book with me; there was so much of healthfulness in the style, and practical life in the subjects, that it would serve as an antidote against the influences of superstitious fancy.

Accordingly, about half-past nine, I put the book into my pocket, and strolled leisurely towards the haunted house. I took with me a favourite dog—an exceedingly sharp, bold, and vigilant bull-terrier—a dog fond of prowling about strange ghostly corners and passages at night in search of rats—a dog of dogs for a ghost.

It was a summer night, but chilly, the sky somewhat gloomy and overcast. Still, there was a moon—faint and sickly, but still a moon—and if the clouds permitted, after midnight it would be brighter.

I reached the house, knocked, and my servant opened with a cheerful smile.

"All right, sir, and very comfortable."

"Oh!" said I, rather disappointed; "have you not seen nor heard anything remarkable?"

"Well, sir, I must own I have heard something queer."

"What?—what?"

"The sound of feet pattering behind me; and once or twice small noises like whispers close at my ear—nothing more."

"You are not at all frightened?"

"I! not a bit of it, sir"; and the man's bold look reassured me on one point—viz. that, happen what might, he would not desert me.

We were in the hall, the street-door closed, and my attention was now drawn to my dog. He had at first ran in eagerly enough, but had sneaked back to the door, and was scratching and whining to get out. After patting him on the head, and encouraging him gently, the dog seemed to reconcile himself to the situation and followed me and F—— through the house, but keeping close at my heels instead of hurrying inquisitively in advance, which was his usual and normal habit in all strange places. We first visited the subterranean apartments, the kitchen and other offices, and especially the cellars, in which last there were two or three bottles of wine still left in a bin, covered with cobwebs, and evidently, by their appearance, undisturbed for many years. It was clear that the ghosts were not wine-bibbers.

For the rest we discovered nothing of interest. There was a gloomy little backyard, with very high walls. The stones of this yard were very damp—and what with the damp, and what with the dust and smoke-grime on the pavement, our feet left a slight impression where we passed. And now appeared the first strange phenomenon witnessed by myself in this strange abode. I saw, just before me, the print of a foot suddenly form itself, as it were. I stopped, caught hold of my servant, and pointed to it. In advance of that footprint as suddenly dropped another. We both saw it. I advanced quickly to the place; the footprint kept advancing before me, a small footprint—the foot of a child: the impression was too faint thoroughly to distinguish the shape, but it seemed to us both that it was the print of a naked foot. This phenomenon ceased when we arrived at the opposite wall, nor did it repeat itself on returning.

We remounted the stairs, and entered the rooms on the ground floor, a dining parlour, a small back-parlour, and a still smaller third room that had been probably appropriated to a footman—all still as death. We then visited the drawing-rooms, which seemed fresh and new. In the front room I seated myself in an armchair. F— — placed on the table the candlestick with which he had lighted us. I told him to shut the door. As he turned to do so, a chair opposite to me moved from the wall quickly and noiselessly, and dropped itself about a yard from my own chair, immediately fronting it.

"Why, this is better than the turning-tables," said I, with a half-laugh— and as I laughed, my dog put back his head and howled.

F— —, coming back, had not observed the movement of the chair. He employed himself now in stilling the dog. I continued to gaze on the chair, and fancied I saw on it a pale blue misty outline of a human figure, but an outline so indistinct that I could only distrust my own vision. The dog now was quiet. "Put back that chair opposite to me," said I to F— —; "put it back to the wall."

F— — obeyed. "Was that you, sir?" said he, turning abruptly.

"I—what!"

"Why, something struck me. I felt it sharply on the shoulder—just here."

"No," said I. "But we have jugglers present, and though we may not discover their tricks, we shall catch *them* before they frighten *us*."

We did not stay long in the drawing-rooms—in fact, they felt so damp and so chilly that I was glad to get to the fire upstairs. We locked the doors of the drawing-rooms—a precaution which, I should observe, we had taken with all the rooms we had searched below. The bedroom my servant had selected for me was the best on the floor—a large one, with two windows fronting the street. The four-posted bed, which took up no inconsiderable space, was opposite to the fire, which burned clear and bright; a door in the wall to the left, between the bed and the window, communicated with the room which my servant appropriated to himself.

This last was a small room with a sofa-bed, and had no communication with the landing-place—no other door but that which conducted to the bedroom I was to occupy. On either side of my fireplace was a cupboard, without locks, flushed with the wall, and covered with the same dull-brown paper. We examined these cupboards—only hooks to suspend female dresses—nothing else; we sounded the walls—evidently solid—the outer walls of the building. Having finished the survey of these apartments, warmed myself a few moments, and lighted my cigar, I then, still accompanied by F——, went forth to complete my reconnoitre. In the landing-place there was another door; it was closed firmly. "Sir," said my servant in surprise, "I unlocked this door with all the others when I first came; it cannot have got locked from the inside, for it is a—"

Before he had finished his sentence the door, which neither of us then was touching, opened quietly of itself. We looked at each other a single instant. The same thought seized both—some human agency might be detected here. I rushed in first, my servant followed. A small blank dreary room without furniture—a few empty boxes and hampers in a corner—a small window—the shutters closed—not even a fireplace—no other door but that by which we had entered—no carpet on the floor, and the floor seemed very old, uneven, worm-eaten, mended here and there, as was shown by the whiter patches on the wood; but no living being, and no visible place in which a living being could have hidden. As we stood gazing around, the door by which we had entered closed as quietly as it had before opened: we were imprisoned.

For the first time I felt a creep of undefinable horror. Not so my servant. "Why, they don't think to trap us, sir; I could break that trumpery door with a kick of my foot."

"Try first if it will open to your hand," said I, shaking off the vague apprehension that had seized me, "while I open the shutters and see what is without."

I unbarred the shutters—the window looked on the little backyard I have before described; there was no ledge without—nothing but sheer descent. No man getting out of that window would have found any footing till he had fallen on the stones below.

F——, meanwhile, was vainly attempting to open the door. He now turned round to me, and asked my permission to use force. And I should here state, in justice to the servant, that, far from evincing any superstitious terrors, his nerve, composure, and even gaiety amidst circumstances so extraordinary compelled my admiration, and made me congratulate myself on having secured a companion in every way fitted to the occasion. I willingly gave him the permission he required. But though he was a remarkably strong man, his force was as idle as his milder efforts; the door did not even shake to his stoutest kick. Breathless and panting, he desisted. I then tried the door myself, equally in vain.

As I ceased from the effort, again that creep of horror came over me; but this time it was more cold and stubborn. I felt as if some strange and ghastly exhalation were rising up from the chinks of that rugged floor, and filling the atmosphere with a venomous influence hostile to human life. The door now very slowly and quietly opened as of its own accord. We precipitated ourselves into the landing-place. We both saw a large pale light—as large as the human figure, but shapeless and unsubstantial—move before us, and ascend the stairs that led from the landing into the attics. I followed the light, and my servant followed me. It entered, to the right of the landing, a small garret, of which the door stood open. I entered in the same instant. The light then collapsed into a small globule, exceedingly brilliant and vivid; rested a moment on a bed in the corner, quivered, and vanished. We approached the bed and examined it—a half-tester, such as is commonly found in attics devoted to servants. On the drawers that stood near it we perceived an old faded silk kerchief, with the needle still left in a rent half repaired. The kerchief was covered with dust; probably it had belonged to the old woman who had last died in that house, and this might have been her sleeping-room.

I had sufficient curiosity to open the drawers; there were a few odds and ends of female dress, and two letters tied round with a narrow ribbon of faded yellow. I took the liberty to possess myself of the letters. We found nothing else in the room worth noticing—nor did the light reappear; but we distinctly heard, as we turned to go, a pattering footfall on the floor—just before us. We went through the other attics (in all, four), the footfall still preceding us. Nothing to be seen—nothing but the footfall heard. I had the letters in my hand; just as I was descending the stairs I distinctly felt my wrist seized, and a faint, soft effort made to draw the letters from my clasp. I only held them the more tightly, and the effort ceased.

We regained the bedchamber appropriated to myself, and I then remarked that my dog had not followed us when we had left it. He was thrusting himself close to the fire, and trembling. I was impatient to examine the letters; and while I read them, my servant opened a little box in which he had deposited the weapons I had ordered him to bring, took them out, placed them on a table close at my bed-head, and then occupied himself in soothing the dog, who, however, seemed to heed him very little.

The letters were short—they were dated; the dates exactly thirty-five years ago. They were evidently from a lover to his mistress, or a husband to some young wife. Not only the terms of expression, but a distinct reference to a former voyage indicated the writer to have been a seafarer. The spelling and handwriting were those of a man imperfectly educated, but still the language itself was forcible. In the expressions of endearment there was a kind of rough wild love; but here and there were dark unintelligible hints at some secret not of love—some secret that seemed of crime. "We ought to love each other," was one of the sentences I remember, "for how everyone else would execrate us if all was known." Again: "Don't let anyone be in the same room with you at night—you talk in your sleep." And again: "What's done can't be undone; and I tell you there's nothing against us unless the dead could come to life." Here there was underlined in a better handwriting (a female's), "They do!" At the end of the letter latest in date the same female hand had written these words: "Lost at sea the 4th of June, the same day as—"

I put down the letters, and began to muse over their contents.

Fearing, however, that the train of thought into which I fell might unsteady my nerves, I fully determined to keep my mind in a fit state to cope with whatever of marvellous the advancing night might bring forth. I roused myself—laid the letters on the table—stirred up the fire, which was still bright and cheering—and opened my volume of Macaulay. I read quietly enough till about half-past eleven. I then threw myself dressed upon the bed, and told my servant he might retire to his own room, but must keep himself awake. I bade him leave open the door between the two rooms. Thus alone, I kept two candles burning on the table by my bed-head. I placed my watch beside the weapons, and calmly resumed my Macaulay.

Opposite to me the fire burned clear; and on the hearth-rug, seemingly asleep, lay the dog. In about twenty minutes I felt an exceedingly cold air pass by my cheek, like a sudden draught. I fancied the door to my right, communicating with the landing-place, must have got open; but no—it was closed. I then turned my glance to my left, and saw the flame of the candles violently swayed as by a wind. At the same moment the watch beside the revolver softly slid from the table—softly, softly—no visible hand—it was gone. I sprang up, seizing the revolver with the one hand, the dagger with the other; I was not willing that my weapons should share the fate of the watch. Thus armed, I looked round the floor—no sign of the watch. Three slow, loud, distinct knocks were now heard at the bed-head; my servant called out, "Is that you, sir?"

"No; be on your guard."

The dog now roused himself and sat on his haunches, his ears moving quickly backwards and forwards. He kept his eyes fixed on me with a look so strange that he concentrated all my attention on himself. Slowly he rose up, all his hair bristling, and stood perfectly rigid, and with the same wild stare. I had no time, however, to examine the dog. Presently my servant emerged from his room; and if ever I saw horror in the human face, it was then. I should not have recognised him had we met in the streets, so altered was every lineament. He passed by me quickly, saying in a whisper that seemed scarcely to come from his lips, "Run—run! it is after me!" He gained the door to the landing, pulled it open, and rushed forth. I followed him into the landing involuntarily, calling him to stop; but, without heeding me, he bounded down the stairs, clinging to the balusters, and taking several steps at a time. I heard, where I stood, the street door open—heard it again clap to. I was left alone in the haunted house.

It was but for a moment that I remained undecided whether or not to follow my servant; pride and curiosity alike forbade so dastardly a flight. I re-entered my room, closing the door after me, and proceeded cautiously into the interior chamber. I encountered nothing to justify my servant's terror. I again carefully examined the walls, to see if there were any concealed door. I could find no trace of one—not even a seam in the dull-brown paper with which the room was hung. How, then, had the Thing, whatever it was, which had so scared him, obtained ingress except through my own chamber?

I returned to my room, shut and locked the door that opened upon the interior one, and stood on the hearth, expectant and prepared. I now perceived that the dog had slunk into an angle of the wall, and was pressing himself close against it, as if literally trying to force his way into it. I approached the animal and spoke to it; the poor brute was evidently beside itself with terror. It showed all its teeth, the slaver dropping from its jaws, and would certainly have bitten me if I had touched it. It did not seem to recognise me. Whoever has seen at the Zoological Gardens a rabbit fascinated by a serpent, cowering in a corner, may form some idea of the anguish which the dog exhibited. Finding all efforts to soothe the animal in vain, and fearing that his bite might be as venomous in that state as if in the madness of hydrophobia, I left him alone, placed my weapons on the table beside the fire, seated myself, and recommenced my Macaulay.

Perhaps in order not to appear seeking credit for a courage, or rather a coolness, which the reader may conceive I exaggerate, I may be pardoned if I pause to indulge in one or two egotistical remarks.

As I hold presence of mind, or what is called courage, to be precisely proportioned to familiarity with the circumstance that lead to it, so I should say that I had been long sufficiently familiar with all experiments that appertain to the Marvellous. I had witnessed many very extraordinary phenomena in various parts of the world—phenomena that would be either totally disbelieved if I stated them, or ascribed to supernatural agencies. Now, my theory is that the Supernatural is the Impossible, and that what is called supernatural is only a something in the laws of nature of which we have been hitherto ignorant. Therefore, if a ghost rise before me, I have not the right to say, "So, then, the supernatural is possible," but rather, "So, then, the apparition of a ghost is, contrary to received opinion, within the laws of nature—*i.e.* not supernatural."

Now, in all that I had hitherto witnessed, and indeed in all the wonders which the amateurs of mystery in our age record as facts, a material living agency is always required. On the Continent you will find still magicians who assert that they can raise spirits. Assume for the moment that they assert truly, still the living material form of the magician is present; and he is the material agency by which from some constitutional peculiarities, certain strange phenomena are represented to your natural senses.

Accept again, as truthful, the tales of Spirit Manifestation in America—musical or other sounds—writings on paper, produced by no discernible hand—articles of furniture moved without apparent human agency—or the actual sight and touch of hands, to which no bodies seem to belong—still there must be found the *medium* or living being, with constitutional peculiarities capable of obtaining these signs. In fine, in all such marvels, supposing even that there is no imposture, there must be a human being like ourselves, by whom, or through whom, the effects presented to human beings are produced. It is so with the now familiar phenomena of mesmerism or electro-biology; the mind of the person operated on is affected through a material living agent. Nor, supposing it true that a mesmerised patient can respond to the will or passes of a mesmeriser a hundred miles distant, is the response less occasioned by a material being; it may be through a material fluid—call it Electric, call it Odic, call it what you will—which has the power of traversing space and passing obstacles, that the material effect is communicated from one to the other.

Hence all that I had hitherto witnessed, or expected to witness, in this strange house, I believed to be occasioned through some agency or medium as mortal as myself; and this idea necessarily prevented the awe with which those who regard as supernatural things that are not within the ordinary operations of nature, might have been impressed by the adventures of that memorable night.

As, then, it was my conjecture that all that was presented, or would be presented, to my senses, must originate in some human being gifted by constitution with the power so to present them, and having some motive so to do, I felt an interest in my theory which, in its way, was rather philosophical than superstitious. And I can sincerely say that I was in as tranquil a temper for observation as any practical experimentalist could be in awaiting the effects of some rare though perhaps perilous chemical combination. Of course, the more I kept my mind detached from fancy, the more the temper fitted for observation would be obtained; and I therefore riveted eye and thought on the strong daylight sense in the page of my Macaulay.

I now became aware that something interposed between the page and the light—the page was overshadowed; I looked up, and I saw what I shall find it very difficult, perhaps impossible, to describe.

It was a Darkness shaping itself out of the air in very undefined outline. I cannot say it was of a human form, and yet it had more resemblance to a human form, or rather shadow, than anything else. As it stood, wholly apart and distinct from the air and the light around it, its dimensions seemed gigantic, the summit nearly touching the ceiling. While I gazed, a feeling of intense cold seized me. An iceberg before me could not more have chilled me; nor could the cold of an iceberg have been more purely physical. I feel convinced that it was not the cold caused by fear. As I continued to gaze, I thought—but this I cannot say with precision—that I distinguished two eyes looking down on me from the height. One moment I seemed to distinguish them clearly, the next they seemed gone; but still two rays of a pale-blue light frequently shot through the darkness, as from the height on which I half-believed, half-doubted, that I had encountered the eyes.

I strove to speak—my voice utterly failed me; I could only think to myself, "Is this fear? it is *not* fear!" I strove to rise—in vain; I felt as if weighed down by an irresistible force. Indeed, my impression was that of an immense and overwhelming Power opposed to my volition; that sense of utter inadequacy to cope with a force beyond men's, which one may feel *physically* in a storm at sea, in a conflagration, or when confronting some terrible wild beast, or rather, perhaps, the shark of the ocean, I felt *morally*. Opposed to my will was another will, as far superior to its strength as storm, fire, and shark are superior in material force to the force of men.

And now, as this impression grew on me, now came, at last, horror—horror to a degree that no words can convey. Still I retained pride, if not courage; and in my own mind I said, "This is horror, but it is not fear; unless I fear, I cannot be harmed; my reason rejects this thing; it is an illusion—I do not fear." With a violent effort I succeeded at last in stretching out my hand towards the weapon on the table; as I did so, on the arm and shoulder I received a strange shock, and my arm fell to my side powerless. And now, to add to my horror, the light began slowly to wane from the candles—they were not, as it were, extinguished, but their flame seemed very gradually withdrawn; it was the same with the fire—the light was extracted from the fuel; in a few minutes the room was in utter darkness.

The dread that came over me, to be thus in the dark with that dark Thing, whose power was so intensely felt, brought a reaction of nerve. In fact, terror had reached that climax, that either my senses must have deserted me, or I must have burst through the spell. I did burst through it. I found voice, though the voice was a shriek. I remember that I broke forth with words like these—"I do not fear, my soul does not fear"; and at the same time I found the strength to rise. Still in that profound gloom I rushed to one of the windows—tore aside the curtain—flung open the shutters; my first thought was—light. And when I saw the moon high, clear, and calm, I felt a joy that almost compensated for the previous terror. There was the moon, there was also the light from the gas-lamps in the deserted slumberous street. I turned to look back into the room; the moon penetrated its shadow very palely and partially—but still there was light. The dark Thing, whatever it might be, was gone—except that I could yet see a dim shadow which seemed the shadow of that shade, against the opposite wall.

My eye now rested on the table, and from under the table (which was without cloth or cover—an old mahogany round table) there rose a hand, visible as far as the wrist. It was a hand, seemingly, as much of flesh and blood as my own, but the hand of an aged person—lean, wrinkled, small too—a woman's hand.

That hand very softly closed on the two letters that lay on the table: hand and letters both vanished. There then came the same three loud measured knocks I had heard at the bed-head before this extraordinary drama had commenced.

As those sounds slowly ceased, I felt the whole room vibrate sensibly; and at the far end there rose, as from the floor, sparks or globules like bubbles of light, many-coloured—green, yellow, fire-red, azure. Up and down, to and fro, hither, thither, as tiny will-o'-the-wisps, the sparks moved, slow or swift, each at its own caprice. A chair (as in the drawing-room below) was now advanced from the wall without apparent agency, and placed at the opposite side of the table. Suddenly, as forth from the chair, there grew a shape—a woman's shape. It was distinct as a shape of life—ghastly as a shape of death. The face was that of youth, with a strange mournful beauty; the throat and shoulders were bare, the rest of the form in a loose robe of cloudy white. It began sleeking its long yellow hair, which fell over its shoulders; its eyes were not turned towards me, but to the door; it seemed listening, watching, waiting. The shadow of the shade in the background grew darker; and again I thought I beheld the eyes gleaming out from the summit of the shadow—eyes fixed upon that shape.

As if from the door, though it did not open, there grew out another shape equally distinct, equally ghastly—a man's shape—a young man's. It was in the dress of the last century, or rather in a likeness of such dress; for both the male shape and the female, though defined, were evidently unsubstantial, impalpable—simulacra—phantasms; and there was something incongruous, grotesque, yet fearful, in the contrast between the elaborate finery, the courtly precision of that old-fashioned garb, with its ruffles and lace and buckles, and the corpse-like aspect and ghost-like stillness of the flitting wearer. Just as the male shape approached the female, the dark Shadow started from the wall, all three for a moment wrapped in darkness. When the pale light returned, the two phantoms were as if in the grasp of the Shadow that towered between them; and there was a bloodstain on the breast of the female; and the phantom-male was leaning on its phantom-sword, and blood seemed trickling fast from the ruffles, from the lace; and the darkness of the intermediate Shadow swallowed them up—they were gone. And again the bubbles of light shot, and sailed, and undulated, growing thicker and thicker and more wildly confused in their movements.

The closet-door to the right of the fireplace now opened, and from the aperture there came the form of a woman, aged. In her hand she held letters—the very letters over which I had seen *the* Hand close; and behind her I heard a footstep. She turned round as if to listen, then she opened the letters and seemed to read; and over her shoulder I saw a livid face, the face as of a man long drowned—bloated, bleached—seaweed tangled in its dripping hair; and at her feet lay a form as of a corpse and beside the corpse there cowered a child, a miserable, squalid child, with famine in its cheeks and fear in its eyes. And as I looked in the old woman's face, the wrinkles and lines vanished, and it became a face of youth—hard-eyed, stony, but still youth; and the Shadow darted forth, and darkened over these phantoms as it had darkened over the last.

Nothing now was left but the Shadow, and on that my eyes were intently fixed, till again eyes grew out of the Shadow—malignant, serpent eyes. And the bubbles of light again rose and fell, and in their disordered, irregular, turbulent maze, mingled with the wan moonlight. And now from these globules themselves as from the shell of an egg, monstrous things burst out; the air grew filled with them; larvæ so bloodless and so hideous that I can in no way describe them except to remind the reader of the swarming life which the solar microscope brings before his eyes in a drop of water—things transparent, supple, agile, chasing each other, devouring each other—forms like nought ever beheld by the naked eye. As the shapes were without symmetry, so their movements were without order. In their very vagrancies there was no sport; they came round me and round, thicker and faster and swifter, swarming over my head, crawling over my right arm, which was outstretched in involuntary command against all evil beings.

Sometimes I felt myself touched, but not by them; invisible hands touched me. Once I felt the clutch as of cold soft fingers at my throat. I was still equally conscious that if I gave way to fear I should be in bodily peril; and I concentrated all my faculties in the single focus of resisting, stubborn will. And I turned my sight from the Shadow—above all, from those strange serpent eyes—eyes that had now become distinctly visible. For there, though in nought else around me, I was aware that there was a *will*, and a will of intense, creative, working evil, which might crush down my own.

The pale atmosphere in the room began now to redden as if in the air of some near conflagration. The larvæ grew lurid as things that live in fire. Again the room vibrated; again were heard the three measured knocks; and again all things were swallowed up in the darkness of the dark Shadow, as if out of that darkness all had come, into that darkness all returned.

As the gloom receded, the Shadow was wholly gone. Slowly as it had been withdrawn, the flame grew again into the candles on the table, again into the fuel in the grate. The whole room came once more calmly, healthfully into sight.

The two doors were still closed, the door communicating with the servants' room still locked. In the corner of the wall, into which he had so convulsively niched himself, lay the dog. I called to him—no movement; I approached—the animal was dead; his eyes protruded; his tongue out of his mouth; the froth gathered round his jaws. I took him in my arms; I brought him to the fire; I felt acute grief for the loss of my poor favourite—acute self-reproach; I accused myself of his death; I imagined he had died of fright. But what was my surprise on finding that his neck was actually broken—

actually twisted out of the vertebræ. Had this been done in the dark?—must it not have been by a hand human as mine?—must there not have been a human agency all the while in that room? Good cause to suspect it. I cannot tell. I cannot do more than state the fact fairly; the reader may draw his own inference.

Another surprising circumstance—my watch was restored to the table from which it had been so mysteriously withdrawn; but it had stopped at the very moment it was so withdrawn; nor, despite all the skill of the watchmaker, has it ever gone since—that is, it will go in a strange erratic way for a few hours, and then comes to a dead stop—it is worthless.

Nothing more chanced for the rest of the night. Nor, indeed, had I long to wait before the dawn broke. Not till it was broad daylight did I quit the haunted house. Before I did so, I revisited the little blind room in which my servant and myself had been for a time imprisoned. I had a strong impression—for which I could not account—that from that room had originated the mechanism of the phenomena—if I may use the term—which had been experienced in my chamber. And though I entered it now in the clear day, with the sun peering through the filmy window, I still felt, as I stood on its floor, the creep of the horror which I had first there experienced the night before, and which had been so aggravated by what had passed in my own chamber. I could not, indeed, bear to stay more than half a minute within those walls. I descended the stairs, and again I heard the footfall before me; and when I opened the street door, I thought I could distinguish a very low laugh. I gained my own home, expecting to find my runaway servant there. But he had not presented himself; nor did I hear more of him for three days, when I received a letter from him, dated from Liverpool, to this effect:—

> "Honoured Sir,—I humbly entreat your pardon, though I can scarcely hope that you will think I deserve it, unless— which Heaven forbid!—you saw what I did. I feel that it will be years before I can recover myself; and as to being fit for service, it is out of the question. I am therefore going to my brother-in-law at Melbourne. The ship sails to-morrow. Perhaps the long voyage may set me up. I do nothing now but start and tremble, and fancy It is behind me. I humbly beg you, honoured sir, to order my clothes, and whatever wages are due to me, to be sent to my mother's, at Walworth—John knows her address."

The letter ended with additional apologies, somewhat incoherent, and explanatory details as to effects that had been under the writer's charge.

This flight may perhaps warrant a suspicion that the man wished to go to Australia, and had been somehow or other fraudulently mixed up with the events of the night. I say nothing in refutation of that conjecture; rather, I suggest it as one that would seem to many persons the most probable solution of improbable occurrences. My own theory remained unshaken. I returned in the evening to the house, to bring away in a hack cab the things I had left there, with my poor dog's body. In this task I was not disturbed, nor did any incident worth note befall me, except that still, on ascending, and descending the stairs I heard the same footfall in advance. On leaving the house, I went to Mr J——'s. He was at home. I returned him the keys, told him that my curiosity was sufficiently gratified, and was about to relate quickly what had passed, when he stopped me, and said, though with much politeness, that he had no longer any interest in a mystery which none had ever solved.

I determined at least to tell him of the two letters I had read, as well as of the extraordinary manner in which they had disappeared, and I then inquired if he thought they had been addressed to the woman who had died in the house, and if there were anything in her early history which could possibly confirm the dark suspicions to which the letters gave rise. Mr J—— seemed startled, and, after musing a few moments, answered, "I know but little of the woman's earlier history, except, as I before told you, that her family were known to mine. But you revive some vague reminiscences to her prejudice. I will make inquiries, and inform you of their result. Still, even if we could admit the popular superstition that a person who had been either the perpetrator or the victim of dark crimes in life could revisit, as a restless spirit, the scene in which those crimes had been committed, I should observe that the house was infested by strange sights and sounds before the old woman died—you smile—what would you say?"

"I would say this, that I am convinced, if we could get to the bottom of these mysteries, we should find a living human agency."

"What! you believe it is all an imposture? For what object?"

"Not an imposture in the ordinary sense of the word. If suddenly I were to sink into a deep sleep, from which you could not awake me, but in that sleep could answer questions with an accuracy which I could not pretend to when awake—tell you what money you had in your pocket—nay, describe your very thoughts—it is not necessarily an imposture, any more than it is necessarily supernatural. I should be, unconsciously to myself, under a mesmeric influence, conveyed to me from a distance by a human being who had acquired power over me by previous *rapport*."

"Granting mesmerism, so far carried, to be a fact, you are right. And you would infer from this that a mesmeriser might produce the extraordinary effects you and others have witnessed over inanimate objects—fill the air with sights and sounds?"

"Or impress our senses with the belief in them—we never having been *en rapport* with the person acting on us? No. What is commonly called mesmerism could not do this; but there may be a power akin to mesmerism, and superior to it—the power that in the old days was called Magic. That such a power may extend to all inanimate objects of matter, I do not say; but if so, it would not be against nature, only a rare power in nature which might be given to constitutions with certain peculiarities, and cultivated by practice to an extraordinary degree. That such a power might extend over the dead—that is, over certain thoughts and memories that the dead may still retain—and compel, not that which ought properly to be called the *soul*, and which is far beyond human reach, but rather a phantom of what has been most earth-stained on earth, to make itself apparent to our senses—is a very ancient though obsolete theory, upon which I will hazard no opinion. But I do not conceive the power would be supernatural.

"Let me illustrate what I mean from an experiment which Paracelsus describes as not difficult, and which the author of the *Curiosities of Literature* cites as credible: A flower perishes; you burn it. Whatever were the elements of that flower while it lived are gone, dispersed, you know not whither; you can never discover nor re-collect them. But you can, by chemistry, out of the burnt dust of that flower, raise a spectrum of the flower, just as it seemed in life. It may be the same with the human being. The soul has so much escaped you as the essence or elements of the flower. Still you may make a spectrum of it. And this phantom, though in the popular superstition it is held to be the soul of the departed, must not be confounded with the true soul; it is but the eidolon of the dead form.

"Hence, like the best-attested stories of ghosts or spirits, the thing that most strikes us is the absence of what we hold to be soul—that is, of superior emancipated intelligence. They come for little or no object—they seldom speak, if they do come; they utter no ideas above that of an ordinary person on earth. These American spirit-seers have published volumes of communications in prose and verse, which they assert to be given in the names of the most illustrious dead—Shakespeare, Bacon—heaven knows whom. Those communications, taking the best, are certainly not a whit of higher order than would be communications from living persons of fair talent and education; they are wondrously inferior to what Bacon, Shakespeare, and Plato said and wrote when on earth.

"Nor, what is more notable, do they ever contain an idea that was not on the earth before. Wonderful, therefore, as such phenomena may be (granting them to be truthful), I see much that philosophy may question, nothing that it is incumbent on philosophy to deny—viz. nothing supernatural. They are but ideas conveyed somehow or other (we have not yet discovered the means) from one mortal brain to another. Whether, in so doing, tables walk of their own accord, or fiend-like shapes appear in a magic circle, or bodyless hands rise and remove material objects, or a Thing of Darkness, such as presented itself to me, freeze our blood—still am I persuaded that these are but agencies conveyed, as by electric wires, to my own brain from the brain of another. In some constitutions there is a natural chemistry, and those may produce chemic wonders—in others a natural fluid, call it electricity, and these produce electric wonders. But they differ in this from Normal Science—they are alike objectless, purposeless, puerile, frivolous. They lead on to no grand results; and therefore the world does not heed, and true sages have not cultivated them. But sure I am, that of all I saw or heard, a man, human as myself, was the remote originator; and I believe unconsciously to himself as to the exact effects produced, for this reason: no two persons, you say, have ever told you that they experienced exactly the same thing. Well, observe, no two persons ever experience exactly the same dream. If this were an ordinary imposture, the machinery would be arranged for results that would but little vary; if it were a supernatural agency permitted by the Almighty, it would surely be for some definite end.

"These phenomena belong to neither class; my persuasion is, that they originate in some brain now far distant; that that brain had no distinct volition in anything that occurred; that what does occur reflects but its devious, motley, ever-shifting, half-formed thoughts; in short, that it has been but the dreams of such a brain put into action and invested with a semisubstance. That this brain is of immense power, that it can set matter into movement, that it is malignant and destructive, I believe: some material force must have killed my dog; it might, for aught I know, have sufficed to kill myself, had I been as subjugated by terror as the dog—had my intellect or my spirit given me no countervailing resistance in my will."

"It killed your dog! that is fearful! indeed, it is strange that no animal can be induced to stay in that house; not even a cat. Rats and mice are never found in it."

"The instincts of the brute creation detect influences deadly to their existence. Man's reason has a sense less subtle, because it has a resisting power more supreme. But enough; do you comprehend my theory?"

"Yes, though imperfectly—and I accept any crotchet (pardon the word), however odd, rather than embrace at once the notion of ghosts and hobgoblins we imbibed in our nurseries. Still, to my unfortunate house the evil is the same. What on earth can I do with the house?"

"I will tell you what I would do. I am convinced from my own internal feelings that the small unfurnished room at right angles to the door of the bedroom which I occupied, forms a starting-point or receptacle for the influences which haunt the house; and I strongly advise you to have the walls opened, the floor removed—nay, the whole room pulled down. I observe that it is detached from the body of the house, built over the small back-yard, and could be removed without injury to the rest of the building."

"And you think, if I did that——"

"You would cut off the telegraph wires. Try it. I am so persuaded that I am right, that I will pay half the expense if you will allow me to direct the operations."

"Nay, I am well able to afford the cost; for the rest, allow me to write to you."

About ten days afterwards I received a letter from Mr J——, telling me that he had visited the house since I had seen him; that he had found the two letters I had described, replaced in the drawer from which I had taken them; that he had read them with misgivings like my own; that he had instituted a cautious inquiry about the woman to whom I rightly conjectured they had been written. It seemed that thirty-six years ago (a year before the date of the letters), she had married against the wish of her relatives, an American of very suspicious character; in fact, he was generally believed to have been a pirate. She herself was the daughter of very respectable tradespeople, and had served in the capacity of a nursery governess before her marriage. She had a brother, a widower, who was considered wealthy, and who had one child of about six years old. A month after the marriage, the body of this brother was found in the Thames, near London Bridge; there seemed some marks of violence about his throat, but they were not deemed sufficient to warrant the inquest in any other verdict than that of "found drowned."

The American and his wife took charge of the little boy, the deceased brother having by his will left his sister the guardian of his only child—and in the event of the child's death, the sister inherited. The child died about six months afterwards—it was supposed to have been neglected and ill-treated. The neighbours deposed to have heard it shriek at night. The surgeon who had examined it after death, said that it was emaciated as if from want of nourishment, and the body was covered with livid bruises. It seemed that one winter night the child had sought to escape—crept out into the backyard—tried to scale the wall—fallen back exhausted, and been found at morning on the stones in a dying state. But though there was some evidence of cruelty, there was none of murder; and the aunt and her husband had sought to palliate cruelty by alleging the exceeding stubbornness and perversity of the child, who was declared to be half-witted. Be that as it may, at the orphan's death the aunt inherited her brother's fortune.

Before the first wedded year was out, the American quitted England abruptly, and never returned to it. He obtained a cruising vessel, which was lost in the Atlantic two years afterwards. The widow was left in affluence; but reverses of various kinds had befallen her: a bank broke—an investment failed—she went into a small business and became insolvent—then she entered into service, sinking lower and lower, from housekeeper down to maid-of-all-work—never long retaining a place, though nothing peculiar against her character was ever alleged. She was considered sober, honest, and peculiarly quiet in her ways; still nothing prospered with her. And so she had dropped into the workhouse, from which Mr J—— had taken her, to be placed in charge of the very house which she had rented as mistress in the first year of her wedded life.

Mr J—— added that he had passed an hour alone in the unfurnished room which I had urged him to destroy, and that his impressions of dread while there were so great, though he had neither heard nor seen anything, that he was eager to have the walls bared and the floors removed as I had suggested. He had engaged persons for the·work, and would commence any day I would name.

The day was accordingly fixed. I repaired to the haunted house—we went into the blind dreary room, took up the skirting, and then the floors. Under the rafters, covered with rubbish, was found a trap-door, quite large enough to admit a man. It was closely nailed down, with clamps and rivets of iron. On removing these we descended into a room below, the existence of which had never been suspected. In this room there had been a window and a flue, but they had been bricked over, evidently for many years. By the help of candles we examined this place; it still retained some mouldering furniture—three chairs, an oak settle, a table—all of the fashion of about eighty years ago. There was a chest of drawers against the wall, in which we found, half-rotted away, old-fashioned articles of a man's dress, such as might have been worn eighty or a hundred years ago by a gentleman of some rank—costly steel buckles and buttons, like those yet worn in court dresses—a handsome court sword—in a waistcoat which had once been rich with gold lace, but which was now blackened and foul with damp, we found five guineas, a few silver coins, and an ivory ticket, probably for some place of entertainment long since passed away. But our main discovery was in a kind of iron safe fixed to the wall, the lock of which it cost us much trouble to get picked.

In this safe were three shelves and two small drawers. Ranged on the shelves were several small bottles of crystal, hermetically stopped. They contained colourless volatile essences, of what nature I shall say no more than that they were not poisons—phosphor and ammonia entered into some of them. There were also some very curious glass tubes, and a small pointed rod of iron, with a large lump of rock-crystal, and another of amber—also a loadstone of great power.

In one of the drawers we found a miniature portrait set in gold, and retaining the freshness of its colours most remarkably, considering the length of time it had probably been there. The portrait was that of a man who might be somewhat advanced in middle life, perhaps forty-seven or forty-eight.

It was a most peculiar face—a most impressive face. If you could fancy some mighty serpent transformed into man, preserving in the human lineaments the old serpent type, you would have a better idea of that countenance than long descriptions can convey: the width and flatness of frontal—the tapering elegance of contour disguising the strength of the deadly jaw—the long, large, terrible eye, glittering and green as the emerald—and withal a certain ruthless calm, as if from the consciousness of an immense power. The strange thing was this—the instant I saw the miniature I recognised a startling likeness to one of the rarest portraits in the world—the portrait of a man of a rank only below that of royalty, who in his own day had made a considerable noise. History says little or nothing of him; but search the correspondence of his contemporaries, and you find reference to his wild daring, his bold profligacy, his restless spirit, his taste for the occult sciences. While still in the meridian of life he died and was buried, so say the chronicles, in a foreign land. He died in time to escape the grasp of the law, for he was accused of crimes which would have given him to the headsman.

After his death, the portraits of him, which had been numerous, for he had been a munificent encourager of art, were bought up and destroyed— it was supposed by his heirs, who might have been glad could they have razed his very name from their splendid line. He had enjoyed a vast wealth; a large portion of this was believed to have been embezzled by a favourite astrologer or soothsayer—at all events, it had unaccountably vanished at the time of his death. One portrait alone of him was supposed to have escaped the general destruction; I had seen it in the house of a collector some months before. It had made on me a wonderful impression, as it does on all who behold it—a face never to be forgotten; and there was that face in the miniature that lay within my hand. True, that in the miniature the man was a few years older than in the portrait I had seen, or than the original was even at the time of his death. But a few years!—why, between the date in which flourished that direful noble and the date in which the miniature was evidently painted, there was an interval of more than two centuries. While I was thus gazing, silent and wondering, Mr J— — said:

"But is it possible? I have known this man."

"How—where?" I cried.

"In India. He was high in the confidence of the Rajah of — —, and wellnigh drew him into a revolt which would have lost the Rajah his dominions. The man was a Frenchman—his name de V— —, clever, bold, lawless. We insisted on his dismissal and banishment: it must be the same man—no two faces like his—yet this miniature seems nearly a hundred years old."

Mechanically I turned round the miniature to examine the back of it, and on the back was engraved a pentacle; in the middle of the pentacle a ladder, and the third step of the ladder was formed by the date 1765. Examining still more minutely, I detected a spring; this, on being pressed, opened the back of the miniature as a lid. Withinside the lid was engraved "Mariana to thee—Be faithful in life and in death to — —." Here follows a name that I will not mention, but it was not unfamiliar to me. I had heard it spoken of by old men in my childhood as the name borne by a dazzling charlatan, who had made a great sensation in London for a year or so, and had fled the country on the charge of a double murder within his own house—that of his mistress and his rival. I said nothing of this to Mr J— —, to whom reluctantly I resigned the miniature.

We had found no difficulty in opening the first drawer within the iron safe; we found great difficulty in opening the second: it was not locked, but it resisted all efforts till we inserted in the chinks the edge of a chisel. When we had thus drawn it forth, we found a very singular apparatus in the nicest order. Upon a small thin book, or rather tablet, was placed a saucer of crystal; this saucer was filled with a clear liquid—on that liquid floated a kind of compass, with a needle shifting rapidly round, but instead of the usual points of a compass were seven strange characters, not very unlike those used by astrologers to denote the planets. A very peculiar, but not strong nor displeasing odour, came from this drawer, which was lined with a wood that we afterwards discovered to be hazel. Whatever the cause of this odour, it produced a material effect on the nerves. We all felt it, even the two workmen who were in the room—a creeping tingling sensation from the tips of the fingers to the roots of the hair. Impatient to examine the tablet, I removed the saucer. As I did so the needle of the compass went round and round with exceeding swiftness, and I felt a shock that ran through my whole frame, so that I dropped the saucer on the floor. The liquid was spilt—the saucer was broken—the compass rolled to the end of the room—and at that instant the walls shook to and fro, as if a giant had swayed and rocked them.

The two workmen were so frightened that they ran up the ladder by which we had descended from the trap-door; but seeing that nothing more happened, they were easily induced to return.

Meanwhile I had opened the tablet: it was bound in a plain red leather, with a silver clasp; it contained but one sheet of thick vellum, and on that sheet were inscribed, within a double pentacle, words in old monkish Latin, which are literally to be translated thus:—"On all that it can reach within these walls—sentient or inanimate, living or dead—as moves the needle, so work my will! Accursed be the house, and restless be the dwellers therein."

We found no more. Mr J—— burnt the tablet and its anathema. He razed to the foundations the part of the building containing the secret room with the chamber over it. He had then the courage to inhabit the house himself for a month, and a quieter, better-conditioned house could not be found in all London. Subsequently he let it to advantage, and his tenant has made no complaints.

But my story is not yet done. A few days after Mr J—— had removed into the house, I paid him a visit. We were standing by the open window and conversing. A van containing some articles of furniture which he was moving from his former house was at the door. I had just urged on him my theory that all those phenomena regarded as supermundane had emanated from a human brain; adducing the charm, or rather curse, we had found and destroyed in support of my philosophy. Mr J—— was observing in reply, "That even if mesmerism, or whatever analogous power it might be called, could really thus work in the absence of the operator, and produce effects so extraordinary, still could those effects continue when the operator himself was dead? and if the spell had been wrought, and, indeed, the room walled up, more than seventy years ago, the probability was, that the operator had long since departed this life"; Mr J——, I say, was thus answering, when I caught hold of his arm and pointed to the street below.

A well-dressed man had crossed from the opposite side, and was accosting the carrier in charge of the van. His face, as he stood, was exactly fronting our window. It was the face of the miniature we had discovered; it was the face of the portrait of the noble three centuries ago.

"Good Heavens!" cried Mr J——, "that is the face of de V——, and scarcely a day older than when I saw it in the Rajah's court in my youth!"

Seized by the same thought, we both hastened downstairs. I was first in the street; but the man had already gone. I caught sight of him, however, not many yards in advance, and in another moment I was by his side.

I had resolved to speak to him, but when I looked into his face I felt as if it were impossible to do so. That eye—the eye of the serpent—fixed and held me spellbound. And withal, about the man's whole person there was a dignity, an air of pride and station and superiority, that would have made anyone, habituated to the usages of the world, hesitate long before venturing upon a liberty or impertinence. And what could I say? what was it I would ask? Thus ashamed of my first impulse, I fell a few paces back, still, however, following the stranger, undecided what else to do. Meanwhile he turned the corner of the street; a plain carriage was in waiting, with a servant out of livery, dressed like a *valet-de-place*, at the carriage door. In another moment he had stepped into the carriage, and it drove off. I returned to the house. Mr J—— was still at the street door. He had asked the carrier what the stranger had said to him.

"Merely asked whom that house now belonged to."

The same evening I happened to go with a friend to a place in town called the Cosmopolitan Club, a place open to men of all countries, all opinions, all degrees. One orders one's coffee, smokes one's cigar. One is always sure to meet agreeable, sometimes remarkable, persons.

I had not been two minutes in the room before I beheld at a table, conversing with an acquaintance of mine, whom I will designate by the initial G——, the man—the Original of the Miniature. He was now without his hat, and the likeness was yet more startling, only I observed that while he was conversing there was less severity in the countenance; there was even a smile, though a very quiet and very cold one. The dignity of mien I had acknowledged in the street was also more striking; a dignity akin to that which invests some prince of the East—conveying the idea of supreme indifference and habitual, indisputable, indolent, but resistless power.

G—— soon after left the stranger, who then took up a scientific journal, which seemed to absorb his attention.

I drew G—— aside. "Who and what is that gentleman?"

"That? Oh, a very remarkable man indeed. I met him last year amidst the caves of Petra—the scriptural Edom. He is the best Oriental scholar I know. We joined company, had an adventure with robbers, in which he showed a coolness that saved our lives; afterwards he invited me to spend a day with him in a house he had bought at Damascus—a house buried amongst almond blossoms and roses—the most beautiful thing! He had lived there for some years, quite as an Oriental, in grand style. I half suspect he is a renegade, immensely rich, very odd; by the by, a great mesmeriser. I have seen him with my own eyes produce an effect on inanimate things. If you take a letter from your pocket and throw it to the other end of the room, he will order it to come to his feet, and you will see the letter wriggle itself along the floor till it has obeyed his command. 'Pon my honour, 'tis true: I have seen him affect even the weather, disperse or collect clouds, by means of a glass tube or wand. But he does not like talking of these matters to strangers. He has only just arrived in England; says he has not been here for a great many years; let me introduce him to you."

"Certainly! He is English, then? What is his name?"

"Oh!—a very homely one—Richards."

"And what is his birth—his family?"

"How do I know? What does it signify?—no doubt some parvenu, but rich—so infernally rich!"

G—— drew me up to the stranger, and the introduction was effected. The manners of Mr Richards were not those of an adventurous traveller. Travellers are in general constitutionally gifted with high animal spirits: they are talkative, eager, imperious. Mr Richards was calm and subdued in tone, with manners which were made distant by the loftiness of punctilious courtesy—the manners of a former age. I observed that the English he spoke was not exactly of our day. I should even have said that the accent was slightly foreign. But then Mr Richards remarked that he had been little in the habit for many years of speaking in his native tongue. The conversation fell upon the changes in the aspect of London since he had last visited our metropolis. G—— then glanced off to the moral changes—literary, social, political—the great men who were removed from the stage within the last twenty years—the new great men who were coming on. In all this Mr Richards evinced no interest. He had evidently read none of our living authors, and seemed scarcely acquainted by name with our younger statesmen. Once and only once he laughed; it was when G—— asked him whether he had any thoughts of getting into Parliament. And the laugh was inward—sarcastic—sinister—a sneer raised into a laugh. After a few minutes G—— left us to talk to some other acquaintances who had just lounged into the room, and I then said quietly:

"I have seen a miniature of you, Mr Richards, in the house you once inhabited, and perhaps built, if not wholly, at least in part, in —— Street. You passed by that house this morning."

Not till I had finished did I raise my eyes to his, and then his fixed my gaze so steadfastly that I could not withdraw it—those fascinating serpent eyes. But involuntarily, and if the words that translated my thought were dragged from me, I added in a low whisper, "I have been a student in the mysteries of life and nature; of those mysteries I have known the occult professors. I have the right to speak to you thus." And I uttered a certain pass-word.

"Well," said he, dryly, "I concede the right—what would you ask?"

"To what extent human will in certain temperaments can extend?"

"To what extent can thought extend? Think, and before you draw breath you are in China!"

"True. But my thought has no power in China."

"Give it expression, and it may have: you may write down a thought which, sooner or later, may alter the whole condition of China. What is a law but a thought? Therefore thought is infinite—therefore thought has power; not in proportion to its value—a bad thought may make a bad law as potent as a good thought can make a good one."

"Yes; what you say confirms my own theory. Through invisible currents one human brain may transmit its ideas to other human brains with the same rapidity as a thought promulgated by visible means. And as thought is imperishable—as it leaves its stamp behind it in the natural world even when the thinker has passed out of this world—so the thought of the living may have power to rouse up and revive the thoughts of the dead—such as those thoughts *were in life*—though the thought of the living cannot reach the thoughts which the dead *now* may entertain. Is it not so?"

"I decline to answer, if, in my judgment, thought has the limit you would fix to it; but proceed. You have a special question you wish to put."

"Intense malignity in an intense will, engendered in a peculiar temperament, and aided by natural means within the reach of science, may produce effects like those ascribed of old to evil magic. It might thus haunt the walls of a human habitation with spectral revivals of all guilty thoughts and guilty deeds once conceived and done within those walls; all, in short, with which the evil will claims *rapport* and affinity—imperfect, incoherent, fragmentary snatches at the old dramas acted therein years ago. Thoughts thus crossing each other haphazard, as in the nightmare of a vision, growing up into phantom sights and sounds, and all serving to create horror, not because those sights and sounds are really visitations from a world without, but that they are ghastly monstrous renewals of what have been in this world itself, set into malignant play by a malignant mortal.

"And it is through the material agency of that human brain that these things would acquire even a human power—would strike as with the shock of electricity, and might kill, if the thought of the person assailed did not rise superior to the dignity of the original assailer—might kill the most powerful animal if unnerved by fear, but not injure the feeblest man, if, while his flesh crept, his mind stood out fearless. Thus, when in old stories we read of a magician rent to pieces by the fiends he had evoked—or still more, in Eastern legends, that one magician succeeds by arts in destroying another—there may be so far truth, that a material being has clothed, from its own evil propensities certain elements and fluids, usually quiescent or harmless, with awful shape and terrific force—just as the lightning that had lain hidden and innocent in the cloud becomes by natural law suddenly visible, takes a distinct shape to the eye, and can strike destruction on the object to which it is attracted."

"You are not without glimpses of a very mighty secret," said Mr Richards, composedly. "According to your view, could a mortal obtain the power you speak of, he would necessarily be a malignant and evil being."

"If the power were exercised as I have said, most malignant and most evil—though I believe in the ancient traditions that he could not injure the good. His will could only injure those with whom it has established an affinity, or over whom it forces unresisted sway. I will now imagine an example that may be within the laws of nature, yet seem wild as the fables of a bewildered monk.

"You will remember that Albertus Magnus, after describing minutely the process by which spirits may be invoked and commanded, adds emphatically that the process will instruct and avail only to the few—that a *man must be born a magician!*—that is, born with a peculiar physical temperament, as a man is born a poet. Rarely are men in whose constitution lurks this occult power of the highest order of intellect;—usually in the intellect there is some twist, perversity, or disease. But, on the other hand, they must possess, to an astonishing degree, the faculty to concentrate thought on a single object— the energic faculty that we call *will*. Therefore, though their intellect be not sound, it is exceedingly forcible for the attainment of what it desires. I will imagine such a person, pre-eminently gifted with this constitution and its concomitant forces. I will place him in the loftier grades of society. I will suppose his desires emphatically those of the sensualist—he has, therefore, a strong love of life. He is an absolute egotist—his will is concentrated in himself—he has fierce passions—he knows no enduring, no holy affections, but he can covet eagerly what for the moment he desires—he can hate implacably what opposes itself to his objects—he can commit fearful crimes, yet feel small remorse—he resorts rather to curses upon others, than to penitence for his misdeeds. Circumstances, to which his constitution guides him, lead him to a rare knowledge of the natural secrets which may serve his egotism. He is a close observer where his passions encourage observation, he is a minute calculator, not from love of truth, but where love of self sharpens his faculties—therefore he can be a man of science.

"I suppose such a being, having by experience learned the power of his arts over others, trying what may be the power of will over his own frame, and studying all that in natural philosophy may increase that power. He loves life, he dreads death; he *wills to live on*. He cannot restore himself to youth, he cannot entirely stay the progress of death, he cannot make himself immortal in the flesh and blood; but he may arrest for a time so prolonged as to appear incredible, if I said it—that hardening of the parts which constitutes old age. A year may age him no more than an hour ages another. His intense will, scientifically trained into system, operates, in short, over the wear and tear of his own frame. He lives on. That he may not seem a portent and a miracle, he *dies* from time to time, seemingly, to certain persons. Having schemed the transfer of a wealth that suffices to his wants, he disappears from one corner of the world, and contrives that his obsequies shall be celebrated. He reappears at another corner of the world, where he resides undetected, and does not revisit the scenes of his former career till all who could remember his features are no more. He would be profoundly miserable if he had affections—he has none but for himself. No good man would accept his longevity, and to no men, good or bad, would he or could he communicate its true secret. Such a man might exist; such a man as I have described I see now before me!—Duke of − −, in the court of − −, dividing time between lust and brawl, alchemists and wizards;—again, in the last century, charlatan and criminal, with name less noble, domiciled in the house at which you gazed to-day, and flying from the law you had outraged, none knew whither; traveller once more revisiting London, with the same earthly passions which filled your heart when races now no more walked through yonder streets; outlaw from the school of all the nobler and diviner mystics; execrable Image of Life in Death and Death in Life, I warn you back from the cities and homes of healthful men; back to the ruins of departed empires; back to the deserts of nature unredeemed!"

There answered me a whisper so musical, so potently musical, that it seemed to enter into my whole being, and subdue me despite myself. Thus it said:

"I have sought one like you for the last hundred years. Now I have found you, we part not till I know what I desire. The vision that sees through the Past, and cleaves through the veil of the Future, is in you at this hour; never before, never to come again. The vision of no puling fantastic girl, of no sick-bed somnambule, but of a strong man, with a vigorous brain. Soar and look forth!"

As he spoke I felt as if I rose out of myself upon eagle wings. All the weight seemed gone from air—roofless the room, roofless the dome of space. I was not in the body—where I knew not—but aloft over time, over earth.

Again I heard the melodious whisper,—"You say right. I have mastered great secrets by the power of Will; true, by Will and by Science I can retard the process of years: but death comes not by age alone. Can I frustrate the accidents which bring death upon the young?"

"No; every accident is a providence. Before a providence snaps every human will."

"Shall I die at last, ages and ages hence, by the slow, though inevitable, growth of time, or by the cause that I call accident?"

"By a cause you call accident."

"Is not the end still remote?" asked the whisper, with a slight tremor.

"Regarded as my life regards time, it is still remote."

"And shall I, before then, mix with the world of men as I did ere I learned these secrets, resume eager interest in their strife and their trouble—battle with ambition, and use the power of the sage to win the power that belongs to kings?"

"You will yet play a part on the earth that will fill earth with commotion and amaze. For wondrous designs have you, a wonder yourself, been permitted to live on through the centuries. All the secrets you have stored will then have their uses—all that now makes you a stranger amidst the generations will contribute then to make you their lord. As the trees and the straws are drawn into a whirlpool—as they spin round, are sucked to the deep, and again tossed aloft by the eddies, so shall races and thrones be plucked into the charm of your vortex. Awful Destroyer—but in destroying, made, against your own will, a Constructor!"

"And that date, too, is far off?"

"Far off; when it comes, think your end in this world is at hand!"

"How and what is the end? Look east, west, south, and north."

"In the north, where you never yet trod towards the point whence your instincts have warned you, there a spectre will seize you. 'Tis Death! I see a ship—it is haunted—'tis chased—it sails on. Baffled navies sail after that ship. It enters the region of ice. It passes a sky red with meteors. Two moons stand on high, over ice-reefs. I see the ship locked between white defiles—they are ice-rocks. I see the dead strew the decks—stark and livid, green mould on their limbs. All are dead but one man—it is you! But years, though so slowly they come, have then scathed you. There is the coming of age on your brow, and the will is relaxed in the cells of the brain. Still that will, though enfeebled, exceeds all that man knew before you, through the will you live on, gnawed with famine; and nature no longer obeys you in that death-spreading region; the sky is a sky of iron, and the air has iron clamps, and the ice-rocks wedge in the ship. Hark how it cracks and groans. Ice will imbed it as amber imbeds a straw. And a man has gone forth, living yet, from the ship and its dead; and he has clambered up the spikes of an iceberg, and the two moons gaze down on his form. That man is yourself; and terror is on you—terror; and terror has swallowed your will. And I see swarming up the steep ice-rock, grey grisly things. The bears of the north have scented their quarry—they come near you and nearer, shambling and rolling their bulk. And in that day every moment shall seem to you longer than the centuries through which you have passed. And heed this—after life, moments continued make the bliss or the hell of eternity."

"Hush," said the whisper; "but the day, you assure me, is far off—very far! I go back to the almond and rose of Damascus!—sleep!"

The room swam before my eyes. I became insensible. When I recovered, I found G—— holding my hand and smiling. He said, "You who have always declared yourself proof against mesmerism have succumbed at last to my friend Richards."

"Where is Mr Richards?"

"Gone, when you passed into a trance—saying quietly to me, 'Your friend will not wake for an hour.'"

I asked, as collectedly as I could, where Mr Richards lodged.

"At the Trafalgar Hotel."

"Give me your arm," said I to G——; "let us call on him; I have something to say."

When we arrived at the hotel, we were told that Mr Richards had returned twenty minutes before, paid his bill, left directions with his servant (a Greek) to pack his effects and proceed to Malta by the steamer that should leave Southampton the next day. Mr Richards had merely said of his own movements that he had visits to pay in the neighbourhood of London, and it was uncertain whether he should be able to reach Southampton in time for that steamer; if not, he should follow in the next one.

The waiter asked me my name. On my informing him, he gave me a note that Mr Richards had left for me, in case I called.

The note was as follows: "I wished you to utter what was in your mind. You obeyed. I have therefore established power over you. For three months from this day you can communicate to no living man what has passed between us—you cannot even show this note to the friend by your side. During three months, silence complete as to me and mine. Do you doubt my power to lay on you this command?—try to disobey me. At the end of the third month, the spell is raised. For the rest I spare you. I shall visit your grave a year and a day after it has received you."

So ends this strange story, which I ask no one to believe. I write it down exactly three months after I received the above note. I could not write it before, nor could I show to G——, in spite of his urgent request, the note which I read under the gas-lamp by his side.

VII
THE BOTATHEN GHOST

By the Rev. S.R. Hawker

The legend of Parson Rudall and the Botathen Ghost will be recognised by many Cornish people as a local remembrance of their boyhood.

It appears from the diary of this learned master of the grammar-school—for such was his office, as well as perpetual curate of the parish,—"that a pestilential disease did break forth in our town in the beginning of the year a.d. 1665; yea, and it likewise invaded my school, insomuch that therewithal certain of the chief scholars sickened and died." "Among others who yielded to the malign influence was Master John Eliot, the eldest son and the worshipful heir of Edward Eliot, Esquire of Trebursey, a stripling of sixteen years of age, but of uncommon parts and hopeful ingenuity. At his own especial motion and earnest desire I did consent to preach his funeral sermon." It should be remembered here that, howsoever strange and singular it may sound to us that a mere lad should formally solicit such a performance at the hands of his master, it was in consonance with the habitual usage of those times. The old services for the dead had been abolished by law, and in the stead of sacrament and ceremony, month's mind and year's mind, the sole substitute which survived was the general desire "to partake," as they called it, of a posthumous discourse, replete with lofty eulogy and flattering remembrance of the living and the dead. The diary proceeds:

"I fulfilled my undertaking and preached over the coffin in the presence of a full assemblage of mourners and lachrymose friends. An ancient gentleman who was then and there in the church, a Mr Bligh of Botathen, was much affected by my discourse, and he was heard to repeat to himself certain parentheses therefrom, especially a phrase from Maro Virgilius, which I had applied to the deceased youth, 'Et puer ipse fuit cantari dignus.'

"The cause wherefore this old gentleman was thus moved by my applications was this: He had a first-born and only son—a child who, but a very few months before, had been not unworthy of the character I drew of young Master Eliot, but who, by some strange accident, had of late quite fallen away from his parent's hopes, and become moody, and sullen, and distraught. When the funeral obsequies were over, I had no sooner come out of the church than I was accosted by this aged parent, and he besought me incontinently, with a singular energy, that I would resort with him forthwith to his abode at Botathen that very night; nor could I have delivered myself from his importunity, had not Mr Eliot urged his claim to enjoy my company at his own house. Hereupon I got loose, but not until I had pledged a fast assurance that I would pay him, faithfully, an early visit the next day."

"The Place," as it was called, of Botathen, where old Mr Bligh resided, was a low-roofed gabled manor-house of the fifteenth century, walled and mullioned, and with clustered chimneys of dark-grey stone from the neighbouring quarries of Ventor-gan. The mansion was flanked by a pleasaunce or enclosure in one space, of garden and lawn, and it was surrounded by a solemn grove of stag-horned trees. It had the sombre aspect of age and of solitude, and looked the very scene of strange and supernatural events. A legend might well belong to every gloomy glade around, and there must surely be a haunted room somewhere within its walls. Hither, according to his appointment, on the morrow, Parson Rudall betook himself. Another clergyman, as it appeared, had been invited to meet him, who, very soon after his arrival, proposed a walk together in the pleasaunce, on the pretext of showing him, as a stranger, the walks and trees, until the dinner-bell should strike. There, with much prolixity, and with many a solemn pause, his brother minister proceeded to "unfold the mystery."

"A singular infelicity," he declared, "had befallen young Master Bligh, once the hopeful heir of his parents and of the lands of Botathen. Whereas he had been from childhood a blithe and merry boy, 'the gladness,' like Isaac of old, of his father's age, he had suddenly of late become morose and silent—nay, even austere and stern—dwelling apart, always solemn, often in tears. The lad had at first repulsed all questions as to the origin of this great change, but of late he had yielded to the importunate researches of his parents, and had disclosed the secret cause. It appeared that he resorted, every day, by a pathway across the fields, to this very clergyman's house, who had charge of his education, and grounded him in the studies suitable to his age. In the course of his daily walk he had to pass a certain heath or down where the road wound along through tall blocks of granite with open spaces of grassy sward between. There in a certain spot and always in one and the same place, the lad declared that he had encountered, every day, a woman with a pale and troubled face, clothed in a long loose garment of frieze, with one hand always stretched forth, and the other pressed against her side. Her name, he said, was Dorothy Dinglet, for he had known her well from his childhood, and she often used to come to his parents' house; but that which troubled him was, that she had now been dead three years, and he himself had been with the neighbours at her burial; so that, as the youth alleged, with great simplicity, since he had seen her body laid in the grave, this that he saw every day must needs be her soul or ghost. 'Questioned again and again,' said the clergyman, 'he never contradicts himself; but he relates the same and the simple tale as a thing that cannot be gainsaid. Indeed, the lad's observance is keen and calm for a boy of his age. The hair of the appearance, sayeth he, is not like anything alive, but it is so soft and light that it seemeth to melt away while you look; but her eyes are set, and never blink—no, not when the sun shineth full upon her face. She maketh no steps, but seemeth to swim along the top of the grass; and her hand, which is stretched out alway, seemeth to point at something far away, out of sight. It is her continual coming; for she never faileth to meet him, and to pass on, that hath quenched his spirits; and although he never seeth her by night, yet cannot he get his natural rest.'

"Thus far the clergyman; whereupon the dinner clock did sound, and we went into the house. After dinner, when young Master Bligh had withdrawn with his tutor, under excuse of their books, the parents did forthwith beset me as to my thoughts about their son. Said I, warily, 'The case is strange, but by no means impossible. It is one that I will study, and fear not to handle, if the lad will be free with me, and fulfil all that I desire.' The mother was overjoyed, but I perceived that old Mr Bligh turned pale, and was downcast with some thought which, however, he did not express. Then they bade that Master Bligh should be called to meet me in the pleasaunce forthwith. The boy came, and he rehearsed to me his tale with an open countenance, and, withal, a modesty of speech. Verily he seemed 'ingenui vultus puer ingenuique pudoris.' Then I signified to him my purpose. 'To-morrow,' said I, 'we will go together to the place; and if, as I doubt not, the woman shall appear, it will be for me to proceed according to knowledge, and by rules laid down in my books.'"

The unaltered scenery of the legend still survives, and, like the field of the forty footsteps in another history, the place is still visited by those who take interest in the supernatural tales of old. The pathway leads along a moorland waste, where large masses of rock stand up here and there from the grassy turf, and clumps of heath and gorse weave their tapestry of golden purple garniture on every side. Amidst all these, and winding along between the rocks, is a natural footway worn by the scant, rare tread of the village traveller. Just midway, a somewhat larger stretch than usual of green sod expands, which is skirted by the path, and which is still identified as the legendary haunt of the phantom, by the name of Parson Rudall's Ghost.

But we must draw the record of the first interview between the minister and Dorothy from his own words. "We met," thus he writes, "in the pleasaunce very early, and before any others in the house were awake; and together the lad and myself proceeded towards the field. The youth was quite composed, and carried his Bible under his arm, from whence he read to me verses, which he said he had lately picked out, to have always in his mind. These were Job vii. 14, 'Thou scarest me with dreams, and terrifiest me through visions'; and Deuteronomy xxviii. 67, 'In the morning thou shalt say, Would to God it were the evening, and in the evening thou shalt say, Would to God it were morning; for the fear of thine heart wherewith thou shalt fear, and for the sight of thine eyes which thou shalt see.'

"I was much pleased with the lad's ingenuity in these pious applications, but for mine own part I was somewhat anxious and out of cheer. For aught I knew this might be a *dæmonium meridianum*, the most stubborn spirit to govern and guide that any man can meet, and the most perilous withal. We had hardly reached the accustomed spot, when we both saw her at once gliding towards us; punctually as the ancient writers describe the motion of their 'lemures, which swoon along the ground, neither marking the sand nor bending the herbage.' The aspect of the woman was exactly that which had been related by the lad. There was the pale and stony face, the strange and misty hair, the eyes firm and fixed, that gazed, yet not on us, but something that they saw far, far away; one hand and arm stretched out, and the other grasping the girdle of her waist. She floated along the field like a sail upon a stream, and glided past the spot where we stood, pausingly. But so deep was the awe that overcame me, as I stood there in the light of day, face to face with a human soul separate from her bones and flesh, that my heart and purpose both failed me. I had resolved to speak to the spectre in the appointed form of words, but I did not. I stood like one amazed and speechless, until she had passed clean out of sight. One thing remarkable came to pass. A spaniel dog, the favourite of young Master Bligh, had followed us, and lo! when the woman drew nigh, the poor creature began to yell and bark piteously, and ran backward and away, like a thing dismayed and appalled. We returned to the house, and after I had said all that I could to pacify the lad, and to soothe the aged people, I took my leave for that time, with a promise that when I had fulfilled certain business elsewhere, which I then alleged, I would return and take orders to assuage these disturbances and their cause.

"January 7, 1665.—At my own house, I find, by my books, what is expedient to be done; and then, Apage, Sathanas!

"January 9, 1665.—This day I took leave of my wife and family, under pretext of engagements elsewhere, and made my secret journey to our diocesan city, wherein the good and venerable bishop then abode.

"January 10.—*Deo gratias*, in safe arrival at Exeter; craved and obtained immediate audience of his lordship; pleading it was for counsel and admonition on a weighty and pressing cause; called to the presence; made obeisance; and then by command stated my case—the Botathen perplexity—which I moved with strong and earnest instances and solemn asseverations of that which I had myself seen and heard. Demanded by his lordship, what was the succour that I had come to entreat at his hands? Replied, licence for my exorcism, that so I might, ministerially, allay this spiritual visitant, and thus render to the living and the dead release from this surprise. 'But,' said our bishop, 'on what authority do you allege that I am intrusted with faculty so to do? Our Church, as is well known, hath abjured certain branches of her ancient power, on grounds of perversion and abuse.' 'Nay, my Lord,' I humbly answered, 'under favour, the seventy-second of the canons ratified and enjoined on us, the clergy, anno Domini 1604, doth expressly provide, that "no minister, *unless he hath* the licence of his diocesan bishop, shall essay to exorcise a spirit, evil or good." Therefore it was,' I did here mildly allege, 'that I did not presume to enter on such a work without lawful privilege under your lordship's hand and seal.' Hereupon did our wise and learned bishop, sitting in his chair, condescend upon the theme at some length with many gracious interpretations from ancient writers and from Holy Scripture, and I did humbly rejoin and reply, till the upshot was that he did call in his secretary and command him to draw the aforesaid faculty, forthwith and without further delay, assigning him a form, insomuch that the matter was incontinently done; and after I had disbursed into the secretary's hands certain moneys for signitary purposes, as the manner of such officers hath always been, the bishop did himself affix his signature under the *sigillum* of his see, and deliver the document into my hands. When I knelt down to receive his benediction, he softly said, 'Let it be secret, Mr R. Weak brethren! weak brethren!'"

This interview with the bishop, and the success with which he vanquished his lordship's scruples, would seem to have confirmed Parson Rudall very strongly in his own esteem, and to have invested him with that courage which he evidently lacked at his first encounter with the ghost.

The entries proceed: "January 11, 1665.—Therewithal did I hasten home and prepare my instruments, and cast my figures for the onset of the next day. Took out my ring of brass, and put it on the index-finger of my right hand, with the *scutum Davidis* traced thereon.

"January 12, 1665.—Rode into the gateway at Botathen, armed at all points, but not with Saul's armour, and ready. There is danger from the demons, but so there is in the surrounding air every day. At early morning then, and alone,—for so the usage ordains,—I betook me towards the field. It was void, and I had thereby due time to prepare. First, I paced and measured out my circle on the grass. Then did I mark my pentacle in the very midst, and at the intersection of the five angles I did set up and fix my crutch of *raun* (rowan). Lastly, I took my station south, at the true line of the meridian, and stood facing due north. I waited and watched for a long time. At last there was a kind of trouble in the air, a soft and rippling sound, and all at once the shape appeared, and came on towards me gradually. I opened my parchment scroll, and read aloud the command. She paused, and seemed to waver and doubt; stood still; then I rehearsed the sentence, sounding out every syllable like a chant. She drew near my ring, but halted at first outside, on the brink. I sounded again, and now at the third time I gave the signal in Syriac,—the speech which is used, they say, where such ones dwell and converse in thoughts that glide.

"She was at last obedient, and swam into the midst of the circle, and there stood still, suddenly. I saw, moreover, that she drew back her pointing hand. All this while I do confess that my knees shook under me, and the drops of sweat ran down my flesh like rain. But now, although face to face with the spirit, my heart grew calm, and my mind was composed. I knew that the pentacle would govern her, and the ring must bind, until I gave the word. Then I called to mind the rule laid down of old, that no angel or fiend, no spirit, good or evil, will ever speak until they have been first spoken to. *N.B.*—This is the great law of prayer. God Himself will not yield reply until man hath made vocal entreaty, once and again. So I went on to demand, as the books advise; and the phantom made answer, willingly. Questioned wherefore not at rest? Unquiet, because of a certain sin. Asked what, and by whom? Revealed it; but it is *sub sigillo*, and therefore *nefas dictu*; more anon. Inquired, what sign she could give that she was a true spirit and not a false fiend? Stated, before next Yule-tide a fearful pestilence would lay waste the land and myriads of souls would be loosened from their flesh, until, as she piteously said, 'our valleys will be full.' Asked again, why she so terrified the lad? Replied: 'It is the law; we must seek a youth or a maiden of clean life, and under age, to receive messages and admonitions.' We conversed with many more words, but it is not lawful for me to set them down. Pen and ink would degrade and defile the thoughts she uttered, and which my mind received that day. I broke the ring, and she passed, but to return once more next day. At even-song, a long discourse with that ancient transgressor, Mr

B. Great horror and remorse; entire atonement and penance; whatsoever I enjoin; full acknowledgment before pardon.

"January 13, 1665.—At sunrise I was again in the field. She came in at once, and, as it seemed, with freedom. Inquired if she knew my thoughts, and what I was going to relate? Answered, 'Nay, we only know what we perceive and hear; we cannot see the heart.' Then I rehearsed the penitent words of the man she had come up to denounce, and the satisfaction he would perform. Then said she, 'Peace in our midst.' I went through the proper forms of dismissal, and fulfilled all as it was set down and written in my memoranda; and then, with certain fixed rites, I did dismiss that troubled ghost, until she peacefully withdrew, gliding towards the west. Neither did she ever afterward appear, but was allayed until she shall come in her second flesh to the valley of Armageddon on the last day."

These quaint and curious details from the "diurnal" of a simple-hearted clergyman of the seventeenth century appear to betoken his personal persuasion of the truth of what he saw and said, although the statements are strongly tinged with what some may term the superstition, and others the excessive belief, of those times. It is a singular fact, however, that the canon which authorises exorcism under episcopal licence is still a part of the ecclesiastical law of the Anglican Church, although it might have a singular effect on the nerves of certain of our bishops if their clergy were to resort to them for the faculty which Parson Rudall obtained. The general facts stated in his diary are to this day matters of belief in that neighbourhood; and it has been always accounted a strong proof of the veracity of the Parson and the Ghost, that the plague, fatal to so many thousands, did break out in London at the close of that very year. We may well excuse a triumphant entry, on a subsequent page of the "diurnal," with the date of July 10, 1665: "How sorely must the infidels and heretics of this generation be dismayed when they know that this Black Death, which is now swallowing its thousands in the streets of the great city, was foretold six months agone, under the exorcisms of a country minister, by a visible and suppliant ghost! And what pleasures and improvements do such deny themselves who scorn and avoid all opportunity of intercourse with souls separate, and the spirits, glad and sorrowful, which inhabit the unseen world!"

VIII
THE GHOST OF LORD CLARENCEUX

By Arnold Bennett [2]

In the chair which stood before the writing-table in the middle of the room sat the figure of Lord Clarenceux. The figure did not move as I went in; its back was towards me. At the other end of the room was the doorway, which led to the small bedroom, little more than an alcove, and the gaze of the apparition was fixed on this doorway. I closed the door behind me and locked it, and then stood still. In the looking-glass over the mantelpiece I saw a drawn, pale, agitated face, in which all the trouble in the world seemed to reside; it was my own face. I was alone in the room with the ghost—the ghost which, jealous of my love for the woman it had loved, meant to revenge itself by my death. The ghost, did I say? I looked at it; no one would have taken it for an apparition. Small wonder that till the previous evening I had never suspected it to be other than a man. It was dressed in black; it had the very aspect of life. I could follow the creases in the black coat, the direction of the nap of the silk hat. How well by this time I knew the faultless black coat and that impeccable hat! Yet it seemed that I could not examine them too closely. I pierced them with the intensity of my fascinated glance. Yes, I pierced them, for, showing faintly through the coat, I could discern the outline of the table which should have been hidden by the man's figure, and through the hat I could see the handle of the French window.

As I stood motionless there, solitary in the glow of the electric light with this fearful visitor, I began to wish that it would move. I wanted to face it—to meet its gaze with my gaze, eye to eye, and will against will. The battle between us must start at once, I thought, if I was to have any chance of victory, for, moment by moment, I felt my resolution, my manliness, my mere physical courage slipping away.

But the apparition did not stir. Impassive, remorseless, sinister, it was content to wait, well aware that all suspense was in its favour. Then I said to myself that I would cross the room and so attain my object. I made a step and drew back, frightened by the sound of a creaking board. Absurd! but it was quite a minute before I dared to move another step. I had meant to walk straight across to the other door, passing in my course close by the occupied chair. I did do not so; I kept round by the wall, creeping on tiptoe, and my eye never leaving the figure in the chair. I did this in spite of myself, and the manner of my action was the first hint of my ultimate defeat.

At length I stood in the doorway leading to the bedroom. I could feel the perspiration on my forehead and at the back of my neck. I fronted the inscrutable white face of Lord Clarenceux, the lover of Rosetta Rosa; I met its awful eyes: dark, invidious, fateful. Ah, those eyes! Even in my terror I could read in them all the history and the characteristics of Lord Clarenceux. They were the eyes of one who could be of the highest and the lowest. Mingled in their hardness was a melting softness, with their cruelty a large benevolence, with their hate a pitying tenderness, with their spirituality a hellish turpitude. They were the eyes of two opposite men, and as I gazed into them they reconciled for me the conflicting accounts of Lord Clarenceux which I had heard from different people.

But, as far as I was concerned, that night the eyes held nothing but cruelty and disaster; though I could detect in them the other qualities, these qualities were not for me. We faced each other, the apparition and I, and the struggle, silent and bitter as the grave, began. Neither of us moved. My arms were folded easily, but my nails pressed into the palms of my clenched hands. My teeth were set, my lips tight together, my glance unswerving. By sheer strength of endeavour I cast aside my fear of defeat, and in my heart I said with the profoundest conviction that I would love Rosa though the seven seas and all the continents give up their dead to frighten me.

So we remained, for how long I do not know. It may have been only minutes—I cannot tell. Then gradually there came over me a feeling that the ghost in the chair was growing larger. The ghastly inhuman sneer on his thin widening lips assaulted me like a giant's malediction, and the light in the room seemed to become more brilliant till it was almost blinding. This went on for a time, and once more I pulled myself together, collected my scattering senses, and seized again the courage of determination which had nearly slipped from me; but I knew that I must get away, out of sight of this moveless and diabolic figure, which did not speak, but which made known its commands by means of its eyes. "Resign her," the eyes said. "Tear your love for her out of your heart! Swear that you will never see her again—or I will ruin you utterly, not now only but for evermore."

I think I trembled; my eyes answered "No." For some reason which I cannot at all explain, I suddenly took off my overcoat, and, drawing aside the screen which ran across the corner of the room at my right hand, forming a primitive sort of wardrobe, I hung it on one of the hooks. I had to feel with my fingers for the hook, because I kept my gaze on the figure. "I will go into the bedroom," I said; and I turned to pass through the doorway. Then I stopped. If I did so, the eyes of the ghost would be upon my back, and I felt that I could only withstand that glance by meeting it. To have it on my back.... Doubtless I was going mad. However, I went backwards to the doorway, and then rapidly stepped out of sight of the apparition and sat down upon the bed. Useless! I must return. The mere idea of the empty sitting-room—empty with the ghost in it—filled me with a new and considerable fear. Horrible happenings might occur in that room, and I must be there to see them! Moreover, the ghost's gaze must now fall on nothing; that would be too appalling (without doubt I was mad). Its gaze must meet something, otherwise it would travel out into space further and further till it had left all the stars and waggled aimless in the ether. The notion of such a calamity was unbearable. Besides, I was hungry for that gaze. My eyes desired those eyes: if that glance did not press against them, they would burst from my head and roll on the floor, and I should be compelled to go down on my hands and knees and grope in search for them. No, no. I must return to the sitting-room. And I returned. The gaze met mine in the doorway, and now there was something novel in it—an added terror, a more intolerable menace, the silent imprecation so frightful that no human being could suffer it. I sank to the ground, and as I did so I shrieked; but it was a weird shriek, sounding only within the brain, and in reply to that unheard shriek I heard an unheard voice of the ghost crying, "Yield!"

I would not yield. Crushed, maddened, tortured, I would not yield. I wanted to die. I felt that death would be sweet and truly desirable. And, so thinking, I faded into a kind of coma, or rather a state which was just short of coma. I had not lost consciousness, but I was conscious of nothing but the gaze. "Good-bye, Rosa," I whispered; "I am beaten, but my love has not been conquered." The next thing I remember was the paleness of the dawn at the window. The apparition had vanished for the night, and I was alive. But I knew that I had touched the skirts of death. I knew that after such another night I should die.

FOOTNOTES

[2] *The Ghost: a Novel* (1911).

IX
DR DUTHOIT'S VISION

By Arthur Machen [3]

I knew a fine specimen of an English abbé when I was at school at Hereford. This was Dr Duthoit, Prebendary of *Consumpta per Sabulum* in Hereford Cathedral, Rector of St Owen's, bookworm and, chiefly, rose-grower. He was a middle-aged man when I was a little boy, but he suffered me to walk with him in his garden sloping down to the Wye, near a pleasaunce of the Vicars Choral, reciting sometimes the poems of Traherne, which he had in manuscript, but, for the most part, demonstrating his progress in the art of growing a coal-black rose. This was the true work of his life, and nearly forty years ago he could show blooms whose copper and crimson tints were very near to utter darkness. I believe that his ideal was never attained in absolute perfection; and perhaps the perfect end and attainment of desire do not prove happiness down here below.

After 1880 Prebendary Duthoit and I rarely saw each other, and rarely wrote. He was at rest among his roses by the quiet Wye, and I dashed to and fro in wilder waters, but each contrived to let the other know that he was still alive, and so I was not altogether surprised to see the Prebendary's queer, niggly writing on an envelope a week or two ago. He said he had heard of a good deal to talk about.... Well, with a popular legend with which I am understood to be in some way concerned, and he thought that an odd experience of his might possibly interest me. I do not give the text of his letter, chiefly because it is full of Latin phrases, which I might be called upon to translate.

But the matter is as follows: On the 4th August, the day of the service at St Paul's, Dr Duthoit was walking up and down and about that pleasant garden on slopes of the Wye. Just above the water his gardener had prepared under direction and instruction a plot of ground in a very special manner. I do not gather the precise purpose of the operation, but it seems that the soil had been very fine and level for a superficies of about ten yards. To this place the Prebendary walked, slowly and reflectively, wishing to assure himself that his orders had been accurately carried out. The plot had been perfectly level the night before, but Dr Duthoit wanted to be more than sure about it. But to his extreme annoyance, when he turned by the fig-tree, he saw that the plot was very far from even. He is an old man, but his sight is good, and at a distance of several yards he could discern quite plainly that there had been mischief. The chosen plot was in a disgraceful state. At first the Prebendary thought that the Custos' sandy tom-cat had scaled the wire entanglement on the top of the wall. Then he felt inclined to consider the ruin done by Scamp, the Bishop's wire-haired fox-terrier, and then, going across, he put on his spectacles and wondered what had been at work. For the level which had been so carefully established was all undone. At first the Doctor thought it was the mischief of some random beast, this confusion of hills and valleys which had taken place of the billiard-table of the night before. And then it reminded him of the raised maps which he had seen in the Diocesan Training Schools, and then it reminded him more distinctly of a sort of picture map which had illustrated his morning paper a day or two before. And then he wondered violently, because he saw that somebody had, with infinite pains, made this garden plot of his into an exact model of Gallipoli Peninsula.

It was all so ingenious and perfect that the old clergyman held his wrath for the moment, and peered into this miniature intricacy of peaks and steeps, and gullies and valleys. He had scarcely gathered himself together to wonder who had had the ingenious impudence for the mischief, when amazement once more seized him. For he saw now, stooping down, that this garden Gallipoli was swarming with life. There were hosts on it and about it, and then Dr Duthoit forgot all about what we call the realities and facts of life, forgot that this sort of thing does not happen, and watched what was happening.

He writes that, queerly enough, he lost all sense of size. He was not a Gulliver looking down upon Lilliput; the mounds ten inches high became to him actual and lofty summits. The tiny precipices were tremendous. And the red ants swarmed to attack the black ants that held the heights with savage and desperate fury. He says he panted with excitement as he watched the courage of the attack and defence, the savagery of the "hand-to-hand" fighting. The black and red fell by myriads, and the doctor had persuaded himself that he observed amazing incidents of individual heroism. One particular range seemed to be the especial aim of the red forces, and they swarmed up victorious and held it for a while, and then retreated. The doctor could not quite make out the reason of this. He started violently when his man called to him. Roberts said he had called for five minutes without getting an answer, and that the Dean was in a hurry, with only five minutes to spare. So the Prebendary went into the house in a kind of dwam, as the Scots put it, and had no notion of what the Dean had to say; and when he got back to the garden he found his gardener smoothing the plot with a long rake, and raking in a lot of dead ants with the mould. The gardener said it was the boys; but the doctor took no notice, and went to the Custos that night, and the Custos reading his paper a fortnight later began to think that the old Prebendary was a prophet.

And the Prebendary? He ends his letter: "Quod superius est sicut quod inferius" ("that which is above is as that which is below"), as the Smaragdine Tablet of Hermes Trismegistus testifies, and it is my belief that this is a world battle in the sense which we do not appreciate. There have been some who have held that the earthly conflict is but a reflection of the war in heaven. What if it be reflected infinitely, if it penetrate to the uttermost depths of creation? And if a speck of dust be a cosmos—the universe—of revolving worlds? There may be battles between creatures that no microscope shall ever discover.

FOOTNOTES

[3] *The Little Nations.*

X
THE SEVEN LIGHTS

From Wilson's "Tales of the Borders"

John M'Pherson was a farmer and grazier in Kintyre—a genuine Highlander. In person, though of rather low stature than otherwise, he was stout, athletic, and active; bold and fearless in disposition, warm in temper, friendly, and hospitable—this last to such a degree that his house was never without as many strangers and visitors of different descriptions, as nearly doubled his own household.

To the vagrant beggar his house and meal-chest were ever open; and to no one, whatever his condition, were a night's quarters ever refused. M'Pherson's house, in short, formed a kind of focus, with a power to draw towards itself all the misery and poverty in the country within a circle whose diameter might be reckoned at somewhere about twenty miles. The wandering mendicant made it one of his regular stages, and the traveller of better degree toiled on his way with increased activity, that he might make it his quarters for the night.

Fortunately for the character and credit of M'Pherson's hospitality, his wife was of an equally kind and generous disposition with himself; so that his absences from home, which were frequent, and sometimes long, did not at all affect the treatment of the stranger under his roof, or make his welcome less cordial.

But the hospitality exercised at Morvane, which was the name of M'Pherson's farm, sometimes, it must be confessed, led to occasional small depredations—such as the loss of a pair of blankets, a sheet, or a pair of stockings, carried off by the ungrateful vagabonds whom he sometimes sheltered. There were, however, one pair of blankets abstracted in this way, that found their road back to their owner in rather a curious manner.

The morning was thick and misty, when the thief (in the case alluded to) decamped with his booty, and continued so during the whole day, so that no object, at any distance, however large, could be seen. After toiling for several hours, under the impression that he was leaving Morvane far behind, the vagabond, who was also a stranger in the country, approached a house, with the stolen blankets snugly and carefully bundled on his back, and knocked at the door, with the view of seeking a night's quarters, as it was now dusk. The door was opened; but by whom, think you, good reader? Why, by M'Pherson!

The thief, without knowing it, had landed precisely at the point from which he had set out. Being instantly recognised, he was politely invited to walk in. To this kind invitation, the thief replied by throwing down the blankets, and taking to his heels—thus making, with his own hands, a restitution which was very far from being intended. Poor M'Pherson, however, did not get all his stolen blankets back in this way.

This, however, is a digression. To proceed with our tale. One night, when M'Pherson was absent, attending a market at some distance, an elderly female appeared at the door, with the usual demand of a night's lodging, which, with the usual hospitality of Morvane, was at once complied with. The stranger, who was a remarkably tall woman, was dressed in widow's weeds, and of rather respectable appearance; her deportment was grave, even stern, and altogether she seemed as if suffering from some recent affliction.

During the whole of the early part of the evening she sat before the fire, with her face buried between her hands, heedless of what was passing around her, and was occasionally observed rocking to and fro, with that kind of motion that bespeaks great internal anguish. It was noticed, however, that she occasionally stole a look at those who were in the apartment with her; and it was marked by all (but whether this was merely the effect of imagination, for all *felt* that there was something singular and mysterious about the stranger, or was really the case, we cannot decide) that, in these furtive glances, there was a peculiarly wild and appalling expression. The stranger spoke none, however, during the whole night; but continued, from time to time, rocking to and fro in the manner already described. Neither could she be prevailed upon to partake of any refreshment, although repeatedly pressed to do so. All invitations of this kind she declined, with a wave of the hand, or a melancholy, yet determined inclination of the head. In words she made no reply.

The singular conduct of this woman threw a damp over all who were present. They felt chilled, they knew not how; and were sensible of the influence of an indefinable terror, for which they could not account. For once, therefore, the feeling of comfort and security, of which all were conscious who were seated around M'Pherson's cheerful and hospitable hearth, was banished, and a scene of awe and dread supplied its place.

No one could conjecture who this strange personage was, whence she had come, nor whither she was going; nor were there any means of acquiring this information, as it was a rule of the house—one of M'Pherson's special points of etiquette—that no stranger should ever be questioned on such subjects. All being allowed to depart as they came, without question or inquiry, there was never anything more known at Morvane, regarding any stranger who visited it, than what he himself chose to communicate.

Under the painful feelings already described, the inmates of M'Pherson's house found, with more than usual satisfaction, the hour for retiring to rest arrive. The general attention being called to this circumstance by the hostess, everyone hastened to his appointed dormitory, with an alacrity which but too plainly showed how glad they were to escape from the presence of the mysterious stranger who, however, also retired to bed with the rest. The place appointed for her to sleep in, was the loft of an outbuilding, as there was no room for her accommodation within the house itself; all the spare beds being occupied.

We have already said that M'Pherson was from home on the evening of which we are speaking, attending a market at some distance. He, however, returned shortly after midnight. On arriving at his own house, he was much surprised, and not a little alarmed, to perceive a window in one of the outhouses blazing with light (it was that in which the stranger slept), while all around and within the house was as silent as the tomb. Afraid that some accident from fire had taken place, he rode up to the building, and standing up in his stirrups—which brought his head on a level with the window— looked in, when a sight presented itself that made even the stout heart of M'Pherson beat with unusual violence.

In the middle of the floor, extended on her pallet, lay the mysterious stranger, surrounded by seven bright and shining lights, arranged at equal distances—three on one side of the bed, three on the other, and one at the head. M'Pherson gazed steadily at the extraordinary and appalling sight for a few seconds, when three of the lights suddenly vanished. In an instant afterwards, two more disappeared, and then another. There was now only that at the head of the bed remaining. When this light had alone been left, M'Pherson saw the person who lay on the pallet, raise herself slowly up, and gaze intently on the portentous beam, whose light showed, to the terrified onlooker, a ghastly and unearthly countenance, surrounded with dishevelled hair, which hung down in long, thick, irregular masses over her pale, clayey visage, so as almost to conceal it entirely. This light, like all the others, at length suddenly disappeared, and with its last gleam the person on the couch sank down with a groan that startled M'Pherson from the trance of horror into which the extraordinary sight had thrown him.

He was a bold and fearless man, however; and, therefore, though certainly appalled by what he had seen, he made no outcry, nor evinced any other symptom of alarm. He resolutely and calmly awaited the conclusion of the extraordinary scene; and when the last light had disappeared, he deliberately dismounted, led his horse into the stable, put him up, entered the house without disturbing any one, and slipped quietly into bed, trusting that the morning would bring some explanation of the mysterious occurrence of the night; but resolving, at the same time that, if it should not, he would mention the circumstance to no one.

On awaking in the morning, M'Pherson asked his wife what strangers were in the house, and how they were disposed of, and particularly, who it was that slept in the loft of the outhouse. He was told that it was a woman in widow's dress, of rather a respectable appearance, but whose conduct had been very singular. M'Pherson inquired no further, but desired that the woman might be detained till he should see her, as he wished to speak with her.

On some one of the domestics, however, going up to her apartment, shortly after, to invite her to breakfast, it was found that she was gone, no one could tell when or where, as her departure had not been seen by any person about the house.

Baulked in his intention of eliciting some explanation of the extraordinary circumstance of the preceding night, from the person who seemed to have been a party to it, M'Pherson became more strengthened in the resolution of keeping the secret to himself, although it made an impression upon him which all his natural strength of mind could not remove.

At this precise period of our story, M'Pherson had three sons employed in the herring fishing, a favourite pursuit in its season, because often a lucrative one, of those who live upon or near the coasts of the West Highlands.

The three brothers had a boat of their own; and, desirous of making their employment as profitable as possible, they, though in sufficiently good circumstances to have hired assistance, manned her themselves, and, with laudable industry, performed all the drudgery of their laborious occupation with their own hands.

Their boat, like all the others employed in the business we are speaking of, by the natives of the Highlands, was wherry-rigged; her name—she was called after the betrothed of the elder of the three brothers—*The Catherine*. The *take* of herrings, as it is called, it is well known, appears in different seasons in different places, sometimes in one loch, or arm of the sea, sometimes in another.

In the season to which our story refers, the fishing was in the sound of Kilbrannan, where several scores of boats, and amongst those that of the M'Phersons, were busily employed in reaping the ocean harvest. When the take of herrings appears in this sound, Campbelton Loch, a well-known harbour on the west coast of Scotland, is usually made the headquarters — a place of rendezvous of the little herring fleet — and to this loch they always repair when threatened with a boisterous night, although it was not always that they could, in such circumstances, succeed in making it.

Such a night as the one alluded to, was that that succeeded the evening on which M'Pherson saw the strange lights that form the leading feature of our tale. Violent gusts of wind came in rapid succession down the sound of Kilbrannan; and a skifting rain, flung fitfully but fiercely from the huge black clouds as they hurried along before the tempest that already raged above, swept over the face of the angry sea, and seemed to impart an additional bitterness to the rising wrath of the incipient storm. It was evident, in short, that what sailors call a "dirty night" was approaching; and, under this impression, the herring boats left their station, and were seen, in the dusk of the evening in question, hurrying towards Campbelton Loch. But the storm had arisen in all its fury long before the desired haven could be gained. The little fleet was dispersed. Some succeeded, however, in making the harbour; others, finding this impossible, ran in for the Saddle and Carradale shores, and were fortunate enough to effect a landing. All, in short, with the exception of one single boat, ultimately contrived to gain a place of shelter of some kind. This unhappy exception was *The Catherine*. Long after all the others had disappeared from the face of the raging sea, she was seen struggling alone with the warring elements, her canvas down to within a few feet of her gunwale, and her keel only at times being visible. The gallant brothers who manned her, however, had not yet lost either heart or hope, although their situation at this moment was but too well calculated to deprive them of both. Gravely and steadily, and in profound silence, they kept each by his perilous post, and endeavoured to make the land on the Campbelton side; but, finding this impossible, they put about, and ran before the wind for the island of Arran, which lay at the distance of about eight miles. But alarmed, as they approached that rugged shore, by the tremendous sea which was breaking on it, and which would have instantly dashed their frail bark to pieces, they again put about, and made to windward. While the hardy brothers were thus contending with their fate, a person mounted on horseback was seen galloping wildly along the Carradale shore, his eyes ever and anon turned towards the struggling boat with a look of despair and mortal agony. It was M'Pherson, the hapless father of the unfortunate youths by whom she was manned. There were others, too, of their kindred, looking, with failing hearts, on the dreadful sight; for all felt that the unequal contest could not continue long, and that the boat must eventually go down.

Amongst those who were thus watching, with intense interest and speechless agony, the struggle of the doomed bark, was Catherine, the beloved of the elder of the brothers, who ran, in wild distraction, along the shore, uttering the most heart-rending cries. "Oh, my Duncan!" she exclaimed, stretching out her arms towards the pitiless sea. "Oh, my beloved, my dearest, come to me, or allow me to come to you that I may perish with you!" But Duncan heard her not, although it was very possible he might see her, as the distance was not great.

There were, at this moment also, several persons on horseback, friends of the young men, galloping along the shore, from point to point, as the boat varied her direction, in the vain and desperate hope of being able to render, though they knew not how, some assistance to the sufferers. But the distracted father, urged on by the wild energy of despair, outrode them all, as they made, on one occasion, for a rising ground near Carradale, from whence a wider view of the sea could be commanded. For this height M'Pherson now pushed, and gained it just in time to see his gallant sons, with their little bark, buried in the waves. He had not taken his station an instant on the height, when *The Catherine* went down, and all on board perished.

The distracted father, when he had seen the last of his unfortunate sons, covered his eyes with his hands, and for a moment gave way to the bitter agony that racked his soul. His manly breast heaved with emotion, and that most affecting of all sounds, the audible sorrowing of a strong man, might have been heard at a great distance. It was, however, of short continuance. M'Pherson prayed to his God to strengthen him in this dread hour of trial, and to enable him to bear with becoming fortitude the affliction with which it had pleased Him to visit him; and the distressed man derived comfort from the appeal.

"My brave, my beautiful boys!" he said, "you are now with your God, and have entered, I trust, on a life of everlasting happiness." Saying this, he rode slowly from the fatal spot from which he had witnessed the death of his children. It was at this moment, and while musing on the misfortune that had befallen him, that the strange occurrence of the preceding night recurred, for the first time, to M'Pherson's mind. It was obtruded on his recollection by the force of association.

"Can it be possible," he inquired of himself, "that the appearances of last night can have any connection with the dreadful events of to-day? It must be so," he said; "for three of the lights of my eyes, three of the guiding stars of my life, have been this day extinguished." Thus reasoned M'Pherson; and, in the mysterious lights which he had seen, he saw that the doom of his children had been announced. But there were seven, he recollected, and his heart sunk within him as he thought of the three gallant boys who were still spared to him. One of them, the youngest, was at home with himself, the other two were in the Army—soldiers in the 42nd Regiment, which then boasted of many privates of birth and education. M'Pherson, however, still kept the appalling secret of the mysterious lights to himself, and determined to await, with resignation, the fulfilment of the destiny which had been read to him, and which he now felt convinced to be inevitable.

The gallant regiment to which M'Pherson's sons belonged was, at this period, abroad on active service. It was in America, and formed a part of the army which was employed in resisting the encroachments of the French on the British territories in that quarter.

The 42nd had, during the campaigns in the western world of that period— viz. 1754 and 1758,—distinguished themselves in many a sanguinary contest, for their singular bravery and general good conduct; and the fame of their exploits rung through their native glens, and was spread far and wide over their hills and mountains; for dear was the honour of their gallant regiment to the warlike Highlanders. Many accounts had arrived, from time to time, in the country, of their achievements, and joyfully were they received. But, on the very day after the loss of *The Catherine*, a low murmur began to arise, in that part of the country which is the scene of our story, of some dreadful disaster having befallen the national regiment. No one could say of what nature this calamity was; but a buzz went round, whose ominous whispering of fearful slaughter made the friends of the absent soldiers turn pale. Mothers and sisters wept, and fathers and brothers looked grave and shook their heads. The rumour bore that, though there had been no loss of honour, there had been a dreadful loss of life. Nay, it was said that the regiment had made a mighty acquisition to its fame, but that it had been dearly bought.

At length, however, the truth arrived, in a distinct and intelligible shape. The well-known and sanguinary affair of Ticonderago had been fought; and, in that murderous contest, the 42nd Regiment, which had behaved with a gallantry unmatched before in the annals of war, had suffered dreadfully— no less than forty-three officers, commissioned and non-commissioned, and six hundred and three privates having been killed and wounded in that corps alone.

To many a heart and home in the Highlands did this disastrous, though glorious intelligence, bring desolation and mourning; and amongst those on whom it brought these dismal effects, was M'Pherson of Morvane.

On the third day after the occurrence of the events related at the outset of our narrative, a letter, which had come, in the first instance, to a gentleman in the neighbourhood, and who also had a son in the 42nd, was put into M'Pherson's hands, by a servant of the former.

The man looked feelingly grave as he delivered it, and hurried away before it was opened. The letter was sealed with black wax. Poor M'Pherson's hand trembled as he opened it. It was from the captain of the company to which his sons belonged, informing him that both had fallen in the attack on Ticonderago. There was an attempt in the letter to soothe the unfortunate father's feelings, and to reconcile him to the loss of his gallant boys, in a lengthened detail of their heroic conduct during the sanguinary struggle. "Nobly," said the writer, "did your two brave sons maintain the honour of their country in the bloody strife. Both Hugh and Alister fell—their broadswords in their hands—on the very ramparts of Ticonderago, whither they had fought their way with a dauntlessness of heart, and a strength of arm, that might have excited the envy and admiration of the son of Fingal."

In this account of the noble conduct of his sons the broken-hearted father did find some consolation. "Thank God!" he exclaimed, though in a tremulous voice, "my brave boys have done their duty, and died as became their name, with their swords in their hands, and their enemies in their front." But there was one circumstance mentioned in the letter, that affected the poor father more than all the rest—this was the intimation, that the writer had, in his hands, a sum of money and a gold brooch, which his son Alister had bequeathed, the first to his father, the latter to his mother, as a token of remembrance. "These," he said, "had been deposited with him by the young man previous to the engagement, under a presentiment that he should fall."

When he had finished the perusal of the letter, M'Pherson sought his wife, whom he found weeping bitterly, for she had already learned the fate of her sons. On entering the apartment where she was, he flung his arms around her, in an agony of grief, and, choking with emotion, exclaimed, that two more of his fair lights had been extinguished by the hand of heaven. "One yet remains," he said, "but that, too, must soon pass away from before mine eyes. His doom is sealed; but God's will be done."

"What mean ye, John?" said his sobbing wife, struck with the prophetic tone of his speech—"is the measure of our sorrows not yet filled? Are we to lose him, too, who is now our only stay, my fair-haired Ian. Why this foreboding of more evil—and whence have you it, John?" she said, now looking her husband steadfastly in the face; and with an expression of alarm that indicated that entire belief in supernatural intelligence regarding coming events, then so general in the Highlands.

Urged by his wife, who implored him to tell her whence he had the tidings of her Ian's approaching fate, M'Pherson related to her the circumstance of the mysterious lights.

"But there were seven, John," she said, when he had concluded—"how comes that?—our children were but six." And immediately added, as if some fearful conviction had suddenly forced itself on her mind—"God grant that the seventh light may have meant me!"

"God forbid!" exclaimed her husband, on whose mind a similar conviction with that with which his wife was impressed, now obtruded itself for the first time; that conviction was, that he himself was indicated by the seventh light. But neither of the sorrowing pair communicated their fears to the other.

Two days subsequent to this, the fair hair of Ian was seen floating on the surface of a deep pool, in the water of Bran; a small river that ran past the house of Morvane. By what accident the poor boy had fallen into the river, was never ascertained. But the pool in which his body was found was known to have been one of his favourite fishing stations. One only of the mysterious lights now remained without its counterpart; but this was not long wanting. Ere the week had expired, M'Pherson was killed by a fall from his horse, when returning from the funeral of his son, and the symbolical prophecy was fulfilled—and thus concludes the story of "The Seven Lights."

XI
THE SPECTRAL COACH OF BLACKADON

"You have heard of such a spirit, and well you know
The superstitious, idle-headed eld
Received and did deliver to our age
This tale of Herne the Hunter for a truth."

Merry Wives of Windsor.

The old vicarage-house at Talland, as seen from the Looe road, its low roof and grey walls peeping prettily from between the dense boughs of ash and elm that environed it, was as picturesque an object as you could desire to see. The seclusion of its situation was enhanced by the character of the house itself. It was an odd-looking, old-fashioned building, erected apparently in an age when asceticism and self-denial were more in vogue than at present, with a stern disregard of the comfort of the inhabitant, and in utter contempt of received principles of taste. As if not secure enough in its retirement, a high wall, enclosing a courtelage in front, effectually protected its inmates from the prying passenger, and only revealed the upper part of the house, with its small Gothic windows, its slated roof, and heavy chimneys partly hidden by the evergreen shrubs which grew in the enclosure. Such was it until its removal a few years since; and such was it as it lay sweetly in the shadows of an autumnal evening one hundred and thirty years ago, when a stranger in the garb of a country labourer knocked hesitatingly at the wicket gate which conducted to the court. After a little delay a servant-girl appeared, and finding that the countryman bore a message to the vicar, admitted him within the walls, and conducted him along a paved passage to the little, low, damp parlour where sat the good man. The Rev. Mr Dodge was in many respects a remarkable man. You would have judged as much of him as he sat before the fire in his high-back chair, in an attitude of thought, arranging, it may have been, the heads of his next Sabbath's discourse. His heavy eyebrows, throwing into shade his spacious eyes, and indeed the whole contour of his face, marked him as a man of great firmness of character and of much moral and personal courage. His suit of sober black and full-bottomed periwig also added to his dignity, and gave him an appearance of greater age. He was then verging on sixty. The time and the place gave him abundant exercise for the qualities we have mentioned, for many of his parishioners obtained their livelihood by the contraband trade, and were mostly men of unscrupulous and daring character, little likely to bear with patience, reflections on the dishonesty of their calling. Nevertheless the vicar was fearless in reprehending it, and his frank exhortations were, at least, listened to on account of the simple honesty of the man, and his well-known kindness of heart. The eccentricity of his life, too, had a wonderful effect in procuring him the respect, not to say the awe, of a people superstitious in a more than ordinary degree. Ghosts in those days had more freedom accorded them, or had more business with the visible world than at present; and the parson was frequently required by his parishioners to draw from the uneasy spirit the dread secret which troubled it, or by the aid of the solemn prayers of the church to set it at rest for ever. Mr Dodge had a fame as an exorcist, which was not confined to the bounds of his parish, nor limited to the age in which he lived.

"Well, my good man, what brings you hither?" said the clergyman to the messenger.

"A letter, may it please your reverence, from Mr Mills of Lanreath," said the countryman, handing him a letter.

Mr Dodge opened it and read as follows:—

"My dear brother Dodge,—I have ventured to trouble you, at the earnest request of my parishioners, with a matter, of which some particulars have doubtless reached you, and which has caused, and is causing, much terror in my neighbourhood. For its fuller explication, I will be so tedious as to recount to you the whole of this strange story as it has reached my ears, for as yet I have not satisfied my eyes of its truth. It has been told me by men of honest and good report (witnesses of a portion of what they relate), with such strong assurances, that it behoves us to look more closely into the matter. There is in the neighbourhood of this village a barren bit of moor which had no owner, or rather more than one, for the lords of the adjoining manors debated its ownership between themselves, and both determined to take it from the poor, who have for many years past regarded it as a common. And truly, it is little to the credit of these gentlemen, that they should strive for a thing so worthless as scarce to bear the cost of law, and yet of no mean value to poor labouring people. The two litigants, however, contested it with as much violence as if it had been a field of great price, and especially one, an old man, (whose thoughts should have been less set on earthly possessions, which he was soon to leave,) had so set his heart on the success of his suit, that the loss of it, a few years back, is said to have much hastened his death. Nor, indeed, after death, if current reports are worthy of credit, does he quit his claim to it; for at night-time his apparition is seen on the moor, to the great terror of the neighbouring villagers. A public path leads by at no great distance from the spot, and on divers occasions has the labourer, returning from his work, been frightened nigh unto lunacy by sight and sounds of a very dreadful character. The appearance is said to be that of a man habited in black, driving a carriage drawn by headless horses. This is, I avow, very marvellous to believe, but it has had so much credible testimony, and has gained so many believers in my parish, that some steps seem necessary to allay the excitement it causes. I have been applied to for this purpose, and my present business is to ask your assistance in this matter, either to reassure the minds of the country people if it be only a simple terror; or, if there be truth in it, to set the troubled spirit of the man at rest. My messenger, who is an industrious, trustworthy man, will give you more information if it be needed, for, from report, he is acquainted with most of the circumstances, and will bring back your advice and promise of assistance.

"Not doubting of your help herein, I do with my very hearty commendation commit you to God's protection and blessing, and am, — Your very loving brother,   Abraham Mills."

This remarkable note was read and re-read, while the countryman sat watching its effects on the parson's countenance, and was surprised that it changed not from its usual sedate and settled character. Turning at length to the man, Mr Dodge inquired, "Are you, then, acquainted with my good friend Mills?"

"I should know him, sir," replied the messenger, "having been sexton to the parish for fourteen years, and being, with my family, much beholden to the kindness of the rector."

"You are also not without some knowledge of the circumstances related in this letter. Have you been an eye-witness to any of those strange sights?"

"For myself, sir, I have been on the road at all hours of the night and day, and never did I see anything which I could call worse than myself. One night my wife and I were awoke by the rattle of wheels, which was also heard by some of our neighbours, and we are all assured that it could have been no other than the black coach. We have every day such stories told in the villages by so many creditable persons, that it would not be proper in a plain, ignorant man like me to doubt it."

"And how far," asked the clergyman, "is the moor from Lanreath?"

"About two miles, and please your reverence. The whole parish is so frightened, that few will venture far after nightfall, for it has of late come much nearer the village. A man who is esteemed a sensible and pious man by many, though an Anabaptist in principle, went a few weeks back to the moor ('tis called Blackadon) at midnight, in order to lay the spirit, being requested thereto by his neighbours, and he was so alarmed at what he saw, that he hath been somewhat mazed ever since."

"A fitting punishment for his presumption, if it hath not quite demented him," said the parson. "These persons are like those addressed by St Chrysostom, fitly called the golden-mouthed, who said, 'Miserable wretches that ye be! ye cannot expel a flea, much less a devil!' It will be well if it serves no other purpose but to bring back these stray sheep to the fold of the Church. So this story has gained much belief in the parish?"

"Most believe it, sir, as rightly they should, what hath so many witnesses," said the sexton, "though there be some, chiefly young men, who set up for being wiser than their fathers, and refuse to credit it, though it be sworn to on the book."

"If those things are disbelieved, friend," said the parson, "and without inquiry, which your disbeliever is ever the first to shrink from, of what worth is human testimony? That ghosts have returned to the earth, either for the discovery of murder, or to make restitution for other injustice committed in the flesh, or compelled thereto by the incantations of sorcery, or to communicate tidings from another world, has been testified to in all ages, and many are the accounts which have been left us both in sacred and profane authors. Did not Brutus, when in Asia, as is related by Plutarch, see— —"

Just at this moment the parson's handmaid announced that a person waited on him in the kitchen,—or the good clergyman would probably have detailed all those cases in history, general and biblical, with which his reading had acquainted him, not much, we fear to the edification and comfort of the sexton, who had to return to Lanreath, a long and dreary road, after nightfall. So, instead, he directed the girl to take him with her, and give him such refreshment as he needed, and in the meanwhile he prepared a note in answer to Mr Mills, informing him that on the morrow he was to visit some sick persons in his parish, but that on the following evening he should be ready to proceed with him to the moor.

On the night appointed the two clergymen left the Lanreath rectory on horseback, and reached the moor at eleven o'clock. Bleak and dismal did it look by day, but then there was the distant landscape dotted over with pretty homesteads to relieve its desolation. Now, nothing was seen but the black patch of sterile moor on which they stood, nothing heard but the wind as it swept in gusts across the bare hill, and howled dismally through a stunted grove of trees that grew in a glen below them, except the occasional baying of dogs from the farmhouses in the distance. That they felt at ease, is more than could be expected of them; but as it would have shown a lack of faith in the protection of Heaven, which it would have been unseemly in men of their holy calling to exhibit, they managed to conceal from each other their uneasiness. Leading their horses, they trod to and fro through the damp fern and heath with firmness in their steps, and upheld each other by remarks on the power of that Great Being whose ministers they were, and the might of whose name they were there to make manifest. Still slowly and dismally passed the time as they conversed, and anon stopped to look through the darkness for the approach of their ghostly visitor. In vain. Though the night was as dark and murky as ghost could wish, the coach and its driver came not.

After a considerable stay, the two clergymen consulted together, and determined that it was useless to watch any longer for that night, but that they would meet on some other, when perhaps it might please his ghostship to appear. Accordingly, with a few words of leave-taking, they separated, Mr Mills for the rectory, and Mr Dodge, by a short ride across the moor, which shortened his journey by half a mile, for the vicarage at Talland.

The vicar rode on at an ambling pace, which his good mare sustained up hill and down vale without urging. At the bottom of a deep valley, however, about a mile from Blackadon, the animal became very uneasy, pricked up her ears, snorted, and moved from side to side of the road, as if something stood in the path before her. The parson tightened the reins, and applied whip and spur to her sides, but the animal, usually docile, became very unruly, made several attempts to turn, and, when prevented, threw herself upon her haunches. Whip and spur were applied again and again, to no other purpose than to add to the horse's terror. To the rider nothing was apparent which could account for the sudden restiveness of his beast. He dismounted, and attempted in turns to lead or drag her, but both were impracticable, and attended with no small risk of snapping the reins. She was remounted with great difficulty, and another attempt was made to urge her forward, with the like want of success. At length the eccentric clergyman, judging it to be some special signal from Heaven, which it would be dangerous to neglect, threw the reins on the neck of his steed, which, wheeling suddenly round, started backward in a direction towards the moor, at a pace which rendered the parson's seat neither a pleasant nor a safe one. In an astonishingly short space of time they were once more at Blackadon.

By this time the bare outline of the moor was broken by a large black group of objects, which the darkness of the night prevented the parson from defining. On approaching this unaccountable appearance, the mare was seized with fresh fury, and it was with considerable difficulty that she could be brought to face this new cause of fright. In the pauses of the horse's prancing, the vicar discovered to his horror the much-dreaded spectacle of the black coach and the headless steeds, and, terrible to relate, his friend Mr Mills lying prostrate on the ground before the sable driver. Little time was left him to call up his courage for this fearful emergency; for just as the vicar began to give utterance to the earnest prayers which struggled to his lips, the spectre shouted, "Dodge is come! I must begone!" and forthwith leaped into his chariot, and disappeared across the moor.

The fury of the mare now subsided, and Mr Dodge was enabled to approach his friend, who was lying motionless and speechless, with his face buried in the heather.

Meanwhile the rector's horse, which had taken fright at the apparition, and had thrown his rider to the ground on or near the spot where we have left him lying, made homeward at a furious speed, and stopped not until he had reached his stable door. The sound of his hoofs as he galloped madly through the village awoke the cottagers, many of whom had been some hours in their beds. Many eager faces, staring with affright, gathered round the rectory, and added, by their various conjectures, to the terror and apprehensions of the family.

The villagers, gathering courage as their numbers increased, agreed to go in search of the missing clergyman, and started off in a compact body, a few on horseback, but the greater number on foot, in the direction of Blackadon. There they discovered their rector, supported in the arms of Parson Dodge, and recovered so far as to be able to speak. Still there was a wildness in his eye, and an incoherency in his speech, that showed that his reason was, at least, temporarily unsettled by the fright. In this condition he was taken to his home, followed by his reverend companion.

Here ended this strange adventure; for Mr Mills soon completely regained his reason, Parson Dodge got safely back to Talland, and from that time to this nothing has been heard or seen of the black ghost or his chariot. [4]

FOOTNOTES

[4] The Parson Dodge, whose adventure is related, was vicar of Talland from 1713 till his death. So that the name as well as the story is true to tradition. Bond (*History of East and West Looe*) says of him: "About a century since the Rev. Richard Dodge was vicar of this parish of Talland, and was, by traditionary account, a very singular man. He had the reputation of being deeply skilled in the black art, and would raise ghosts, or send them into the Dead Sea, at the nod of his head. The common people, not only in his own parish, but throughout the neighbourhood, stood in the greatest awe of him, and to meet him on the highway at midnight produced the utmost horror; he was then driving about the evil spirits; many of them were seen, in all sorts of shapes, flying and running before him, and he pursuing them with his whip in a most daring manner. Not unfrequently he would be seen in the churchyard at dead of night to the terror of passers-by. He was a worthy man, and much respected, but had his eccentricities."

XII
DRAKE'S DRUM

By William Hunt

Sir Francis Drake—who appears to have been especially befriended by his demon—is said to drive at night a black hearse drawn by headless horses, and urged on by running devils and yelping, headless dogs, through Jump, on the road from Tavistock to Plymouth.

Sir Francis, according to tradition, was enabled to destroy the Spanish Armada by the aid of the devil. The old admiral went to Devil's Point, a well-known promontory jutting into Plymouth Sound. He there cut pieces of wood into the water, and by the power of magic and the assistance of his demon these became at once well-armed gunboats.

Queen Elizabeth gave Sir Francis Drake Buckland Abbey; and on every hand we hear of Drake and his familiars.

An extensive building attached to the abbey—which was no doubt used as barns and stables after the place had been deprived of its religious character—was said to have been built by the devil in three nights. After the first night, the butler, astonished at the work done, resolved to watch and see how it was performed. Consequently, on the second night, he mounted into a large tree, and hid himself between the forks of its five branches. At midnight the devil came, driving several teams of oxen; and as some of them were lazy, he plucked this tree from the ground and used it as a goad. The poor butler lost his senses, and never recovered them.

Drake constructed the channel, carrying the waters from Dartmoor to Plymouth. Tradition says he went with his demon to Dartmoor, walked into Plymouth, and the waters followed him. Even now—as old Betty Donithorne, formerly the housekeeper at Buckland Abbey, told me,—if the warrior hears the drum which hangs in the hall of the abbey, and which accompanied him round the world, he rises and has a revel.

Some few years since a small box was found in a closet which had been long closed, containing, it is supposed, family papers. This was to be sent to the residence of the inheritor of this property. The carriage was at the abbey door, and a man easily lifted the box into it. The owner having taken his seat, the coachman attempted to start his horses, but in vain. They would not—they could not move. More horses were brought, and then the heavy farm-horses, and eventually all the oxen. They were powerless to start the carriage. At length a mysterious voice was heard, declaring that the box could never be moved from Buckland Abbey. It was taken from the carriage easily by one man, and a pair of horses galloped off with the carriage.

XIII
THE SPECTRE BRIDEGROOM

By William Hunt

Long, long ago a farmer named Lenine lived in Boscean. He had but one son, Frank Lenine, who was indulged into waywardness by both his parents. In addition to the farm servants, there was one, a young girl, Nancy Trenoweth, who especially assisted Mrs Lenine in all the various duties of a small farmhouse.

Nancy Trenoweth was very pretty, and although perfectly uneducated, in the sense in which we now employ the term education, she possessed many native graces, and she had acquired much knowledge, really useful to one whose aspirations would probably never rise higher than to be mistress of a farm of a few acres. Educated by parents who had certainly never seen the world beyond Penzance, her ideas of the world were limited to a few miles around the Land's-End. But although her book of nature was a small one, it had deeply impressed her mind with its influences. The wild waste, the small but fertile valley, the rugged hills, with their crowns of cairns, the moors rich in the golden furze and the purple heath, the sea-beaten cliffs and the silver sands, were the pages she had studied, under the guidance of a mother who conceived, in the sublimity of her ignorance, that everything in nature was the home of some spirit form. The soul of the girl was imbued with the deeply religious dye of her mother's mind, whose religion was only a sense of an unknown world immediately beyond our own. The elder Nancy Trenoweth exerted over the villagers around her considerable power. They did not exactly fear her. She was too free from evil for that; but they were conscious of a mental superiority, and yielded without complaining to her sway.

The result of this was, that the younger Nancy, although compelled to service, always exhibited some pride, from a feeling that her mother was a superior woman to any around her.

She never felt herself inferior to her master and mistress, yet she complained not of being in subjection to them. There were so many interesting features in the character of this young servant girl that she became in many respects like a daughter to her mistress. There was no broad line of division in those days, in even the manorial hall, between the lord and his domestics, and still less defined was the position of the employer and the employed in a small farmhouse. Consequent on this condition of things, Frank Lenine and Nancy were thrown as much together as if they had been brother and sister. Frank was rarely checked in anything by his over-fond parents, who were especially proud of their son, since he was regarded as the handsomest young man in the parish. Frank conceived a very warm attachment for Nancy, and she was not a little proud of her lover. Although it was evident to all the parish that Frank and Nancy were seriously devoted to each other, the young man's parents were blind to it, and were taken by surprise when one day Frank asked his father and mother to consent to his marrying Nancy.

The Lenines had allowed their son to have his own way from his youth up; and now, in a matter which brought into play the strongest of human feelings, they were angry because he refused to bend to their wills.

The old man felt it would be a degradation for a Lenine to marry a Trenoweth, and, in the most unreasoning manner, he resolved it should never be.

The first act was to send Nancy home to Alsia Mill, where her parents resided; the next was an imperious command to his son never again to see the girl.

The commands of the old are generally powerless upon the young where the affairs of the heart are concerned. So were they upon Frank. He who was rarely seen of an evening beyond the garden of his father's cottage, was now as constantly absent from his home. The house, which was wont to be a pleasant one, was strangely altered. A gloom had fallen over all things; the father and son rarely met as friends—the mother and her boy had now a feeling of reserve. Often there were angry altercations between the father and son, and the mother felt she could not become the defender of her boy, in his open acts of disobedience, his bold defiance of his parents' commands.

Rarely an evening passed that did not find Nancy and Frank together in some retired nook. The Holy Well was a favourite meeting-place, and here the most solemn vows were made. Locks of hair were exchanged; a wedding-ring, taken from the finger of a corpse, was broken, when they vowed that they would be united either dead or alive; and they even climbed at night the granite-pile at Treryn, and swore by the Logan Rock the same strong vow.

Time passed onward unhappily, and as the result of the endeavours to quench out the passion by force, it grew stronger under the repressing power, and, like imprisoned steam, eventually burst through all restraint.

Nancy's parents discovered at length that moonlight meetings between two untrained, impulsive youths, had a natural result, and they were now doubly earnest in their endeavours to compel Frank to marry their daughter.

The elder Lenine could not be brought to consent to this, and he firmly resolved to remove his son entirely from what he considered the hateful influences of the Trenoweths. He resolved to go to Plymouth, to take his son with him, and, if possible, to send him away to sea, hoping thus to wean him from his folly, as he considered this love-madness. Frank, poor fellow, with the best intentions, was not capable of any sustained effort, and consequently he at length succumbed to his father; and, to escape his persecution, he entered a ship bound for India, and bade adieu to his native land.

Frank could not write, and this happened in days when letters could be forwarded only with extreme difficulty, consequently Nancy never heard from her lover.

A babe had been born into a troublesome world, and the infant became a real solace to the young mother. As the child grew, it became an especial favourite with its grandmother; the elder Nancy rejoiced over the little prattler, and forgot her cause of sorrow. Young Nancy lived for her child, and on the memory of its father. Subdued in spirit she was, but her affliction had given force to her character, and she had been heard to declare that wherever Frank might be, she was ever present with him, whatever might be the temptations of the hour, that her influence was all powerful over him for good. She felt that no distance could separate their souls, that no time could be long enough to destroy the bond between them.

A period of distress fell upon the Trenoweths, and it was necessary that Nancy should leave her home once more, and go again into service. Her mother took charge of the babe, and she found a situation in the village of Kimyall, in the parish of Paul. Nancy, like her mother, contrived by force of character to maintain an ascendancy amongst her companions. She had formed an acquaintance, which certainly never grew into friendship, with some of the daughters of the small farmers around. These girls were all full of the superstitions of the time and place.

The winter was coming on, and nearly three years had passed away since Frank Lenine left his country. As yet there was no sign. Nor father, nor mother, nor maiden had heard of him, and they all sorrowed over his absence. The Lenines desired to have Nancy's child, but the Trenoweths would not part with it. They went so far even as to endeavour to persuade Nancy to live again with them, but Nancy was not at all disposed to submit to their wishes.

It was All-Hallows' eve, and two of Nancy's companions persuaded her,—no very difficult task,—to go with them and sow hemp-seed.

At midnight the three maidens stole out unperceived into Kimyall town-place to perform their incantation. Nancy was the first to sow, the others being less bold than she.

Boldly she advanced, saying, as she scattered the seed,—

> "Hemp-seed I sow thee,
> Hemp-seed grow thee;
> And he who will my true love be,
> Come after me
> And shaw thee."

This was repeated three times, when, looking back over her left shoulder, she saw Lenine; but he looked so angry that she shrieked with fear, and broke the spell. One of the other girls, however, resolved now to make trial of the spell, and the result of her labours was the vision of a white coffin. Fear now fell on all, and they went home sorrowful, to spend, each one, a sleepless night.

November came with its storms, and during one terrific night a large vessel was thrown upon the rocks in Bernowhall Cliff, and, beaten by the impetuous waves, she was soon in pieces. Amongst the bodies of the crew washed ashore, nearly all of whom had perished, was Frank Lenine. He was not dead when found, but the only words he lived to speak were begging the people to send for Nancy Trenoweth, that he might make her his wife before he died.

Rapidly sinking, Frank was borne by his friends on a litter to Boscean, but he died as he reached the town-place. His parents, overwhelmed in their own sorrows, thought nothing of Nancy, and without her knowing that Lenine had returned, the poor fellow was laid in his last bed, in Burian Churchyard.

On the night of the funeral, Nancy went, as was her custom, to lock the door of the house, and as was her custom too, she looked out into the night. At this instant a horseman rode up in hot haste, called her by name, and hailed her in a voice that chilled her blood.

The voice was the voice of Lenine. She could never forget that; and the horse she now saw was her sweetheart's favourite colt, on which he had often ridden at night to Alsia.

The rider was imperfectly seen; but he looked very sorrowful, and deathly pale, still Nancy knew him to be Frank Lenine.

He told her that he had just arrived home, and that the first moment he was at liberty he had taken horse to fetch his loved one, and to make her his bride.

Nancy's excitement was so great, that she was easily persuaded to spring on the horse behind him, that they might reach his home before the morning.

When she took Lenine's hand a cold shiver passed through her, and as she grasped his waist to secure herself in her seat, her arm became as stiff as ice. She lost all power of speech, and suffered deep fear, yet she knew not why. The moon had arisen, and now burst out in a full flood of light, through the heavy clouds which had obscured it. The horse pursued its journey with great rapidity, and whenever in weariness it slackened its speed, the peculiar voice of the rider aroused its drooping energies. Beyond this no word was spoken since Nancy had mounted behind her lover. They now came to Trove Bottom, where there was no bridge at that time; they dashed into the river. The moon shone full in their faces. Nancy looked into the stream, and saw that the rider was in a shroud and other grave-clothes. She now knew that she was being carried away by a spirit, yet she had no power to save herself; indeed, the inclination to do so did not exist.

On went the horse at a furious pace, until they came to the blacksmith's shop, near Burian Church-town, when she knew by the light from the forge fire thrown across the road that the smith was still at his labours. She now recovered speech. "Save me! save me! save me!" she cried with all her might. The smith sprang from the door of the smithy, with a red-hot iron in his hand, and as the horse rushed by, caught the woman's dress, and pulled her to the ground. The spirit, however, also seized Nancy's dress in one hand, and his grasp was like that of a vice. The horse passed like the wind, and Nancy and the smith were pulled down as far as the old Alms-houses, near the churchyard. Here the horse for a moment stopped. The smith seized that moment, and with his hot iron burned off the dress from the rider's hand, thus saving Nancy, more dead than alive; while the rider passed over the wall of the churchyard, and vanished on the grave in which Lenine had been laid but a few hours before.

The smith took Nancy into his shop, and he soon aroused some of his neighbours, who took the poor girl back to Alsia. Her parents laid her on her bed. She spoke no word, but to ask for her child, to request her mother to give up her child to Lenine's parents, and her desire to be buried in his grave. Before the morning light fell on the world Nancy had breathed her last breath.

A horse was seen that night to pass through the Church-town like a ball from a musket, and in the morning Lenine's colt was found dead in Bernowhall Cliff, covered with foam, its eyes forced from its head, and its swollen tongue hanging out of its mouth. On Lenine's grave was found the piece of Nancy's dress which was left in the spirit's hand when the smith burnt her from his grasp.

It is said that one or two of the sailors who survived the wreck related after the funeral, how, on the 30th of October, at night, Lenine was like one mad; they could scarcely keep him in the ship. He seemed more asleep than awake, and, after great excitement, he fell as if dead upon the deck, and lay so for hours. When he came to himself, he told them that he had been taken to the village of Kimyall, and that if he ever married the woman who had cast the spell, he would make her suffer the longest day she had to live for drawing his soul out of his body.

Poor Nancy was buried in Lenine's grave, and her companion in sowing hemp-seed, who saw the white coffin, slept beside her within the year.

XIV
THE POOL IN THE GRAVEYARD

By Greville MacDonald [5]

By this corner of the graveyard the red dawn discovered to Jonas a little pool of clear water, with mosses and parsley-ferns all around it, and so clear and cool-looking that he must drink. The larger part of it was still shadowed by the wall. On knees and hands, he put his lips to it and drank. The refreshment was wonderful. He rose with a sense that he should find the lost sheep yet and bring her home. He looked down once more into the clear pool. It was wider than he had thought—indeed, he had been mistaken; it was a great tarn on the mountain-side! Then he saw that wonderful things were happening on the face of and all round the water. What appeared to be little glow-worms were lying motionless in groups on the mosses in a still-shadowed region by the side of the water. From beneath a low arch in the wall, where the water was slowly flowing away in a river, there came, against stream and wave and wind, a fishing-boat. Its great red sail was spread, and its pennant shone silvery blue in the sun. It came alongside a pier of mossy stones, and cast anchor. From it leapt twelve strong young fishermen, all with bright faces. They took up the little creatures with the glowing lights, and carried them aboard; then back again to other groups, until all were gathered in. For they were all sleeping human forms, close-wrapped in grave-clothes, but with their light still living, as might be seen by anyone who had suffered. When all were safe aboard, the men cast off and the boat disappeared under the arch.

FOOTNOTES

[5] From *How Jonas Found his Enemy: a Romance of the South Downs* (1916).

XV
THE LIANHAN SHEE

By Will Carleton

One summer evening Mary Sullivan was sitting at her own well-swept hearthstone, knitting feet to a pair of sheep's-grey stockings for Bartley, her husband. It was one of those serene evenings in the month of June when the decline of day assumes a calmness and repose, resembling what we might suppose to have irradiated Eden when our first parents sat in it before their fall. The beams of the sun shone through the windows in clear shafts of amber light, exhibiting millions of those atoms which float to the naked eye within its mild radiance. The dog lay barking in his dream at her feet, and the grey cat sat purring placidly upon his back, from which even his occasional agitation did not dislodge her.

Mrs Sullivan was the wife of a wealthy farmer, and niece to the Rev. Felix O'Rourke; her kitchen was consequently large, comfortable, and warm. Over where she sat, jutted out the "brace" well lined with bacon; to the right hung a well-scoured salt-box, and to the left was the jamb, with its little paneless window to admit the light. Within it hung several ash rungs, seasoning for flail-sooples, or boulteens, a dozen of eel-skins, and several stripes of horse-skin, as hangings for them. The dresser was a "parfit white," and well furnished with the usual appurtenances. Over the door and on the "threshel" were nailed, "for luck," two horse-shoes, that had been found by accident. In a little "hole" in the wall, beneath the salt-box, lay a bottle of holy water to keep the place purified; and against the copestone of the gable, on the outside, grew a large lump of house-leek, as a specific for sore eyes and other maladies.

In the corner of the garden were a few stalks of tansy "to kill the thievin' worms in the childhre, the crathurs," together with a little Rosenoble, Solomon's Seal, and Bugloss, each for some medicinal purpose. The "lime wather" Mrs Sullivan could make herself, and the "bog bane" for the *linh roe*, or heartburn, grew in their own meadow-drain; so that, in fact, she had within her reach a very decent pharmacopœia, perhaps as harmless as that of the profession itself. Lying on the top of the salt-box was a bunch of fairy flax, and sewed in the folds of her own scapular was the dust of what had once been a four-leaved shamrock, an invaluable specific "for seein' the good people," if they happened to come within the bounds of vision. Over the door in the inside, over the beds, and over the cattle in the outhouses, were placed branches of withered palm, that had been consecrated by the priest on Palm Sunday; and when the cows happened to calve, this good woman tied, with her own hands, a woollen thread about their tails, to prevent them from being overlooked by evil eyes, or *elf-shot* by the fairies, who seem to possess a peculiar power over females of every species during the period of parturition. It is unnecessary to mention the variety of charms which she possessed for that obsolete malady the colic, for toothache, headaches, or for removing warts, and taking motes out of the eyes; let it suffice to inform our readers that she was well stocked with them; and, that in addition to this, she, together with her husband, drank a potion made up and administered by an herb-doctor, for preventing for ever the slightest misunderstanding or quarrel between man and wife. Whether it produced this desirable object or not, our readers may conjecture, when we add, that the herb-doctor, after having taken a very liberal advantage of their generosity, was immediately compelled to disappear from the neighbourhood, in order to avoid meeting with Bartley, who had a sharp look-out for him, not exactly on his own account, but "in regard," he said, "that it had no effect upon *Mary*, at all at all"; whilst Mary, on the other hand, admitted its efficacy upon herself, but maintained, "that *Bartley* was worse nor ever afther it."

Such was Mary Sullivan, as she sat at her own hearth, quite alone, engaged as we have represented her. What she may have been meditating on, we cannot pretend to ascertain; but after some time, she looked sharply into the "backstone," or hob, with an air of anxiety and alarm. By and by she suspended her knitting, and listened with much earnestness, leaning her right ear over to the hob, from whence the sounds to which she paid such deep attention proceeded. At length she crossed herself devoutly, and exclaimed, "Queen of saints about us!—is it back ye are? Well sure there's no use in talkin' bekase they say you know what's said of you, or to you— an' we may as well spake yez fair. Hem—musha yez are welcome back, crickets, avour-neenee! I hope that, not like the last visit ye ped us, yez are comin' for luck now! Moolyeen died, any way, soon afther your other *kailyee*, ye crathurs ye. Here's the bread, an' the salt, an' the male for yez, an' we wish ye well. Eh?—saints above, if it isn't listenin' they are jist like a Christhien! Wurrah, but ye are the wise an' the quare crathurs all out!"

She then shook a little holy water over the hob, and muttered to herself an Irish charm or prayer against the evils which crickets are often supposed by the peasantry to bring with them, and requested, still in the words of the charm, that their presence might, on that occasion, rather be a presage of good fortune to man and beast belonging to her.

"There now, ye *dhonans* ye, sure ye can't say that ye're ill-thrated here, anyhow, or ever was mocked or made game of in the same family. You have got your hansel, an' full an' plenty of it; hopin' at the same time that you'll have no rason in life to cut our best clothes from revinge. Sure an' I didn't desarve to have my brave stuff *long body* riddled the way it was the last time ye wor here, an' only bekase little Barny, that has but the sinse of a *gorsoon*, tould yez in a joke to pack off wid yourselves somewhere else. Musha, never heed what the likes of him says; sure he's but a *caudy*, that doesn't mane ill, only the bit o' divarsion wid yez."

She then resumed her knitting, occasionally stopping, as she changed her needles, to listen, with her ear set, as if she wished to augur from the nature of their chirping, whether they came for good or evil. This, however, seemed to be beyond her faculty of translating their language; for after sagely shaking her head two or three times, she knit more busily than before.

At this moment, the shadow of a person passing the house darkened the window opposite which she sat, and immediately a tall female, of a wild dress and aspect, entered the kitchen.

"*Gho manhy dhea ghud, a ban chohr*! the blessin' o' goodness upon you, dacent woman," said Mrs Sullivan, addressing her in those kindly phrases so peculiar to the Irish language.

Instead of making her any reply, however, the woman, whose eye glistened with a wild depth of meaning, exclaimed in low tones, apparently of much anguish, "*Husht, husht, dherum*! husht, husht, I say—let me alone—I will do it—will you husht? I will, I say—I will—there now—that's it—be quiet, an' I will do it—be quiet!" and as she thus spoke she turned her face back over her left shoulder, as if some invisible being dogged her steps, and stood bending over her.

"*Gho manhy dhea ghud, a ban chohr, dherhum areesht*! the blessin' o' God on you, honest woman, I say again," said Mrs Sullivan, repeating that *sacred* form of salutation with which the peasantry address each other. "'Tis a fine evenin', honest woman, glory be to Him that sent the same, and amin! If it was cowld, I'd be axin' you to draw your chair in to the fire; but, any way, won't you sit down?"

As she ceased speaking the piercing eye of the strange woman became riveted on her with a glare, which, whilst it startled Mrs Sullivan, seemed full of an agony that almost abstracted her from external life. It was not, however, so wholly absorbing as to prevent it from expressing a marked interest, whether for good or evil, in the woman who addressed her so hospitably.

"Husht, now—husht," she said, as if aside—"husht, won't you—sure I may speak *the thing* to her—you said it—there now, husht!" And then fastening her dark eyes on Mrs Sullivan, she smiled bitterly and mysteriously.

"I know you well," she said, without, however, returning the *blessing* contained in the usual reply to Mrs Sullivan's salutation—"I know you well, Mary Sullivan—husht, now, husht—yes, I know you well, and the power of all that you carry about you; but you'd be better than you are—and that's well enough *now*—if you had sense to know—ah, ah, ah!—what's this!" she exclaimed abruptly, with three distinct shrieks, that seemed to be produced by sensations of sharp and piercing agony.

"In the name of goodness, what's over you, honest woman?" inquired Mrs Sullivan, as she started from her chair, and ran to her in a state of alarm, bordering on terror—"Is it sick you are?"

The woman's face had got haggard, and its features distorted; but in a few minutes they resumed their peculiar expression of settled wildness and mystery. "Sick!" she replied, licking her parched lips; "*awirck, awirck!* look! look!" and she pointed with a shudder that almost convulsed her whole frame, to a lump that rose on her shoulders; this, be it what it might, was covered with a red cloak, closely pinned and tied with great caution about her body—"'tis here!—I have it!"

"Blessed mother!" exclaimed Mrs Sullivan, tottering over to her chair, as finished a picture of horror as the eye could witness, "this day's Friday: the saints stand betwixt me an' all harm! Oh, holy Mary, protect me! *Nhanim an airh*," in the name of the Father, etc., and she forthwith proceeded to bless herself, which she did thirteen times in honour of the blessed virgin and the twelve apostles.

"Ay, it's as you see!" replied the stranger bitterly. "It is here—husht, now—husht, I say—I will say *the thing* to her, mayn't I? Ay, indeed, Mary Sullivan, 'tis with me always—always. Well, well, no, I won't I won't—easy. Oh, blessed saints, easy, and I won't!"

In the meantime Mrs Sullivan had uncorked her bottle of holy water, and plentifully bedewed herself with it, as a preservative against this mysterious woman and her dreadful secret.

"Blessed mother above!" she ejaculated, "the *Lianhan Shee!*" And as she spoke, with the holy water in the palm of her hand, she advanced cautiously, and with great terror, to throw it upon the stranger and the unearthly thing she bore.

"Don't attempt it!" shouted the other, in tones of mingled fierceness and terror; "do you want to give *me* pain without keeping *yourself* anything at all safer? Don't you know *it* doesn't care about your holy water? But I'd suffer for it, an' perhaps so would you."

Mrs Sullivan, terrified by the agitated looks of the woman, drew back with affright, and threw the holy water with which she intended to purify the other on her own person.

"Why thin, you lost crathur, who or what are you at all?—don't, don't—for the sake of all the saints and angels of heaven, don't come next or near me—keep your distance—but what are you, or how did you come to get that 'good thing' you carry about wid you?"

"Ay, indeed!" replied the woman bitterly, "as if I would or could tell you that! I say, you woman, you're doing what's not right in asking me a question you ought not let to cross your lips—look to yourself, and what's over you."

The simple woman, thinking her meaning literal, almost leaped off her seat with terror, and turned up her eyes to ascertain whether or not any dreadful appearance had approached her, or hung over her where she sat.

"Woman," said she, "I spoke you kind an' fair, an' I wish you well—but——"

"But what?" replied the other—and her eyes kindled into deep and profound excitement, apparently upon very slight grounds.

"Why—hem—nothin' at all sure, only——"

"Only what?" asked the stranger, with a face of anguish that seemed to torture every feature out of its proper lineaments.

"Dacent woman," said Mrs Sullivan, whilst the hair began to stand with terror upon her head, "sure it's no wondher in life that I'm in a perplexity, whin a *Lianhan Shee* is undher the one roof wid me. 'Tisn't that I want to know anything at all about it—the dear forbid I should; but I never hard of a person bein' tormented wid it as you are. I always used to hear the people say that it thrated its friends well."

"Husht!" said the woman, looking wildly over her shoulder, "I'll not tell: it's on myself I'll leave the blame! Why, will you never pity me? Am I to be night and day tormented? Oh, you're wicked and cruel for no reason!"

"Thry," said Mrs Sullivan, "an' bless yourself; call on God."

"Ah!" shouted the other, "are you going to get me killed?" and as she uttered the words, a spasmodic working which must have occasioned great pain, even to torture, became audible in her throat; her bosom heaved up and down, and her head was bent repeatedly on her breast, as if by force.

"Don't mention that name," said she, "in my presence, except you mean to drive me to utter distraction. I mean," she continued, after considerable effort to recover her former tone and manner—"hear me with attention—I mean, woman—you, Mary Sullivan—that if you mention that holy name, you might as well keep plunging sharp knives into my heart! Husht! peace to me for one minute, tormentor! Spare me something, I'm in your power!"

"Will you ate anything?" said Mrs Sullivan; "poor crathur, you look like hunger an' distress; there's enough in the house, blessed be them that sent it! an' you had betther thry an' take some nourishment, any way"; and she raised her eyes in a silent prayer of relief and ease for the unhappy woman, whose unhallowed association had, in her opinion, sealed her doom.

"Will I?—will I?—oh!" she replied, "may you never know misery for offering it! Oh, bring me something—some refreshment—some food—for I'm dying with hunger."

Mrs Sullivan, who, with all her superstition, was remarkable for charity and benevolence, immediately placed food and drink before her, which the stranger absolutely devoured—taking care occasionally to secrete under the protuberance which appeared behind her neck, a portion of what she ate. This, however, she did, not by stealth, but openly; merely taking means to prevent the concealed thing from being, by any possible accident, discovered.

When the craving of hunger was satisfied, she appeared to suffer less from the persecution of her tormentor than before; whether it was, as Mrs Sullivan thought, that the food with which she plied it appeased in some degree its irritability, or lessened that of the stranger, it was difficult to say; at all events, she became more composed; her eyes resumed somewhat of a natural expression; each sharp ferocious glare, which shot from them with such intense and rapid flashes, partially disappeared; her knit brows dilated, and part of a forehead, which had once been capacious and handsome, lost the contractions which deformed it by deep wrinkles. Altogether the change was evident, and very much relieved Mrs Sullivan, who could not avoid observing it.

"It's not that I care much about it, if you'd think it not right o' me, but it's odd enough for you to keep the lower part of your face muffled up in that black cloth, an' then your forehead, too, is covered down on your face a bit. If they're part of the *bargain*,"—and she shuddered at the thought,— "between you an' anything that's not good—hem!—I think you'd do well to throw thim off o' you, an' turn to thim that can protect you from everything that's bad. Now, a scapular would keep all the divils in hell from one; an' if you'd——"

On looking at the stranger she hesitated, for the wild expression of her eyes began to return.

"Don't begin my punishment again," replied the woman; "make no allus——don't make mention in my presence of anything that's good. Husht—husht—it's beginning—easy now—easy! No," said she, "I came to tell you, that only for my breaking a vow I made to this thing upon me, I'd be happy instead of miserable with it. I say, it's a good thing to have, if the person will use this bottle," she added, producing one, "as I will direct them."

"I wouldn't wish, for my part," replied Mrs Sullivan, "to have anything to do wid it—neither act nor part"; and she crossed herself devoutly, on contemplating such an unholy alliance as that at which her companion hinted.

"Mary Sullivan," replied the other, "I can put good fortune and happiness in the way of you and yours. It is for you the good is intended; if *you* don't get both, *no other* can," and her eyes kindled as she spoke like those of the Pyrhoness in the moment of inspiration.

Mrs Sullivan looked at her with awe, fear, and a strong mixture of curiosity; she had often heard that the *Lianhan Shee* had, through means of the person to whom it was bound, conferred wealth upon several, although it could never render this important service to those who exercised direct authority over it. She therefore experienced something like a conflict between her fears and a love of that wealth, the possession of which was so plainly intimated to her.

"The money," said she, "would be one thing, but to have the *Lianhan Shee* planted over a body's shouldher—och! the saints preserve us!—no, not for oceans of hard goold would I have it in my company one minnit. But in regard to the money—hem!—why, if it could be managed without havin' act or part wid *that thing*, people would do anything in reason and fairity."

"You have this day been kind to me," replied the woman, "and that's what I can't say of many—dear help me!—husht! Every door is shut in my face! Does not every cheek get pale when I am seen? If I meet a fellow-creature on the road, they turn into the field to avoid me; if I ask for food, it's to a deaf ear I speak; if I am thirsty, they send me to the river. What house would shelter me? In cold, in hunger, in drought, in storm, and in tempest, I am alone and unfriended, hated, feared, an' avoided; starving in the winter's cold, and burning in the summer's heat. All this is my fate here;

and—oh! oh! oh!—have mercy, tormentor—have mercy! I will not lift my thoughts *there*—I'll keep the paction—but spare me *now*!"

She turned round as she spoke, seeming to follow an invisible object, or, perhaps, attempting to get a more complete view of the mysterious being which exercised such a terrible and painful influence over her. Mrs Sullivan, also, kept her eye fixed upon the lump, and actually believed that she saw it move. Fear of incurring the displeasure of what it contained, and a superstitious reluctance harshly to thrust a person from her door who had eaten of her food, prevented her from desiring the woman to depart.

"In the name of Goodness," she replied, "I will have nothing to do wid your gift. Providence, blessed be His name, has done well for me an' mine; an' it mightn't be right to go beyant what it has pleased *Him* to give me."

"A rational sentiment!—I mean there's good sense in what you say," answered the stranger: "but you need not be afraid," and she accompanied the expression by holding up the bottle and kneeling. "Now," she added, "listen to me, and judge for yourself, if what I say, when I swear it, can be a lie." She then proceeded to utter oaths of the most solemn nature, the purport of which was to assure Mrs Sullivan that drinking of the bottle would be attended with no danger.

"You see this little bottle? Drink it. Oh, for my sake and your own, drink it; it will give wealth without end to you and to all belonging to you. Take one-half of it before sunrise, and the other half when he goes down. You must stand while drinking it, with your face to the east, in the morning; and at night, to the west. Will you promise to do thus?"

"How would drinkin' the bottle get me money?" inquired Mrs Sullivan, who certainly felt a strong tendency of heart to the wealth.

"That I can't tell you now, nor would you understand it, even if I could; but you will know all when what I say is complied with."

"Keep your bottle, dacent woman. I wash my hands out of it: the saints above guard me from the timptation! I'm sure it's not right, for as I'm a sinner, 'tis gettin' stronger every minute widin me! Keep it! I'm loth to bid any one that *ett* o' my bread to go from my hearth, but if you go, I'll make it worth your while. Saints above! what's comin' over me? In my whole life I never had such a hankerin' afther money! Well, well, but it's quare entirely!"

"Will you drink it?" asked her companion. "If it does hurt or harm to you or yours, or anything but good, may what is hanging over me be fulfilled!" and she extended a thin, but, considering her years, not ungraceful arm, in the act of holding out the bottle to her kind entertainer.

"For the sake of all that's good and gracious, take it without scruple—it is not hurtful, a child might drink every drop that's in it. Oh, for the sake of all you love, and of all that love you, take it!" and as she urged her the tears streamed down her cheeks.

"No, no," replied Mrs Sullivan, "it'll never cross my lips; not if it made me as rich as ould Hendherson, that airs his guineas in the sun, for fraid they'd get light by lyin' past."

"I entreat you to take it," said the strange woman.

"Never, never!—once for all—I say, I won't; so spare your breath."

The firmness of the good housewife was not, in fact, to be shaken; so, after exhausting all the motives and arguments with which she could urge the accomplishment of her design, the strange woman, having again put the bottle into her bosom, prepared to depart.

She had now once more become calm, and resumed her seat with the languid air of one who has suffered much exhaustion and excitement. She put her hand upon her forehead for a few moments, as if collecting her faculties, or endeavouring to remember the purport of their previous conversation. A slight moisture had broken through her skin, and altogether, notwithstanding her avowed criminality in entering into an unholy bond, she appeared an object of deep compassion.

In a moment her manner changed again, and her eyes blazed out once more, as she asked her alarmed hostess, —

"Again, Mary Sullivan, will you take the gift that I have it in my power to give you? ay or no? speak, poor mortal, if you know what is for your own good."

Mrs Sullivan's fears, however, had overcome her love of money, particularly as she thought that wealth obtained in such a manner could not prosper; her only objection being to the means of acquiring it.

"Oh!" said the stranger, "am I doomed never to meet with anyone who will take the promise off me by drinking of this bottle. Oh! but I am unhappy! What it is to fear—ah! ah!—and keep *His* commandments. Had *I* done so in my youthful time, I wouldn't now—ah—merciful mother, is there no relief? kill me, tormentor; kill me outright, for surely the pangs of eternity cannot be greater than those you now make me suffer. Woman," said she, and her muscles stood out in extraordinary energy—"woman, Mary Sullivan—ay, if you should kill me—blast me—where I stand, I will say the word—woman—you have daughters—teach them—to fear——" Having got so far, she stopped—her bosom heaved up and down—her frame shook dreadfully—her eyeballs became lurid and fiery—her hands were clenched, and the spasmodic throes of inward convulsion worked the white froth up to her mouth; at length she suddenly became like a statue, with this wild supernatural expression intense upon her, and with an awful calmness, by far more dreadful than excitement could be, concluded by pronouncing in deep husky tones the name of God.

Having accomplished this with such a powerful struggle, she turned round with pale despair in her countenance and manner, and with streaming eyes slowly departed, leaving Mrs Sullivan in a situation not at all to be envied.

In a short time the other members of the family, who had been out at their evening employments, returned. Bartley, her husband, having entered somewhat sooner than his three daughters from milking, was the first to come in; presently the girls followed, and in a few minutes they sat down to supper, together with the servants, who dropped in one by one, after the toil of the day. On placing themselves about the table, Bartley as usual took his seat at the head; but Mrs Sullivan, instead of occupying hers, sat at the fire in a state of uncommon agitation. Every two or three minutes she would cross herself devoutly, and mutter such prayers against spiritual influences of an evil nature as she could compose herself to remember.

"Thin, why don't you come to your supper, Mary," said the husband, "while the sowans are warm? Brave and thick they are this night, any way."

His wife was silent, for so strong a hold had the strange woman and her appalling secret upon her mind, that it was not till he repeated his question three or four times—raising his head with surprise, and asking, "Eh, thin, Mary, what's come over you—is it unwell you are?"—that she noticed what he said.

"Supper!" she exclaimed; "unwell! 'tis a good right I have to be unwell,—I hope nothing bad will happen, any way. Feel my face, Nannie," she added, addressing one of her daughters; "it's as cowld an' wet as a limestone—ay, an' if you found me a corpse before you, it wouldn't be at all strange."

There was a general pause at the seriousness of this intimation. The husband rose from his supper, and went up to the hearth where she sat.

"Turn round to the light," said he; "why, Mary dear, in the name of wondher, what ails you? for you're like a corpse sure enough. Can't you tell us what has happened, or what put you in such a state? Why, childhre, the cowld sweat's teemin' off her!"

The poor woman, unable to sustain the shock produced by her interview with the stranger, found herself getting more weak, and requested a drink of water; but before it could be put to her lips, she laid her head upon the back of the chair and fainted. Grief, and uproar, and confusion followed this alarming incident. The presence of mind, so necessary on such occasions, was wholly lost; one ran here, and another there, all jostling against each other, without being cool enough to render her proper assistance. The daughters were in tears, and Bartley himself was dreadfully shocked by seeing his wife apparently lifeless before him.

She soon recovered, however, and relieved them from the apprehension of her death, which they thought had actually taken place. "Mary," said the husband, "something quare entirely has happened, or you wouldn't be in this state!"

"Did any of you see a strange woman lavin' the house a minute or two before ye came in?" she inquired.

"No," they replied, "not a stim of anyone did we see."

"Wurrah dheelish! No?—now is it possible ye didn't?" She then described her, but all declared they had seen no such person.

"Bartley, whisper," said she, and beckoning him over to her, in a few words she revealed the secret. The husband grew pale and crossed himself. "Mother of Saints! childhre," said he, "a *Lianhan Shee*!" The words were no sooner uttered than every countenance assumed the pallidness of death; and every right hand was raised in the act of blessing the person, and crossing the forehead. "*The Lianhan Shee!!*" all exclaimed in fear and horror—"This day's Friday; God betwixt us an' harm!"

It was now after dusk, and the hour had already deepened into the darkness of a calm, moonless, summer night; the hearth, therefore, in a short time, became surrounded by a circle, consisting of every person in the house; the door was closed and securely bolted;—a struggle for the safest seat took place; and to Bartley's shame be it spoken, he lodged himself on the hob within the jamb, as the most distant situation from the fearful being known as the *Lianhan Shee*. The recent terror, however, brooded over them all; their topic of conversation was the mysterious visit, of which Mrs Sullivan gave a painfully accurate detail; whilst every ear of those who composed her audience was set, and every single hair of their heads bristled up, as if awakened into distinct life by the story. Bartley looked into the fire soberly, except when the cat, in prowling about the dresser, electrified him into a start of fear, which sensation went round every link of the living chain about the hearth.

The next day the story spread through the whole neighbourhood, accumulating in interest and incident as it went. Where it received the touches, embellishments, and emendations, with which it was amplified, it would be difficult to say: every one told it, forsooth, *exactly* as he heard it from another, but indeed it is not improbable that those through whom it passed were unconscious of the additions it had received at their hands. It is not unreasonable to suppose that imagination in such cases often colours highly without a premeditated design of falsehood. Fear and dread, however, accompanied its progress; such families as had neglected to keep holy water in their houses borrowed some from their neighbours; every old prayer which had become rusty from disuse was brightened up—charms were hung about the necks of cattle, and gospels about those of children— crosses were placed over the doors and windows;—no unclean water was thrown out before sunrise or after dusk—

> "E'en those prayed now who never prayed before,
> And those who always prayed, still prayed the more."

The inscrutable woman who caused such general dismay in the parish was an object of much pity. Avoided, feared, and detested, she could find no rest for her weary feet, nor any shelter for her unprotected head. If she was seen approaching a house, the door and windows were immediately closed against her; if met on the way she was avoided as a pestilence. How she lived no one could tell, for none would permit themselves to know. It was asserted that she existed without meat or drink, and that she was doomed to remain possessed of life, the prey of hunger and thirst, until she could get some one weak enough to break the spell by drinking her hellish draught, to taste which, they said, would be to change places with herself, and assume her despair and misery.

There had lived in the country about six months before her appearance in it, a man named Stephenson. He was unmarried, and the last of his family. This person led a solitary and secluded life, and exhibited during the last years of his existence strong symptoms of eccentricity, which for some months before his death assumed a character of unquestionable derangement. He was found one morning hanging by a halter in his own stable, where he had, under the influence of his malady, committed suicide. At this time the public press had not, as now, familiarised the minds of the people to that dreadful crime, and it was consequently looked upon *then* with an intensity of horror of which we can scarcely entertain any adequate notion. His farm remained unoccupied, for while an acre of land could be obtained in any other quarter, no man would enter upon such unhallowed premises. The house was locked up, and it was currently reported that Stephenson and the devil each night repeated the hanging scene in the stable; and that when the former was committing the "hopeless sin," the halter slipped several times from the beam of the stable-loft, when Satan came, in the shape of a dark-complexioned man with a hollow voice, and secured the rope until Stephenson's end was accomplished.

In this stable did the wanderer take up her residence at night; and when we consider the belief of the people in the night-scenes which were supposed to occur in it, we need not be surprised at the new features of horror which this circumstance superadded to her character. Her presence and appearance in the parish were dreadful; a public outcry was soon raised against her, which, were it not from fear of her power over their lives and cattle, might have ended in her death. None, however, had courage to grapple with her, or to attempt expelling her by violence, lest a signal vengeance might be taken on any who dared to injure a woman that could call in the terrible aid of the *Lianhan Shee*.

In this state of feeling they applied to the parish priest, who, on hearing the marvellous stories related concerning her, and on questioning each man closely upon his authority, could perceive that, like most other reports, they were to be traced principally to the imagination and fears of the people. He ascertained, however, enough from Bartley Sullivan to justify a belief that there was something certainly uncommon about the woman; and being of a cold, phlegmatic disposition, with some humour, he desired them to go home, if they were wise—he shook his head mysteriously as he spoke— "and do the woman no injury, if they didn't wish"—and with this abrupt hint he sent them about their business.

This, however, did not satisfy them. In the same parish lived a suspended priest, called Father Philip O'Dallaghy, who supported himself, as most of them do, by curing certain diseases of the people—miraculously! He had no other means of subsistence, nor, indeed, did he seem strongly devoted to life, or to the pleasures it afforded. He was not addicted to those intemperate habits which characterise "Blessed Priests" in general; spirits he never tasted, nor any food that could be termed a luxury, or even a comfort. His communion with the people was brief, and marked by a tone of severe contemptuous misanthropy. He seldom stirred abroad except during morning, or in the evening twilight, when he might be seen gliding amidst the coming darkness, like a dissatisfied spirit. His life was an austere one, and his devotional practices were said to be of the most remorseful character. Such a man, in fact, was calculated to hold a powerful sway over the prejudices and superstitions of the people. This was true. His power was considered almost unlimited, and his life one that would not disgrace the highest saint in the calendar. There were not wanting some persons in the parish who hinted that Father Felix O'Rourke, the parish priest, was himself rather reluctant to incur the displeasure, or challenge the power of the *Lianhan Shee*, by driving its victim out of the parish. The opinion of these persons was, in its distinct unvarnished reality, that Father Felix absolutely showed the white feather on this critical occasion—that he became shy, and begged leave to decline being introduced to this intractable pair—seeming to intimate that he did not at all relish adding them to the stock of his acquaintances.

Father Philip they considered as a decided contrast to him on this point. His stern and severe manner, rugged, and, when occasion demanded, daring, they believed suitable to the qualities requisite for sustaining such an interview. They accordingly waited on him; and after Bartley and his friends had given as faithful a report of the circumstances as, considering all things, could be expected, he told Bartley he would hear from Mrs Sullivan's own lips the authentic narrative. This was quite satisfactory, and what was expected from him. As for himself, he appeared to take no particular interest in the matter, further than that of allaying the ferment and alarm which had spread through the parish.

"Plase your Reverence," said Bartley, "she came in to Mary, and she alone in the house, and for the matther o' that, I believe she laid hands upon her, and tossed and tumbled the crathur, and she but a sickly woman, through the four corners of the house. Not that Mary lets an so much, for she's afeard; but I know from her way, when she spakes about her, that it's thruth, your Reverence."

"But didn't the *Lianhan Shee*," said one of them, "put a sharp-pointed knife to her breast, wid a divilish intintion of makin' her give the best of atin' an' dhrinkin' the house afforded?"

"She got the victuals, to a sartinty," replied Bartley, "and 'overlooked' my woman for her pains; for she's not the picture of herself since."

Everyone now told some magnified and terrible circumstance, illustrating the formidable power of the *Lianhan Shee*.

When they had finished, the sarcastic lip of the priest curled into an expression of irony and contempt; his brow, which was naturally black and heavy, darkened; and a keen, but rather a ferocious-looking, eye shot forth a glance, which, while it intimated disdain for those to whom it was directed, spoke also of a dark and troubled spirit in himself. The man seemed to brook with scorn the degrading situation of a religious quack, to which some uncontrollable destiny had doomed him.

"I shall see your wife to-morrow," said he to Bartley; "and after hearing the plain account of what happened, I will consider what is best to be done with this dark, perhaps unhappy, perhaps guilty character; but whether dark, or unhappy, or guilty, I, for one, should not, and will not, avoid her. Go, and bring me word to-morrow evening when I can see her on the following day. Begone!"

When they withdrew, Father Philip paced his room for some time in silence and anxiety.

"Ay," said he, "infatuated people! sunk in superstition and ignorance, yet, perhaps, happier in your degradation than those who, in the pride of knowledge, can only look back upon a life of crime and misery. What is a sceptic? What is an infidel? Men who, when they will not submit to moral restraint, harden themselves into scepticism and infidelity, until, in the headlong career of guilt, that which was first adopted to lull the outcry of conscience, is supported by the pretended pride of principle. Principle in a sceptic! Hollow and devilish lie! Would *I* have plunged into scepticism, had I not first violated the moral sanctions of religion? Never. I became an infidel, because I first became a villain! Writhing under a load of guilt, that which I wished might be true, I soon forced myself to think true: and now"—he here clenched his hands and groaned—"now—ay, now—and hereafter—oh, *that* hereafter! Why can I not shake the thoughts of it from my conscience? Religion! Christianity! With all the hardness of an infidel's heart, I feel your truth; because, if every man were the villain that infidelity would make him, then indeed might every man curse God for the existence bestowed upon him—as I would, but dare not do. Yet why can I not believe? Alas! why should God accept an unrepentant heart? Am I not a hypocrite, mocking Him by a guilty pretension to His power, and leading the dark into thicker darkness? Then these hands—blood!—broken vows!—ha! ha! ha! Well, go—let misery have its laugh, like the light that breaks from the thunder-cloud. Prefer Voltaire to Christ; sow the wind, and reap the whirlwind, as I have done—ha, ha, ha! Swim, world—swim about me! I have lost the ways of Providence, and am dark! *She* awaits me; but I broke the chain that galled us: yet it still rankles—still rankles!"

The unhappy man threw himself into a chair in a paroxysm of frenzied agony. For more than an hour he sat in the same posture, until he became gradually hardened into a stiff, lethargic insensibility, callous and impervious to feeling, reason, or religion—an awful transition from a visitation of conscience so terrible as that which he had just suffered. At length he arose, and by walking moodily about, relapsed into his usual gloomy and restless character.

When Bartley went home, he communicated to his wife Father Philip's intention of calling on the following day, to hear a correct account of the *Lianhan Shee.*

"Why, thin," said she, "I'm glad of it, for I intinded myself to go to him, any way, to get my new scapular consecrated. How-an'-ever, as he's to come, I'll get a set of gospels for the boys an' girls, an' he can consecrate all when his hand's in. Aroon, Bartley, they say that man's so holy that he can do anything—ay, melt a body off the face o' the earth, like snow off a ditch. Dear me, but the power they have is strange all out!"

"There's no use in gettin' him anything to ate or dhrink," replied Bartley; "he wouldn't take a glass o' whisky once in seven years. Throth, myself thinks he's a little too dhry; sure he might be holy enough, an' yet take a sup of an odd time. There's Father Felix, an' though we all know he's far from bein' so blessed a man as him, yet he has friendship an' neighbourliness in him, an' never refuses a glass in rason."

"But do you know what I was tould about Father Philip, Bartley?"

"I'll tell you that afther I hear it, Mary, my woman; you won't expect me to tell what I don't know?—ha, ha, ha!"

"Behave, Bartley, an' quit your jokin' now, at all evints; keep it till we're talkin' of somethin' else, an' don't let us be committin' sin, maybe, while we're spakin' of what we're spakin' about; but they say it's as thrue as the sun to the dial:—the Lent afore last itself it was,—he never tasted mate or dhrink durin' the whole seven weeks! Oh, you needn't stare! it's well known by thim that has as much sinse as you—no, not so much as you'd carry on the point o' this knittin'-needle. Well, sure the housekeeper an' the two sarvants wondhered—faix, they couldn't do less—an' took it into their heads to watch him closely; an' what do you think—blessed be all the saints above!—what do you think they *seen*?"

"The Goodness above knows; for me—I don't."

"Why, thin, whin he was asleep they seen a small silk thread in his mouth, that came down through the ceilin' from heaven, an' he suckin' it, just as a child would his mother's breast whin the crathur 'ud be asleep: so that was the way he was supported by the angels! An' I remember myself, though he's a dark, spare, yellow man at all times, yet he never looked half so fat an' rosy as he did the same Lent!"

"Glory be to Heaven! Well, well—*it is* sthrange the power they have! As for him, I'd as *lee* meet St Pether, or St Pathrick himself, as him; for one can't but fear him, somehow."

"Fear him! Och, it 'ud be the pity o' thim that 'ud do anything to vex or anger that man. Why, his very look 'ud wither thim, till there wouldn't be the thrack o' thim on the earth; an' as for his curse, why it 'ud scorch thim to ashes!"

As it was generally known that Father Philip was to visit Mrs Sullivan the next day, in order to hear an account of the mystery which filled the parish with such fear, a very great number of the parishioners were assembled in and about Bartley's long before he made his appearance. At length he was seen walking slowly down the road, with an open book in his hand, on the pages of which he looked from time to time. When he approached the house, those who were standing about it assembled in a body, and, with one consent, uncovered their heads, and asked his blessing. His appearance bespoke a mind ill at ease; his face was haggard, and his eyes bloodshot. On seeing the people kneel, he smiled with his usual bitterness, and, shaking his hand with an air of impatience over them, muttered some words, rather in mockery of the ceremony than otherwise. They then rose, and, blessing themselves, put on their hats, rubbed the dust off their knees, and appeared to think themselves recruited by a peculiar accession of grace.

On entering the house the same form was repeated; and when it was over, the best chair was placed for him by Mary's own hands, and the fire stirred up, and a line of respect drawn, within which none was to intrude, lest he might feel in any degree incommoded.

"My good neighbour," said he to Mrs Sullivan, "what strange woman is this, who has thrown the parish into such a ferment? I'm told she paid you a visit? Pray sit down."

"I humbly thank your Reverence," said Mary, curtseying lowly, "but I'd rather not sit, sir, if you, plase. I hope I know what respect manes, your Reverence. Barny Bradagh, I'll thank you to stand up, if you plase, an' his Reverence to the fore, Barny."

"I ax your Reverence's pardon, an' yours, too, Mrs Sullivan; sure we didn't mane the disrespect, anyhow, sir, plase your Reverence."

"About this woman, and the *Lianhan Shee*," said the priest, without noticing Barny's apology. "Pray what do you precisely understand by a *Lianhan Shee*?"

"Why, sir," replied Mary, "some sthrange bein' from the good people, or fairies, that sticks to some persons. There's a bargain, sir, your Reverence, made atween thim; an' the divil, sir, that is, the ould boy—the saints about us!—has a hand in it. The *Lianhan Shee*, your Reverence, is never seen only by thim it keeps wid; but—hem!—it always, wid the help of the ould boy, conthrives, sir, to make the person brake the agreement, an' thin it has *thim* in *its* power; but if they *don't* brake the agreement, thin *it's* in *their* power. If they can get anybody to put in their place, they may get out o' the bargain; for they can, of a sartainty, give oceans o' money to people, but can't take any themselves, plase your Reverence. But sure, where's the use o' me to be tellin' your Reverence what you know betther nor myself?—an' why shouldn't you, or any one that has the power you have?"

He smiled again at this in his own peculiar manner, and was proceeding to inquire more particularly into the nature of the interview between them, when the noise of feet, and sounds of general alarm, accompanied by a rush of people into the house, arrested his attention, and he hastily inquired into the cause of the commotion. Before he could receive a reply, however, the house was almost crowded; and it was not without considerable difficulty that, by the exertions of Mrs Sullivan and Bartley, sufficient order and quiet were obtained to hear distinctly what was said.

"Plase your Reverence," said several voices at once, "they're comin', hot-foot, into the very house to us! Was ever the likes seen! an' they must know right well, sir, that you're widin it."

"Who are coming?" he inquired.

"Why, the woman, sir, an' her *good pet*, the *Lianhan Shee*, your Reverence!"

"Well," said he, "but why should you all appear so blanched with terror? Let her come in, and we shall see how far she is capable of injuring her fellow-creatures: some maniac," he muttered, in a low soliloquy, "whom the villainy of the world has driven into derangement—some victim to a hand like m— —. Well, they say there *is* a Providence, yet such things are permitted!"

"He's sayin' a prayer now," observed one of them; "haven't we a good right to be thankful that he's in the place wid us while she's in it, or dear knows what harm she might do us—maybe *rise* the wind!"

As the latter speaker concluded, there was a dead silence. The persons about the door crushed each other backwards, their feet set out before them, and their shoulders laid with violent pressure against those who stood behind, for each felt anxious to avoid all danger of contact with a being against whose power even a blessed priest found it necessary to guard himself by a prayer.

At length a low murmur ran among the people—"Father O'Rourke!—here's Father O'Rourke!—he has turned the corner after her, an' they're both comin' in." Immediately they entered, but it was quite evident, from the manner of the worthy priest, that he was unacquainted with the person of this singular being. When they crossed the threshold, the priest advanced, and expressed his surprise at the throng of people assembled.

"Plase your Reverence," said Bartley, "*that's* the woman," nodding significantly towards her as he spoke, but without looking at her person, lest the evil eye he dreaded so much might meet his, and give him "the blast."

The dreaded female, on seeing the house in such a crowded state, started, paused, and glanced with some terror at the persons assembled. Her dress was not altered since her last visit; but her countenance, though more meagre and emaciated, expressed but little of the unsettled energy which then flashed from her eyes, and distorted her features by the depth of that mysterious excitement by which she had been agitated. Her countenance was still muffled as before, the awful protuberance rose from her shoulders, and the same band which Mrs Sullivan had alluded to during their interview, was bound about the upper part of her forehead.

She had already stood upwards of two minutes, during which the fall of a feather might be heard, yet none bade God bless her—no kind hand was extended to greet her—no heart warmed in affection towards her; on the contrary, every eye glanced at her, as a being marked with enmity towards God. Blanched faces and knit brows, the signs of fear and hatred, were turned upon her; her breath was considered pestilential, and her touch paralysis. There she stood, proscribed, avoided, and hunted like a tigress, all fearing to encounter, yet wishing to exterminate her! Who could she be?—or what had she done, that the finger of the Almighty marked her out for such a fearful weight of vengeance?

Father Philip rose and advanced a few steps, until he stood confronting her. His person was tall, his features dark, severe, and solemn: and when the nature of the investigation about to take place is considered, it need not be wondered at, that the moment was, to those present, one of deep and impressive interest—such as a visible conflict between a supposed champion of God and a supernatural being was calculated to excite.

"Woman," said he, in his deep stern voice, "tell me who and what you are, and why you assume a character of such a repulsive and mysterious nature, when it can entail only misery, shame, and persecution on yourself? I conjure you, in the name of Him after whose image you are created, to speak truly!"

He paused, and the tall figure stood mute before him. The silence was dead as death—every breath was hushed—and the persons assembled stood immovable as statues! Still she spoke not; but the violent heaving of her breast evinced the internal working of some dreadful struggle. Her face before was pale—it was now ghastly; her lips became blue, and her eyes vacant.

"Speak!" said he; "I conjure you in the name of the power by whom you live!"

It is probable that the agitation under which she laboured was produced by the severe effort made to sustain the unexpected trial she had to undergo.

For some minutes her struggle continued; but having begun at its highest pitch, it gradually subsided until it settled in a calmness which appeared fixed and awful as the resolution of despair. With breathless composure she turned round, and put back that part of her dress which concealed her face, except the band on her forehead, which she did not remove; having done this, she turned again, and walked calmly towards Father Philip, with a deadly smile upon her thin lips. When within a step of where he stood, she paused, and, riveting her eyes upon him, exclaimed,—

"Who and what am I? The victim of infidelity and you, the bearer of a cursed existence, the scoff and scorn of the world, the monument of a broken vow and a guilty life, a being scourged by the scorpion lash of conscience, blasted by periodical insanity, pelted by the winter's storm, scorched by the summer's heat, withered by starvation, hated by man, and touched into my inmost spirit by the anticipated tortures of future misery. I have no rest for the sole of my foot, no repose for a head distracted by the contemplation of a guilty life; I am the unclean spirit which walketh to seek rest and findeth none; I am—*what you have made me*! Behold," she added, holding up the bottle, "this failed, and I live to accuse you. But no, you are my husband—though our union was but a guilty form, and I will bury that in silence. You thought me dead, and you flew to avoid punishment; did you avoid it? No; the finger of God has written pain and punishment upon your brow. I have been in all characters, in all shapes, have spoken with the tongue of a peasant, moved in my natural sphere, but my knees were smitten, my brain stricken, and the wild malady which banishes me from society has been upon me for years. Such I am, and such, I say, have you made me. As for you, kind-hearted woman, there was nothing in this bottle but pure water. The interval of reason returned this day, and having remembered glimpses of our conversation, I came to apologise to you, and to explain the nature of my unhappy distemper, and to beg a little bread, which I have not tasted for two days. I at times conceive myself attended by an evil spirit, shaped out by a guilty conscience, and this is the only familiar which attends me, and by it I have been dogged into madness through every turning of life. Whilst it lasts I am subject to spasms and convulsive starts which are exceedingly painful. The lump on my back is the robe I wore when innocent in my peaceful convent."

The intensity of general interest was now transferred to Father Philip; every face was turned towards him, but he cared not. A solemn stillness yet prevailed among all present. From the moment she spoke, her eye drew his with the power of a basilisk. His pale face became like marble, not a muscle moved; and when she ceased speaking, his bloodshot eyes were still fixed upon her countenance with a gloomy calmness like that which precedes a tempest. They stood before each other, dreadful counterparts in guilt, for truly his spirit was as dark as hers.

At length he glanced angrily around him:—"Well," said he, "what is it now, ye poor infatuated wretches, to trust in the sanctity *of man*? Learn from me to place the same confidence *in God* which you place in His *guilty creatures*, and you will not lean on a broken reed. Father O'Rourke, you, too, witness my disgrace, but not my punishment. It is pleasant, no doubt, to have a topic for conversation at your Conferences; enjoy it. As for you, Margaret, if society lessen misery, we may be less miserable. But the band of your order, and the remembrance of your vow is on your forehead, like the mark of Cain—tear it off, and let it not blast a man who is the victim of prejudice still, nay, of superstition, as well as of guilt; tear it from my sight." His eyes kindled fearfully as he attempted to pull it away by force.

She calmly took it off, and he immediately tore it into pieces, and stamped upon the fragments as he flung them on the ground.

"Come," said the despairing man—"come—there is a shelter for you, *but no peace*!—food, and drink, and raiment, but *no peace*!—no peace!" As he uttered these words, in a voice that sank to its deepest pitch, he took her hand, and they both departed to his own residence.

The amazement and horror of those who were assembled in Bartley's house cannot be described. Our readers may be assured that they deepened in character as they spread through the parish. An undefined fear of this mysterious pair seized upon the people, for their images were associated in their minds with darkness and crime, and supernatural communion. The departing words of Father Philip rang in their ears: they trembled, and devoutly crossed themselves, as fancy again repeated the awful exclamation of the priest—"No peace! no peace!"

When Father Philip and his unhappy associate went home, he instantly made her a surrender of his small property; but with difficulty did he command sufficient calmness to accomplish even this. He was distracted— his blood seemed to have been turned to fire—he clenched his hands, and he gnashed his teeth, and exhibited the wildest symptoms of madness. About ten o'clock he desired fuel for a large fire to be brought into the kitchen, and got a strong cord, which he coiled, and threw carelessly on the table. The family were then ordered to bed. About eleven they were all asleep; and at the solemn hour of twelve he heaped additional fuel upon the living turf, until the blaze shone with scorching light upon everything around.

Dark and desolating was the tempest within him, as he paced, with agitated steps, before the crackling fire.

"She is risen!" he exclaimed—"the spectre of all my crimes is risen to haunt me through life! I *am* a murderer—yet she lives, and my guilt is not the less! The stamp of eternal infamy is upon me—the finger of scorn will mark me out—the tongue of reproach will sting me like that of the serpent—the deadly touch of shame will cover me like a leper—the laws of society will crush the murderer, not the less that his wickedness in blood has miscarried: after that comes the black and terrible tribunal of the Almighty's vengeance—of His fiery indignation! Hush!—What sounds are those? They deepen—they deepen! Is it thunder? It cannot be the crackling of the blaze! It *is* thunder!—but it speaks only to *my* ear! Hush!—Great God, there is a change in my voice! It is hollow and supernatural! Could a change have come over me? Am I living? Could I have—Hah!—Could I have departed? and am I now at length given over to the worm that never dies? If it be at my heart, I may feel it. God!—I am damned! Here is a viper twined about my limbs, trying to dart its fangs into my heart! Hah!—there are feet pacing in the room, too, and I hear voices! I am surrounded by evil spirits! Who's there?—What are you?—Speak!—They are silent!—There is no answer! Again comes the thunder! But perchance this is not my place of punishment, and I will try to leave these horrible spirits!"

He opened the door, and passed out into a small green field that lay behind the house. The night was calm, and the silence profound as death. Not a cloud obscured the heavens;—the light of the moon fell upon the stillness of the scene around him, with all the touching beauty of a moonlit midnight in summer. Here he paused a moment, felt his brow, then his heart, the palpitations of which fell audibly upon his ear. He became somewhat cooler; the images of madness which had swept through his stormy brain disappeared, and were succeeded by a lethargic vacancy of thought, which almost deprived him of the consciousness of his own identity. From the green field he descended mechanically to a little glen which opened beside it. It was one of those delightful spots to which the heart clingeth. Its sloping sides were clothed with patches of wood, on the leaves of which the moonlight glanced with a soft lustre, rendered more beautiful by their stillness. That side on which the light could not fall, lay in deep shadow, which occasionally gave to the rocks and small projecting precipices an appearance of monstrous and unnatural life. Having passed through the tangled mazes of the glen, he at length reached its bottom, along which ran a brook, such as, in the description of the poet,—

"In the leafy month of June,
Unto the sleeping woods all night,
Singeth a quiet tune."

Here he stood, and looked upon the green winding margin of the streamlet—but its song he heard not. With the workings of a guilty conscience, the beautiful in nature can have no association. He looked up the glen, but its picturesque windings, soft vistas, and wild underwood mingling with grey rocks and taller trees, all mellowed by the moon-beams, had no charms for him. He maintained a profound silence—but it was not the silence of peace or reflection. He endeavoured to recall the scenes of the past day, but could not bring them back to his memory. Even the fiery tide of thought, which, like burning lava, seared his brain a few moments before, was now cold and hardened. He could remember nothing. The convulsion of his mind was over, and his faculties were impotent and collapsed.

In this state he unconsciously retraced his steps, and had again reached the paddock adjoining his house, when, as he thought, the figure of his paramour stood before him. In a moment his former paroxysm returned, and with it the gloomy images of a guilty mind, charged with the extravagant horrors of brain-struck madness.

"What!" he exclaimed, "the band still on your forehead! Tear it off!"

He caught at the form as he spoke, but there was no resistance to his grasp. On looking again towards the spot, it had ceased to be visible. The storm within him arose once more; he rushed into the kitchen, where the fire blazed out with fiercer heat; again he imagined that the thunder came to his ears, but the thunderings which he heard were only the voice of conscience. Again his own footsteps and his voice sounded in his fancy as the footsteps and voices of fiends, with which his imagination peopled the room. His state and his existence seemed to him a confused and troubled dream; he tore his hair—threw it on the table—and immediately started back with a hollow groan; for his locks, which but a few hours before had been as black as the raven's wing, were now white as snow!

On discovering this, he gave a low but frantic laugh. "Ha, ha, ha!" he exclaimed; "here is another mark—here is food for despair. Silently, but surely, did the hand of God work this, as a proof that I am hopeless! But I will bear it; I will bear the sight! I now feel myself a man blasted by the eye of God Himself! Ha, ha, ha! Food for despair! Food for despair!"

Immediately he passed into his own room, and approaching the looking-glass beheld a sight calculated to move a statue. His hair had become literally white, but the shades of his dark complexion, now distorted by terror and madness, flitted, as his features worked under the influence of his tremendous passions, into an expression so frightful, that deep fear came over himself. He snatched one of his razors, and fled from the glass to the kitchen. He looked upon the fire, and saw the white ashes lying around its edge.

"Ha!" said he, "the light is come! I see the sign. I am directed, and I will follow it. There is yet one hope. The immolation! I shall be saved, yet so as by fire. It is for this my hair has become white;—the sublime warning for my self-sacrifice! The colour of ashes!—white—white! It is so!—I will sacrifice my body in material fire, to save my soul from that which is eternal! But I had anticipated the Sign! The self-sacrifice is accepted!"

We must here draw a veil over that which ensued, as the description of it would be both unnatural and revolting. Let it be sufficient to say, that the next morning he was found burnt to a cinder, with the exception of his feet and legs, which remained as monuments of, perhaps, the most dreadful suicide that ever was committed by man. His razor, too, was found bloody, and several clots of gore were discovered about the hearth; from which circumstances it was plain that he had reduced his strength so much by loss of blood, that when he committed himself to the flames, he was unable, even had he been willing, to avoid the fiery and awful sacrifice of which he made himself the victim. If anything could deepen the impression of fear and awe, already so general among the people, it was the unparalleled nature of his death. Its circumstances are yet remembered in the parish and county wherein it occurred—*for it is no fiction*, gentle reader! and the titular bishop who then presided over the diocese declared, that while he lived no person bearing the unhappy man's name should ever be admitted to the clerical order.

The shock produced by his death struck the miserable woman into the utter darkness of settled derangement. She survived him some years, but wandered about through the province, still, according to the superstitious belief of the people, tormented by the terrible enmity of the *Lianhan Shee*.

XVI
THE HAUNTED COVE

By Sir George Douglas, Bart

Commonplace in itself and showing positive vulgarity in the style in which its pleasure-grounds are laid out, Clyffe, near Berwick-on-Tweed, has yet one delightful feature of its own,—to wit, a private bay to which access is obtained by a tunnel seventy or eighty yards long, cut through the soft formation of the cliff from the sloping gardens above. The result is that, if you are a visitor at Clyffe, you have your own private bathing ground, your own private beach where the children may play, without fear of being encroached upon, unless, indeed, a boat should be run in among the rocks from seaward. In the early nineties of the last century, the only daughter of the house of Clyffe was engaged to be married to a young officer quartered at the military depot at Berwick. They were a blameless but not particularly interesting couple, and one of their hobbies was to meet and promenade on the smooth sands of Clyffe bay in the brilliant autumn moonlight. In order to prevent possible intrusion from the sea, the seaward end of the tunnel was closed by a heavy iron gate, and upon the inner side of this gate the Lieutenant was to wait until his fiancée should steal forth bringing with her the key which should give access to the beach. It was all very foolish and romantic, no doubt, for they might have met just as conveniently in the conservatory of Clyffe House, where their privacy would have been equally respected, and where Miss Alix's satin shoes and diaphanous draperies would have exposed her to no risk of a chill. Lovers are like that, however, and had they not been so on this occasion, I should have had no story to tell.

Like the exemplary swain he was, Dick arrived early at the rendezvous,—that is to say, early in respect to the time agreed upon, though, as a matter of fact, it was nearly eleven o'clock. There he lit a cigarette, and approaching the heavy iron bars of the locked gate, looked forth upon the peaceful scene beyond. It was a perfect night, the harvest moon riding through fleecy cloud aloft, whilst the breaking of the sea between the rocky points to right and left was soothing in its gentle iteration. Dick had been on parade extremely early that morning, and, tell it not in Gath! his eyes involuntarily closed.

Starting awake again, he saw with surprise that, though Alix had not yet come forward, he was no longer alone. No! the sacred beach had been invaded, and a female figure clad in light draperies was pacing slowly in the moonlight betwixt himself and the distant rocks. Who on earth could she be, and how had she got there? were the questions he asked himself, his first sensation being one of annoyance at so unexpected and so ill-timed an intrusion. But as the moments passed and the figure came more clearly into view, impatience gave way to curiosity, and curiosity to something like awe.

What he saw was the tall and slender form of a young girl whose hands were clasped in front of her, and whose eyes were fixed on the ground in a pensive, not to say sorrowful, attitude. Clear as was the moonlight, at least in the intervals of the moon's passage through the broken clouds, her features were not plainly visible; but her every movement was instinct with grace. What could she be doing there? Under other circumstances, possibly Dick might have felt inclined to pass the gate and himself step forth on to the sands. But, besides that the gate was locked, he gradually became conscious of a singular delicacy or unwillingness to intrude upon the privacy of this solitary, inexplicable, and impressive figure. He was content, therefore, to watch her noiseless progress, and, as he did so, even his untrained masculine eye seemed to note something unusual—out of date, it might be—in the fashion of her garments. So perhaps might some old-world portrait have appeared, had it stept down from its frame against the wall. This, however, stirred him little. What he was not prepared for was the gesture of anguish, nay, of positive despair, with which, when about opposite him, the figure threw her head back and her arms aloft, as if in mute and agonised appeal to Heaven. The action was heart-rending even to look on; nor, to a male eye, did it lose aught from the fact that, as the moonlight now fell for the first time on her upturned face, it showed it to be deathly pale indeed, but also exquisitely lovely. Another moment or two, and the graceful and appealing form had passed beyond his field of vision, for, as the locked gate stood some little way back from the mouth of the tunnel, his view was restricted.

A short time only, though he knew not exactly how long, had passed when Alix stood beside him.

"I had some difficulty," she archly explained, "in eluding prying eyes."

For an ardent lover, Dick's greetings were perfunctory; after which, being still powerfully under the impression of what he had just seen, he told Alix all about it.

"We shall soon see who she is," replied that practical young lady, as she placed the heavy key in the cumbrous lock, "and I shall also take leave to inform her that this bit of coast is strictly private."

And strictly private it appeared to be when they emerged from the tunnel. For though their eyes swept the beach to right and left, and though the moon just then was unobscured, they saw no trace of any living form.

"She must have landed from a boat," said Alix; but as little trace of a boat could they discover.

Still it was quite possible that she might pass unobserved against the dark rocks, so they turned first to the right, then to the left, keeping a keen look-out for any sign of motion.

They detected nothing.

And by this time I am bound to confess that a slightly uncomplimentary suspicion had more than once crossed the brain of Alix. She knew that, as a rule, her Dick was a pattern of moderation. But even the most prudent may be liable to be occasionally overtaken. And she recalled his having mentioned that this was to be a guest-night at the mess. Indeed, it was chiefly upon that account that the assignation had been fixed so late. This present portentous solemnity was certainly most unlike him. Was it possible that the poor fellow had taken just one more whisky-and-soda than he could conveniently carry? Outspoken by nature, she blurted out her suspicion, which was strengthened rather than the reverse by the great earnestness with which he repelled it.

Less convinced than before, Alix then exclaimed: "Look here, Dick! If, as you say, the young woman passed this way, she must have left tracks on the smooth sand. Where do you say the place was?"

With some uncertainty, Dick then led her to what he took to be the place. No tracks were there. He then tried further back from the mouth of the tunnel, and with as little success. It was true the tide was coming up, but it could scarcely yet have reached footmarks which had been imprinted so far inshore as he supposed these to have been.

In a spirit of levity which jarred on him, Alix now recommended her lover to go back to his quarters and have a good sleep; and then, having again passed through the gate and pushed their way up the tunnel, the two young people parted in something very like a tiff.

Dick did not call at Clyffe House the next day, and when he called on the day following, Alix met him in a complaisant mood. After all, she had no wish to quarrel with him. And very soon she said, "Going back to what you told me you had seen the other night, Dick, it occurred to me, after you were gone, that it fits in rather curiously with an old story connected with this place." And then, at his request, she proceeded to tell him how, some thirty years ago, her grandmother had had a favourite maid, a friendless orphan girl named Barbara, to whom attached a mystery. Barbara was a very lovely creature of refinement and education above her station, and she had of course numerous admirers. Young as she was, her discretion was faultless, with the sole exception that her native amiability and desire to please sometimes betrayed her into conduct which meant less than her admirers wished to think it did. Well, at last Barbara became plighted to a respectable young fisherman, part-owner of a boat sailing from The Greenses, and, though details were vague, it was generally understood that, as a consequence, several hearts were severely damaged. As Barbara had no relatives, it was arranged by her employer that she should remain in her situation until the wedding-day and should be married from Clyffe House. Considerable preparations had also been made to do honour to the occasion, when—judge of the consternation of the inmates of the house!—upon the morning of the wedding-day Barbara was not to be found. She was believed to have retired to rest on the previous night as usual, yet her bed had not been slept in. Nor, although most of her clothes were packed in anticipation of her change of domicile, had she apparently taken anything with her. Nothing in the least unusual had been observed in her demeanour; nor could the unhappy bridegroom suggest any possible motive for her conduct. Exhaustive inquiries and exhaustive search were made; but, to cut the story short, nothing had ever again been seen or heard of the fair Barbara to that day. Her mistress, who had been sincerely attached to her, had long mourned for her, and in after times would often sing her praises. But, in order to be quite candid, it must be acknowledged that there were others, not a few, who declined to believe that the girl had come to an untimely end; and, who, knowing that she had several suitors, and had sometimes appeared uncertain which to favour, preferred to think that she had changed her mind at the last moment, and, deciding to throw over her fisherman, had made her escape from Clyffe House during the night to join some more eligible swain. This would have been a desperate step indeed; nor could her conduct in withholding subsequent explanations be absolved of heartlessness. But, after all, she was the sort of girl who, where no actual misconduct was involved, might easily allow herself to be over-persuaded. And certainly the tangled skein of love does sometimes present a knot which must be cut rather than untied.

The Lieutenant professed himself profoundly interested in this narrative, which he and Alix then proceeded to discuss in all its bearings, and more particularly, of course, in its relation to the figure seen by him in the cove. It is true that Alix never quite believed in the genuineness of the apparition; but, seeing that Dick really wished to have it taken seriously, she decided tactfully to humour him, and made quite a nine days' wonder of the mysterious occurrence. Their own wedding-day was, however, fast drawing on, so they soon found other things to talk and think of. To be brief, they were in due course married, and, amid the cares and pleasures of wedded life, the story, though not forgotten, came to be very seldom referred to. So twenty years passed; at the end of which time the Colonel (as he now was), accompanied by his wife and several youngsters, paid one of his not very frequent visits to his wife's parents at Clyffe House.

On the first night of the visit, after dinner, Alix's father had significantly recalled the story of the maid Barbara's disappearance, and, after stating that the mystery had now been finally cleared up, had gone on to relate the following particulars:—A few days previously there had lain at the point of death in the infirmary at Berwick an aged fisherman, who had long been known in the seaport town for his solitary habits and morose and violent ways. As death drew near, it became evident that his mind was sorely troubled, and to one of the nurses or doctors who had sought to comfort him he had been led to make the acknowledgment that a guilty secret weighed upon his soul, making him fearful to confront his Maker. He then told how, as a young man, he had passionately loved a pretty servant-girl employed at Clyffe House. Misled by those smiles and that graciousness of manner which in the guileless amiability of her nature the girl lavished upon all alike, he had for a moment imagined himself her favoured suitor. How bitter, then, was the blow, and how rude the awakening when he learned that a younger brother of his own, a mere boy, was preferred before himself! Nor was it only unrequited love that grieved him. No, he believed, or managed to persuade himself, that an unfair advantage had been taken of him, by which he had been made the lovers' dupe. A silent man, he took no one into his confidence, but abode his time until the eve of the wedding-day. On that day he had accidentally intercepted a note from the girl Barbara, addressed to his brother, in which she had agreed to meet her bridegroom of the morrow in the cove below Clyffe House one hour before midnight, to spend a final hour together before the momentous crisis in their lives. Instantly it had occurred to the elder brother to use the knowledge gained from the note in order to make one last desperate appeal on his own account to the sweet girl he loved so madly. Accordingly he kept back the missive, and, to make assurance doubly sure, mixed a soporific drug with his brother's drink when the latter came in from fishing. Then, whilst the youngster slumbered heavily, he himself embarked in a cockle-boat and, unobserved, rowed quietly round the headland, into Clyffe cove, where he ran his boat into a safe creek he knew of, and jumped ashore. Poor Barbara had come down to the water's edge to meet the boat, and great was her consternation on finding herself confronted by the wrong brother.

Then an impassioned scene was enacted, in which the seaman used every means of persuasion known to him to get the girl to give up his brother and plight herself to him. But though alternately distressed and terrified, Barbara had stood her ground, and, gentle and yielding though she appeared to be, neither threats nor vows had had the slightest effect upon her constancy. And then, of a sudden, the reckless brother had "seen red." If he could not have this girl to wife, then neither should another, and a moment later her white form lay stretched upon the dark rocks at his feet.

The sight brought him to himself. There was no room for doubt that life was extinct; and if he was to escape suspicion, he must act at once, for the summer night was short and the dread interview had lasted long. He accordingly placed the body in the boat, and, having collected several heavy stones, proceeded to make use of his seacraft by binding them closely and firmly about the poor girl's body by means of her clothing. Then he rowed out to sea, some mile or more, and there quietly dropped the body overboard. Such, in essentials, was the story told by the dying fisherman, and so it had come about that the bride of that fatal morning was never seen or heard of more. Though possibly intended to be regarded as confidential, certain it is that the confession had leaked out, and very soon became public property. For a few days it attracted great attention; and then, like other more important things which had preceded it, it ceased, save very occasionally, to be alluded to at all. But the Colonel never forgot it, any more than he ever forgot the lovely and inexplicable vision which had appeared to him for so brief an interval, in the moonlight, on the shore below Clyffe House. It is true that he seldom referred to it. Nor did that stately dame, who had once been Miss Alix and who was now believed to command the regiment, encourage him to do so. For she had observed that he was always most ready to tell the story after an exceptionally good dinner. And, with her high sense of what was due to his rank, she fancied that it made him mildly ridiculous. Neither, it might be, had her earliest doubts been ever wholly laid to rest. But members of the fair sex, when they are practical, are apt to be very practical indeed.

XVII
WANDERING WILLIE'S TALE

By Sir Walter Scott

Ye maun have heard of Sir Robert Redgauntlet of that Ilk, who lived in these parts before the dear years. The country will lang mind him; and our fathers used to draw breath thick if ever they heard him named. He was out wi' the Hielandmen in Montrose's time; and again he was in the hills wi' Glencairn in the saxteen hundred and fifty-twa; and sae when King Charles the Second came in, wha was in sic favour as the Laird of Redgauntlet? He was knighted at Lonon court, wi' the King's ain sword; and being a redhot prelatist, he came down here, rampauging like a lion, with commissions of lieutenancy (and of lunacy, for what I ken), to put down a' the Whigs and Covenanters in the country. Wild wark they made of it; for the Whigs were as dour as the Cavaliers were fierce, and it was which should first tire the other. Redgauntlet was aye for the strong hand; and his name is kend as wide in the country as Claverhouse's or Tam Dalyell's. Glen, nor dargle, nor mountain, nor cave, could hide the puir hill-folk when Redgauntlet was out with bugle and bloodhound after them, as if they had been sae mony deer. And troth when they fand them, they didna mak muckle mair ceremony than a Hielandman wi' a roebuck—It was just, "Will ye tak the test?"—if not, "Make ready—present—fire!"—and there lay the recusant.

Far and wide was Sir Robert hated and feared. Men thought he had a direct compact with Satan—that he was proof against steel—and that bullets happed aff his buff-coat like hailstanes from a hearth—that he had a mear that would turn a hare on the side of Carrifragawns[6]—and muckle to the same purpose, of whilk mair anon. The best blessing they wared on him was, "Deil scowp wi' Redgauntlet!" He wasna a bad maister to his ain folk, though, and was weel aneugh liked by his tenants; and as for the lackies and troopers that rade out wi' him to the persecutions, as the Whigs caa'd those killing times, they wad hae drunken themsells blind to his health at ony time.

Now you are to ken that my gudesire lived on Redgauntlet's grund— they ca' the place Primrose-Knowe. We had lived on the grund, and under the Redgauntlets, since the riding days, and lang before. It was a pleasant bit; and I think the air is callerer and fresher there than ony where else in the country. It's a' deserted now; and I sat on the broken door-cheek three days since, and was glad I couldna see the plight the place was in; but that's a' wide o' the mark. There dwelt my gudesire, Steenie Steenson, a rambling, rattling chiel he had been in his young days, and could play weel on the pipes; he was famous at "Hoopers and Girders"—a' Cumberland couldna touch him at "Jockie Lattin"—and he had the finest finger for the backlilt between Berwick and Carlisle. The like o' Steenie wasna the sort that they made Whigs o'. And so he became a Tory, as they ca' it, which we now ca' Jacobites, just out of a kind of needcessity, that he might belang to some side or other. He had nae ill-will to the Whig bodies, and liked little to see the blude rin, though, being obliged to follow Sir Robert in hunting and hosting, watching and warding, he saw muckle mischief, and maybe did some, that he couldna avoid.

Now Steenie was a kind of favourite with his master, and kend a' the folks about the Castle, and was often sent for to play the pipes when they were at their merriment. Auld Dougal MacCallum, the butler, that had followed Sir Robert through gude and ill, thick and thin, pool and stream, was specially fond of the pipes, and aye gae my gudesire his gude word wi' the Laird; for Dougal could turn his master round his finger.

Weel, round came the Revolution, and it had like to have broken the hearts baith of Dougal and his master. But the change was not a'thegether sae great as they feared, and other folk thought for. The Whigs made an unco crawing what they wad do with their auld enemies, and in special wi' Sir Robert Redgauntlet. But there were ower mony great folks dipped in the same doings, to mak a spick and span new warld. So Parliament passed it a' ower easy; and Sir Robert, bating that he was held to hunting foxes instead of Covenanters, remained just the man he was. His revel was as loud, and his hall as weel lighted, as ever it had been, though maybe he lacked the fines of the nonconformists, that used to come to stock his larder and cellar; for it is certain he began to be keener about the rents than his tenants used to find him before, and they behoved to be prompt to the rent-day, or else the Laird wasna pleased. And he was sic an awsome body, that naebody cared to anger him; for the oaths he swore, and the rage that he used to get into, and the looks that he put on, made men sometimes think him a devil incarnate.[7]

Weel, my gudesire was nae manager—no that he was a very great misguider—but he hadna the saving gift, and he got twa terms' rent in arrear. He got the first brash at Whitsunday put ower wi' fair word and piping; but when Martinmas came, there was a summons from the grund-officer to come wi' the rent on a day preceese, or else Steenie behoved to flit. Sair wark he had to get the siller; but he was weel-freended, and at last he got the haill scraped thegether—a thousand merks—the maist of it was from a neighbour they caa'd Laurie Lapraik—a sly tod. Laurie had walth o' gear—could hunt wi' the hound and rin wi' the hare—and be Whig or Tory, saunt or sinner, as the wind stood. He was a professor in this Revolution warld, but he liked an orra sough of this warld, and a tune on the pipes weel aneugh at a by time; and abune a', he thought he had a gude security for the siller he lent my gudesire ower the stocking at Primrose-Knowe.

Away trots my gudesire to Redgauntlet Castle, wi' a heavy purse and a light heart, glad to be out of the Laird's danger. Weel, the first thing he learned at the Castle was, that Sir Robert had fretted himself into a fit of the gout, because he did not appear before twelve o'clock. It wasna a'thegether for sake of the money, Dougal thought; but because he didna like to part wi' my gudesire aff the grund. Dougal was glad to see Steenie, and brought him into the great oak parlour, and there sat the Laird his leesome lane, excepting that he had beside him a great, ill-favoured jackanape, that was a special pet of his; a cankered beast it was, and mony an ill-natured trick it played—ill to please it was, and easily angered—ran about the haill castle, chattering and yowling, and pinching, and biting folk, especially before ill-weather, or disturbances in the state. Sir Robert caa'd it Major Weir, after the warlock that was burnt;[8] and few folk liked either the name or the conditions of the creature—they thought there was something in it by ordinar—and my gudesire was not just easy in his mind when the door shut on him, and he saw himself in the room wi' naebody but the Laird, Dougal MacCallum, and the Major, a thing that hadna chanced to him before.

Sir Robert sat, or, I should say, lay, in a great armchair, wi' his grand velvet gown, and his feet on a cradle; for he had baith gout and gravel, and his face looked as gash and ghastly as Satan's. Major Weir sat opposite to him, in a red laced coat, and the Laird's wig on his head; and aye as Sir Robert girned wi' pain, the jackanape girned too, like a sheep's-head between a pair of tangs—an ill-faur'd, fearsome couple they were. The Laird's buff-coat was hung on a pin behind him, and his broadsword and his pistols within reach; for he keepit up the auld fashion of having the weapons ready, and a horse saddled day and night, just as he used to do when he was able to loup on horseback, and away after ony of the hill-folk he could get speerings of. Some said it was for fear of the Whigs taking vengeance, but I judge it was just his auld custom—he wasna gien to fear ony thing. The rental-book, wi' its black cover and brass clasps, was lying beside him; and a book of sculduddry sangs was put betwixt the leaves, to keep it open at the place where it bore evidence against the Goodman of Primrose-Knowe, as behind the hand with his mails and duties. Sir Robert gave my gudesire a look, as if he would have withered his heart in his bosom. Ye maun ken he had a way of bending his brows, that men saw the visible mark of a horse-shoe in his forehead, deep-dinted, as if it had been stamped there.

"Are ye come light-handed, ye son of a toom whistle?" said Sir Robert. "Zounds! if you are——"

My gudesire, with as gude a countenance as he could put on, made a leg, and placed the bag of money on the table wi' a dash, like a man that does something clever. The Laird drew it to him hastily—"Is it all here, Steenie, man?"

"Your honour will find it right," said my gudesire.

"Here, Dougal," said the Laird, "gie Steenie a tass of brandy down stairs, till I count the siller and write the receipt."

But they werena weel out of the room, when Sir Robert gied a yelloch that garr'd the Castle rock. Back ran Dougal—in flew the livery men—yell on yell gied the Laird, ilk ane mair awfu' than the ither. My gudesire knew not whether to stand or flee, but he ventured back into the parlour, where a' was gaun hirdy-girdie—naebody to say "come in," or "gae out." Terribly the Laird roared for cauld water to his feet, and wine to cool his throat; and hell, hell, hell, and its flames, was aye the word in his mouth. They brought him water, and when they plunged his swoln feet into the tub, he cried out it was burning; and folk say that it *did* bubble and sparkle like a seething caldron. He flung the cup at Dougal's head, and said he had given him blood instead of burgundy; and, sure aneugh, the lass washed clotted blood aff the carpet the neist day. The jackanape they caa'd Major Weir, it jibbered and cried as if it was mocking its master; my gudesire's head was like to turn—he forgot baith siller and receipt, and down stairs he banged; but as he ran, the shrieks came faint and fainter; there was a deep-drawn shivering groan, and word gaed through the Castle, that the Laird was dead.

Weel, away came my gudesire, wi' his finger in his mouth, and his best hope was, that Dougal had seen the money-bag, and heard the Laird speak of writing the receipt. The young Laird, now Sir John, came from Edinburgh, to see things put to rights. Sir John and his father never gree'd weel. Sir John had been bred an advocate, and afterwards sat in the last Scots Parliament and voted for the Union, having gotten, it was thought, a rug of the compensations—if his father could have come out of his grave, he would have brained him for it on his awn hearthstane. Some thought it was easier counting with the auld rough Knight than the fair-spoken young ane—but mair of that anon.

Dougal MacCallum, poor body, neither grat nor graned, but gaed about the house looking like a corpse, but directing, as was his duty, a' the order of the grand funeral. Now, Dougal looked aye waur and waur when night was coming, and was aye the last to gang to his bed, whilk was in a little round just opposite the chamber of dais, whilk his master occupied while he was living, and where he now lay in state, as they caa'd it, weel-a-day! The night before the funeral, Dougal could keep his awn counsel nae langer; he cam doun with his proud spirit, and fairly asked auld Hutcheon to sit in his room with him for an hour. When they were in the round, Dougal took ae tass of brandy to himsell, and gave another to Hutcheon, and wished him all health and lang life, and said that, for himsell, he wasna lang for this world; for that, every night since Sir Robert's death, his silver call had sounded from the state-chamber, just as it used to do at nights in his lifetime, to call Dougal to help to turn him in his bed. Dougal said, that being alone with the dead on that floor of the tower (for naebody cared to wake Sir Robert Redgauntlet like another corpse), he had never daured to answer the call, but that now his conscience checked him for neglecting his duty; for, "though death breaks service," said MacCallum, "it shall never break my service to Sir Robert; and I will answer his next whistle, so be you will stand by me, Hutcheon."

Hutcheon had nae will to the wark, but he had stood by Dougal in battle and broil, and he wad not fail him at this pinch; so down the carles sat ower a stoup of brandy, and Hutcheon, who was something of a clerk, would have read a chapter of the Bible; but Dougal would hear naething but a blaud of Davie Lindsay, whilk was the waur preparation.

When midnight came, and the house was quiet as the grave, sure aneugh the silver whistle sounded as sharp and shrill as if Sir Robert was blowing it, and up gat the twa auld serving-men, and tottered into the room where the dead man lay. Hutcheon saw aneugh at the first glance; for there were torches in the room, which showed him the foul fiend, in his ain shape, sitting on the Laird's coffin! Over he cowped as if he had been dead. He could not tell how lang he lay in a trance at the door, but when he gathered himself, he cried on his neighbour, and getting nae answer, raised the house, when Dougal was found lying dead within twa steps of the bed where his master's coffin was placed. As for the whistle, it was gaen anes and aye; but mony a time was it heard at the top of the house on the bartizan, and amang the auld chimneys and turrets, where the howlets have their nests. Sir John hushed the matter up, and the funeral passed over without mair bogle-wark.

But when a' was ower, and the Laird was beginning to settle his affairs, every tenant was called up for his arrears, and my gudesire for the full sum that stood against him in the rental-book. Weel, away he trots to the Castle, to tell his story, and there he is introduced to Sir John, sitting in his father's chair, in deep mourning, with weepers and hanging cravat, and a small walking rapier by his side, instead of the auld broadsword, that had a hundred-weight of steel about it, what with blade, chape, and basket-hilt. I have heard their communing so often tauld ower, that I almost think I was there mysell, though I couldna be born at the time. (In fact, Alan, my companion mimicked, with a good deal of humour, the flattering, conciliating tone of the tenant's address, and the hypocritical melancholy of the Laird's reply. His grandfather, he said, had, while he spoke, his eye fixed on the rental-book, as if it were a mastiff-dog that he was afraid would spring up and bite him.)

"I wuss ye joy, sir, of the head seat, and the white loaf, and the braid lairdship. Your father was a kind man to friends and followers; muckle grace to you, Sir John, to fill his shoon—his boots, I suld say, for he seldom wore shoon, unless it were muils when he had the gout."

"Ay, Steenie," quoth the Laird, sighing deeply and putting his napkin to his een, "his was a sudden call, and he will be missed in the country; no time to set his house in order—weel prepared Godward, no doubt, which is the root of the matter—but left us behind a tangled hesp to wind, Steenie.— Hem! hem! We maun go to business, Steenie; much to do, and little time to do it in."

Here he opened the fatal volume. I have heard of a thing they call Doomsday-book—I am clear it has been a rental of back-ganging tenants.

"Stephen," said Sir John, still in the same soft, sleekit tone of voice— "Stephen Stevenson, or Steenson, ye are down here for a year's rent behind the hand—due at last term."

Stephen. "Please your honour, Sir John, I paid it to your father."

Sir John. "Ye took a receipt then, doubtless, Stephen; and can produce it?"

Stephen. "Indeed I hadna time, an it like your honour; for nae sooner had I set doun the siller, and just as his honour Sir Robert, that's gaen, drew it till him to count it, and write out the receipt, he was ta'en wi' the pains that removed him."

"That was unlucky," said Sir John, after a pause. "But you maybe paid it in the presence of somebody. I want but a *talis qualis* evidence, Stephen. I would go ower strictly to work with no poor man."

Stephen. "Troth, Sir John, there was naebody in the room but Dougal MacCallum the butler. But, as your honour kens, he has e'en followed his auld master."

"Very unlucky again, Stephen," said Sir John, without altering his voice a single note. "The man to whom ye paid the money is dead—and the man who witnessed the payment is dead too—and the siller, which should have been to the fore, is neither seen nor heard tell of in the repositories. How am I to believe a' this?"

Stephen. "I dinna ken, your honour; but there is a bit memorandum note of the very coins; for, God help me! I had to borrow out of twenty purses; and I am sure that ilka man there set down will take his grit oath for what purpose I borrowed the money."

Sir John. "I have little doubt ye *borrowed* the money, Steenie. It is the *payment* to my father that I want to have some proof of."

Stephen. "The siller maun be about the house, Sir John. And since your honour never got it, and his honour that was canna have ta'en it wi' him, maybe some of the family may have seen it."

Sir John. "We will examine the servants, Stephen; that is but reasonable."

But lackey and lass, and page and groom, all denied stoutly that they had ever seen such a bag of money as my gudesire described. What was waur, he had unluckily not mentioned to any living soul of them his purpose of paying his rent. Ae quean had noticed something under his arm, but she took it for the pipes.

Sir John Redgauntlet ordered the servants out of the room, and then said to my gudesire, "Now, Steenie, ye see you have fair play; and, as I have little doubt ye ken better where to find the siller than any other body, I beg, in fair terms, and for your own sake, that you will end this fasherie; for, Stephen, ye maun pay or flit."

"The Lord forgie your opinion," said Stephen, driven almost to his wit's end—"I am an honest man."

"So am I, Stephen," said his honour; "and so are all the folks in the house, I hope. But if there be a knave amongst us, it must be he that tells the story he cannot prove." He paused, and then added, mair sternly, "If I understand your trick, sir, you want to take advantage of some malicious reports concerning things in this family, and particularly respecting my father's sudden death, thereby to cheat me out of the money, and perhaps take away my character, by insinuating that I have received the rent I am demanding.—Where do you suppose this money to be?—I insist upon knowing."

My gudesire saw everything look sae muckle against him, that he grew nearly desperate—however, he shifted from one foot to another, looked to every corner of the room and made no answer.

"Speak out, sirrah," said the Laird, assuming a look of his father's, a very particular ane, which he had when he was angry—it seemed as if the wrinkles of his frown made that self-same fearful shape of a horse's shoe in the middle of his brow;—"Speak out, sir! I *will* know your thoughts;—do you suppose that I have this money?"

"Far be it frae me to say so," said Stephen.

"Do you charge any of my people with having taken it?"

"I wad be laith to charge them that may be innocent," said my gudesire; "and if there be anyone that is guilty, I have nae proof."

"Somewhere the money must be, if there is a word of truth in your story," said Sir John; "I ask where you think it is—and demand a correct answer?"

"In hell, if you *will* have my thoughts of it," said my gudesire, driven to extremity,—"in hell! with your father, his jackanape, and his silver whistle."

Down the stairs he ran (for the parlour was nae place for him after such a word), and he heard the Laird swearing blood and wounds behind him, as fast as ever did Sir Robert, and roaring for the bailie and the baron-officer.

Away rode my gudesire to his chief creditor (him they caa'd Laurie Lapraik), to try if he could make ony thing out of him; but when he tauld his story, he got but the warst word in his wame—thief, beggar, and dyvour, were the saftest terms; and to the boot of these hard terms, Laurie brought up the auld story of his dipping his hand in the blood of God's saunts, just as if a tenant could have helped riding with the Laird, and that a laird like Sir Robert Redgauntlet. My gudesire was, by this time, far beyond the bounds of patience, and, while he and Laurie were at deil speed the liars, he was wanchancie aneugh to abuse Lapraik's doctrine as weel as the man, and said things that garr'd folk's flesh grue that heard them;—he wasna just himsell, and he had lived wi' a wild set in his day.

At last they parted, and my gudesire was to ride hame through the wood of Pitmurkie, that is a' fou of black firs, as they say.—I ken the wood, but the firs may be black or white for what I can tell.—At the entry of the wood there is a wild common, and on the edge of the common, a little lonely change-house, that was keepit then by an ostler-wife, they suld hae caa'd her Tibbie Faw, and there puir Steenie cried for a mutchkin of brandy, for he had had no refreshment the haill day. Tibbie was earnest wi' him to take a bite of meat, but he couldna think o't, nor would he take his foot out of the stirrup, and took off the brandy wholely at twa draughts, and named a toast at each:—the first was, the memory of Sir Robert Redgauntlet, and might he never lie quiet in his grave till he had righted his poor bond-tenant; and the second was, a health to Man's Enemy, if he would but get him back the pock of siller, or tell him what came o't, for he saw the haill world was like to regard him as a thief and a cheat, and he took that waur than even the ruin of his house and hauld.

On he rode, little caring where. It was a dark night turned, and the trees made it yet darker, and he let the beast take its ain road through the wood; when, all of a sudden, from tired and wearied that it was before, the nag began to spring, and flee, and stend, that my gudesire could hardly keep the saddle.—Upon the whilk, a horseman, suddenly riding up beside him, said, "That's a mettle beast of yours, freend; will you sell him?"—So saying, he touched the horse's neck with his riding-wand, and it fell into its auld heigh-ho of a stumbling trot. "But his spunk's soon out of him, I think," continued the stranger, "and that is like mony a man's courage, that thinks he wad do great things till he come to the proof."

My gudesire scarce listened to this, but spurred his horse, with "Gude e'en to you, freend."

But it's like the stranger was ane that doesna lightly yield his point; for, ride as Steenie liked, he was aye beside him at the self-same pace. At last my gudesire, Steenie Steenson, grew half angry; and, to say the truth, half feared.

"What is it that ye want with me, freend?" he said. "If ye be a robber, I have nae money; if ye be a leal man, wanting company, I have nae heart to mirth or speaking; and if ye want to ken the road, I scarce ken it mysell."

"If you will tell me your grief," said the stranger, "I am one that, though I have been sair miscaa'd in the world, am the only hand for helping my freends."

So my gudesire, to ease his ain heart, mair than from any hope of help, told him the story from beginning to end.

"It's a hard pinch," said the stranger; "but I think I can help you."

"If you could lend the money, sir, and take a lang day—I ken nae other help on earth," said my gudesire.

"But there may be some under the earth," said the stranger. "Come, I'll be frank wi' you; I could lend you the money on bond, but you would maybe scruple my terms. Now, I can tell you, that your auld Laird is disturbed in his grave by your curses, and the wailing of your family, and if ye daur venture to go to see him, he will give you the receipt."

My gudesire's hair stood on end at this proposal, but he thought his companion might be some humorsome chield that was trying to frighten him, and might end with lending him the money. Besides, he was bauld wi' brandy, and desperate wi' distress; and he said, he had courage to go to the gate of hell, and a step farther, for that receipt.—The stranger laughed.

Weel, they rode on through the thickest of the wood, when, all of a sudden, the horse stopped at the door of a great house; and, but that he knew the place was ten miles off, my father would have thought he was at Redgauntlet Castle. They rode into the outer courtyard, through the muckle faulding yetts, and aneath the auld portcullis; and the whole front of the house was lighted, and there were pipes and fiddles, and as much dancing and deray within as used to be in Sir Robert's house at Pace and Yule, and such high seasons. They lap off, and my gudesire, as seemed to him, fastened his horse to the very ring he had tied him to that morning, when he gaed to wait on the young Sir John.

"God!" said my gudesire, "if Sir Robert's death be but a dream!"

He knocked at the ha' door just as he was wont, and his auld acquaintance, Dougal MacCallum,—just after his wont, too,—came to open the door, and said, "Piper Steenie, are ye there, lad? Sir Robert has been crying for you."

My gudesire was like a man in a dream—he looked for the stranger, but he was gane for the time. At last he just tried to say, "Ha! Dougal Driveower, are ye living? I thought ye had been dead."

"Never fash yoursell wi' me," said Dougal, "but look to yoursell; and see ye tak naething frae onybody here, neither meat, drink, or siller, except just the receipt that is your ain."

So saying, he led the way out through halls and trances that were weel kend to my gudesire, and into the auld oak parlour; and there was as much singing of profane sangs, and birling of red wine, and speaking blasphemy and sculduddry, as had ever been in Redgauntlet Castle when it was at the blithest.

But, Lord take us in keeping! what a set of ghastly revellers they were that sat round that table!—My gudesire kend mony that had long before gane to their place, for often had he piped to the most part in the hall of Redgauntlet. There was the fierce Middleton, and the dissolute Rothes, and the crafty Lauderdale; and Dalyell, with his bald head and a beard to his girdle; and Earlshall, with Cameron's blude on his hand; and wild Bonshaw, that tied blessed Mr Cargill's limbs till the blude sprang; and Dunbarton Douglas, the twice-turned traitor baith to country and king. There was the Bluidy Advocate MacKenyie, who, for his worldly wit and wisdom, had been to the rest as a god. And there was Claverhouse, as beautiful as when he lived, with his long, dark, curled locks, streaming down over his laced buff-coat, and his left hand always on his right spule-blade, to hide the wound that the silver bullet had made. He sat apart from them all, and looked at them with a melancholy, haughty countenance; while the rest hallooed, and sung, and laughed, that the room rang. But their smiles were fearfully contorted from time to time; and their laughter passed into such wild sounds, as made my gudesire's very nails grow blue, and chilled the marrow in his banes.

They that waited at the table were just the wicked serving-men and troopers, that had done their work and cruel bidding on earth. There was the Lang Lad of the Nethertown, that helped to take Argyle; and the Bishop's summoner, that they called the Deil's Rattle-bag; and the wicked guardsmen, in their laced coats; and the savage Highland Amorites, that shed blood like water; and many a proud serving-man, haughty of heart and bloody of hand, cringing to the rich, and making them wickeder than they would be; grinding the poor to powder, when the rich had broken them to fragments. And mony, mony mair were coming and ganging, a' as busy in their vocation as if they had been alive.

Sir Robert Redgauntlet, in the midst of a' this fearful riot, cried, wi' a voice like thunder, on Steenie Piper, to come to the board-head where he was sitting; his legs stretched out before him, and swathed up with flannel, with his holster pistols aside him, while the great broadsword rested against his chair, just as my gudesire had seen him the last time upon earth—the very cushion for the jackanape was close to him, but the creature itsell was not there—it wasna its hour, it's likely; for he heard them say as he came forward, "Is not the Major come yet?" And another answered, "The jackanape will be here betimes the morn." And when my gudesire came forward, Sir Robert, or his ghaist, or the deevil in his likeness, said, "Weel, piper, hae ye settled wi' my son for the year's rent?"

With much ado my father gat breath to say, that Sir John would not settle without his honour's receipt.

"Ye shall hae that for a tune of the pipes, Steenie," said the appearance of Sir Robert—"Play us up 'Weel hoddled, Luckie.'"

Now this was a tune my gudesire learned frae a warlock, that heard it when they were worshipping Satan at their meetings; and my gudesire had sometimes played it at the ranting suppers in Redgauntlet Castle, but never very willingly; and now he grew cauld at the very name of it, and said, for excuse, he hadna his pipes wi' him.

"MacCallum, ye limb of Beelzebub," said the fearfu' Sir Robert, "bring Steenie the pipes that I am keeping for him!"

MacCallum brought a pair of pipes might have served the piper of Donald of the Isles. But he gave my gudesire a nudge as he offered them; and looking secretly and closely, Steenie saw that the chanter was of steel, and heated to a white heat; so he had fair warning not to trust his fingers with it. So he excused himself again, and said, he was faint and frightened, and had not wind aneugh to fill the bag.

"Then ye maun eat and drink, Steenie," said the figure; "for we do little else here; and it's ill speaking between a fou man and a fasting."

Now these were the very words that the bloody Earl of Douglas said to keep the King's messenger in hand, while he cut the head off MacLellan of Bombie, at the Threave Castle;[9] and that put Steenie mair and mair on his guard. So he spoke up like a man, and said he came neither to eat, or drink, or make minstrelsy; but simply for his ain—to ken what was come o' the money he had paid, and to get a discharge for it; and he was so stout-hearted by this time, that he charged Sir Robert for conscience-sake—(he had no power to say the holy name)—and as he hoped for peace and rest, to spread no snares for him, but just to give him his ain.

The appearance gnashed its teeth and laughed, but it took from a large pocket-book the receipt, and handed it to Steenie. "There is your receipt, ye pitiful cur; and for the money, my dog-whelp of a son may go look for it in the Cat's Cradle."

My gudesire uttered mony thanks, and was about to retire, when Sir Robert roared aloud, "Stop, though, thou sack-doudling son of a whore! I am not done with thee. Here we do nothing for nothing; and you must return on this very day twelvemonth, to pay your master the homage that you owe me for my protection."

My father's tongue was loosed of a suddenty, and he said aloud, "I refer mysell to God's pleasure, and not to yours."

He had no sooner uttered the word than all was dark around him; and he sunk on the earth with such a sudden shock, that he lost both breath and sense.

How lang Steenie lay there, he could not tell; but when he came to himsell, he was lying in the auld kirkyard of Redgauntlet parochine, just at the door of the family aisle, and the scutcheon of the auld knight, Sir Robert, hanging over his head. There was a deep morning fog on grass and gravestane around him, and his horse was feeding quietly beside the minister's twa cows. Steenie would have thought the whole was a dream, but he had the receipt in his hand, fairly written and signed by the auld

Laird; only the last letters of his name were a little disorderly, written like one seized with sudden pain.

Sorely troubled in his mind, he left that dreary place, rode through the mist to Redgauntlet Castle, and with much ado he got speech of the Laird.

"Well, you dyvour bankrupt," was the first word, "have you brought me my rent?"

"No," answered my gudesire, "I have not; but I have brought your honour Sir Robert's receipt for it."

"How, sirrah?—Sir Robert's receipt!—You told me he had not given you one."

"Will your honour please to see if that bit line is right?"

Sir John looked at every line, and at every letter, with much attention; and at last, at the date, which my gudesire had not observed,—*"From my appointed place,"* he read, *"this twenty-fifth of November."* —"What!—That is yesterday!—Villain, thou must have gone to hell for this!"

"I got it from your honour's father—whether he be in heaven or hell, I know not," said Steenie.

"I will delate you for a warlock to the Privy Council!" said Sir John. "I will send you to your master, the devil, with the help of a tar-barrel and a torch!"

"I intend to delate mysell to the Presbytery," said Steenie, "and tell them all I have seen last night, whilk are things fitter for them to judge of than a borrel man like me."

Sir John paused, composed himself, and desired to hear the full history; and my gudesire told it him from point to point, as I have told it you—word for word, neither more nor less.

Sir John was silent again for a long time, and at last he said, very composedly, "Steenie, this story of yours concerns the honour of many a noble family besides mine; and if it be a leasing-making, to keep yourself out of my danger, the least you can expect is to have a red-hot iron driven through your tongue, and that will be as bad as scaulding your fingers with a redhot chanter. But yet it may be true, Steenie; and if the money cast up, I shall not know what to think of it.—But where shall we find the Cat's Cradle? There are cats enough about the old house, but I think they kitten without the ceremony of bed or cradle."

"We were best ask Hutcheon," said my gudesire; "he kens a' the odd corners about as weel as—another serving-man that is now gane, and that I wad not like to name."

Aweel, Hutcheon, when he was asked, told them, that a ruinous turret, lang disused, next to the clock-house, only accessible by a ladder, for the opening was on the outside, and far above the battlements, was called of old the Cat's Cradle.

"There will I go immediately," said Sir John; and he took (with what purpose, Heaven kens) one of his father's pistols from the hall-table, where they had lain since the night he died, and hastened to the battlements.

It was a dangerous place to climb, for the ladder was auld and frail, and wanted ane or twa rounds. However, up got Sir John, and entered at the turret door, where his body stopped the only little light that was in the bit turret. Something flees at him wi' a vengeance, maist dang him back ower— bang gaed the knight's pistol, and Hutcheon, that held the ladder, and my gudesire that stood beside him, hears a loud skelloch. A minute after, Sir John flings the body of the jackanape down to them, and cries that the siller is fund, and that they should come up and help him. And there was the bag of siller sure aneugh, and mony orra things besides, that had been missing for mony a day. And Sir John, when he had riped the turret weel, led my gudesire into the dining-parlour, and took him by the hand, and spoke kindly to him, and said he was sorry he should have doubted his word, and that he would hereafter be a good master to him, to make amends.

"And now, Steenie," said Sir John, "although this vision of yours tends, on the whole, to my father's credit, as an honest man, that he should, even after his death, desire to see justice done to a poor man like you, yet you are sensible that ill-dispositioned men might make bad constructions upon it, concerning his soul's health. So, I think, we had better lay the haill dirdum on that ill-deedie creature, Major Weir, and say naething about your dream in the wood of Pitmurkie. You had taken ower muckle brandy to be very certain about onything; and, Steenie, this receipt," (his hand shook while he held it out,)—"it's but a queer kind of document, and we will do best, I think, to put it quietly in the fire."

"Od, but for as queer as it is, it's a' the voucher I have for my rent," said my gudesire, who was afraid, it may be, of losing the benefit of Sir Robert's discharge.

"I will bear the contents to your credit in the rental-book, and give you a discharge under my own hand," said Sir John, "and that on the spot. And, Steenie, if you can hold your tongue about this matter, you shall sit, from this term downward, at an easier rent."

"Mony thanks to your honour," said Steenie, who saw easily in what corner the wind was; "doubtless I will be conformable to all your honour's commands; only I would willingly speak wi' some powerful minister on the subject, for I do not like the sort of soumons of appointment whilk your honour's father——"

"Do not call the phantom my father!" said Sir John, interrupting him.

"Weel, then, the thing that was so like him,"—said my gudesire; "he spoke of my coming back to him this time twelvemonth, and it's a weight on my conscience."

"Aweel, then," said Sir John, "if you be so much distressed in mind, you may speak to our minister of the parish; he is a douce man, regards the honour of our family, and the mair that he may look for some patronage from me."

Wi' that, my gudesire readily agreed that the receipt should be burnt, and the Laird threw it into the chimney with his ain hand. Burn it would not for them, though; but away it flew up the lum, wi' a lang train of sparks at its tail, and a hissing noise like a squib.

My gudesire gaed down to the manse, and the minister, when he had heard the story, said, it was his real opinion, that though my gudesire had gaen very far in tampering with dangerous matters, yet, as he had refused the devil's arles (for such was the offer of meat and drink), and had refused to do homage by piping at his bidding, he hoped, that if he held a circumspect walk hereafter, Satan could take little advantage by what was come and gane. And, indeed, my gudesire, of his ain accord, long forswore baith the pipes and the brandy—it was not even till the year was out, and the fatal day passed, that he would so much as take the fiddle, or drink usquebaugh or tippenny.

Sir John made up his story about the jackanape as he liked himself; and some believe till this day there was no more in the matter than the filching nature of the brute. Indeed, ye'll no hinder some to threap, that it was nane o' the Auld Enemy that Dougal and my gudesire saw in the Laird's room, but only that wanchancy creature, the Major, capering on the coffin; and that, as to the blawing on the Laird's whistle that was heard after he was dead, the filthy brute could do that as weel as the Laird himself, if no better. But Heaven kens the truth, whilk first came out by the minister's wife, after Sir John and her ain gudeman were baith in the moulds. And then my gudesire, wha was failed in his limbs, but not in his judgment or memory—at least nothing to speak of—was obliged to tell the real narrative to his freends, for the credit of his good name. He might else have been charged for a warlock.

FOOTNOTES

[6] A precipitous side of a mountain in Moffatdale.

[7] The caution and moderation of King William III., and his principles of unlimited toleration, deprived the Cameronians of the opportunity they ardently desired, to retaliate the injuries which they had received during the reign of prelacy, and purify the land, as they called it, from the pollution of blood. They esteemed the Revolution, therefore, only a half measure, which neither comprehended the rebuilding the Kirk in its full splendour, nor the revenge of the death of the Saints on their persecutors.

[8] A celebrated wizard, executed at Edinburgh for sorcery and other crimes.

[9] The reader is referred for particulars to Pitscottie's *History of Scotland.*

II
GHOST STORIES FROM LOCAL RECORDS, FOLK LORE AND LEGEND

XVIII
GLAMIS CASTLE

Local Records

"The Castle of Glamis, a venerable and majestic pile of buildings," says an old Scots Gazetteer, "is situate about one mile north from the village, on the flat grounds at the confluence of the Glamis Burn and the Dean. There is a print of it given by Slezer in Charles II.'s reign—by which it appears to have been anciently much more extensive, being a large quadrangular mass of buildings, having two courts in front, with a tower in each, and gateway through below them; and on the northern side was the principal tower, which now constitutes the central portion of the present castle upwards of 100 feet in height. The building received the addition of a tower, in one of its angles, for a spiral staircase from bottom to top, with conical roofs. The wings were added, at the same time, by Patrick Earl of Strathmore, who repaired and modernised the structure, under the directions of Inigo Jones. One of the wings has been renovated within the last forty years, and other additions made, but not in harmony with Earl Patrick's repairs.

"There is also a secret room in it, only known to two or at most three individuals, at the same time, who are bound not to reveal it, unless to their successors in the secret. It has been frequently the object of search with the inquisitive, but the search has been in vain. There are no records of the castle prior to the tenth century, when it is first noticed in connection with the death of Malcolm II. in 1034. Tradition says that he was murdered in this castle, and in a room which is still pointed out, in the centre of the principal tower; and that the murderers lost their way in the darkness of the night, and by the breaking

of the ice, were drowned in the loch of Forfar. Fordun's account is, however, somewhat different and more probable. He states that the King was mortally wounded in a skirmish, in the neighbourhood, by some of the adherents of Kenneth V."

Let us turn now to the ghosts of Glamis Castle.

A lady, well known in London society, an artistic and social celebrity, wealthy beyond all doubts of the future, a cultivated, clear-headed, and indeed slightly matter-of-fact woman, went to stay at Glamis Castle for the first time. She was allotted very handsome apartments, just on the point of junction between the new buildings—perhaps a hundred or two hundred years old—and the very ancient part of the castle. The rooms were handsomely furnished; no gaunt carvings grinned from the walls; no grim tapestry swung to and fro, making strange figures look still stranger by the flickering fire-light; all was smooth, cosy, and modern, and the guest retired to bed without a thought of the mysteries of Glamis.

In the morning she appeared at the breakfast table quite cheerful and self-possessed. To the inquiry how she had slept, she replied: "Well, thanks, very well, up to four o'clock in the morning. But your Scottish carpenters seem to come to work very early. I suppose they put up their scaffolding quickly, though, for they are quiet now." This speech produced a dead silence, and the speaker saw with astonishment that the faces of members of the family were very pale.

She was asked, as she valued the friendship of all there, never to speak to them on that subject again; there had been no carpenters at Glamis Castle for months past. This fact, whatever it may be worth, is absolutely established, so far as the testimony of a single witness can establish anything. The lady was awakened by a loud knocking and hammering, as if somebody were putting up a scaffold, and the noise did not alarm her in the least. On the contrary, she took it for an accident, due to the presumed matutinal habits of the people. She knew, of course, that there were stories about Glamis, but had not the remotest idea that the hammering she had heard was connected with any story. She had regarded it simply as an annoyance, and was glad to get to sleep after an unrestful time; but had no notion of the noise being supernatural until informed of it at the breakfast-table.

With what particular event in the stormy annals of the Lyon family the hammering is connected is quite unknown, except to members of the family, but there is no lack of legends, possible and impossible, to account for any sights or sounds in the magnificent old feudal edifice.

It is said that once a visitor stayed at Glamis Castle for a few days, and, sitting up late one moonlight night, saw a face appear at the window opposite to him. The owner of the face—it was very pale, with great sorrowful eyes—appeared to wish to attract attention; but vanished suddenly from the window, as if plucked suddenly away by superior strength. For a long while the horror-stricken guest gazed at the window, in the hope that the pale face and great sad eyes would appear again. Nothing was seen at the window, but presently horrible shrieks penetrated even the thick walls of the castle, and rent the night air. An hour later, a dark huddled figure, like that of an old decrepit woman, carrying something in a bundle, came into the waning moonlight, and presently vanished.

There is a modern story of a stonemason, who was engaged at Glamis Castle last century, and who, having discovered more than he should have done, was supplied with a handsome competency, upon the conditions that he emigrated and kept inviolable the secret he had learned.

The employment of a stonemason is explained by the conditions under which the mystery is revealed to successive heirs and factors. The abode of the dread secret is in a part of the castle, also haunted by the apparition of a bearded man, who flits about at night, but without committing any other objectionable action. What connection, if any, the bearded spectre may have with the mystery is not even guessed. He hovers at night over the couches of children for an instant, and then vanishes. The secret itself abides in a room—a secret chamber—the very situation of which, beyond a general idea that it is in the most ancient part of the castle, is unknown. Where walls are fifteen feet thick, it is not impossible to have a chamber so concealed, that none but the initiated can guess its position. It was once attempted by a madcap party of guests to discover the locality of the secret chamber, by hanging their towels out of the window, and thus deciding in favour of any window from which no spotless banner waved; but this escapade, which is said to have been ill-received by the owners, ended in nothing but a vague conclusion that the old square tower must be the spot sought.

XIX
POWYS CASTLE

Local Records

It had been for some time reported in the neighbourhood that a poor unmarried woman, who was a member of the Methodist society; and had become serious under their ministry, had seen and conversed with the apparition of a gentleman, who had made a strange discovery to her. Mr Hampson, being desirous to ascertain if there was any truth in the story, sent for the woman, and desired her to give an exact relation of the whole affair from her own mouth, and as near the truth as she possibly could. She said she was a poor woman who got her living by spinning hemp and line; that it was customary for the farmers and gentlemen of that neighbourhood to grow a little hemp or line in the corner of their fields, for their own home consumption, and as she had a good hand at spinning the materials she used to go from house to house to inquire for work; that her method was, where they employed her, during her stay to have meat and lodging (if she had occasion to sleep with them) for her work, and what they pleased to give her besides. That, among other places, she happened to call in one day at the Welsh Earl Powis's country seat, called Redcastle, to inquire for work, as she usually had done before. The quality were at this time in London, and had left the steward and his wife, with other servants, as usual, to take care of their country residence in their absence. The steward's wife set her to work, and in the evening told her that she must stay all night with them, as they had more work for her to do next day. When bed-time arrived, two or three of the servants in company, with each a lighted candle in her hand, conducted her to her lodging. They led her to a grand room, with a boarded floor and two sash windows. The room was grandly furnished, and had a genteel bed in one corner of it. They had made her a good fire, and had placed her a chair and a table before it, and a large lighted candle upon the table. They told her that was her bedroom, and she might go to sleep when she pleased, they then wished a good night and withdrew all together, pulling the door quickly after them, so as to hasp the springsneck in the brass lock that was upon it. When they were gone she gazed a while at the fine furniture, under no small astonishment that they should put such a poor person as her in so grand a room and bed, with all the apparatus of fire, chair, table, and candle. She was also surprised at the circumstance of the servants coming so many together, with each of them a candle; however, after gazing about her some little time, she sat down and took out of her pocket a small Welsh Bible which she always carried about with her, and in which she usually read a chapter—chiefly in the New Testament—before she said her prayers and went to bed. While she was reading she heard the room door open, and, turning her head, saw a gentleman enter in a gold-laced hat and waistcoat, and the rest of his dress corresponding therewith. (I think she was very particular in describing the rest of his dress to Mr Hampson, and he to me at the time, but I have now forgot the other particulars.) He walked down by the sash window to the corner of the room, and then returned. When he came at the first window in his return (the bottom of which was nearly breast-high) he rested his elbow on the bottom of the window, and the side of his face upon the palm of his hand, and stood in that leaning posture for some time, with his side partly towards her. She looked at him earnestly to see if she knew him, but though, from her frequent intercourse with them, she had a personal knowledge of all the present family, he appeared a stranger to her. She supposed afterwards that he stood in this manner to encourage her to speak; but as she did not, after some little time he walked off, pulling the door after him as the servants had done before. She began now to be much alarmed, concluding it to be an apparition and that they had put her there on purpose. This was really the case. The room, it seems, had been disturbed for a long time, so that nobody could sleep peaceably in it; and as she passed for a very serious woman, the servants took it in their heads to put the Methodist and spirit together, to see what they would make out of it. Startled at this thought, she rose from her chair, and kneeled down by the bedside to say her prayers. While she was praying he came in again, walked round the room and came close behind her. She had it on her mind to speak, but when she attempted it she was so very much agitated that she could not utter a word. He walked out of the room again, pulling the door shut as before. She begged that God would strengthen her, and not suffer her to be tried beyond what she was able to bear; she recovered her surprise and thought she felt more confidence and resolution, and determined if he came in again she would speak to him if possible. He presently came in again, walked round, and came behind her as before; she turned her head and said, "Pray, sir, who are you, and what do you want?" He put up his finger and said, "Take up the candle and follow me, and I will tell you." She got up, took up the candle and followed him out of the room. He led her through a long boarded passage, till they came to the door of another room which he opened and went in; it was a small room, or what might be called a large closet. "As the room was small, and I believed him to be a spirit," said she, "I stopped at the door; he turned and said, 'Walk in, I will not hurt you'; so I walked in. He said, 'Observe what I do'; I said, 'I will.' He stooped and tore up one of the boards of the floor, and there appeared under it a box with an iron handle in the lid. He said, 'Do you see that box?' I said, 'Yes, I do.' He then stepped to one side of the room and showed me a crevice in the wall, where he said a key was hid that would open it. He said, 'This box and key must be taken out, and sent to the Earl in London' (naming the Earl and his residence in the city). He said, 'Will you see it done?' I said, 'I will do my best to get it done'; and he said, 'Do, and I will trouble the house no longer!' He then walked out of the room and left me. (He seems to have been a very civil spirit, and to have been very careful to affright her as little as possible.) I stepped to the room door, and set up a shout. The steward and his wife, with the other servants, came to me immediately; all clinging together, with a number of lights in their hands. It seems they had all been waiting to see the issue of the interview betwixt me and the apparition. They asked me what was the matter. I told them the foregoing circumstances, and showed them the box. The steward durst not meddle with it, but his wife had more courage, and, with the help of the other servants, tugged it out, and found the key. She said by their lifting it appeared to be pretty heavy, but that she did not see it opened, and therefore did not know what it contained—perhaps money, or writings of consequence to the family, or both." They took it away with them, and she then went to bed and slept peaceably till morning.

It appeared that they sent the box to the Earl in London, with an account of the manner of its discovery, and by whom; as the Earl sent down orders immediately to his steward to inform the poor woman who had been the occasion of its discovery that if she would come and reside in his family she would be comfortably provided for during her remaining days; or, if she did not choose to reside constantly with them, if she would let them know when she wanted assistance, she would be liberally supplied at his lordship's expense as long as she lived. And Mr Hampson said it was a known fact in the neighbourhood that she had been supplied from his lordship's family, from the time the affair was said to have happened, and continued to be so at the time she gave Mr Hampson this account. She told him that she was so often solicited by curious people to relate the story that she was weary of repeating it; but, to oblige him, she once more related the particulars, wishing now to have done with it. Mr Hampson said she appeared to be a sensible, intelligent person, and that he saw no reason to doubt her veracity. I know many persons in the present day laugh at such stories, and affect very much to doubt their reality, while others totally deny the possibility of their existence. However, Scripture and many well-attested relations seem to favour the idea, and the present story appeared so singular and so well attested, and I had it so near the fountain-head, that I thought it might perhaps be worth preserving, and I have therefore taken pains to record it. Admitting it to be true, it should seem that the consequence to the family of what the hidden box contained was the formal cause of the spirit's disquiet, and of its disturbing the house so much and so long, in order to bring about the discovery; but why the departed spirit should concern itself in the affairs of this world after it has left it—or why they should disquiet it so as to cause it to reappear and make disturbances, in order to discover and have things righted, as in the preceding case,—or why this should be done in some cases of apparently less moment, while in other cases much greater family injuries seem to be suffered, and no spirit appears to interest itself in the case—are circumstances for which we can by no means account. A cloud sits deep on futurity; and we are so little acquainted with the laws of the spiritual world that we are perhaps incapable, in our present state, of comprehending its nature or of giving any satisfactory account of these matters.

XX
CROGLIN GRANGE

From Archdeacon Hare's Autobiography [10]

"Fisher," said the Captain, "may sound a very plebeian name, but this family is of very ancient lineage, and for many hundreds of years they have possessed a very curious old place in Cumberland, which bears the weird name of Croglin Grange. The great characteristic of the house is that never at any period of its very long existence has it been more than one story high, but it has a terrace from which large grounds sweep away towards the church in the hollow, and a fine distant view.

"When, in lapse of years, the Fishers outgrew Croglin Grange in family and fortune, they were wise enough not to destroy the long-standing characteristic of the place by adding another story to the house, but they went away to the south, to reside at Thorncombe near Guildford, and they let Croglin Grange.

"They were extremely fortunate in their tenants, two brothers and a sister. They heard their praises from all quarters. To their poorer neighbours they were all that is most kind and beneficent, and their neighbours of a higher class spoke of them as a welcome addition to the little society of the neighbourhood. On their part the tenants were greatly delighted with their new residence. The arrangement of the house, which would have been a trial to many, was not so to them. In every respect Croglin Grange was exactly suited to them.

"The winter was spent most happily by the new inmates of Croglin Grange, who shared in all the little social pleasures of the district, and made themselves very popular. In the following summer there was one day which was dreadfully, annihilatingly hot. The brothers lay under the trees with their books, for it was too hot for any active occupation. The sister sat in the verandah and worked, or tried to work, for in the intense sultriness of that summer day work was next to impossible. They dined early, and after dinner they still sat out in the verandah, enjoying the cool air which came with evening, and they watched the sun set, and the moon rise over the belt of trees which separated the grounds from the churchyard, seeing it mount the heavens till the whole lawn was bathed in silver light, across which the long shadows from the shrubbery fell as if embossed, so vivid and distinct were they.

"When they separated for the night, all retiring to their rooms on the ground-floor (for, as I said, there was no upstairs in that house), the sister felt that the heat was still so great that she could not sleep, and having fastened her window, she did not close the shutters—in that very quiet place it was not necessary—and, propped against the pillows, she still watched the wonderful, the marvellous beauty of that summer night. Gradually she became aware of two lights, two lights which flickered in and out in the belt of trees which separated the lawn from the churchyard; and, as her gaze became fixed upon them, she saw them emerge, fixed in a dark substance, a definite ghastly *something*, which seemed every moment to become nearer, increasing in size and substance as it approached. Every now and then it was lost for a moment in the long shadows which stretched across the lawn from the trees, and then it emerged larger than ever, and still coming on—on. As she watched it, the most uncontrollable horror seized her. She longed to get away, but the door was close to the window and the door was locked on the inside, and while she was unlocking it, she must be for an instant nearer to *it*. She longed to scream, but her voice seemed paralysed, her tongue glued to the roof of her mouth.

"Suddenly, she never could explain why afterwards, the terrible object seemed to turn to one side, seemed to be going round the house, not to be coming to her at all, and immediately she jumped out of bed and rushed to the door; but as she was unlocking it, she heard scratch, scratch, scratch upon the window, and saw a hideous brown face with flaming eyes glaring in at her. She rushed back to the bed, but the creature continued to scratch, scratch, scratch upon the window. She felt a sort of mental comfort in the knowledge that the window was securely fastened on the inside. Suddenly the scratching sound ceased, and a kind of pecking sound took its place. Then, in her agony, she became aware that the creature was unpicking the lead! The noise continued, and a diamond pane of glass fell into the room. Then a long bony finger of the creature came in and turned the handle of the window, and the window opened, and the creature came in; and it came across the room, and her terror was so great that she could not scream, and it came up to the bed, and it twisted its long, bony fingers into her hair, and it dragged her head over the side of the bed, and—it bit her violently in the throat.

"As it bit her, her voice was released, and she screamed with all her might and main. Her brothers rushed out of their rooms, but the door was locked on the inside. A moment was lost while they got a poker and broke it open. Then the creature had already escaped through the window, and the sister, bleeding violently from a wound in the throat, was lying unconscious over the side of the bed. One brother pursued the creature, which fled before him through the moonlight with gigantic strides, and eventually seemed to disappear over the wall into the churchyard. Then he rejoined his brother by the sister's bedside. She was dreadfully hurt, and her wound was a very definite one; but she was of strong disposition, not either given to romance or superstition, and when she came to herself she said, 'What has happened is most extraordinary, and I am very much hurt. It seems inexplicable, but of course there is an explanation, and we must wait for it. It will turn out that a lunatic has escaped from some asylum and found his way here.' The wound healed, and she appeared to get well, but the doctor who was sent for would not believe that she could bear so terrible a shock so easily, and insisted that she must have change, mental and physical; so her brothers took her to Switzerland.

"Being a sensible girl, when she went abroad she threw herself at once into the interests of the country she was in. She dried plants, she made sketches, she went up mountains, and, as autumn came on, she was the person who urged that they should return to Croglin Grange. 'We have taken it,' she said, 'for seven years, and we have only been there one; and we shall always find it difficult to let a house which is only one story high, so we had better return there; lunatics do not escape every day.' As she urged it, her brothers wished nothing better, and the family returned to Cumberland. From there being no upstairs to the house it was impossible to make any great change in their arrangements. The sister occupied the same room, but it is unnecessary to say she always closed her shutters, which, however, as in many old houses, always left one top pane of the window uncovered. The brothers moved, and occupied a room together, exactly opposite that of their sister, and they always kept loaded pistols in their room.

"The winter passed most peacefully and happily. In the following March the sister was suddenly awakened by a sound she remembered only too well—scratch, scratch, scratch upon the window, and, looking up, she saw quite clearly in the topmost pane of the window the same hideous brown shrivelled face, with glaring eyes, looking in at her. This time she screamed as loud as she could. Her brothers rushed out of their room with pistols, and out of the front door. The creature was already scudding away across the lawn. One of the brothers fired and hit it in the leg, but still with the other leg it continued to make way, scrambled over the wall into the churchyard, and seemed to disappear into a vault which belonged to a family long extinct.

"The next day the brothers summoned all the tenants of Croglin Grange, and in their presence the vault was opened. A horrible scene revealed itself. The vault was full of coffins; they had been broken open, and their contents, horribly mangled and distorted, were scattered over the floor. One coffin alone remained intact. Of that the lid had been lifted, but still lay loose upon the coffin. They raised it, and there, brown, withered, shrivelled, mummified, but quite entire, was the same hideous figure which had looked in at the windows of Croglin Grange, with the marks of a recent pistol-shot in the leg; and they did—the only thing that can lay a vampire— they burnt it."

FOOTNOTES

[10] *The Story of my Life* (Allen & Unwin).

XXI
THE GHOST OF MAJOR SYDENHAM

By Joseph Glanvil [11]

Concerning the apparition of the Ghost of Major George Sydenham, (late of Dulverton in the County of Somerset) to Captain William Dyke, late of Skilgate in this County also, and now likewise deceased: Be pleased to take the Relation of it as I have it from the worthy and learned Dr Tho. Dyke, a near kinsman of the Captain's, thus: Shortly after the Major's Death, the Doctor was desired to come to the House, to take care of a Child that was there sick, and in his way thither he called on the Captain, who was very willing to wait on him to the place, because he must, as he said, have gone thither that night, though he had not met with so encouraging an opportunity. After their arrival there at the House, and the Civility of the People shewn them in that Entertainment, they were seasonably conducted to their Lodging, which they desired might be together in the same Bed: Where after they had lain a while, the Captain knocked, and bids the Servant bring him two of the largest and biggest Candles lighted that he could get. Whereupon the Doctor enquires what he meant by this? The Captain answers, You know Cousin what Disputes my Major and I have had touching the Being of a God, and the Immortality of the Soul; in which points we could never yet be resolv'd, though we so much sought for and desired it; and therefore it was at length fully agreed between us, That he of us that died first, should the third Night after his Funeral, between the Hours of Twelve and one, come to the little House that is here in the Garden, and there give a full account to the Survivor touching these Matters, who should be sure to be present there at the set time, and so receive a full satisfaction; and this, says the Captain, is the very Night, and I am come on purpose to fulfil my promise. The Doctor dissuaded him, minding him of the danger of following those strange Counsels, for which we could have no Warrant, and that the Devil might by some cunning Device make such an advantage of this rash attempt, as might work his utter Ruin. The Captain replies, That he had solemnly engag'd, and that nothing should discourage him, and adds, that if the Doctor would wake awhile with him, he would thank him, if not, he might compose himself to his rest; but for his own part he was resolv'd to watch, that he might be sure to be present at the Hour appointed: To that purpose he sets his watch by him, and as soon as he perceived by it that it was half an Hour past 11, he rises, and taking a Candle in each Hand, goes out by a back-door, of which he had before gotten the Key, and walks to the Garden-house, where he continued two hours and a half, and at his return declared, that he had neither saw not heard any thing more than what was usual. But I know, said he, that my Major would surely have come, had he been able.

About 6 weeks after, the Captain rides to *Eaton* to place his Son a Scholar there, when the Doctor went thither with him. They lodged there at an Inn, the Sign was the *Christopher*, and tarried two or three Nights, not lying together now as before at *Dulverton*, but in two several Chambers. The morning before they went thence, the Captain staid in his Chamber longer than he was wont to do before he called upon the Doctor. At length he comes into the Doctor's Chamber, but in a Visage and Form much differing from himself, with his Hair and Eyes staring, and his whole Body shaking and trembling: Whereupon at the Doctor wondering, presently demanded: What is the matter Cousin Captain? The Captain replies, I have seen my Major: At which the Doctor seeming to smile, the Captain immediately confirms it, saying, If ever I saw him in my life, I saw him but now: And then he related to the Doctor what had passed, thus: This morning after it was light, someone comes to my bedside, and suddenly drawing back the Curtains, calls, *Cap. Cap.* (which was the term of familiarity that the Major used to call the Captain by). To whom I replied, *What my Major?* To which he returns, *I could not come at the time appointed, but I am now come to tell you, That there is a God, and a very just and terrible one, and if you do not turn over a new leaf*, (the very Expressions as is by the Doctor punctually remembered) *you will find it so.* The Captain proceeded: On the Table by there lay a Sword, which the Major had formerly given me. Now after the Apparition had walked a turn or two about the Chamber, he took up the Sword, drew it out, and finding it not so clean and bright as it ought, *Cap. Cap.* says he, *this Sword did not use to be kept after this manner when it was mine.* After which Words he suddenly disappeared.

The Captain was not only thoroughly persuaded of what he had thus seen and heard, but was from that time observed to be very much affected with it: and the Humour that before in him was brisk and jovial, was then strangely alter'd; insomuch, as very little Meat would pass down with him at Dinner, though at the taking leave of their Friends there was a very handsome Treat provided: Yea it was observed that what the Captain had thus seen and heard, had a more lasting Influence upon him, and 'tis judged by those who were well acquainted with his Conversation, that the remembrance of this Passage stuck close to him, and that those words of his dead Friend were frequently sounding fresh in his Ears, during the remainder of his Life, which was about Two Years.

FOOTNOTES

[11] *Sadducismus Triumphatus.*

XXII
THE MIRACULOUS CASE OF JESCH CLAES

From Christmas' "Phantom World"

In the year 1676, about the 13th or 14th of this Month October, in the Night, between one and two of the Clock, this *Jesch Claes*, a cripple, being in bed with her Husband, who was a Boatman, she was three times pulled by her Arm, with which she awaked and cried out, "O Lord! what may this be?"

Hereupon she heard an answer in plain words: "Be not afraid, I come in the Name of the Father, Son, and Holy Ghost. Your malady which hath for many years been upon you shall cease, and it shall be given you from God Almighty to walk again. But keep this good news to yourself!" Whereupon she cried aloud, "O Lord! that I had a light that I might know what this is." Then had she this answer: "There needs no light, the light shall be given you from God."

Then came light all over the Room, and she saw a beautiful Youth about ten Years of Age, with curled yellow Hair, cloathed in white to the Feet, who went from the Bed's-Head to the Chimney with a light, which a little after vanished. Hereupon did there did shoot something through her Leg, like water, from hip to toe, and when she did find life rising up in her dead limb, she fell to crying out, "Lord give me now again the feeling, which I have not had in so many years." And farther she continued crying and praying to the Lord according to her weak measure.

Yet she continued that day, Wednesday, and the next day Thursday, as before till Evening at six a clock. At which time she sate at the Fire dressing the Food. Then came as like rushing noise in both her Ears with which it was said to her, "*Stand.* Your going is given you again."

Then did she immediately stand up, that had so many years crept, and went to the door. Her Husband meeting her, being exceedingly afraid, drew back. In the mean time while she cried out, "My dear Husband, I can go again."

He thinking it was a Spirit, drew back, saying, "You are not my Wife."

His Wife taking hold of him, said, "My dear Husband, I am the self-same that hath been married these thirty years to you. The Almighty God hath given me my going again."

But her Husband being amazed, drew back to the side of the Room, till at last she clasped her Hand about his Neck. And yet he doubted, and said to his Daughter, "Is this your Mother?"

She answered, "Yes, Father! this we plainly see. I had seen her go also before you came in."

This befell upon Prince's-Island in Amsterdam, where Jesch Claes lived with her husband.

XXIII
THE RADIANT BOY OF CORBY CASTLE

Local Records

The haunted room forms part of the old house, with windows looking into the court. It adjoins a tower built for defence, for Corby was, properly, more a border tower than a castle of any consideration. There is a winding staircase in this tower, and the walls are from eight to ten feet thick.

When the times became more peaceable, our ancestors enlarged the arrow-slit windows, and added to that part of the building which looks towards the river Eden; the view of which, with its beautiful banks, we now enjoy. But many additions and alterations have been made since that.

To return to the room in question: I must observe that it is by no means remote or solitary, being surrounded on all sides by chambers that are constantly inhabited. It is accessible by a passage cut through a wall eight feet in thickness, and its dimensions are twenty-one by eighteen. One side of the wainscotting is covered with tapestry, the remainder is decorated with old family pictures, and some ancient pieces of embroidery, probably the handiwork of nuns. Over a press, which has doors of Venetian glass, is an ancient oaken figure, with a battle-axe in his hand, which was one of those formerly placed on the walls of the City of Carlisle, to represent guards. There used to be also an old-fashioned bed and some dark furniture in this room; but so many were the complaints of those who slept there, that I was induced to replace some of these articles of furniture by more modern ones, in the hope of removing a certain air of gloom, which I thought might have given rise to the unaccountable reports of apparitions and extraordinary noises which were constantly reaching us. But I regret to say, I did not succeed in banishing the nocturnal visitor, which still continues to disturb our friends.

I shall pass over numerous instances, and select one as being especially remarkable, from the circumstance of the apparition having been seen by a clergyman well known and highly respected in this county, who, not six weeks ago, repeated the circumstances to a company of twenty persons, amongst whom were some who had previously been entire disbelievers in such appearances.

The best way of giving you these particulars will be by subjoining an extract from my journal, entered at the time the event occurred.

Sept. 8, 1803. — Amongst other guests invited to Corby Castle came the Rev. Henry A., of Redburgh, and rector of Greystoke, with Mrs A., his wife, who was a Miss S., of Ulverstone. According to previous arrangements, they were to have remained with us some days; but their visit was cut short in a very unexpected manner. On the morning after their arrival we were all assembled at breakfast, when a chaise and four dashed up to the door in such haste that it knocked down part of the fence of my flower garden. Our curiosity was, of course, awakened to know who could be arriving at so early an hour; when, happening to turn my eyes towards Mr A., I observed that he appeared extremely agitated. "It is our carriage," said he; "I am very sorry, but we must absolutely leave you this morning."

We naturally felt and expressed considerable surprise, as well as regret, at this unexpected departure, representing that we had invited Colonel and Mrs S., some friends whom Mr A. particularly desired to meet, to dine with us on that day. Our expostulations, however, were vain; the breakfast was no sooner over than they departed, leaving us in consternation to conjecture what could possibly have occasioned so sudden an alteration in their arrangements. I really felt quite uneasy lest anything should have given them offence; and we reviewed all the occurrences of the preceding evening in order to discover, if offence there was, whence it had arisen. But our pains were vain; and after talking a great deal about it for some days, other circumstances banished the matter from our minds.

It was not till we some time afterwards visited the part of the county in which Mr A. resides that we learnt the real cause of his sudden departure from Corby. The relation of the fact, as it here follows, is in his own words: —

"Soon after we went to bed, we fell asleep; it might be between one and two in the morning when I awoke. I observed that the fire was totally extinguished; but, although that was the case, and we had no light, I saw a glimmer in the centre of the room, which suddenly increased to a bright flame. I looked out, apprehending that something had caught fire, when, to my amazement, I beheld a beautiful boy, clothed in white, with bright locks resembling gold, standing by my bedside, in which position he remained some minutes, fixing his eyes upon me with a mild and benevolent expression. He then glided gently towards the side of the chimney, where it is obvious there is no possible egress, and entirely disappeared. I found myself again in total darkness, and all remained quiet until the usual hour of rising. I declare this to be a true account of what I saw at Corby Castle, upon my word as a clergyman."

Mrs Crowe, alluding to this story in her "Night Side of Nature," said that she was acquainted with some of the family and several of the friends of the Rev. Henry A., who, she continued, "is still alive, though now an old man; and I can most positively assert that his own conviction with regard to the nature of this appearance has remained ever unshaken. The circumstance made a lasting impression upon his mind, and he never willingly speaks of it; but when he does, it is always with the greatest seriousness, and he never shrinks from avowing his belief that what he saw admits of no other interpretation than the one he then put upon it."

XXIV
CLERK SAUNDERS

"Border Minstrelsy"

Clerk Saunders and May Margaret
Walked owre yon garden green;
And sad and heavy was the love
That fell them twa between.

And thro' the dark, and thro' the mirk,
And thro' the leaves o' green,
He cam that night to Margaret's door,
And tirléd at the pin.

"O wha is that at my bower door,
Sae weel my name does ken?"
"'Tis I, Clerk Saunders, your true love;
You'll open and let me in?"

"But in may come my seven bauld brithers,
Wi' torches burning bright;
They'll say—'We hae but ae sister,
And behold she's wi' a knight!'"

"Ye'll tak my brand I bear in hand,
And wi' the same ye'll lift the pin;
Then ye may swear, and save your aith,
That ye ne'er let Clerk Saunders in.

"Ye'll tak the kerchief in your hand,
And wi' the same tie up your een;
Then ye may swear and save your aith,
Ye saw me na since yestere'en."

It was about the midnight hour,
When they asleep were laid,

When in and cam her seven brothers,
Wi' torches burning red.

When in and cam her seven brothers,
Wi' torches burning bright;
They said, "We hae but ae sister,
And behold she's wi' a knight."

Then out and spak the first o' them,
"We'll awa' and lat them be."
And out and spak the second o' them,
"His father has nae mair than he!"

And out and spak the third o' them,
"I wot they are lovers dear!"
And out and spak the fourth o' them,
"They hae lo'ed this mony a year!"

Then out and spak the fifth o' them,
"It were sin true love to twain!"
"'Twere shame," out spak the sixth o' them,
"To slay a sleeping man!"

Then up and gat the seventh o' them,
And never a word spak he;
But he has striped his bright brown brand
Through Saunders' fair bodie.

Clerk Saunders started, and Margaret she turned,
Into his arms as asleep she lay;
And sad and silent was the night,
That was atween thir twae.

And they lay still and sleepit sound,
Till the day began to daw;
And kindly to him she did say,
"It is time, love, you were awa'."

But he lay still, and sleepit sound,
Till the sun began to sheen;
She looked atween her and the wa',
And dull, dull were his een.

She turned the blankets to the foot,
The sheets unto the wa',
And there she saw his bloody wound,
And her tears fast doun did fa'.

Then in and cam her father dear,
Said, "Let a' your mournin' be;
I'll carry the dead corpse to the clay
And then come back and comfort thee.

"Hold your tongue, my daughter dear,
And let your mourning be;
I'll wed you to a higher match

Than his father's son could be."

"Gae comfort weel your seven sons, father,
For man sall ne'er comfort me;
Ye'll marry me wi' the Queen o' Heaven,
For wedded I ne'er sall be!"

The clinking bell gaed through the toun,
To carry the dead corse to the clay;
And Clerk Saunders stood at Margaret's window,
'Twas an hour before the day.

"O'are ye sleeping, Margaret?" he says,
"Or are ye waking presentlie?
Gie me my faith and troth again,
I wot, true love, I gied to thee.

"I canna rest, Margaret," he says,
"Doun in the grave where I must be,
Till ye gie me my faith and troth again,
I wot, true love, I gied to thee."

"Your faith and troth ye sall never get,
Nor our true love sall never twin,
Until ye come within my bower,
And kiss me cheek and chin."

"My mouth it is full cold, Margaret,
It has the smell, now, of the ground;

And if I kiss thy comely mouth,
To the grave thou will be bound.

"O, cocks are crawing a merry midnight,
I wot the wild-fowls are boding day;
Gie me my faith and troth again,
And let me fare me on my way."

"Thy faith and troth thou sall na get,
And our true love shall never twin,
Until ye tell what comes of women,
I wot, who die in strong travailing."

"Their beds are made in the heavens high,
Down at the foot of our good Lord's knee,
Weel set about wi' gillyflowers;
I wot sweet company for to see.

"O, cocks are crawing a merry midnight,
I wot the wild-fowl are boding day;
The psalms of heaven will soon be sung,
And I, ere now, will be missed away."

Then she has ta'en a crystal wand,
And she has stroken her troth thereon,
She has given it him out at the shot-window,
Wi' mony a sigh and heavy groan.

"I thank ye, Margaret; I thank ye, Margaret;
And aye I thank ye heartilie;
Gin ever the dead come for the quick,
Be sure, Margaret, I'll come for thee."

It's hosen, and shoon, and gown, alane,
She clam the wa' and after him;
Until she cam to the green forest,
And there she lost the sight o' him.

"Is there ony room at your head, Saunders,
Is there ony room at your feet?
Or ony room at your side, Saunders,
Where fain, fain, I wad sleep?"

"There's nae room at my head, Margaret,
There's nae room at my feet;
My bed it is full lowly now:
'Mang the hungry worms I sleep.

"Cauld mould is my covering now,
But and my winding-sheet;
The dew it falls nae sooner down,
Than my resting-place is weet.

"But plait a wand o' the bonnie birk
And lay it on my breast;
And shed a tear upon my grave,
And wish my saul gude rest.

"And fair Margaret, and rare Margaret,
And Margaret o' veritie,
Gin e'er ye love anither man,
Ne'er love him as ye did me."

Then up and crew the milk-white cock,
And up and crew the gray;
Her lover vanished in the air,
And she gaed weeping away.

XXV
DOROTHY DURANT

By Mrs Crowe

A schoolboy named Bligh, who went to Launceston Grammar School, of which the Rev. John Ruddle was headmaster, from being a lad of bright parts and no common attainments, became on a sudden moody, dejected, and melancholy. His friends, seeing the change without being able to find the cause, attributed it to laziness, an aversion to school, or to some other motive which he was ashamed to avow. He was led, however, to tell his brother, after some time, that in a field through which he passed to and from school, he invariably met the apparition of a woman, whom he personally knew while living, and who had been dead about eight years. Ridicule, threats, persuasions, were alike used in vain by the family to induce him to dismiss these absurd ideas. Finally, Mr Ruddle was sent for, and to him the boy ingenuously told the time, manner, and frequency of this appearance. It was in a field called Higher Broomfield. The apparition, he said, appeared dressed in female attire, met him two or three times while he passed through the field, glided hastily by him, but never spoke. He had thus been occasionally met about two months before he took any particular notice of it; at length the appearance became more frequent, meeting him both morning and evening, but always in the same field, yet invariably moving out of the path when it came close to him. He often spoke, but could never get any reply. To avoid this unwelcome visitor he forsook the field, and went to school and returned from it through a lane, in which place, between the quarry pack and nursery, it always met him. Unable to disbelieve the evidence of his own senses, or to obtain credit with any of his family, he prevailed upon Mr Ruddle to accompany him to the place.

"I arose," says this clergyman, "the next morning, and went with him. The field to which he led me I guessed to be about twenty acres, in an open country, and about three furlongs from any house. We went into the field, and had not gone a third part before the spectrum in the shape of a woman, with all the circumstances he had described the day before, so far as the suddenness of its appearance and transition would permit me to discover, passed by.

"I was a little surprised at it, and though I had taken up a firm resolution to speak to it, I had not the power, nor durst I look back; yet I took care not to show any fear to my pupil and guide, and therefore, telling him I was satisfied of the truth of his statement, we walked to the end of the field and returned—nor did the ghost meet us that time but once.

"On the 27th July, 1665, I went to the haunted field by myself, and walked the breadth of it without any encounter. I then returned and took the other walk, and then the spectre appeared to me, much about the same place in which I saw it when the young gentleman was with me. It appeared to move swifter than before, and seemed to be about ten feet from me on my right hand, insomuch that I had not time to speak to it, as I had determined with myself beforehand. The evening of this day, the parents, the son, and myself, being in the chamber where I lay, I proposed to them our going altogether to the place next morning. We accordingly met at the stile we had appointed; thence we all four walked into the field together. We had not gone more than half the field before the ghost made its appearance. It then came over the stile just before us, and moved with such rapidity that by the time we had gone six or seven steps it passed by. I immediately turned my head and ran after it, with the young man by my side. We saw it pass over the stile at which we entered, and no farther. I stepped upon the hedge at one place and the young man at another, but we could discern nothing; whereas I do aver that the swiftest horse in England could not have conveyed himself out of sight in that short space of time. Two things I observed in this day's appearance: first, a spaniel dog, which had followed the company unregarded, barked and ran away as the spectrum passed by; whence it is easy to conclude that it was not our fear or fancy which made the apparition. Secondly, the motion of the spectrum was not *gradatim* or by steps, or moving of the feet, but by a kind of gliding, as children upon ice, or as a boat down a river, which punctually answers the description the ancients give of the motion of these Lamures. This ocular evidence clearly convinced, but withal strangely affrighted, the old gentleman and his wife. They well knew this woman, Dorothy Durant, in her life-time; were at her burial, and now plainly saw her features in this apparition.

"The next morning, being Thursday, I went very early by myself, and walked for about an hour's space in meditation and prayer in the field next adjoining. Soon after five I stepped over the stile into the haunted field, and had not gone above thirty or forty paces before the ghost appeared at the further stile. I spoke to it in some short sentences with a loud voice; whereupon it approached me, but slowly, and when I came near it moved not. I spoke again, and it answered in a voice neither audible nor very intelligible. I was not in the least terrified, and therefore persisted until it spoke again and gave me satisfaction; but the work could not be finished at this time. Whereupon the same evening, an hour after sunset, it met me again near the same place, and after a few words on each side it quietly vanished, and neither doth appear now, nor hath appeared since, nor ever will more to any man's disturbance. The discourse in the morning lasted about a quarter of an hour.

"These things are true," concludes the Rev. John Ruddle, "and I know them to be so, with as much certainty as eyes and ears can give me; and until I can be persuaded that my senses all deceive me about their proper objects, and by that persuasion deprive me of the strongest inducement to believe the Christian religion, I must and will assert that the things contained in this paper are true."

XXVI
PEARLIN JEAN

By Charles Kirkpatrick Sharpe

It was Charles Kirkpatrick Sharpe, the antiquary, who furnished this account of Pearlin Jean's hauntings at Allanbank.

"In my youth," he says, "Pearlin Jean was the most remarkable ghost in Scotland, and my terror when a child. Our old nurse, Jenny Blackadder, had been a servant at Allanbank, and often heard her rustling in silks up and down stairs, and along the passages. She never saw her; but her husband did.

"She was a French woman, whom the first baronet of Allanbank, then Mr Stuart, met with at Paris, during his tour to finish his education as a gentleman. Some people said she was a nun; in which case she must have been a Sister of Charity, as she appears not to have been confined to a cloister. After some time, young Stuart either became faithless to the lady or was suddenly recalled to Scotland by his parents, and had got into his carriage at the door of the hotel, when his Dido unexpectedly made her appearance, and stepping on the forewheel of the coach to address her lover, he ordered the postilion to drive on; the consequence of which was that the lady fell, and one of the wheels going over her forehead, killed her.

"In a dusky autumnal evening, when Mr Stuart drove under the arched gateway of Allanbank, he perceived Pearlin Jean sitting on the top, her head and shoulders covered with blood.

"After this, for many years, the house was haunted; doors shut and opened with great noise at midnight; the rustling of silks and pattering of high-heeled shoes were heard in bedrooms and passages. Nurse Jenny said there were seven ministers called in together at one time to *lay* the spirit; 'but they did no mickle good, my dear.'

"The picture of the ghost was hung between those of her lover and his lady, and kept her comparatively quiet; but when taken away, she became worse-natured than ever. This portrait was in the present Sir J.G.'s possession. I am unwilling to record its fate.

"The ghost was designated Pearlin, from always wearing a great quantity of that sort of lace.

"Nurse Jenny told me that when Thomas Blackadder was her lover (I remember Thomas very well), they made an assignation to meet one moonlight night in the orchard at Allanbank. True Thomas, of course, was the first comer; and seeing a female figure in a light-coloured dress, at some distance, he ran forward with open arms to embrace his Jenny; when lo and behold! as he neared the spot where the figure stood, it vanished; and presently he saw it again at the very end of the orchard, a considerable way off. Thomas went home in a fright; but Jenny, who came last, and saw nothing, forgave him, and they were married.

"Many years after this, about the year 1790, two ladies paid a visit at Allanbank—I think the house was then let—and passed the night there. They had never heard a word about the ghost; but they were disturbed the whole night with something walking backwards and forwards in their bed-chamber. This I had from the best authority."

To this account may be added that a housekeeper, called Betty Norrie, who, in more recent times, lived many years at Allanbank, positively averred that she, and many other persons, had frequently seen Pearlin Jean; and, moreover, stated that they were so used to her as to be no longer alarmed at the noises she made.

XXVII
THE DENTON HALL GHOST

Local Records

A day or two after my arrival at Denton Hall, when all around was yet new to me, I had accompanied my friends to a ball given in the neighbourhood, and returned heartily fatigued. At this time I need not blush, nor you smile, when I say that on that evening I had met, for the second time, one with whose destinies my own were doomed to become connected.

I think I was sitting upon an antique carved chair, near to the fire, in the room where I slept, busied in arranging my hair, and thinking over some of the events of the day. Whether I had dropped into a half-slumber, I cannot say; but on looking up—for I had my face bent toward the fire—there seemed sitting on a similar highbacked chair, on the other side of the ancient tiled fireplace, an old lady, whose air and dress were so remarkable that to this hour they seem as fresh in my memory as they were the day after the vision. She appeared to be dressed in a flowered satin gown, of a cut then out of date. It was peaked and long-waisted. The fabric of the satin had that extreme of glossy stiffness which old fabrics of this kind exhibit. She wore a stomacher. On her wrinkled fingers appeared some rings of great size and seeming value; but, what was most remarkable, she wore also a satin hood of a peculiar shape. It was glossy like the gown, but seemed to be stiffened either by whalebone or some other material. Her age seemed considerable, and the face, though not unpleasant, was somewhat hard and severe and indented with minute wrinkles. I confess that so entirely was my attention engrossed by what was passing in my mind, that, though I felt mightily confused, I was not startled (in the emphatic sense) by the apparition. In fact, I deemed it to be some old lady, perhaps a housekeeper, or dependent in the family, and, therefore, though rather astonished, was by no means frightened by my visitant, supposing me to be awake, which I am convinced was the case, though few persons believe me on this point.

My own impression is that I stared somewhat rudely, in the wonder of the moment, at the hard, but lady-like features of my aged visitor. But she left me small time to think, addressing me in a familiar half-whisper and with a constant restless motion of the hand which aged persons, when excited, often exhibit in addressing the young. "Well, young lady," said my mysterious companion, "and so you've been at yon hall to-night! and highly ye've been delighted there! Yet if you could see as I can see, or could know as I can know, troth! I guess your pleasure would abate. 'Tis well for you, young lady, peradventure, ye see not with my eyes"—and at the moment, sure enough, her eyes, which were small, grey, and in no way remarkable, twinkled with a light so severe that the effect was unpleasant in the extreme. "'Tis well for you and them," she continued, "that ye cannot count the cost. Time was when hospitality could be kept in England, and the guest not ruin the master of the feast—but that's all vanished now: pride and poverty—pride and poverty, young lady, are an ill-matched pair, Heaven kens!" My tongue, which had at first almost faltered in its office, now found utterance. By a kind of instinct, I addressed my strange visitant in her own manner and humour. "And are we, then, so much poorer than in days of yore?" were the words that I spoke. My visitor seemed half startled at the sound of my voice, as at something unaccustomed, and went on, rather answering my question by implication than directly: "'Twas not all hollowness then," she exclaimed, ceasing somewhat her hollow whisper; "the land was then the lord's, and that which *seemed, was*. The child, young lady, was not then mortgaged in the cradle, and, mark ye, the bride, when she kneeled at the altar, gave not herself up, body and soul, to be the bondswoman of the Jew, but to be the helpmate of the spouse." "The Jew!" I exclaimed in surprise, for then I understood not the allusion. "Ay, young lady! the Jew," was the rejoinder. "'Tis plain ye know not who rules. 'Tis all hollow yonder! all hollow, all hollow! to the very glitter of the side-board, all false! all false! all hollow! Away with such make-believe finery!" And here again the hollow voice rose a little, and the dim grey eye glistened. "Ye mortgage the very oaks of your ancestors—I saw the planting of them; and now 'tis all painting, gilding, varnishing and veneering. Houses call ye them? Whited sepulchres, young lady, whited sepulchres. Trust not all that seems to glisten. Fair though it seems, 'tis but the product of disease—even as is the pearl in your hair, young lady, that glitters in the mirror yonder,—not more specious than is all,—ay, *all* ye have seen to-night."

As my strange visitor pronounced these words, I instinctively turned my gaze to a large old-fashioned mirror that leaned from the wall of the chamber. 'Twas but for a moment. But when I again turned my head, my visitant was no longer there! I heard plainly, as I turned, the distinct rustle of the silk, as if she had risen and was leaving the room. I seemed distinctly to hear this, together with the quick, short, easy footstep with which females of rank of that period were taught to glide rather than to walk; this I seemed to hear, but of what appeared the antique old lady I saw no more. The suddenness and strangeness of this event for a moment sent the blood back to my heart. Could I have found voice, I should, I think, have screamed, but that was, for a moment, beyond my power. A few seconds recovered me. By a sort of impulse I rushed to the door, outside which I now heard the footsteps of some of the family, when, to my utter astonishment, I found it was—locked! I now recollected that I myself locked it before sitting down.

Though somewhat ashamed to give utterance to what I really believed as to this matter, the strange adventure of the night was made a subject of conversation at the breakfast-table next morning. On the words leaving my lips, I saw my host and hostess exchange looks with each other, and soon found that the tale I had to tell was not received with the air which generally meets such relations. I was not repelled by an angry or ill-bred incredulity, or treated as one of diseased fancy, to whom silence is indirectly recommended as the alternative of being laughed at. In short, it was not attempted to be denied or concealed that I was not the first who had been alarmed in a manner, if not exactly similar, yet just as mysterious; that visitors, like myself, had actually given way to these terrors so far as to quit the house in consequence; and that servants were sometimes not to be prevented from sharing in the same contagion. At the same time they told me this, my host and hostess declared that custom and continued residence had long exempted all regular inmates of the mansion from any alarms or terrors. The visitations, whatever they were, seemed to be confined to newcomers, and to them it was by no means a matter of frequent occurrence.

In the neighbourhood, I found, this strange story was well known; that the house was regularly set down as "haunted" all the country round, and that the spirit, or goblin, or whatever it was that was embodied in these appearances, was familiarly known by the name of "Silky."

At a distance, those to whom I have related my night's adventure have one and all been sceptical, and accounted for the whole by supposing me to have been half asleep, or in a state resembling somnambulism. All I can say is, that my own impressions are directly contrary to this supposition; and that I feel as sure that I saw the figure that sat before me with my bodily eyes, as I am sure I now see you with them. Without affecting to deny that I was somewhat shocked by the adventure, I must repeat that I suffered no unreasonable alarm, nor suffered my fancy to overcome my better spirit of womanhood.

I certainly slept no more in that room, and in that to which I removed I had one of the daughters of my hostess as a companion; but I have never, from that hour to this, been convinced that I did not actually encounter something more than is natural—if not an actual being in some other state of existence. My ears have not been deceived, if my eyes were—which, I repeat, I cannot believe.

The warnings so strongly shadowed forth have been too true. The gentleman at whose house I that night was a guest has long since filled an untimely grave! In that splendid hall, since that time, strangers have lorded it—and I myself have long since ceased to think of such scenes as I partook of that evening—the envied object of the attention of one whose virtues have survived the splendid inheritance to which he seemed destined.

Whether this be a tale of delusion and superstition, or something more than that, it is, at all events, not without a legend for its foundation. There is some obscure and dark rumour of secrets strangely obtained and enviously betrayed by a rival sister, ending in deprivation of reason and death; and that the betrayer still walks by times in the deserted Hall which she rendered tenantless, always prophetic of disaster to those she encounters. So has it been with me, certainly; and more than me, if those who say it say true. It is many, many years since I saw the scene of this adventure; but I have heard that since that time the same mysterious visitings have more than once been renewed; that midnight curtains have been drawn by an arm clothed in rustling silks; and the same form, clad in dark brocade, has been seen gliding along the dark corridors of that ancient, grey, and time-worn mansion, ever prophetic of death or misfortune.

XXVIII
THE GOODWOOD GHOST STORY

(Doubtfully attributed to Charles Dickens)

My wife's sister, Mrs M——, was left a widow at the age of thirty-five, with two children, girls, of whom she was passionately fond. She carried on the draper's business at Bognor, established by her husband. Being still a very handsome woman, there were several suitors for her hand. The only favoured one amongst them was a Mr Barton. My wife never liked this Mr Barton, and made no secret of her feelings to her sister, whom she frequently told that Mr Barton only wanted to be master of the little haberdashery shop in Bognor. He was a man in poor circumstances, and had no other motive in his proposal of marriage, so my wife thought, than to better himself.

On the 23rd of August 1831 Mrs M—— arranged to go with Barton to a picnic party at Goodwood Park, the seat of the Duke of Richmond, who had kindly thrown open his grounds to the public for the day. My wife, a little annoyed at her going out with this man, told her she had much better remain at home to look after her children and attend to the business. Mrs M——, however, bent on going, made arrangements about leaving the shop, and got my wife to promise to see to her little girls while she was away.

The party set out in a four-wheeled phaeton, with a pair of ponies driven by Mrs M——, and a gig for which I lent the horse.

Now we did not expect them to come back till nine or ten o'clock, at any rate. I mention this particularly to show that there could be no expectation of their earlier return in the mind of my wife, to account for what follows.

At six o'clock that bright summer's evening my wife went out into the garden to call the children. Not finding them, she went all round the place in her search till she came to the empty stable; thinking they might have run in there to play, she pushed open the door; there, standing in the darkest corner, she saw Mrs M——. My wife was surprised to see her, certainly; for she did not expect her return so soon; but, oddly enough, it did not strike her as being singular to see her *there*. Vexed as she had felt with her all day for going, and rather glad, in her woman's way, to have something entirely different from the genuine *casus belli* to hang a retort upon, my wife said: "Well, Harriet, I should have thought another dress would have done quite as well for your picnic as that best black silk you have on." My wife was the elder of the twain, and had always assumed a little of the air of counsellor to her sister. Black silks were thought a great deal more of at that time than they are just now, and silk of any kind was held particularly inconsistent wear for Wesleyan Methodists, to which denomination we belonged.

Receiving no answer, my wife said: "Oh, well, Harriet, if you can't take a word of reproof without being sulky, I'll leave you to yourself"; and then she came into the house to tell me the party had returned and that she had seen her sister in the stable, not in the best of tempers. At the moment it did not seem extraordinary to me that my wife should have met her sister in the stable.

I waited indoors some time, expecting them to return my horse. Mrs M—— was my neighbour, and, being always on most friendly terms, I wondered that none of the party had come in to tell us about the day's pleasure. I thought I would just run in and see how they had got on. To my great surprise the servant told me they had not returned. I began, then, to feel anxiety about the result. My wife, however, having seen Harriet in the stable, refused to believe the servant's assertion; and said there was no doubt of their return, but that they had probably left word to say they were not come back, in order to offer a plausible excuse for taking a further drive, and detaining my horse for another hour or so.

At eleven o'clock Mr Pinnock, my brother-in-law, who had been one of the party, came in, apparently much agitated. As soon as she saw him, and before he had time to speak, my wife seemed to know what he had to say.

"What is the matter?" she said; "something has happened to Harriet, I know!"

"Yes" replied Mr Pinnock; "if you wish to see her alive, you must come with me directly to Goodwood."

From what he said it appeared that one of the ponies had never been properly broken in; that the man from whom the turn-out was hired for the day had cautioned Mrs M—— respecting it before they started; and that he had lent it reluctantly, being the only pony to match in the stable at the time, and would not have lent it at all had he not known Mrs M—— to be a remarkably good whip.

On reaching Goodwood, it seems, the gentlemen of the party had got out, leaving the ladies to take a drive round the park in the phaeton. One or both of the ponies must then have taken fright at something in the road, for Mrs M—— had scarcely taken the reins when the ponies shied. Had there been plenty of room she would readily have mastered the difficulty; but it was in a narrow road, where a gate obstructed the way. Some men rushed to open the gate—too late. The three other ladies jumped out at the beginning of the accident; but Mrs M—— still held on to the reins, seeking to control her ponies, until, finding it was impossible for the men to get the gate open in time, she too sprang forward; and at the same instant the ponies came smash on to the gate. She had made her spring too late, and fell heavily to the ground on her head. The heavy, old-fashioned comb of the period, with which her hair was looped up, was driven into her skull by the force of the fall. The Duke of Richmond, a witness to the accident, ran to her assistance, lifted her up, and rested her head upon his knees. The only words Mrs M—— had spoken were uttered at the time: "Good God, my children!" By direction of the Duke she was immediately conveyed to a neighbouring inn, where every assistance, medical and otherwise, that forethought or kindness could suggest was afforded her.

At six o'clock in the evening, the time at which my wife had gone into the stable and seen what we now knew had been her spirit, Mrs M——, in her sole interval of returning consciousness, had made a violent but unsuccessful attempt to speak. From her glance having wandered round the room, in solemn awful wistfulness, it had been conjectured she wished to see some relative or friend not then present. I went to Goodwood in the gig with Mr Pinnock, and arrived in time to see my sister-in-law die at two o'clock in the morning. Her only conscious moments had been those in which she laboured unsuccessfully to speak, which had occurred at six o'clock. She wore a black silk dress.

When we came to dispose of her business, and to wind up her affairs, there was scarcely anything left for the two orphan girls. Mrs M——'s father, however, being well-to-do, took them to bring up. At his death, which happened soon afterwards, his property went to his eldest son, who speedily dissipated the inheritance. During a space of two years the children were taken as visitors by various relations in turn, and lived an unhappy life with no settled home.

For some time I had been debating with myself how to help these children, having many boys and girls of my own to provide for. I had almost settled to take them myself, bad as trade was with me, at the time, and bring them up with my own family, when one day business called me to Brighton. The business was so urgent that it necessitated my travelling at night.

I set out from Bognor in a close-headed gig on a beautiful moonlight winter's night, when the crisp frozen snow lay deep over the earth, and its fine glistening dust was whirled about in little eddies on the bleak night-wind—driven now and then in stinging powder against my tingling cheek, warm and glowing in the sharp air. I had taken my great "Bose" (short for "Boatswain") for company. He lay, blinking wakefully, sprawled out on the spare seat of the gig beneath a mass of warm rugs.

Between Littlehampton and Worthing is a lonely piece of road, long and dreary, through bleak and bare open country, where the snow lay knee-deep, sparkling in the moonlight. It was so cheerless that I turned round to speak to my dog, more for the sake of hearing the sound of a voice than anything else. "Good Bose," I said, patting him, "there's a good dog!" Then suddenly I noticed he shivered, and shrank underneath the wraps. Then the horse required my attention, for he gave a start, and was going wrong, and had nearly taken me into the ditch.

Then I looked up. Walking at my horse's head, dressed in a sweeping robe, so white that it shone dazzling against the white snow, I saw a lady, her back turned to me, her head bare; her hair dishevelled and strayed, showing sharp and black against her white dress.

I was at first so much surprised at seeing a lady, so dressed, exposed to the open night, and such a night as this, that I scarcely knew what to do. Recovering myself, I called out to know if I could render assistance—if she wished to ride? No answer. I drove faster, the horse blinking, and shying, and trembling the while, his ears laid back in abject terror. Still the figure maintained its position close to my horse's head. Then I thought that what I saw was no woman, but perchance a man disguised for the purpose of robbing me, seeking an opportunity to seize the bridle and stop the horse. Filled with this idea, I said, "Good Bose! hi! look at it, boy!" but the dog only shivered as if in fright. Then we came to a place where four cross-roads meet.

Determined to know the worst, I pulled up the horse. I fetched Bose, unwilling, out by the ears. He was a good dog at anything from a rat to a man, but he slunk away that night into the hedge, and lay there, his head between his paws, whining and howling. I walked straight up to the figure, still standing by the horse's head. As I walked, the figure turned, and I saw *Harriet's face* as plainly as I see you now—white and calm—placid, as idealised and beautified by death. I must own that, though not a nervous man, in that instant I felt sick and faint. Harriet looked me full in the face with a long, eager, silent look. I knew then it was her spirit, and felt a strange calm come over me, for I knew it was nothing to harm me. When I could speak, I asked what troubled her. She looked at me still, never changing that cold fixed stare. Then I felt in my mind it was her children, and I said:

"Harriet! is it for your children you are troubled?"

No answer.

"Harriet," I continued, "if for these you are troubled, be assured they shall never want while I have power to help them. Rest in peace!"

Still no answer.

I put up my hand to wipe from my forehead the cold perspiration which had gathered there. When I took my hand away from shading my eyes, the figure was gone. I was alone on the bleak snow-covered ground. The breeze, that had been hushed before, breathed coolly and gratefully on my face, and the cold stars glimmered and sparkled sharply in the far blue heavens. My dog crept up to me and furtively licked my hand, as who would say, "Good master, don't be angry. I have served you in all but this."

I took the children and brought them up till they could help themselves.

XXIX
CAPTAIN WHEATCROFT

From Dale Owen's "Footfalls"

In the month of September 1857 Captain German Wheatcroft, of the 6th (Inniskilling) Dragoons, went out to India to join his regiment.

His wife remained in England, residing at Cambridge. On the night between the 14th and 15th of November 1857, towards morning, she dreamed that she saw her husband, looking anxious and ill; upon which she immediately awoke, much agitated. It was bright moonlight; and, looking up, she perceived the same figure standing by her bedside. He appeared in his uniform, the hands pressed across the breast, the hair dishevelled, the face very pale. His large dark eyes were fixed full upon her; their expression was that of great excitement, and there was a peculiar contraction of the mouth, habitual to him when agitated. She saw him, even to each minute particular of his dress, as distinctly as she had ever done in her life; and she remembers to have noticed between his hands the white of his shirt-bosom, unstained, however, with blood. The figure seemed to bend forward, as if in pain, and to make an effort to speak; but there was no sound. It remained visible, the wife thinks, as long as a minute, and then disappeared.

Her first idea was to ascertain if she was actually awake. She rubbed her eyes with the sheet, and felt that the touch was real. Her little nephew was in bed with her; she bent over the sleeping child and listened to its breathing; the sound was distinct, and she became convinced that what she had seen was no dream. It need hardly be added that she did not again go to sleep that night.

Next morning she related all this to her mother, expressing her conviction, though she had noticed no marks of blood on his dress, that Captain Wheatcroft was either killed or grievously wounded. So fully impressed was she with the reality of that apparition, that she thenceforth refused all invitations. A young friend urged her soon afterwards to go with her to a fashionable concert, reminding her that she had received from Malta, sent by her husband, a handsome dress cloak, which she had never yet worn. But she positively declined, declaring that, uncertain as she was whether she was not already a widow, she would never enter a place of amusement until she had letters from her husband (if indeed he still lived) of a later date than the 14th of November.

It was on a Tuesday, in the month of December 1857, that the telegram regarding the actual fate of Captain Wheatcroft was published in London. It was to the effect that he was killed before Lucknow on the *fifteenth* of November.

This news, given in the morning paper, attracted the attention of Mr Wilkinson, a London solicitor, who had in charge Captain Wheatcroft's affairs. When at a later period this gentleman met the widow, she informed him that she had been quite prepared for the melancholy news, but that she had felt sure her husband could not have been killed on the 15th of November, inasmuch as it was during the night between the 14th and 15th that he appeared to her.

The certificate from the War Office, however, which it became Mr Wilkinson's duty to obtain, confirmed the date given in the telegram, its tenor being as follows:—

"No. 9579/1   War Office,
30th January 1858.

"These are to certify that it appears, by the records in this office, that Captain German Wheatcroft of the 6th Dragoon Guards, was killed in action on the 15th of November 1857.

"(*Signed*) B. Hawes."

The difference of longitude between London and Lucknow being about five hours, three or four o'clock a.m. in London would be eight or nine o'clock a.m. at Lucknow. But it was in the *afternoon* not in the *morning*, as will be seen in the sequel, that Captain Wheatcroft was killed. Had he fallen on the 15th, therefore, the apparition to his wife would have appeared several hours before the engagement in which he fell, and while he was yet alive and well.

XXX
THE IRON CAGE

From Mrs Crowe's "Night Side of Nature"

[As you express a wish to know what credit is to be attached to a tale sent forth after a lapse of between thirty and forty years, I will state the facts as they were recalled last year by a daughter of Sir William A. C——.]

Sir James, my mother, with myself and my brother Charles, went abroad towards the end of the year 1786. After trying several different places, we determined to settle at Lille, where we had letters of introduction to several of the best French families. There Sir James left us, and after passing a few days in an uncomfortable lodging, we engaged a nice large family house, which we liked much, and which we obtained at a very low rent, even for that part of the world.

About three weeks after we were established there, I walked one day with my mother to the bankers, for the purpose of delivering our letter of credit from Sir Robert Herries and drawing some money, which being paid in heavy five-frank pieces, we found we could not carry, and therefore requested the banker to send, saying, "We live in the Place du Lion d'Or." Whereupon he looked surprised, and observed that he knew of no house there fit for us, "except, indeed," he added, "the one that has been long uninhabited on account of the *revenant* that walks about it."

He said this quite seriously, and in a natural tone of voice; in spite of which we laughed, and were quite entertained at the idea of a ghost; but, at the same time, we begged him not to mention the thing to our servants, lest they should take any fancies into their heads; and my mother and I resolved to say nothing about the matter to anyone. "I suppose it is the ghost," said my mother, laughing, "that wakes us so often by walking over our heads." We had, in fact, been awakened several nights by a heavy foot, which we supposed to be that of one of the men-servants, of whom we had three English and four French. The English ones, men and women, every one of them, returned ultimately to England with us.

A night or two afterwards, being again awakened by the step, my mother asked Creswell: "Who slept in the room above us?" "No one, my lady," she replied, "it is a large empty garret."

About a week or ten days after this, Creswell came to my mother, one morning, and told her that all the French servants talked of going away, because there was a *revenant* in the house; adding, that there seemed to be a strange story attached to the place, which was said, together with some other property, to have belonged to a young man, whose guardian, who was also his uncle, had treated him cruelly, and confined him in an iron cage; and as he had subsequently disappeared, it was conjectured he had been murdered. This uncle, after inheriting the property, had suddenly quitted the house, and sold it to the father of the man of whom we had hired it. Since that period, though it had been several times let, nobody had ever stayed in it above a week or two; and, for a considerable time past, it had had no tenant at all.

"And do you really believe all this nonsense, Creswell?" said my mother.

"Well, I don't know, my lady," answered she, "but there is the iron cage in the garret over your bedroom, where you may see it, if you please."

Of course we rose to go, and just at that moment an old officer, with his Croix de St Louis, called on us, we invited him to accompany us, and we ascended together. We found, as Creswell had said, a large empty garret, with bare brick walls, and in the further corner of it stood an iron cage, such as wild beasts are kept in, only higher; it was about four feet square, and eight in height, and there was an iron ring in the wall at the back, to which was attached an old rusty chain, with a collar fixed to the end of it! I confess it made my blood creep, when I thought of the possibility of any human being having inhabited it! And our old friend expressed as much horror as ourselves, assuring us that it must certainly have been constructed for some such dreadful purpose. As, however, we were no believer in ghosts, we all agreed that the noises must proceed from somebody who had an interest in keeping the house empty; and since it was very disagreeable to imagine that there were secret means of entering it by night, we resolved, as soon as possible, to look out for another residence, and, in the meantime, to say nothing about the matter to anybody. About ten days after this determination, my mother, observing one morning that Creswell, when she came to dress her, looked exceedingly pale and ill, inquired if anything was the matter with her? "Indeed, my lady," answered she, "we have been frightened to death; and neither I nor Mrs Marsh can sleep again in the room we are now in."

"Well," returned my mother, "you shall both come and sleep in the little spare room next us; but what has alarmed you?"

"Someone, my lady, went through our room in the night; we both saw the figure, but we covered our heads with the bed-clothes, and lay in a dreadful fright till morning."

On hearing this, I could not help laughing, upon which Creswell burst into tears; and seeing how nervous she was, we comforted her by saying we had heard of a good house, and that we should very soon abandon our present habitation.

A few nights afterwards, my mother requested me and Charles to go into her bedroom, and fetch her frame, that she might prepare her work for the next day. It was after supper; and we were ascending the stairs by the light of a lamp which was always kept burning, when we saw going up before us, a tall, thin figure, with hair flowing down his back, and wearing a loose powdering gown. We both at once concluded it was my sister Hannah, and called out: "It won't do, Hannah! you cannot frighten us!" Upon which the figure turned into a recess in the wall; but as there was nobody there when we passed, we concluded that Hannah had contrived, somehow or other, to slip away and make her escape by the back stairs. On telling this to my mother, however, she said, "It is very odd, for Hannah went to bed with a headache before you came in from your walk"; and sure enough, on going to her room, there we found her fast asleep; and Alice, who was at work there, assured us that she had been so for more than an hour. On mentioning this circumstance to Creswell, she turned quite pale, and exclaimed that that was precisely the figure she and Marsh had seen in their bedroom.

About this time my brother Harry came to spend a few days with us, and we gave him a room up another pair of stairs, at the opposite end of the house. A morning or two after his arrival, when he came down to breakfast, he asked my mother, angrily, whether she thought he went to bed drunk and could not put out his own candle, that she sent those French rascals to watch him. My mother assured him that she had never thought of doing such a thing; but he persisted in the accusation, adding, "last night I jumped up and opened the door, and by the light of the moon, through the skylight, I saw the fellow in his loose gown at the bottom of the stairs. If I had not been in my shirt, I would have gone after him, and made him remember coming to watch me."

We were now preparing to quit the house, having secured another, belonging to a gentleman who was going to spend some time in Italy; but a few days before our removal, it happened that a Mr and Mrs Atkyns, some English friends of ours, called, to whom we mentioned these strange circumstances, observing how extremely unpleasant it was to live in a house that somebody found means of getting into, though how they contrived it we could not discover, nor what their motive could be, except it was to frighten us; observing that nobody could sleep in the room Marsh and Creswell had been obliged to give up. Upon this, Mrs Atkyns laughed heartily, and said that she should like, of all things, to sleep there, if my mother would allow her, adding that, with her little terrier, she should not be afraid of any ghost that ever appeared. As my mother had, of course, no objection to this fancy of hers, Mrs Atkyns requested her husband to ride home with the groom, in order that the latter might bring her night-things before the gates of the town were shut, as they were then residing a little way in the country. Mr Atkyns smiled, and said she was very bold; but he made no difficulties, and sent the things, and his wife retired with her dog to her room when we retired to ours, apparently without the least apprehension.

When she came down in the morning we were immediately struck at seeing her look very ill; and, on inquiring if she, too, had been frightened, she said she had been awakened in the night by something moving in her room, and that, by the light of the night lamp, she saw most distinctly a figure, and that the dog, which was very spirited and flew at everything, never stirred, although she endeavoured to make him. We saw clearly that she had been very much alarmed; and when Mr Atkyns came and endeavoured to dissipate the feeling by persuading her that she might have dreamt it, she got quite angry. We could not help thinking that she had actually seen something; and my mother said, after she was gone, that though she could not bring herself to believe it was really a ghost, still she earnestly hoped that she might get out of the house without seeing this figure which frightened people so much.

We were now within three days of the one fixed for our removal; I had been taking a long ride, and being tired, had fallen asleep the moment I lay down, but in the middle of the night I was suddenly awakened—I cannot tell by what, for the step over our heads we had become so used to that it no longer disturbed us. Well, I awoke; I had been lying with my face towards my mother, who was asleep beside me, and, as one usually does on awaking, I turned to the other side, where, the weather being warm, the curtain of the bed was undrawn, as it was also at the foot, and I saw standing by a chest of drawers, which were betwixt me and the window, a thin, tall figure, in a loose powdering gown, one arm resting on the drawers, and the face turned towards me. I saw it quite distinctly by the night-light, which burnt clearly; it was a long, thin, pale, young face, with oh! such a melancholy expression as can never be effaced from my memory! I was, certainly, very much frightened; but my great horror was lest my mother should awake and see the figure. I turned my head gently towards her, and heard her breathing high in a sound sleep. Just then the clock on the stairs struck four. I daresay it was nearly an hour before I ventured to look again; and when I did take courage to turn my eyes towards the drawers there was nothing, yet I had not heard the slightest sound, though I had been listening with the greatest intensity.

As you may suppose, I never closed my eyes again; and glad I was when Creswell knocked at the door, as she did every morning, for we always locked it, and it was my business to get out of bed and let her in. But on this occasion, instead of doing so, I called out, "Come in, the door is not fastened"; upon which she answered that it was, and I was obliged to get out of bed and admit her as usual.

When I told my mother what had happened she was very grateful to me for not waking her, and commended me much for my resolution; but as she was always my first object, that was not to be wondered at. She, however, resolved not to risk another night in the house, and we got out of it that very day, after instituting, with the aid of the servants, a thorough search, with a view to ascertain whether there was any possible means of getting into the rooms except by the usual modes of ingress; but our search was vain; none could be discovered.

Considering the number of people that were in the house, the fearlessness of the family, and their disinclination to believe in what is called the *supernatural*, together with the great interest the owner of this large and handsome house must have had in discovering the trick, if there had been one, I think it is difficult to find any other explanation of this strange story than that the sad and disappointed spirit of this poor injured, and probably murdered boy, had never been disengaged from its earthly relations, to which regret for its frustrated hopes and violated rights still held it attached.

XXXI
THE GHOST OF ROSEWARNE

From Hunt's "Romances of the West of England"

"Ezekiel Grosse, gent., attorney-at-law," bought the lands of Rosewarne from one of the De Rosewarnes, who had become involved in debt by endeavouring, without sufficient means, to support the dignity of his family. There is reason for believing that Ezekiel was the legal adviser of this unfortunate Rosewarne, and that he was not over-honest in his transactions with his client. However this may be, Ezekiel Grosse had scarcely made Rosewarne his dwelling-place, before he was alarmed by noises, at first of an unearthly character, and subsequently, one very dark night, by the appearance of the ghost himself in the form of a worn and aged man. The first appearance was in the park, but he subsequently repeated his visits in the house, but always after dark. Ezekiel Grosse was not a man to be terrified at trifles, and for some time he paid but slight attention to his nocturnal visitor. Howbeit the repetition of visits, and certain mysterious indications on the part of the ghost, became annoying to Ezekiel. One night, when seated in his office examining some deeds, and being rather irritable, having lost an important suit, his visitor approached him, making some strange indications which the lawyer could not understand. Ezekiel suddenly exclaimed, "In the name of God, what wantest thou?"

"To show thee, Ezekiel Grosse, where the gold for which thou longest lies buried."

No one ever lived upon whom the greed of gold was stronger than on Ezekiel, yet he hesitated now that his spectral friend had spoken so plainly, and trembled in every limb as the ghost slowly delivered himself in sepulchral tones of this telling speech.

The lawyer looked fixedly on the spectre; but he dared not utter a word. He longed to obtain possession of the secret, yet he feared to ask him where he was to find this treasure. The spectre looked as fixedly at the poor trembling lawyer, as if enjoying the sight of his terror. At length, lifting his finger, he beckoned Ezekiel to follow him, turning at the same time to leave the room. Ezekiel was glued to his seat; he could not exert strength enough to move, although he desired to do so.

"Come!" said the ghost, in a hollow voice. The lawyer was powerless to come.

"Gold!" exclaimed the old man, in a whining tone, though in a louder key.

"Where?" gasped Ezekiel.

"Follow me, and I will show thee," said the ghost. Ezekiel endeavoured to rise; but it was in vain.

"I command thee, come!" almost shrieked the ghost. Ezekiel felt that he was compelled to follow his friend; and by some supernatural power rather than his own, he followed the spectre out of the room, and through the hall, into the park.

They passed onward through the night—the ghost gliding before the lawyer, and guiding him by a peculiar phosphorescent light, which appeared to glow from every part of the form, until they arrived at a little dell, and had reached a small cairn formed of granite boulders. By this the spectre rested; and when Ezekiel had approached it, and was standing on the other side of the cairn, still trembling, the aged man, looking fixedly in his face, said, in low tones, "Ezekiel Grosse, thou longest for gold, as I did. I won the glittering prize, but I could not enjoy it. Heaps of treasure are buried beneath those stones; it is thine, if thou diggest for it. Win the gold, Ezekiel. Glitter with the wicked ones of the world; and when thou art the most joyous, I will look in upon thy happiness." The ghost then disappeared, and as soon as Grosse could recover himself from the extreme trepidation,—the result of mixed feelings,—he looked about him, and finding himself alone, he exclaimed, "Ghost or devil, I will soon prove whether or not thou liest!" Ezekiel is said to have heard a laugh, echoing between the hills, as he said those words.

The lawyer noted well the spot; returned to his house; pondered on all the circumstances of his case; and eventually resolved to seize the earliest opportunity, when he might do so unobserved, of removing the stones, and examining the ground beneath them.

A few nights after this, Ezekiel went to the little cairn, and by the aid of a crowbar, he soon overturned the stones, and laid the ground bare. He then commenced digging, and had not proceeded far when his spade struck against some other metal. He carefully cleared away the earth, and he then felt—for he could not see, having no light with him—that he had uncovered a metallic urn of some kind. He found it quite impossible to lift it, and he was therefore compelled to cover it up again, and to replace the stones sufficiently to hide it from the observation of any chance wanderer.

The next night Ezekiel found that this urn, which was of bronze, contained gold coins of a very ancient date. He loaded himself with his treasure, and returned home. From time to time, at night, as Ezekiel found he could do so without exciting the suspicions of his servants, he visited the urn, and thus by degrees removed all the treasure to Rosewarne House. There was nothing in the series of circumstances which had surrounded Ezekiel which he could less understand than the fact, that the ghost of the old man had left off troubling him from the moment when he had disclosed to him the hiding-place of this treasure.

The neighbouring gentry could not but observe the rapid improvements which Ezekiel Grosse made in his mansion, his grounds, in his personal appearance, and indeed in everything by which he was surrounded. In a short time he abandoned the law, and led in every respect the life of a country gentleman. He ostentatiously paraded his power to procure all earthly enjoyments, and, in spite of his notoriously bad character, he succeeded in drawing many of the landed proprietors around him.

Things went well with Ezekiel. The man who could in those days visit London in his own carriage and four was not without a large circle of flatterers. The lawyer who had struggled hard, in the outset of life, to secure wealth, and who did not always employ the most honest means for doing so, now found himself the centre of a circle to whom he could preach honesty, and receive from them expressions of the admiration in which the world holds the possessor of gold. His old tricks were forgotten, and he was put in places of honour. This state of things continued for some time; indeed, Grosse's entertainments became more and more splendid, and his revels more and more seductive to those he admitted to share them with him. The Lord of Rosewarne was the Lord of the West. To him everyone bowed the knee: he walked the earth as the proud possessor of a large share of the planet.

It was Christmas Eve, and a large gathering there was at Rosewarne. In the hall the ladies and gentlemen were in the full enjoyment of the dance, and in the kitchen all the tenantry and the servants were emulating their superiors. Everything went joyously; but when the mirth was in full swing, and Ezekiel felt to the full the influence of wealth, it appeared as if all in a moment the chill of death had fallen over everyone. The dancers paused, and looked one at another, each one struck with the other's paleness; and there, in the middle of the hall, everyone saw a strange old man looking angrily, but in silence, at Ezekiel Grosse, who was fixed in terror, blank as a statue.

No one had seen this old man enter the hall, yet there he was in the midst of them. It was but for a minute, and he was gone. Ezekiel, as if a frozen torrent of water had thawed in an instant, recovered himself, and roared at them.

"What do you think of that for a Christmas play? Ha, ha, ha! How frightened you all look! Butler, hand round the spiced wines! On with the dancing, my friends! It was only a trick, ay, and a clever one, which I have put upon you. On with your dancing, my friends!"

But with all his boisterous attempts to restore the spirit of the evening, Ezekiel could not succeed. There was an influence stronger than any he could command; and one by one, framing sundry excuses, his guests took their departure, every one of them satisfied that all was not right at Rosewarne.

From that Christmas Eve Grosse was a changed man. He tried to be his former self; but it was in vain. Again and again he called his gay companions around him; but at every feast there appeared one more than was desired. An aged man—weird beyond measure—took his place at the table in the middle of the feast; and although he spoke not, he exerted a miraculous power over all. No one dared to move; no one ventured to speak. Occasionally Ezekiel assumed an appearance of courage, which he felt not; rallied his guests, and made sundry excuses for the presence of his aged friend, whom he represented as having a mental infirmity, as being deaf and dumb. On all such occasions the old man rose from the table, and looking at the host, laughed a demoniac laugh of joy, and departed as quietly as he came.

The natural consequence of this was that Ezekiel Grosse's friends fell away from him, and he became a lonely man, amidst his vast possessions—his only companion being his faithful clerk, John Call.

The persecuting presence of the spectre became more and more constant; and wherever the poor lawyer went, there was the aged man at his side. From being one of the finest men in the county, he became a miserably attenuated and bowed old man. Misery was stamped on every feature—terror was indicated in every movement. At length he appears to have besought his ghostly attendant to free him of his presence. It was long before the ghost would listen to any terms; but when Ezekiel at length agreed to surrender the whole of his wealth to anyone whom the spectre might indicate, he obtained a promise that upon this being carried out, in a perfectly legal manner, in favour of John Call, that he should no longer be haunted.

This was, after numerous struggles on the part of Ezekiel to retain his property, or at least some portion of it, legally settled, and John Call became possessor of Rosewarne and the adjoining lands. Grosse was then informed that this evil spirit was one of the ancestors of the Rosewarne, from whom by his fraudulent dealings he obtained the place, and that he was allowed to visit the earth again for the purpose of inflicting the most condign punishment on the avaricious lawyer. His avarice had been gratified, his pride had been pampered to the highest; and then he was made a pitiful spectacle, at whom all men pointed, and no one pitied. He lived on in misery, but it was for a short time. He was found dead; and the country people ever said that his death was a violent one; they spoke of marks on his body, and some even asserted that the spectre of De Rosewarne was seen rejoicing amidst a crowd of devils, as they bore the spirit of Ezekiel over Carn Brea.

XXXII
THE IRON CHEST OF DURLEY

By Joseph Glanvil [12]

Mr *John Bourne*, for his Skill, Care and Honesty, was made by his Neighbour *John Mallet*, Esq., of *Enmore*, the chief of his Trustees, for his Son *John Mallet* (Father to Elizabeth, now Countess Dowager of *Rochester*) and the rest of his Children in Minority. He had the reputation of a worthy good Man, and was commonly taken notice of for an habitual Saying, by way of Interjection almost to anything, viz. *You say true, you say true, you are in the right.* This Mr Bourne fell sick at his House at Durley, in the year 1654, and Dr *Raymond of Oak* was sent for to him, who after some time, gave the said Mr Bourne over. And he had not now spoken in twenty-four Hours, when the said Dr Raymond, and Mrs *Carlisle* (Mr Bourne's Nephew's Wife, whose Husband he had made one of his Heirs) sitting by his bedside, the Doctor opened the Bed-curtains at the Bed's-feet, to give him air; when on a sudden, to the Horror and Amazement of Dr Raymond, and Mrs Carlisle, the great Iron Chest by the Window, at his Bed's-feet, with three Locks to it (in which were all the Writings and Evidences of the said Mr Mallet's Estate), began to open, first one Lock, and then another, then the third; afterwards the Lid of the Chest, lifted up of itself, and stood wide open. Then the patient, Mr Bourne, who had not spoke in 24 Hours, lifted himself up also, and looking upon the Chest, cry'd: *You say true, you say true, you are in the right, I'll be with you by and by.* So the Patient lay down, and spake no more. Then the Chest fell again of itself, and lock'd itself, one Lock after another, as the 3 Locks opened; and they tried to knock it open, and could not, and Mr Bourne died within an Hour after.

N.B. — This Narrative was sent in a Letter to J.C., directed for Dr H. More from Mr Thomas Alcock, of Shear-Hampton; of which in a Letter to the said Doctor, he gives this Account. I am, said he, very confident of the truth of the Story; for I had it from a very good Lady, the eldest daughter of the said John Mallet (whose Trustee Mr Bourne was) and only Aunt to the Countess of Rochester, who knew all the parties; and I have heard Dr Raymond, and Mr Carlisle, relate it often with amazement, being both Persons of Credit.

The curious may be inquisitive what the meaning of the opening of the Chest may be, and of Mr Bourne his saying *You say true, etc., I'll be with you by and by*. As for the former, it is noted by Paracelsus especially, and by others, that there are signs often given of the Departure of sick Men lying on their death beds, of which this opening of the Iron Coffer or Chest, and closing again, is more than ordinary significant, especially if we recall to mind that of Virgil:

"Olli dura quies oculos & *ferreus* urget
Somnus——"

Though this quaintness is more than is requisite in these Prodigies presaging the sick Man's Death. As for the latter, it seems to be nothing else but the saying *Amen* to the Presage, uttered in his accustomary form of Speech, as if he should say, you of the invisible Kingdom of Spirits, have given the Token of my sudden Departure, and you say true, I shall be with you by and by. Which he was enabled so assuredly to assent to, upon the advantage of the relaxation of his Soul now departing from the Body: Which Diodorus Siculus, lib. 18, notes to be the Opinion of Pythagoras and his followers, that it is the privilege of the Soul near her Departure, to exercise a fatidical Faculty, and to pronounce truly touching things future.

FOOTNOTES

[12] *Sadducismus Triumphatus.*

XXXIII
THE STRANGE CASE OF M. BEZUEL

From Christmas' "Phantom World"

"In 1695," said M. Bezuel, "being a schoolboy of about fifteen years of age, I became acquainted with the two children of M. Abaquene, attorney, schoolboys like myself. The eldest was of my own age, the second was eighteen months younger; he was named Desfontaines; we took all our walks and all our parties of pleasure together, and whether it was that Desfontaines had more affection for me, or that he was more gay, obliging, and clever than his brother, I loved him the best.

"In 1696, we were walking both of us in the cloister of the Capuchins. He told me that he had lately read a story of two friends who had promised each other that the first of them who died should come and bring news of his condition to the one still living; that the one who died came back to earth, and told his friend surprising things. Upon that, Desfontaines told me that he had a favour to ask me; that he begged me to grant it instantly; it was to make him a similar promise, and on his part he would do the same. I told him that I would not. For several months he talked to me of it, often and seriously; I always resisted his wish. At last, towards the month of August 1696, as he was to leave to go and study at Caen, he pressed me so much with tears in his eyes, that I consented to it. He drew out at that moment two little papers which he had ready written; one was signed with his blood, in which he promised me that in case of his death he would come and bring me news of his condition; in the other, I promised him the same thing. I pricked my finger; a drop of blood came with which I signed my name. He was delighted to have my billet, and embracing me, thanked me a thousand times.

"Some time after, he set off with his tutor. Our separation caused us much grief, but we wrote to each other now and then, and it was but six weeks since I had had a letter from him, when what I am going to relate to you happened to me.

"The 31st of July, 1697, one Thursday,—I shall remember it all my life,—the late M. Sorteville, with whom I lodged, and who had been very kind to me, begged of me to go to a meadow near the Cordeliers, and help his people, who were making hay, and to make haste. I had not been there a quarter of an hour, when, about half-past two, I all of a sudden felt giddy and weak. In vain I lent upon my hay-fork; I was obliged to place myself on a little hay, where I was nearly half an hour recovering my senses. That passed off; but as nothing of the kind had ever occurred to me before, I was surprised at it, and I feared it might be the commencement of an illness. Nevertheless, it did not make much impression upon me during the remainder of the day. It is true, I did not sleep that night so well as usual.

"The next day, at the same hour, as I was conducting to the meadow M. de St Simon, the grandson of M. de Sorteville, who was then ten years old, I felt myself seized on the way with a similar faintness, and I sat down on a stone in the shade. That passed off, and we continued our way; nothing more happened to me that day, and at night I had hardly any sleep.

"At last, on the morrow, the second day of August, being in the loft where they laid up the hay they brought from the meadow, I was taken with a similar giddiness and a similar faintness, but still more violent than the other. I fainted away completely; one of the men perceived it. I have been told that I was asked what was the matter with me, and that I replied, 'I have seen what I never should have believed'; but I have no recollection of either the question or the answer. That, however, accords with what I do remember to have seen just then; as it were someone naked to the middle, but whom, however, I did not recognise. They helped me down from the ladder. The faintness seized me again; my head swam as I was between two rounds of the ladder, and again I fainted. They took me down and placed me on a beam which served for a seat in the large square of the Capuchins. I sat down on it, and then I no longer saw M. de Sorteville nor his domestics, although present; but perceiving Desfontaines near the foot of the ladder, who made me a sign to come to him, I moved on my seat as if to make room for him; and those who saw me and whom I did not see, although my eyes were open, remarked this movement.

"As he did not come, I rose to go to him. He advanced towards me, took my left arm with his right arm, and led me about thirty paces from thence into a retired street, holding me still under the arm. The domestics, supposing that my giddiness had passed off, and that I had purposely retired, went everyone to their work, except a little servant who went and told M. de Sorteville that I was talking all alone. M. de Sorteville thought I was tipsy; he drew near, and heard me ask some questions, and make some answers, which he has told me since.

"I was there nearly three-quarters of an hour, conversing with Desfontaines. 'I promised you,' said he to me, 'that if I died before you I would come and tell you of it. I was drowned the day before yesterday in the river of Caen, at nearly this same hour. I was out walking with such and such a one. It was very warm, and we had a wish to bathe; a faintness seized me in the water, and I fell to the bottom. The Abbé de Menil-Jean, my comrade, dived to bring me up. I seized hold of his foot; but whether he was afraid it might be a salmon, because I held him so fast, or that he wished to remount promptly to the surface of the water, he shook his legs so roughly, that he gave me a violent kick on the breast, which sent me to the bottom of the river, which is there very deep.'

"Desfontaines related to me afterwards all that had occurred to them in their walk, and the subjects they had conversed upon. It was in vain for me to ask him questions—whether he was saved, whether he was damned, if he was in purgatory, if I was in a state of grace, and if I should soon follow him; he continued to discourse as if he had not heard me, and as if he would not hear me.

"I approached him several times to embrace him, but it seemed to me that I embraced nothing, and yet I felt very sensibly that he held me tightly by the arm, and that when I tried to turn away my head that I might not see him, because I could not look at him without feeling afflicted, he shook my arm as if to oblige me to look at and listen to him.

"He always appeared to me taller than I had seen him, and taller even than he was at the time of his death, although he had grown during the eighteen months in which we had not met. I beheld him always naked to the middle of his body, his head uncovered, with his fine hair, and a white scroll twisted in his hair over his forehead, on which there was some writing, but I could only make out the word *In*....

"It was his usual tone of voice. He appeared to me neither gay nor sad, but in a calm and tranquil state. He begged of me, when his brother returned, to tell him certain things to say to his father and mother. He begged me to say the Seven Psalms which had been given him as a penance the preceding Sunday, which he had not yet recited; again he recommended me to speak to his brother, and then he bade me adieu, saying, as he left me, '*Jusques*, *jusques*' (*till, till*), which was the usual term he made use of when at the end of our walk we bade each other good-bye, to go home.

"He told me that at the time he was drowned, his brother, who was writing a translation, regretted having let him go without accompanying him, fearing some accident. He described to me so well where he was drowned, and the tree in the avenue of Louvigni on which he had written a few words, that two years afterwards, being there with the late Chevalier de Getel, one of these who were with him at the time he was drowned, I pointed out to him the very spot; and by counting the trees in a particular direction which Desfontaines had specified to me, I went straight up to the tree, and I found his writing. He (the Chevalier) told me also that the article of the Seven Psalms was true, and that on coming from confession that they had told each other their penance; and since then his brother has told me that it was quite true that at that hour he was writing his exercise, and he reproached himself for not having accompanied his brother. As nearly a month passed by without my being able to do what Desfontaines had told me in regard to his brother, he appeared to me again twice before dinner at a country house whither I had gone to dine a league from hence. I was very faint. I told them not to mind me, that it was nothing, and that I should soon recover myself; and I went to a corner of the garden. Desfontaines having appeared to me, reproached me for not having yet spoken to his brother, and again conversed with me for a quarter of an hour without answering any of my questions.

"As I was going in the morning to Notre-Dame de la Victoire, he appeared to me again, but for a shorter time, and pressed me always to speak to his brother, and left me, saying still, '*Jusques, jusques*,' without choosing to reply to my questions.

"It is a remarkable thing that I always felt a pain in that part of my arm which he had held me by the first time, until I had spoken to his brother. I was three days without being able to sleep, from the astonishment and agitation I felt. At the end of the first conversation, I told M. de Varonville, my neighbour and schoolfellow, that Desfontaines had been drowned; that he himself had just appeared to me and told me so. He went away and ran to the parents' house to know if it was true; they had just received the news, but by a mistake he understood that it was the eldest. He assured me that he had read the letter of Desfontaines, and he believed it; but I maintained always that it could not be, and that Desfontaines himself had appeared to me. He returned, came back, and told me in tears that it was but too true."

XXXIV
THE MARQUIS DE RAMBOUILLET

"The Phantom World"

The Marquis de Rambouillet, eldest brother of the Duchess of Montauzier, and the Marquis de Precy, eldest son of the family of Nantouillet, both of them between twenty and thirty, were intimate friends, and went to the wars, as in France do all men of quality. As they were conversing one day together on the subject of the other world, they promised each other that the first who died should come and bring the news to his companion. At the end of three months the Marquis de Rambouillet set off for Flanders, where the war was then being carried on; and de Precy, detained by a high fever, remained at Paris. Six weeks afterwards de Precy, at six in the morning, heard the curtains of his bed drawn, and turning to see who it was, he perceived the Marquis de Rambouillet in his buff vest and boots; he sprung out of bed to embrace him to show his joy at his return, but Rambouillet, retreating a few steps, told him that these caresses were no longer seasonable, for he only came to keep his word with him; that he had been killed the day before on such an occasion; that all that was said of the other world was certainly true; that he must think of leading a different life; and that he had no time to lose, as he would be killed the first action he was engaged in.

It is impossible to express the surprise of the Marquis de Precy at this discourse; as he could not believe what he heard, he made several efforts to embrace his friend, whom he thought desirous of deceiving him, but he embraced only air; and Rambouillet, seeing that he was incredulous, showed the wound he had received, which was in the side, whence the blood still appeared to flow. After that the phantom disappeared, and left de Precy in a state of alarm more easy to comprehend than describe; he called at the same time his *valet de chambre*, and awakened all the family with his cries. Several persons ran to his room, and he related to them what he had just seen. Everyone attributed this vision to the violence of the fever, which might have deranged his imagination; they begged of him to go to bed again, assuring him that he must have dreamt what he told them.

The Marquis, in despair, on seeing that they took him for a visionary, related all the circumstances I have just recounted; but it was in vain for him to protest that he had seen and heard his friend, being wideawake; they persisted in the same idea until the arrival of the post from Flanders, which brought the news of the death of the Marquis de Rambouillet.

This first circumstance being found true, and in the same manner as de Precy had said, those to whom he had related the adventure began to think that there might be something in it, because Rambouillet having been killed precisely on the eve of the day he had said it, it was impossible de Precy should have known of it in a natural way. This event having spread in Paris, they thought it was the effect of a disturbed imagination, or a made-up story; and whatever might be said by the persons who examined the thing seriously, there remained in people's minds a suspicion, which time alone could disperse: this depended upon what might happen to Marquis de Precy, who was threatened that he should be slain in the first engagement; thus everyone regarded his fate as the *dénouement* of the piece; but he soon confirmed everything they had doubted the truth of, for as soon as he recovered from his illness he would go to the combat of St Antoine, although his father and mother, who were afraid of the prophecy, said all they could to prevent him; he was killed there, to the great regret of all his family.

XXXV
THE ALTHEIM REVENANT

"The Phantom World"

A monk of the Abbey of Toussaints relates that on the 9th of September 1625 a man named John Steinlin died at a place called Altheim, in the diocese of Constance. Steinlin was a man in easy circumstances, and a common-councilman of his town. Some days after his death he appeared during the night to a tailor, named Simon Bauh, in the form of a man surrounded by a sombre flame, like that of lighted sulphur, going and coming in his own house, but without speaking. Bauh, who was disquieted by this sight, resolved to ask him what he could do to serve him. He found an opportunity to do so, the 17th of November in the same year, 1625; for, as he was reposing at night near his stove, a little after eleven o'clock, he beheld this spectre environed by fire like sulphur, who came into his room, going and coming, shutting and opening the windows. The tailor asked him what he desired. He replied, in a hoarse interrupted voice, that he could help very much, if he would; "but," added he, "do not promise me to do so, if you are not resolved to execute your promises." "I will execute them, if they are not beyond my power," replied he.

"I wish, then," replied the spirit, "that you would cause a mass to be said, in the Chapel of the Virgin at Rotembourg; I made a vow to that intent during my life, and I have not acquitted myself of it. Moreover, you must have two masses said at Altheim, the one of the Defunct and the other of the Virgin; and as I did not always pay my servants exactly, I wish that a quarter of corn should be distributed to the poor." Simon promised to satisfy him on all these points. The spectre held out his hand, as if to ensure his promise; but Simon, fearing that some harm might happen to himself, tendered him the board which came to hand, and the spectre having touched it, left the print of his hand with the four fingers and thumb, as if fire had been there, and had left a pretty deep impression. After that he vanished with so much noise that it was heard three houses off.

XXXVI
SERTORIUS AND HIS HIND

North's "Plutarch"

So soone as Sertorius arriued from Africa, he straight leauied men of warre, and with them subdued the people of Spaine fronting upon his marches, of which the more part did willingly submit themselues, upon the bruit that ran of him to be merciful and courteous, and a valiant man besides in present danger. Furthermore, he lacked no fine deuises and subtilties to win their goodwills: as among others, the policy, and deuise of the hind. There was a poore man of the countrey called Spanus, who meeting by chance one day with a hind in his way that had newly calued, flying from the hunters, he let the damme go, not being able to take her; and running after her calfe tooke it, which was a young hind, and of a strange haire, for she was all milk-white. It chanced so, that Sertorius was at that time in those parts. So, this poore man presented Sertorius with his young hind, which he gladly receiued, and which with time he made so tame, that she would come to him when he called her, and follow him whereeuer he went, being nothing the wilder for the daily sight of such a number of armed souldiers together as they were, nor yet afraid of the noise and tumult of the campe. Insomuch as Sertorius by little and little made it a miracle, making the simple barbarous people beleeue that it was a gift that Diana had sent him, by the which she made him understand of many and sundrie things to come: knowing well inough of himselfe, that the barbarous people were men easily deceiued, and quickly caught by any subtill superstition, besides that by art also he brought them to beleeue it as a thing verie true. For when he had any secret intelligence giuen him, that the enemies would inuade some part of the countries and prouinces subject vnto him, or that they had taken any of his forts from him by any intelligence or sudden attempt, he straight told them that his hind spake to him as he slept, and had warned him both to arme his men, and put himselfe in strength. In like manner if he had heard any newes that one of his lieutenants had wonne a battell, or that he had any aduantage of his enemies, he would hide the messenger, and bring his hind abroad with a garland and coller of nosegayes: and then say, it was a token of some good newes comming towards him, perswading them withall to be of good cheare; and so did sacrifice to the gods, to giue them thankes for the good tidings he should heare before it were long. Thus by putting this superstition into their heades, he made them the more tractable and obedient to his will, in so much as they thought they were not now gouerned any more by a stranger wiser than themselues, but were steadfastly perswaded that they were rather led by some certaine god.——

Now was Sertorius very heauie, that no man could tell him what was become of his white hind: for thereby all his subtilltie and finenesse to keepe the barbarous people in obedience was taken away, and then specially when they stood in need of most comfort. But by good hap, certaine of his souldiers that had lost themselves in the night, met with the hind in their way, and knowing her by her colour, tooke her and brought her backe againe. Sertorius hearing of her, promised them a good reward, so that they would tell no liuing creature that they brought her againe, and thereupon made her to be secretly kept. Then within a few dayes after, he came abroad among them, and with a pleasant countenance told the noble men and chiefe captaines of these barbarous people, how the gods had reuealed it to him in his dreame, that he should shortly haue a maruellous good thing happen to him: and with these words sate downe in his chaire to giue audience. Whereupon they that kept the hind not farre from thence, did secretly let her go. The hind being loose, when she had spied Sertorius, ranne straight to his chaire with great joy, and put her head betwixt his legges, and layed her mouth in his right hand, as she before was wont to do. Sertorius also made very much of her, and of purpose appeared maruellous glad, shewing much tender affection to the hind, as it seemed the water stood in his eyes for joy. The barbarous people that stood there by and beheld the same, at the first were much amazed therewith, but afterwards when they had better bethought themselues, for ioy they clapped their hands together, and waited upon Sertorius to his lodging with great and ioyfull shouts, saying, and steadfastly beleeuing, that he was a heavenly creature, and beloued of the gods.

XXXVII
ERICHTHO

By E.W. Godwin. (From Lucan.)

When Sextus sought Erichtho he chose his time in the depth of the night, when the sun is at its lowermost distance from the upper sky. He took for companions the associates of his crimes. Wandering among broken graves and crumbling sepulchres, they discovered her, sitting sublime on a ragged rock, where Mount Hæmus stretches its roots to the Pharsalic field. She was mumbling charms of the Magi and the magical gods. For she feared that the war might yet be transferred to other than the Emathian fields. The sorceress was busy therefore enchanting the soil of Philippi, and scattering on its surface the juice of potent herbs, that it might be heaped with carcasses of the dead, and saturated with their blood, that Macedon, and not Italy, might receive the bodies of departed kings and the bones of the noble, and might be amply peopled with the shades of men. Her choicest labour was as to the earth where should be deposited the prostrate Pompey, or the limbs of the mighty Cæsar.

Sextus approached, and bespoke her thus: "Oh, glory of Hæmonia, that hast the power to divulge the fates of men, or canst turn aside fate itself from its prescribed course, I pray thee to exercise thy gift in disclosing events to come. Not the meanest of the Roman race am I, the offspring of an illustrious chieftain, lord of the world in the one case, or in the other the destined heir to my father's calamity. I stand on a tremendous and giddy height: snatch me from this posture of doubt; let me not blindly rush on, and blindly fall; extort this secret from the gods, or force the dead to confess what they know."

To whom the Thessalian crone replied: "If you asked to change the fate of an individual, though it were to restore an old man, decrepit with age, to vigorous youth, I could comply; but to break the eternal chain of causes and consequences exceeds even our power. You seek, however, only a foreknowledge of events to come, and you shall be gratified. Meanwhile it were best, where slaughter has afforded so ample a field, to select the body of one newly deceased, and whose flexible organs shall be yet capable of speech, not with lineaments already hardened in the sun."

Saying thus, Erichtho proceeded (having first with her art made the night itself more dark, and involved her head in a pitchy cloud), to explore the field, and examine one by one the bodies of the unburied dead. As she approached, the wolves fled before her, and the birds of prey, unwillingly sheathing their talons, abandoned their repast, while the Thessalian witch, searching into the vital parts of the frames before her, at length fixed on one whose lungs were uninjured, and whose organs of speech had sustained no wound. The fate of many hung in doubt, till she had made her selection. Had the revival of whole armies been her will, armies would have stood up obedient to her bidding. She passed a hook beneath the jaw of the selected one, and, fastening it to a cord, dragged him along over rocks and stones, till she reached a cave, overhung by a projecting ridge. A gloomy fissure in the ground was there, of a depth almost reaching to the infernal gods, where the yew-tree spread thick its horizontal branches, at all times excluding the light of the sun. Fearful and withering shade was there, and noisome slime cherished by the livelong night. The air was heavy and flagging as that of the Tænarian promontory; and hither the god of hell permits his ghosts to extend their wanderings. It is doubtful whether the sorceress called up the dead to attend her here, or herself descended to the abodes of Pluto. She put on a fearful and variegated robe; she covered her face with her dishevelled hair, and bound her brow with a wreath of vipers.

Meanwhile she observed Sextus afraid, with his eyes fixed on the ground, and his companions trembling; and thus she reproached them. "Lay aside," she said, "your vainly-conceived terrors! You shall behold only a living and a human figure, whose accents you may listen to with perfect security. If this alarms you, what would you say if you should have seen the Stygian lakes, and the shores burning with sulphur unconsumed, if the Furies stood before you, and Cerberus with his mane of vipers, and the Giants chained in eternal adamant? Yet all these you might have witnessed unharmed; for all these would quail at the terror of my brow."

She spoke, and next plied the dead body with her arts. She supples his wounds, and infuses fresh blood into his veins: she frees his scars from the clotted gore, and penetrates them with froth from the moon. She mixes whatever nature has engendered in its most fearful caprices, foam from the jaws of a mad dog, the entrails of the lynx, the backbone of the hyena, and the marrow of a stag that had dieted on serpents, the sinews of the remora, and the eyes of a dragon, the eggs of the eagle, the flying serpent of Arabia, the viper that guards the pearl in the Red Sea, the slough of the hooded snake, and the ashes that remain when the phœnix has been consumed. To these she adds all venom that has a name, the foliage of herbs over which she has sung her charms, and on which she had voided her rheum as they grew.

At length she chants her incantation to the Stygian Gods, in a voice compounded of all discords, and altogether alien to human organs. It resembles at once the barking of a dog and the howl of a wolf; it consists of the hooting of the screech-owl, the yelling of a ravenous wild beast, and the fearful hiss of a serpent. It borrows somewhat from the roar of tempestuous waves, the hollow rushing of the winds among the branches of the forest, and the tremendous crash of deafening thunder.

"Ye Furies," she cries, "and dreadful Styx, ye sufferings of the damned, and Chaos, for ever eager to destroy the fair harmony of worlds, and thou, Pluto, condemned, to an eternity of ungrateful existence, Hell, and Elysium, of which no Thessalian witch shall partake, Proserpine, for ever cut off from thy health-giving mother, and horrid Hecate, Cerberus curst with incessant hunger, ye Destinies, and Charon endlessly murmuring at the task I impose of bringing back the dead again to the land of the living, hear me!—if I call on you with a voice sufficiently impious and abominable, if I have never sung this chaunt, unsated with human gore, if I have frequently laid on your altars the fruit of the pregnant mother, bathing its contents with the reeking brain, if I have placed on a dish before you the head and entrails of an infant on the point to be born——

"I ask not of you a ghost, already a tenant of the Tartarean abodes, and long familiarised to the shades below, but one who has recently quitted the light of day, and who yet hovers over the mouth of hell; let him hear these incantations, and immediately after descend to his destined place! Let him articulate suitable omens to the son of his general, having so late been himself a soldier of the great Pompey! Do this, as you love the very sound and rumour of a civil war!"

Saying this, behold, the ghost of the dead man stood erect before her, trembling at the view of his own unanimated limbs, and loth to enter again the confines of his wonted prison. He shrinks to invest himself with the gored bosom, and the fibres from which death had separated him. Unhappy wretch, to whom death had not given the privilege to die! Erichtho, impatient at the unlooked-for delay, lashes the unmoving corpse with one of her serpents. She calls anew on the powers of hell, and threatens to pronounce the dreadful name, which cannot be articulated without consequences never to be thought of, nor without the direst necessity to be ventured upon.

At length the congealed blood becomes liquid and warm; it oozes from the wounds, and creeps steadily along the veins and the members; the fibres are called into action beneath the gelid breast, and the nerves once more become instinct with life. Life and death are there at once. The arteries beat; the muscles are braced; the body raises itself, not by degrees, but at a single impulse, and stands erect. The eyelids unclose. The countenance is not that of a living subject, but of the dead. The paleness of the complexion, the rigidity of the lines, remain; and he looks about with an unmeaning stare, but utters no sound. He waits on the potent enchantress.

"Speak!" said she, "and ample shall be your reward. You shall not again be subject to the art of the magician. I will commit your members to such a sepulchre; I will burn your form with such wood, and will chaunt such a charm over your funeral pyre, that all incantations shall thereafter assail you in vain. Be it enough, that you have once been brought back to life! Tripods, and the voice of oracles deal in ambiguous responses; but the voice of the dead is perspicuous and certain to him who receives it with an unshrinking spirit. Spare not! Give names to things; give places a clear designation, speak with a full and articulate voice."

Saying this, she added a further spell, qualified to give to him who was to answer, a distinct knowledge of that respecting which he was about to be consulted. He accordingly delivers the responses demanded of him; and, that done, earnestly requires of the witch to be dismissed. Herbs and magic rites are necessary, that the corpse may be again unanimated, and the spirit never more be liable to be recalled to the realms of day. The sorceress constructs the funeral pile; the dead man places himself upon it; Erichtho applies the torch, and the charm is ended for ever.

III
OMENS AND PHANTASMS

XXXVIII
PATROKLOS

Homer's *Iliad* (E.H. Blakeney's translation [13])

Then there came unto him the ghost of poor Patroklos, in all things like unto the very man, in stature, and fair eyes, and voice; and he was arrayed in vesture such as in life he wore. He stood above the hero's head and challenged him:—

"Thou sleepest, Achilles, unmindful of me. Not in my lifetime wert thou neglectful, but in death. Bury me with all speed; let me pass the gates of Hades. Far off the souls, wraiths of the dead, keep me back, nor suffer me yet to join them beyond the river; forlorn I wander up and down the wide-doored house of Hades. And now give me thy hand, I entreat; for never more shall I return from Hades, when once ye have given me my meed of fire. Nay, never more shall we sit, at least in life, apart from our comrades, taking counsel together; but upon me hateful doom hath gaped—doom which was my portion even at birth. Aye and to thee thyself also, Achilles, thou peer of the gods, it is fated to perish beneath the wall of the wealthy Trojans. Another thing I will tell thee, and will straitly charge thee, if peradventure thou wilt hearken: lay not my bones apart from thine, Achilles, but side by side; for we were brought up together in thy house, when Menoitios brought me, a child, from Opöeis to thy father's house because of woeful bloodshed on the day when I slew the son of Amphidamas, myself a child, unwittingly, but in wrath over our games. Then did Peleus, the knight, take me into his home and rear me kindly and name me thy squire. So let one urn also hide the bones of us both."

And swift-footed Achilles answered him and said:—

"Why, dearest and best-beloved, hast thou come hither to lay upon me these thy several behests? Of a truth I will accomplish all, and bow to thy command. But stand nearer, I pray; for a little space let us cast our arms about each other, and take our fill of dire sorrow."

With these words he stretched forth his hands to clasp him, but could not; for, like a smoke, the spirit vanished earthward with a wailing cry. Amazed, Achilles sprang up, and smote his hands together, and spake a piteous word:—

"O ye heavens! surely, even among the dead, the soul and wraith are something (yet is there no life therein at all). For all night long the soul of poor Patroklos stood beside me, crying and making lamentation, and bade me do his will; it was the perfect image of himself."

So he spake, and in the hearts of them all roused desire for lamentation; and while they yet were mourning about the pitiful corpse appeared rosy-fingered dawn.

FOOTNOTES

[13] George Bell & Sons.

XXXIX
VISION OF CROMWELL

By "Arise Evans"

A vision that I had presently after the king's death—I thought that I was in a great hall, like the king's hall, or the castle in Winchester, and there was none there but a judge that sat upon the bench and myself; and as I turned to a window in the north-westward, and looking into the palm of my hand, there appeared to me a face, head and shoulders like the Lord Fairfax's, and presently it vanished. Again, there arose the Lord Cromwell, and he vanished likewise; then arose a young face and he had a crown upon his head, and he vanished also; and another young face arose with a crown upon his head, and he vanished also; and another young face arose with a crown upon his head, and vanished in like manner; and as I turned the palm of my hand back again to me and looked, there did appear no more in it. Then I turned to the judge and said to him, there arose in my hand seven, and five of them had crowns; but when I turned my hand, the blood turned to its veins, and these appeared no more: so I awoke. The interpretation of this vision is, that after the Lord Cromwell, there shall be kings again in England, which thing is signified unto us by those that arose after him, who were all crowned, but the generations to come may look for a change of the blood, and of the name in the royal seat, after five kings once passed, 2 Kings x. 30. (The words referred to in this text are these:) "And the Lord said unto Jehu, because thou hast done well, etc., thy children of the fourth generation shall sit upon the throne of Israel."

XL
LORD STRAFFORD'S WARNING

By the Rev. John Mastin

In the Rev. John Mastin's *History of Naseby* is cited a story of an apparition that was supposed to have appeared to Charles the First at Daintree, near Naseby, previous to the famous battle of that name.

The army of Charles, says the historian, consisting of less than 5000 foot, and about as many horse, was ordered to Daintree, whither the King went with a thorough resolution of fighting. The next day, however, to the surprise of Prince Rupert and all the rest of the army, this design was given up, and the former one of going to the north resumed. The reason of this alteration in his plans was alleged to be some presages of ill-fortune which the King had received, and which were related to me, says Mr Mastin's authority, by a person of Newark, at that time in His Majesty's horse. About two hours after the King had retired to rest, said the narrator, some of his attendants hearing an uncommon noise in his chamber, went into it, where they found His Majesty sitting up in bed and much agitated, but nothing which could have produced the noise they fancied they had heard. The King, in a tremulous voice, inquired after the cause of their alarm, and told them how much he had been disturbed, apparently by a dream, by thinking he had seen an apparition of Lord Strafford, who, after upbraiding him for his cruelty, told him he was come to return him good for evil, and that he advised him by no means to fight the Parliament army that was at that time quartered at Northampton, for it was one which the King could never conquer by arms. Prince Rupert, in whom courage was the predominant quality, rated the King out of his apprehensions the next day, and a resolution was again taken to meet the enemy. The next night, however, the apparition appeared to him a second time, but with looks of anger assuring him that would be the last advice he should be permitted to give him, but that if he kept his resolution of fighting he was undone. If His Majesty had taken the advice of the friendly ghost, and marched northward the next day, where the Parliament had few English forces, and where the Scots were becoming very discontented, his affairs might, perhaps, still have had a prosperous issue, or if he had marched immediately into the west he might afterwards have fought on more equal terms. But the King, fluctuating between the apprehensions of his imagination and the reproaches of his courage, remained another whole day at Daintree in a state of inactivity. The battle of Naseby, fought 14th June 1645, put a finishing stroke to the King's affairs. After this he could never get together an army fit to look the enemy in the face. He was often heard to say that he wished he had taken *the warning*, and not fought at Naseby; the meaning of which nobody knew but those to whom he had told of the apparition which he had seen at Daintree, and all of whom were, subsequently, charged to keep the affair secret.

XLI
KOTTER'S RED CIRCLE

From Ferrier's "Apparitions"

Kotter's first vision was detailed by him, on oath, before the magistrates of Sprottaw, in 1619. While he was travelling on foot, in open daylight, in June 1616, a man appeared to him, who ordered him to inform the civil and ecclesiastical authorities, that great evils were impending over Germany, for the punishment of the sins of the people; after which he vanished. The same apparition met him at different times, and compelled him at length, by threats, to make this public declaration.

After this, his visions assumed a more imposing appearance: on one occasion the angel (for such he was now confessed to be) showed him three suns, filling one half of the heavens; and nine moons, with their horns turned towards the east, filling the other half. At the same time, a superb fountain of pure water spouted from the arid soil, under his feet.

At another time, he beheld a mighty lion, treading on the moon, and seven other lions around him, in the clouds.

Sometimes he beheld the encounter of hostile armies, splendidly accoutred; sometimes he wandered through palaces, whose only inhabitants were devouring monsters; or beheld dragons of enormous size, in various scenes of action.

He was at length attended by two angels, in his ecstasy; one of his visions at this time was of the most formidable and impressive kind. "On the 13th day of September, says he, both the youths returned to me, saying, be not afraid, but observe the thing which will be shewn to thee. And I suddenly beheld a circle, like the sun, red, and as it were, bloody: in which were black and white lines, or spots, so intermingled, that sometimes there appeared a greater number of blacks, sometimes of white; and this sight continued for some space of time. And when they had said to me, Behold!

Attend! Fear not! No evil will befal thee! Lo, there were three successive peals of thunder, at short intervals, so loud and dreadful, that I shuddered all over. But the circle stood before me, and the black and white spots were disunited, and the circle approached so near that I could have touched it with my hand. And it was so beautiful, that I had never in my life seen any thing more agreeable: and the white spots were so bright and pleasant, that I could not contain my admiration. But the black spots were carried away in cloud of horrible darkness, in which I heard a dismal outcry, though I could see no one. Yet these words of lamentation were audible: Woe unto us, who have committed ourselves unto the black cloud, to be withdrawn from the circle coloured with the blood of divine grace, in which the grace of God, in his well-beloved Son, had inclosed us."

After several other piteous exclamations, he saw a procession of many thousand persons, bearing palms, and singing hymns, but of very small stature, enter the red circle, from the black cloud, chanting halleluiah.

XLII
THE VISION OF CHARLES XI. OF SWEDEN

From a *Procés-verbal*

The authenticity of the following narrative rests upon a *procés-verbal*, drawn out in form, and attested by the signatures of four credible witnesses.

Charles XI. was one of the most despotic and, at the same time, one of the ablest monarchs that ever ruled the destinies of Sweden. History represents him as brave and enlightened, but of a harsh and inflexible disposition; regulating his opinions by positive facts, and wholly ungifted with imagination. At the period of which we are about to speak, death had bereaved him of his Queen, Ulrica Eleonora. Notwithstanding the harshness which had marked his conduct to the Princess during her lifetime, and which, in the opinion of his subjects, had precipitated her into the grave, Charles revered her memory, and appeared more affected by her loss than might have been imagined from the natural sternness of his character. Subsequently to this event, he became more gloomy and taciturn than before, and devoted himself to study with an intensity of application that evinced his anxiety to escape the tortures of his own painful reflections. Towards the close of a dreary autumnal evening, the king, in slippers and *robe de chambre*, was seated before a large fire, in a private cabinet of his palace at Stockholm. Near him were his grand chamberlain, the Count de Brahe, who was honoured with the favourite estimation of his sovereign, and the principal state physician, Baumgarten, a learned disciple of Hippocrates, who aimed at the reputation of an *esprit fort*, and who would have pardoned a disbelief in anything except in the efficacy of his own prescriptions. The last-mentioned personage had on that evening been hastily summoned to the presence of the monarch, who felt or fancied himself in need of his professional skill. The evening was already far advanced, and the king, contrary to his wont, delayed bidding the customary "goodnight to all," — the well-understood signal at which his guests always retired. With his head bent down, and his eyes fixed upon the decaying embers, that gradually withdrew even their mockery of warmth from the spacious fireplace, he maintained a strict silence, evidently fatigued with his company, yet dreading, though he scarcely knew why, to be left alone. The grand chamberlain, who perceived that even his profound remarks failed to excite the attention of the monarch, ventured to hint that his majesty would do well to seek repose; a gesture of the king retained him in his place. The physician, in his turn, hazarded a casual observation on the injurious tendency of late hours. The significant innuendoes were, however, thrown away on Charles, who replied to them by muttering between his teeth, "You may remain; I have no wish to sleep." This permission, with which the drowsy courtiers would willingly have dispensed, but which was really equivalent to a command, was succeeded by an attempt on their part to enliven his majesty with different subjects of conversation. No topic, however, that they introduced could outlive the second or third phrase. The king was in one of his gloomy moods; for royalty, with reverence be it spoken, has its moments of merriment and ill-humour, its mixture of sunshine and of cloud; and be it known to thee, gentle reader, that ticklish is the position of a courtier when majesty is in the dumps. To mend, or rather to mar the matter, the grand chamberlain, imagining that the sadness which overshadowed the royal brow came from regret, fixed his eyes upon a portrait of the queen, hung up in the cabinet, and with a sigh of pathos exclaimed, "How striking the resemblance! and who could not recognise the expression of majesty and gentleness, that—" "Fudge!" cried the king. Conscience had probably something to do with the abruptness of the exclamation. The old chamberlain had unwittingly touched a tender chord; every allusion to the queen appearing like a tacit reproach to the august and widowed spouse. "That portrait," added the king, "is too flattering, the queen was far from handsome"; then, as if inwardly repentant of his harshness, he rose from his seat and paced the apartment with hasty strides, to conceal the tears that had well-nigh betrayed his emotion. He sat in the embrasure of a window which looked upon the court; the moon was obscured by a thick veil of clouds; not even a solitary star twinkled through the darkness. The palace at present inhabited by the kings of Sweden was not at that time finished; and Charles XI., in whose reign it had been commenced, usually resided in an old-fashioned edifice, built something in the shape of a horseshoe, and situated at the point of Ritterholm, commanding a view of Lake Mader. The royal cabinet was at one of the extremities, nearly opposite to the grand hall or council-chamber, in which the States were accustomed to assemble when a message or communication from the crown was expected. Just at this moment the windows of the council-chamber appeared brilliantly illuminated. The king was lost in surprise. He at first imagined the light to proceed from the torch of some domestic. Yet what could occasion so unseasonable a visit to a place that for a considerable time had been closed? Besides, the light was too vivid to be produced by one single torch, it might have been attributed to a conflagration; but no smoke was perceptible, no noise was heard, the window glasses were not broken, everything in short seemed to indicate an illumination, such as takes place on public and solemn occasions. Charles, without uttering a word, remained gazing at the windows of the council-chamber. The Count Brahe, who had already grasped the bell-cord, was on the point of summoning a page, in order to ascertain the cause of this singular illumination, when the king suddenly prevented him. "I will visit the chamber myself," said his majesty; the seriousness of his deportment and the paleness of his countenance indicating a strange mixture of determination and superstitious awe. He quitted the cabinet with the unhesitating step of one resolved to obtain mastery over himself; the legislator of etiquette, and the regulator of bodies, each with a lighted taper, followed him with fear and trembling. The keeper of the keys had already retired to rest; Baumgarten was despatched by the king to awaken him, and to order him forthwith to open the doors of the council-chamber. Unbounded was the worthy keeper's surprise at the unexpected intimation. Benign Providence, however, has ordained monarchs to command, and created keepers of keys to obey. The prudent Cerberus yawned, dressed himself in haste, and presented himself before his sovereign with the insignia of his office, a bunch of keys of various dimensions suspended at his girdle. He commenced by opening the door of a gallery, which served as a sort of ante-room to the council-chamber. The king entered; but his astonishment may be conceived, on finding the walls of the building entirely hung with black. "By whose order has this been done?" demanded the king in a tone of anger. "Sire," replied the trembling keeper of the keys, "I am ignorant; the last time the gallery was opened it was wainscoted with oak, as usual, most assuredly these hangings are not from your majesty's wardrobe." The king, however, had by this time traversed at a rapid pace two-thirds of the gallery, without stopping to avail himself of the worshipful warden's conjectures. The latter personage and the grand chamberlain followed his majesty, whilst the learned doctor lingered a little in the rear. "Sire," cried the keeper of the keys, "I beseech your majesty to go no farther. As I have a living soul, there is witchcraft in this matter. At this hour ... and since the death of the queen, God be gracious to us! It is said that her majesty walks every night in this gallery." "Hold, Sire!" cried the Count in his turn, "do you not hear a strange noise which seems to proceed from the council-chamber? Who can foresee the danger to which your majesty may expose your sacred person?" "Forward!" replied the resolute monarch in an imperative tone; and as he stopped before the door of the council-chamber, "Quick! your keys!" said he to the keeper. He pushed the door violently with his foot, and the noise, repeated by the echoes of the vaulted roof, resounded through the gallery like the report of a cannon. The old keeper trembled; he tried one key, then another, but without success; his hand shook, his sight was confused. "A soldier, and afraid?" cried Charles with a smile. "Come, Count, you must be our usher: open that door." "Sire," replied the grand chamberlain stepping backwards, "if your majesty command me to walk up to the mouth of a Danish cannon, I will obey on the instant; but you will not order me to combat with the devil and his imps?" The monarch snatched the keys from the palsied hands of the infirm old keeper. "I see," said his majesty in a tone of contempt, "that I must finish this adventure"; and before his terrified suite could prevent his design, he had already opened the massy oaken door, and penetrated into the council-chamber, first pronouncing the usual formula, "with the help of God." The companions of his midnight excursion entered along with him, prompted by a sentiment of curiosity, stronger on this occasion even than terror; their courage too was reinforced by a feeling of shame, which forbade them to abandon their sovereign in the hour of peril. The council-chamber was illuminated with an immense number of torches. The ancient figured tapestry had been replaced by a black drapery suspended on the walls, along which were ranged, in regular order, and according to the custom of those days, German, Danish, and Muscovite banners, trophies of the victories won by the soldiers of Gustavus Adolphus. In the middle were distinguished the banners of Sweden, covered with black crape. A numerous assemblage was seated on the benches of the hall. The four orders of the state—the nobility, the clergy, the citizens, and the peasants,—were ranged according to the respective disposition assigned to each. All were clothed in black; and the multitude of human faces, that shone like so many luminous rays upon a dark ground, dazzled the sight to such a degree that, of the four individuals who witnessed this extraordinary scene, not one could discern amidst the crowd a countenance with which he was familiar; the position of the four spectators might have been compared to that of actors, who, in presence of a numerous audience, were incapable of distinguishing a single face among the confused mass. On the elevated throne whence the monarch habitually harangued the assembly of the States, was seated a bleeding corpse, invested with the emblems of royalty. On the right of this apparition stood a child, a crown upon his head and the sceptre in his hand; on the left an aged man, or rather another phantom, leaned upon the throne, opposite to which were several personages of austere and solemn demeanour, clothed in long black robes, and seated before a table covered with thick folios and parchments; from the gravity of their deportment the latter seemed to be judges. Between the throne and the portion of the council-chamber above which it was elevated, were placed an axe and a block covered with black crape. In this unearthly assembly none seemed at all conscious of the presence of Charles, or of the three individuals by whom he was accompanied. At last the oldest of the judges in black robes—he who appeared to discharge the functions of president—rising with dignity, struck three times with his hand upon an open folio. Profound silence immediately succeeded; some youths of distinguished appearance, richly dressed, and with their hands fettered behind their backs, were led into the council-chamber by a door opposite to that which Charles had opened. Behind them a man of vigrous mould held the extremity of the cord with which their hands were pinioned. The prisoner who marched in the foremost rank, and whose air was more imposing than that of the others, stopped in the midst of the council-chamber before the block which he seemed to contemplate with haughty disdain. At the same instant the corse seated on the throne was agitated by a convulsive tremor, and the purple tide flowed afresh from his wounds. The youthful prisoner knelt upon the ground, and laid his head upon the block; the fatal axe glittering in the air descended swiftly; a stream of blood forced its way even to the platform of the throne, and mingled with that of the royal corse; whilst the head of the victim, rebounding from the crimson pavement, rolled to the feet of Charles, and stained them with blood. Hitherto, astonishment had rendered the monarch dumb; but at this horrid spectacle his tongue was unloosed. He advanced a few steps towards the platform, and addressing himself to the apparition on the left of the corse, boldly pronounced the customary abjuration, "If thou art of God, speak; if of the Evil One, depart in peace." The phantom replied in slow and emphatic accents, "Charles, not under thy reign shall this blood be shed [here the voice became indistinct]; five monarchs succeeding thee shall first sit on the throne of Sweden. Woe, woe, woe to the blood of Wasa!" Upon this the numerous figures composing this extraordinary assemblage became less distinct, till at last they resembled a mass of coloured shadows, soon after which they disappeared altogether. The fantastic torches were extinguished of themselves, and those of Charles and his suite cast their dim, flickering light upon the old-fashioned tapestry with which the chamber was usually hung, and which was now slightly moved by the wind. During some minutes longer a strange sort of melody was heard, a harmony compared by one of the eye-witnesses of this unparalleled scene to the murmur of the breeze agitating the foliage, and by another to the sound emitted by the breaking of a harp-string. All agreed upon one point, the duration of the apparition, which they stated to have lasted about ten minutes. The black drapery, the decapitated victim, the stream of blood which had inundated the platform, all had disappeared with the phantoms; every trace had vanished except a crimson spot, which still stained the slipper of Charles, and which alone would have sufficed to remind him of the horrid vision, had it been possible for any effort to erase it from his memory. Returning to his private cabinet, the king committed to paper an exact relation of what he had seen, signed it, and ordered his companions to do the same. Spite of the precautions taken to conceal the contents of this statement from the public, they soon transpired, and were generally known, even during the lifetime of Charles XI. The original document is still in existence, and its authenticity has never been questioned; it concludes with the following remarkable words:—"If," says the king, "all that I have just declared is not the exact truth, I renounce my hopes of a happier existence which I may have merited by some good actions, and by my zeal for the welfare of my people and for the maintenance of the religion of my fathers." If the reader will call to mind the death of Gustavus III., and the trial of his assassin, Ankarstroem, he will observe the intimate connection between these events and the circumstances of the extraordinary prediction which we have just detailed. The apparition of the young man beheaded in the presence of the assembled States prognosticated the execution of Ankarstroem. The crowned corse represented Gustavus III., the child, his son and successor, Gustavus Adolphus IV.; and lastly, by the old man was designated the uncle of Gustavus IV., the Duke of Sudermania, regent of the kingdom and afterwards king, upon the deposition of his nephew.

XLIII
BEN JONSON'S PREVISION

Drummond's "Conversations"

Ben Jonson told Drummond of Hawthornden that "when the king came to England, about the time that plague was in London, he being in the country, at Sir Robert Cotton's house with old Cambden, he saw in a vision his eldest son, then a young child and at London, appear unto him with the mark of a bloody cross on his forehead, as if it had been cut with a sword, at which amazed he prayed unto God, and in the morning he came unto Mr Cambden's chamber to tell him, who persuaded him it was but an apprehension, at which he should not be dejected. In the meantime there came letters from his wife of the death of that boy in the plague. He appeared to him, he said, of a manly shape, and of that growth he thinks he shall be at the resurrection."

XLIV
QUEEN ULRICA AND THE COUNTESS STEENBOCK

"Court Records"

When Queen Ulrica was dead, her corpse was placed in the usual way in an open coffin, in a room hung with black and lighted with numerous wax candles; a company of the king's guards did duty in the ante-room. One afternoon, the carriage of the Countess Steenbock, first lady of the palace, and a particular favourite of the queen's, drove up from Stockholm. The officers commanding the guard of honour went to meet the countess, and conducted her from the carriage to the door of the room where the dead queen lay, which she closed after her.

The long stay of the lady in the death-chamber caused some uneasiness; but it was ascribed to the vehemence of her grief; and the officers on duty, fearful of disturbing the further effusion of it by their presence, left her alone with the corpse. At length, finding that she did not return, they began to apprehend that some accident had befallen her, and the captain of the guard opened the door. He instantly started back, with a face of the utmost dismay. The other officers ran up, and plainly perceived, through the half-open door, the deceased queen standing upright in her coffin, and ardently embracing the countess. The apparition seemed to move, and soon after became enveloped in a dense smoke or vapour. When this had cleared away, the body of the queen lay in the same position as before, but the countess was nowhere to be found. In vain did they search that and the adjoining apartments, while some of the party hastened to the door, thinking she must have passed unobserved to her carriage; but neither carriage, horses, driver, or footmen were to be seen. A messenger was quickly despatched with a statement of this extraordinary circumstance to Stockholm, and there he learnt that the Countess Steenbock had never quitted the capital, and that she died at the very moment when she was seen in the arms of the deceased queen.

XLV
DENIS MISANGER

"The Phantom World"

On Friday, the first day of May 1705, about five o'clock in the evening, Denis Misanger de la Richardiere, eighteen years of age, was attacked with an extraordinary malady, which began by a sort of lethargy. They gave him every assistance that medicine and surgery could afford. He fell afterwards into a kind of furor or convulsion, and they were obliged to hold him, and have five or six persons to keep watch over him, for fear that he should throw himself out of the windows, or break his head against the wall. The emetic which they gave him made him throw up a quantity of bile, and for four or five days he remained pretty quiet.

At the end of the month of May, they sent him into the country, to take the air; and some other circumstances occurred, so unusual, that they judged he must be bewitched. And what confirmed this conjecture was, that he never had any fever, and retained all his strength, notwithstanding all the pains and violent remedies which he had been made to take. They asked him if he had not had some dispute with a shepherd or some other person suspected of sorcery, or malpractices.

He declared that on the 18th of April preceding, when he was going through the village of Noysi on horseback for a ride, his horse stopped short in the midst of the *Rue Feret*, opposite the chapel, and he could not make him go forward, though he touched him several times with the spur. There was a shepherd standing leaning against the chapel, with his crook in his hand, and two black dogs at his side. This man said to him, "Sir, I advise you to return home, for your horse will not go forward." The young La Richardiere, continuing to spur his horse, said to the shepherd, "I do not understand what you say." The shepherd replied, in a low tone, "I will make you understand." In effect, the young man was obliged to get down from his horse, and lead it back by the bridle to his father's dwelling in the same village. Then the shepherd cast a spell upon him, which was to take effect on the 1st of May, as was afterwards known.

During this malady, they caused several masses to be said in different places, especially at St Maur des Fosses, at St Amable, and at St Esprit.

Young La Richardiere was present at some of these masses which were said at St Maur; but he declared that he should not be cured till Friday, 26th June, on his return from St Maur. On entering his chamber, the key of which he had in his pocket, he found there that shepherd, seated in his armchair, with his crook, and his two black dogs. He was the only person who saw him; none other in the house could perceive him. He said even that this man was called Damis, although he did not remember that anyone had before this revealed his name to him. He beheld him all that day, and all the succeeding night. Towards six o'clock in the evening, as he felt his usual sufferings, he fell on the ground, exclaiming that the shepherd was upon him, and crushing him; at the same time he drew his knife, and aimed five blows at the shepherd's face, of which he retained the marks. The invalid told those who were watching over him that he was going to be very faint at five different times, and begged of them to help him, and move him violently. The thing happened as he had predicted.

On Friday, the 26th June, M. de la Richardiere, having gone to the mass at St Maur, asserted that he should be cured on that day. After mass, the priest put the stole upon his head, and recited the Gospel of St John, during which prayer the young man saw St Maur standing, and the unhappy shepherd at his left, with his face bleeding from the five knife-wounds which he had given him. At that moment the youth cried out, unintentionally, "A miracle! a miracle!" and asserted that he was cured, as in fact he was.

On the 29th of June, the same M. de la Richardiere returned to Noysi, and amused himself with shooting. As he was shooting in the vineyards, the shepherd presented himself before him; he hit him on the head with the butt-end of his gun. The shepherd cried out, "Sir, you are killing me!" and fled. The next day this man presented himself again before him, and asked his pardon, saying, "I am called Damis; it was I who cast a spell over you which was to have lasted a year. By the aid of masses and prayers which have been said for you, you have been cured at the end of eight weeks. But the charm has fallen back upon myself, and I can be cured of it only by a miracle. I implore you then to pray for me."

During all these reports, the *maréchaussée* had set off in pursuit of the shepherd; but he escaped them, having killed his two dogs and thrown away his crook. On Sunday, the 13th of September, he came to M. de la Richardiere, and related to him his adventure; that after having passed twenty years without approaching the sacraments, God had given him grace to confess himself at Troyes; and that after divers delays he had been admitted to the holy communion. Eight days after, M. de la Richardiere received a letter from a woman who said she was a relation of the shepherd's, informing him of his death, and begging him to cause a requiem mass to be said for him, which was done.

XLVI
THE PIED PIPER

"The Phantom World"

The following instance is so extraordinary, that I should not repeat it if the account were not attested by more than one writer, and also preserved in the public monuments of a considerable town of Upper Saxony; this town is Hamelin in the principality of Kalenberg, at the confluence of the rivers Hamel and Weser.

In the year 1384, this town was infested by such a prodigious multitude of rats, that they ravaged all the corn which was laid up in the granaries; everything was employed that art and experience could invent to chase them away, and whatever is usually employed against this kind of animals. At that time there came to the town an unknown person, of taller stature than ordinary, dressed in a robe of divers colours, who engaged to deliver them from that scourge, for a certain recompense which was agreed upon.

Then he drew from his sleeve a flute, at the sound of which all the rats came out of their holes and followed him; he led them straight to the river, into which they ran and were drowned. On his return he asked for the promised reward, which was refused him, apparently on account of the facility with which he had exterminated the rats. The next day, which was a fête day, he chose the moment when the older inhabitants were at church, and by means of another flute which he began to play, all the boys in the town above the age of fourteen, to the number of a hundred and thirty, assembled round him; he led them to the neighbouring mountain, named Kopfelberg, under which is a sewer for the town, and where criminals are executed; these boys disappeared and were never seen afterwards.

A young girl, who had followed at a distance, was witness of the matter, and brought the news of it to the town.

XLVII
JEANNE D'ARC

Ferrier's "Apparitions"

Upon her trial, as it is repeated by Chartier, she spoke with the utmost simplicity and firmness of her visions: "Que souvent alloit a une belle fontaine au pays de Lorraine, laquelle elle nommoit bonne fontaine aux Feés Nostre Seigneur, at en icelluy lieu tous ceulx de pays quand ils avoient fiebvre ils alloient pour recouvrer garison; et la alloit souvent ladite Jehanne la Pucelle sous un grand arbre qui la fontaine ombroit; et s'apparurent a elle Ste Katerine et Ste Marguerite qui lui dirent qu'elle allast a ung Cappitaine qu'elles lui nommerent, laquelle y alla sans prendre congé ni a pere ni a mere; lequel Cappitaine la vestit en guise d'homme et l'armoit et lui ceint l'epeé, et luy bailla un escuyer et quatre varlets; et en ce point fut monteé sur un bon cheval; et en ce point vint aut Roy de France, et lui dit que du Commandement de lui estoit venue a lui, et qu'elle le feroit le plus grand Seigneur du Monde, et qu'il fut ordonné que tretou ceulx qui lui desobeiroient fussent occis sans mercy, et que St Michel et plusieurs anges lui avoient baillé une Couronne moult riche pour lui."

XLVIII
ANNE WALKER

Local Records

In the year 1680, at Lumley, a hamlet near Chester-le-Street in the county of Durham, there lived one Walker, a man well to do in the world, and a widower. A young relation of his, whose name was Anne Walker, kept his house, to the great scandal of the neighbourhood, and that with but too good cause. A few weeks before this young woman expected to become a mother, Walker placed her with her aunt, one Dame Clare, in Chester-le-Street, and promised to take care both of her and her future child. One evening in the end of November, this man, in company with Mark Sharp, an acquaintance of his, came to Dame Clare's door, and told her that they had made arrangements for removing her niece to a place where she could remain in safety till her confinement was over. They would not say where it was; but as Walker bore, in most respects, an excellent character, she was allowed to go with him; and he professed to have sent her off with Sharp into Lancashire. Fourteen days after, one Graeme, a fuller, who lived about six miles from Lumley, had been engaged till past midnight in his mill; and on going downstairs to go home, in the middle of the ground floor he saw a woman, with dishevelled hair, covered with blood, and having five large wounds on her head. Graeme, on recovering a little from his first terror, demanded what the spectre wanted. "I," said the apparition, "am the spirit of Anne Walker"; and proceeded accordingly to tell Graeme the particulars which I have already related to you. "When I was sent away with Mark Sharp, he slew me on such a moor," naming one that Graeme knew, "with a collier's pick, threw my body into a coal-pit, and hid the pick under the bank; and his shoes and stockings, which were covered with blood, he left in a stream." The apparition proceeded to tell Graeme that he must give information of this to the nearest justice of peace, and that till this was done, he must look to be continually haunted. Graeme went home very sad; he dared not bring such a charge against a man of so unimpeachable a character as Walker; and yet he as little dared to incur the anger of the spirit that had appeared to him. So, as all weak minds will do, he went on procrastinating;

only he took care to leave his mill early, and while in it never to be alone. Notwithstanding this caution on his part, one night, just as it began to be dark, the apparition met him again in a more terrible shape, and with every circumstance of indignation. Yet he did not even then fulfil its injunction; till on St Thomas's eve, as he was walking in his garden just after sunset, it threatened him so effectually that in the morning he went to a magistrate and revealed the whole thing. The place was examined; the body and the pickaxe found; and a warrant was granted against Walker and Sharp. They were, however, admitted to bail; but in August, 1681, their trial came on before Judge Davenport at Durham. Meanwhile the whole circumstances were known over all the north of England, and the greatest interest was excited by the case. Against Sharp the fact was strong, that his shoes and stockings, covered with blood, were found in the place where the murder had been committed; but against Walker, except the account received from the ghost, there seemed not a shadow of evidence. Nevertheless the judge summed up strongly against the prisoners, the jury found them guilty, and the judge pronounced sentence upon them that night, a thing which was unknown in Durham, either before or after. The prisoners were executed, and both died professing their innocence to the last. Judge Davenport was much agitated during the trial; and it was believed, says the historian, that the spirit had also appeared to him, as if to supply in his mind the want of legal evidence. This case is certainly a solemn illustration of the mal-administration of justice in an ancient court; yet the circumstantial evidence, arising from the appearance of the spirit, appears very strong—the finding of the body, and the boots and stockings. Yet we need perhaps to live more immediately within the circle of the circumstance to pronounce upon it. None of us, however, reading this book, would like to take upon ourselves the responsibility of those daring jurymen, who durst venture to throw away life upon evidence which, strong as it appears to have been, did not come to them, but only to one who had borne witness to them.

XLIX
THE HAND OF GLORY

Henderson's "Folk Lore"

One evening, between the years 1790 and 1800, a traveller, dressed in woman's clothes, arrived at the Old Spital Inn, the place where the mail coach changed horses, in High Spital, on Bowes Moor. The traveller begged to stay all night, but had to go away so early in the morning that if a mouthful of food were set ready for breakfast there was no need the family should be disturbed by her departure. The people of the house, however, arranged that a servant maid should sit up till the stranger was out of the premises, and then went to bed themselves. The girl lay down for a nap on the longsettle by the fire, but before she shut her eyes she took a good look at the traveller, who was sitting on the opposite side of the hearth, and espied a pair of man's trousers peeping out from under the gown. All inclination for sleep was now gone; however, with great self-command, she feigned it, closed her eyes, and even began to snore. On this the traveller got up, pulled out of his pocket a dead man's hand, fitted a candle to it, lighted the candle, and passed hand and candle several times before the servant girl's face, saying as he did so: "Let those who are asleep be asleep, and let those who are awake be awake." This done, he placed the light on the table, opened the outer door, went down two or three of the steps which led from the house to the road, and began to whistle for his companions. The girl (who had hitherto had presence of mind enough to remain perfectly quiet) now jumped up, rushed behind the ruffian, and pushed him down the steps. She then shut the door, locked it, and ran upstairs to try and wake the family, but without success: calling, shouting, and shaking were alike in vain. The poor girl was in despair, for she heard the traveller and his comrades outside the house. So she ran down again, seized a bowl of blue (*i.e.* skimmed milk), and threw it over the hand and candle; after which she went upstairs again, and awoke the sleepers without any difficulty. The landlord's son went to the window, and asked the men outside what they wanted. They answered that if the dead man's hand were but given them, they would go away quietly, and do no harm to anyone. This he refused, and fired among them, and the shot must have taken effect, for in the morning stains of blood were traced to a considerable distance.

These circumstances were related to my informant, Mr Charles Wastell, in the spring of 1861, by an old woman named Bella Parkin, who resided close to High Spital, and was actually the daughter of the courageous servant-girl.

It is interesting to compare them with the following narrations, communicated to me by the Rev. S. Baring Gould:—"Two magicians having come to lodge in a public-house with a view to robbing it, asked permission to pass the night by the fire, and obtained it. When the house was quiet, the servant-girl, suspecting mischief, crept downstairs and looked through the keyhole. She saw the men open a sack, and take out a dry, withered hand. They anointed the fingers with some unguent, and lighted them. Each finger flamed, but the thumb they could not light; that was because one of the household was not asleep. The girl hastened to her master, but found it impossible to arouse him. She tried every other sleeper, but could not break the charmed sleep. At last, stealing down into the kitchen, while the thieves were busy over her master's strong box, she secured the hand, blew out the flames, and at once the whole household was aroused."[14]

But the next story bears a closer resemblance to the Stainmore narrative. One dark night, when all was shut up, there came a tap at the door of a lone inn in the middle of a barren moor. The door was opened, and there stood without, shivering and shaking, a poor beggar, his rags soaked with rain, and his hands white with cold. He asked piteously for a lodging, and it was cheerfully granted him; there was not a spare bed in the house, but he could lie on the mat before the kitchen fire, and welcome.

So this was settled, and everyone in the house went to bed except the cook, who from the back kitchen could see into the large room through a pane of glass let into the door. She watched the beggar, and saw him, as soon as he was left alone, draw himself up from the floor, seat himself at the table, extract from his pocket a brown withered human hand, and set it upright in the candlestick. He then anointed the fingers, and applying a match to them, they began to flame. Filled with horror, the cook rushed up the back stairs, and endeavoured to arouse her master and the men of the house. But all was in vain—they slept a charmed sleep; so in despair she hastened down again, and placed herself at her post of observation.

She saw the fingers of the hand flaming, but the thumb remained unlighted, because one inmate of the house was awake. The beggar was busy collecting the valuables around him into a large sack, and having taken all he cared for in the large room, he entered another. On this the

The Haunters & The Haunted | 263

woman ran in, and, seizing the light, tried to extinguish the flames. But this was not so easy. She blew at them, but they burnt on as before. She poured the dregs of a beer-jug over them, but they blazed up the brighter. As a last resource, she caught up a jug of milk, and dashed it over the four lambent flames, and they died out at once. Uttering a loud cry, she rushed to the door of the apartment the beggar had entered, and locked it. The whole family was aroused, and the thief easily secured and hanged. This tale is told in Northumberland.

FOOTNOTES

[14] Delrio. See also Thorpe's *Mythology*, vol. iii. p. 274.

L
THE BLOODY FOOTSTEP

Local Records

On the threshold of one of the doors of Smithills Hall there is a bloody footstep impressed into the door-step, and ruddy as if the bloody foot had just trodden there; and it is averred that, on a certain night of the year, and at a certain hour of the night, if you go and look at the door-step you will see the mark wet with fresh blood. Some have pretended to say that this appearance of blood was but dew; but can dew redden a cambric handkerchief? Will it crimson the finger-tips when you touch it? And that is what the bloody footstep will surely do when the appointed night and hour come round....

It is needless to tell you all the strange stories that have survived to this day about the old Hall, and how it is believed that the master of it, owing to his ancient science, has still a sort of residence there and control of the place, and how in one of the chambers there is still his antique table, and his chair, and some rude old instruments and machinery, and a book, and everything in readiness, just as if he might still come back to finish some experiment.... One of the chief things to which the old lord applied himself was to discover the means of prolonging his own life, so that its duration should be indefinite, if not infinite; and such was his science that he was believed to have attained this magnificent and awful purpose....

The object of the Lord of Smithills Hall was to take a life from the course of Nature, and Nature did not choose to be defrauded; so that, great as was the power of this scientific man over her, she would not consent that he should escape the necessity of dying at his proper time, except upon condition of sacrificing some other life for his; and this was to be done once for every thirty years that he chose to live, thirty years being the account of a generation of man; and if in any way, in that time, this lord could be the death of a human being, that satisfied the requisition, and he might live on....

There was but one human being whom he cared for—that was a beautiful kinswoman, an orphan, whom his father had brought up, and dying, left to his care.... He saw that she, if anyone, was to be the person whom the sacrifice demanded, and that he might kill twenty others without effect, but if he took the life of this one it would make the charm strong and good.... He did slay this pure young girl; he took her into the wood near the house, an old wood that is standing yet, with some of its magnificent oaks, and there he plunged a dagger into her heart....

He buried her in the wood, and returned to the house; and, as it happened, he had set his right foot in her blood, and his shoe was wet in it, and by some miraculous fate it left a track all along the wood-path, and into the house, and on the stone steps of the threshold, and up into his chamber. The servants saw it the next day, and wondered, and whispered, and missed the fair young girl, and looked askance at their lord's right foot, and turned pale, all of them....

Next, the legend says, that Sir Forrester was struck with horror at what he had done ... and fled from his old Hall, and was gone full many a day. But all the while he was gone there was the mark of a bloody footstep impressed upon the stone door-step of the Hall.... The legend says that wherever Sir Forrester went, in his wanderings about the world, he left a bloody track behind him.... Once he went to the King's Court, and, there being a track up to the very throne, the King frowned upon him, so that he never came there any more. Nobody could tell how it happened; his foot was not seen to bleed, only there was the bloody track behind him....

At last this unfortunate lord deemed it best to go back to his own Hall, where, living among faithful old servants born in the family, he could hush the matter up better than elsewhere.... So home he came, and there he saw the bloody track on the door-step, and dolefully went into the Hall, and up the stairs, an old servant ushering him into his chamber, and half a dozen others following him behind, gazing, shuddering, pointing with quivering fingers, looking horror-stricken in one another's pale faces....

By and by he vanished from the old Hall, but not by death; for, from generation to generation, they say that a bloody track is seen around that house, and sometimes it is traced up into the chambers, so fresh that you see he must have passed a short time before.

This is the legend of the Bloody Footstep, which I myself have seen at the Hall door.

LI
THE GHOSTLY WARRIORS OF WORMS

"The Phantom World"

The abbot of Ursperg, in his Chronicle, year 1123, says that in the territory of Worms they saw during many days a multitude of armed men, on foot and on horseback, going and coming with great noise, like people who are going to a solemn assembly. Every day they marched, towards the hour of noon, to a mountain, which appeared to be their place of rendezvous. Someone in the neighbourhood, bolder than the rest, having guarded himself with the sign of the cross, approached one of these armed men, conjuring him in the name of God, to declare the meaning of this army, and their design. The soldier or phantom replied, "We are not what you imagine; we are neither vain phantoms nor true soldiers, we are the spirits of those who were killed on this spot a long time ago. The arms and horses which you behold are the instruments of our punishment, as they were of our sins. We are all on fire, though you can see nothing about us which appears inflamed." It is said that they remarked in this company the Count Emico, who had been killed a few years before, and who declared that he might be extricated from that state by alms and prayers.

LII
THE WANDERING JEW IN ENGLAND

"Notes and Queries"

When on the weary way to Golgotha, Christ fainting, and overcome under the burden of the cross, asked Salathiel, as he was standing at his door, for a cup of water to cool His parched throat, he spurned the supplication, and bade Him on the faster.

"I go," said the Saviour, "but thou shalt thirst and tarry till I come."

And ever since then, by day and night, through the long centuries he has been doomed to wander about the earth, ever craving for water, and ever expecting the day of judgment which shall end his toils:

> "Mais toujours le soleil se lève,
> Toujours, toujours
> Tourne la terre où moi je cours,
> Toujours, toujours, toujours, toujours!"

Sometimes, during the cold winter nights, the lonely cottager will be awoke by a plaintive demand for "Water, good Christian! water for the love of God!" And if he looks out into the moonlight, he will see a venerable old man in antique raiment, with grey flowing beard, and a tall staff, who beseeches his charity with the most earnest gesture. Woe to the churl who refuses him water or shelter. My old nurse, who was a Warwickshire woman, and, as Sir Walter said of his grandmother, "a most *awfu' le'er,*" knew a man who boldly cried out, "All very fine, Mr Ferguson, but you can't lodge here." And it was decidedly the worst thing he ever did in his life, for his best mare fell dead lame, and corn went down, I am afraid to say how much per quarter. If, on the contrary, you treat him well, and refrain from indelicate inquiries respecting his age—on which point he is very touchy—his visit is sure to bring good luck. Perhaps years afterwards, when you are on your death-bed, he may happen to be passing; and if he *should,* you are safe; for three knocks with his staff will make you hale, and he never forgets any kindnesses. Many stories are current of his wonderful cures; but there is one to be found in Peck's *History of Stamford* which possesses the rare merit of being written by the patient himself. Upon Whitsunday, in the year of our Lord 1658, "about six of the clock, just after evensong," one Samuel Wallis, of Stamford, who had been long wasted with a lingering consumption, was sitting by the fire, reading in that delectable book called *Abraham's Suit for Sodom.* He heard a knock at the door; and, as his nurse was absent, he crawled to open it himself. What he saw there, Samuel shall say in his own style:—"I beheld a proper, tall, grave old man. Thus he said: 'Friend, I pray thee, give an old pilgrim a cup of small beere!' And I said, 'Sir, I pray you, come in and welcome.' And he said, 'I am no Sir, therefore call me not Sir; but come in I must, for I cannot pass by thy doore.'"

After finishing the beer: "Friend," he said, "thou art not well." "I said, 'No, truly Sir, I have not been well this many yeares.' He said, 'What is thy disease?' I said, 'A deep consumption, Sir; our doctors say, past cure: for, truly, I am a very poor man, and not able to follow doctors' councell.' 'Then,' said he, 'I will tell thee what thou shalt do; and, by the help and power of Almighty God above, thou shalt be well. To-morrow, when thou risest up, go into thy garden, and get there two leaves of red sage, and one of bloodworte, and put them into a cup of thy small beere. Drink as often as need require, and when the cup is empty fill it again, and put in fresh leaves every fourth day, and thou shalt see, through our Lord's great goodness and mercy, before twelve dayes shall be past, thy disease shall be cured and thy body altered.'"

After this simple prescription, Wallis pressed him to eat: "But he said, 'No, friend, I will not eat; the Lord Jesus is sufficient for me. Very seldom doe I drinke any beere neither, but that which comes from the rocke. So, friend, the Lord God be with thee.'"

So saying, he departed, and was never more heard of; but the patient got well within the given time, and for many a long day there was war hot and fierce among the divines of Stamford, as to whether the stranger was an angel or a devil. His dress has been minutely described by honest Sam. His coat was purple, and buttoned down to the waist; "his britches of the same couler, all new to see to"; his stockings were very white, but whether linen or jersey, deponent knoweth not; his beard and head were white, and he had a white stick in his hand. The day was rainy from morning to night, "but he had not one spot of dirt upon his cloathes."

Aubrey gives an almost exactly similar relation, the scene of which he places in the Staffordshire Moorlands. The Jew there appears in a "purple shag gown," and prescribes balm-leaves.

LIII
BENDITH EU MAMMAU[15]

By Edmund Jones

They appeared diverse ways, but their most frequent way of appearing was like dancing-companies with musick, or in the form of funerals. When they appeared like dancing-companies, they were desirous to entice persons into their company, and some were drawn among them and remained among them some time, usually a whole year; as did Edmund William Rees, a man whom I well knew, and was a neighbour, who came back at the year's end, and looked very bad. But either they were not able to give much account of themselves, or they durst not give it, only said they had been dancing, and that the time was short. But there were some others who went with them at night, and returned sometimes at night, and sometimes the next morning; especially those persons who took upon them to cure the hurts received from the fairies, as Charles Hugh of Coed yr Pame, in Langybi parish, and Rissiart Cap Dee, of Aberystruth; for the former of these must certainly converse with them, for how else could he declare the words which his visitors had spoken a day or days before they came to him, to their great surprise and wonder?

And as for Rissiart Cap Dee, so called because he wore a black cap, it is said of him that when he lodged in some houses to cure those who were hurt by the fairies, he would suddenly rise up in the night, and make a very hasty preparation to go downstairs; which when one person observ'd, he said, "Go softly, Uncle Richard, least you fall": he made answer, "O, here are some to receive me." But when he was called to one person, who had inadvertently fallen among the fairies, and had been greatly hurt by them, and kept his bed upon it, whose relations had sent for the said Rissiart Cap Dee to cure him; who, when he came up to the sick man's chamber, the sick man took up a pound-weight stone, which was by the bed-side, and threw it at the infernal charmer with all his might, saying, "Thou old villain, wast one of the worst of them to hurt me!" for he had seen him among them acting his part against him; upon which the old charmer went away muttering some words of malevolence against him. He lived at the foot of Rhyw Coelbren, and there was a large hole in the side of the thatch of his house, thro' which the people believed he went out at night to the fairies, and came in from them at night; but he pretended it was that he might see the stars at night. The house is down long ago. He lived by himself, as did the before-mentioned Charles Hugh, who was very famous in the county for his cures, and knowledge of things at a distance; which he could not possibly know without conversing with evil spirits, who walked the earth to and fro. He is yet said to be an affable, friendly man, and cheerful; 'tis then a pity he should be in alliance with hell, and an agent in the kingdom of darkness.

I will only give one instance of his knowledge of things at a distance, and of secret things. Henry John Thomas, of the parish of Aberystruth, a relation of mine, an honest man, went with the water of a young woman whom he courted, and was sick, to the said Charles Hugh, who, as soon as he saw Henry John, pleasantly told him, "Ho! you come with your sweetheart's water to me." And he told him the very words which they had spoken together in a secret place, and described the place where they spoke. It was the general opinion in times past, when these things were very frequent, that the fairies knew whatever was spoken in the air without the houses, not so much what was spoken in the houses. I suppose they chiefly knew what was spoken in the air at night. It was also said they rather appeared to an uneven number of persons, to one, three, five, &c.; and oftener to men than to women. Thomas William Edmund, of Havodavel, an honest, pious man, who often saw them, declared that they appeared with one bigger than the rest, going before them in the company.

But they very often appeared in the form of a funeral before the death of many persons, with a bier and a black cloth, in the midst of a company about it, on every side, before and after it. The instances of this were so numerous, that it is plain, and past all dispute, that they infallibly foreknew the time of men's death: the difficulty is, whence they had this knowledge. It cannot be supposed that either God Himself, or His angels, discovered this to these spirits of darkness. For *the secrets of the Lord are with those that fear Him*, not with His enemies. Psalm xxv. 14. They must therefore have this knowledge from the position of the stars at the time of birth, and their influence, which they perfectly understand beyond what mortal men can do. We have a constant proof of this in the corps candles, whose appearance is an infallible sign that death will follow, and they never fail going the way that the corps will go to be buried, be the way ever so unlikely that it should go through. But to give some instances in Aberystruth Parish.

FOOTNOTES

[15] *A Geographical, Historical, and Religious Account of the Parish of Aberystruth, in the County of Monmouth. To which are added, Memoirs of several persons of Note, who lived in the said Parish.* By Edmund Jones. Trevecka: printed in the Year 1779.

LIV
THE RED BOOK OF APPIN

Campbell's "Tales of the West Highlands"

Once upon a time, there lived a man at Appin, Argyllshire, and he took to his house an orphan boy. When the boy was grown up, he was sent to herd; and upon a day of days, and him herding, there came a fine gentleman where he was, who asked him to become his servant, and that he would give him plenty to eat and drink, clothes, and great wages. The boy told him that he would like very much to get a good suit of clothes, but that he would not engage till he would see his master; but the fine gentleman would have him engaged without any delay; this the boy would not do upon any terms till he would see his master. "Well," says the gentleman, "in the meantime write your name in this book." Saying this, he puts his hand into his oxter pocket, and pulling out a large red book, he told the boy to write his name in the book. This the boy would not do; neither would he tell his name, till he would acquaint his master first. "Now," says the gentleman, "since you will neither engage, or tell your name, till you see your present master, be sure to meet me about sunset to-morrow, at a certain place?" The boy promised that he would be sure to meet him at the place about sunsetting. When the boy came home he told his master what the gentleman said to him. "Poor boy," says he, "a fine master he would make; lucky for you that you neither engaged nor wrote your name in his book; but since you promised to meet him, you must go; but as you value your life, do as I tell you." His master gave him a sword, and at the same time he told him to be sure to be at the place mentioned a while before sunset, and to draw a circle round himself with the point of the sword in the name of Trinity. "When you do this, draw a cross in the centre of the circle, upon which you will stand yourself; and do not move out of that position till the rising of the sun next morning." He also told him that he would wish him to come out of the circle to put his name in the book; but that upon no account he was to leave the circle; "but ask the book till you would write your name yourself, and when once you get hold of the book keep it, he cannot touch a hair of your head, if you keep inside the circle."

So the boy was at the place long before the gentleman made his appearance; but sure enough he came after sunset; he tried all his arts to get the boy outside the circle, to sign his name in the red book, but the boy would not move one foot out from where he stood; but, at the long last, he handed the book to the boy, so as to write his name therein. The book was no sooner inside the circle than it fell out of the gentleman's hand inside the circle; the boy cautiously stretched out his hand for the book, and as soon as he got hold of it, he put it in his oxter. When the fine gentleman saw that he did not mean to give him back the book, he got furious; and at last he transformed himself into great many likenesses, blowing fire and brimstone out of his mouth and nostrils; at times he would appear as a horse, other times a huge cat, and a fearful beast (uille bbeast); he was going round the circle the length of the night; when day was beginning to break he let out one fearful screech; he put himself in the shape of a large raven, and he was soon out of the boy's sight. The boy still remained where he was till he saw the sun in the morning, which no sooner he observed, than he took to his soles home as fast as he could. He gave the book to his master; and this is how the far-famed red book of Appin was got.

LV
THE GOOD O'DONOGHUE

Irish Folk Tales

In an age so distant that the precise period is unknown, a chieftain named O'Donoghue ruled over the country which surrounds the romantic Lough Lean, now called the Lake of Killarney. Wisdom, beneficence, and justice distinguished his reign, and the prosperity and happiness of his subjects were their natural results. He is said to have been as renowned for his warlike exploits as for his pacific virtues; and as a proof that his domestic administration was not the less rigorous because it was mild, a rocky island is pointed out to strangers, called "O'Donoghue's Prison," in which this prince once confined his own son for some act of disorder and disobedience.

His end—for it cannot correctly be called his death—was singular and mysterious. At one of those splendid feasts for which his court was celebrated, surrounded by the most distinguished of his subjects, he was engaged in a prophetic relation of the events which were to happen in ages yet to come. His auditors listened, now rapt in wonder, now fired with indignation, burning with shame, or melted into sorrow, as he faithfully detailed the heroism, the injuries, the crimes, and the miseries of their descendants. In the midst of his predictions he rose slowly from his seat, advanced with a solemn, measured, and majestic tread to the shore of the lake, and walked forward composedly upon its unyielding surface. When he had nearly reached the centre he paused for a moment, then, turning slowly round, looked toward his friends, and waving his arms to them with the cheerful air of one taking a short farewell, disappeared from their view.

The memory of the good O'Donoghue has been cherished by successive generations with affectionate reverence; and it is believed that at sunrise, on every May-day morning, the anniversary of his departure, he revisits his ancient domains: a favoured few only are in general permitted to see him, and this distinction is always an omen of good fortune to the beholders; when it is granted to many it is a sure token of an abundant harvest—a blessing, the want of which during this prince's reign was never felt by his people.

Some years have elapsed since the last appearance of O'Donoghue. The April of that year had been remarkably wild and stormy; but on May-morning the fury of the elements had altogether subsided. The air was hushed and still; and the sky, which was reflected in the serene lake, resembled a beautiful but deceitful countenance, whose smiles, after the most tempestuous emotions, tempt the stranger to believe that it belongs to a soul which no passion has ever ruffled.

The first beams of the rising sun were just gilding the lofty summit of Glenaa, when the waters near the eastern shore of the lake became suddenly and violently agitated, though all the rest of its surface lay smooth and still as a tomb of polished marble, the next morning a foaming wave darted forward, and, like a proud high-crested war-horse, exulting in his strength, rushed across the lake toward Toomies mountain. Behind this wave appeared a stately warrior fully armed, mounted upon a milk-white steed; his snowy plume waved gracefully from a helmet of polished steel, and at his back fluttered a light blue scarf. The horse, apparently exulting in his noble burden, sprung after the wave along the water, which bore him up like firm earth, while showers of spray that glittered brightly in the morning sun were dashed up at every bound.

The warrior was O'Donoghue; he was followed by numberless youths and maidens, who moved lightly and unconstrained over the watery plain, as the moonlight fairies glide through the fields of air; they were linked together by garlands of delicious spring flowers, and they timed their movements to strains of enchanting melody. When O'Donoghue had nearly reached the western side of the lake, he suddenly turned his steed, and directed his course along the wood-fringed shore of Glenaa, preceded by the huge wave that curled and foamed up as high as the horse's neck, whose fiery nostrils snorted above it. The long train of attendants followed with playful deviations the track of their leader, and moved on with unabated fleetness to their celestial music, till gradually, as they entered the narrow strait between Glenaa and Dinis, they became involved in the mists which still partially floated over the lake, and faded from the view of the wondering beholders: but the sound of their music still fell upon the ear, and echo, catching up the harmonious strains, fondly repeated and prolonged them in soft and softer tones, till the last faint repetition died away, and the hearers awoke as from a dream of bliss.

LVI
SARAH POLGRAIN

By William Hunt

A woman, who had lived in Ludgvan, was executed at Bodmin for the murder of her husband. There was but little doubt that she had been urged on to the diabolical deed by a horse-dealer, known as Yorkshire Jack, with whom, for a long period, she was generally supposed to have been criminally acquainted.

Now, it will be remembered that this really happened within the present century. One morning, during my residence in Penzance, an old woman from Ludgvan called on me with some trifling message. While she was waiting for my answer, I made some ordinary remark about the weather.

"It's all owing to Sarah Polgrain," said she.

"Sarah Polgrain," said I; "and who is Sarah Polgrain?"

Then the voluble old lady told me the whole story of the poisoning with which we need not, at present, concern ourselves. By and by the tale grew especially interesting, and there I resume it.

Sarah had begged that Yorkshire Jack might accompany her to the scaffold when she was led forth to execution. This was granted; and on the dreadful morning there stood this unholy pair, the fatal beam on which the woman's body was in a few minutes to swing, before them.

They kissed each other, and whispered words passed between them.

The executioner intimated that the moment of execution had arrived, and that they must part. Sarah Polgrain, looking earnestly into the man's eyes, said:

"You will?"

Yorkshire Jack replied, "I will!" and they separated. The man retired amongst the crowd, the woman was soon a dead corpse, pendulating in the wind.

Years passed on, Yorkshire Jack was never the same man as before, his whole bearing was altered. His bold, his dashing air deserted him.

He walked, or rather wandered, slowly about the streets of the town, or the lanes of the country. He constantly moved his head from side to side, looking first over one, and then over the other shoulder, as though dreading that someone was following him.

The stout man became thin, his ruddy cheeks more pale, and his eyes sunken.

At length he disappeared, and it was discovered—for Yorkshire Jack had made a confidant of some Ludgvan man—that he had pledged himself, "living or dead, to become the husband of Sarah Polgrain, after the lapse of years."

To escape, if possible, from himself, Jack had gone to sea in the merchant service.

Well, the period had arrived when this unholy promise was to be fulfilled. Yorkshire Jack was returning from the Mediterranean in a fruit-ship. He was met by the devil and Sarah Polgrain far out at sea, off the Land's End. Jack would not accompany them willingly, so they followed the ship for days, during all which time she was involved in a storm. Eventually Jack was washed from the deck by such a wave as the oldest sailor had never seen; and presently, amidst loud thunders and flashing lightnings, riding as it were in a black cloud, three figures were seen passing onward. These were the devil, Sarah Polgrain, and Yorkshire Jack; and this was the cause of the storm.

"It is all true, as you may learn if you will inquire," said the old woman; "for many of her kin live in Churchtown."

LVII
ELEANOR COBHAM, DUCHESS
OF GLOUCESTER

Godwin's "Lives of the Necromancers"

This was a period in which the ideas of witchcraft had caught fast hold of the minds of mankind; and those accusations, which by the enlightened part of the species would now be regarded as worthy only of contempt, were then considered as charges of the most flagitious nature. While John, Duke of Bedford, the eldest uncle of King Henry VI., was regent of France, Humphrey of Gloucester, next brother to Bedford, was Lord Protector of the realm of England. Though Henry was now nineteen years of age, yet as he was a prince of slender capacity, Humphrey still continued to discharge the functions of sovereignty. He was eminently endowed with popular qualities, and was a favourite with the majority of the nation. He had, however, many enemies, one of the chief of whom was Henry Beaufort, great-uncle to the king, and Cardinal of Winchester. One of the means employed by this prelate to undermine the power of Humphrey, consisted in a charge of witchcraft brought against Eleanor Cobham, his wife.

This woman had probably yielded to the delusions which artful persons, who saw into the weakness of her character, sought to practise upon her. She was the second wife of Humphrey, and he was suspected to have indulged in undue familiarity with her before he was a widower. His present duchess was reported to have had recourse to witchcraft in the first instance, by way of securing his wayward inclinations. The Duke of Bedford had died in 1435; and Humphrey now, in addition to the actual exercise of the powers of sovereignty, was next heir to the crown in case of the king's decease. This weak and licentious woman, being now Duchess of Gloucester, and wife to the Lord Protector, directed her ambition to the higher title and prerogatives of a queen, and, by way of feeding her evil passions, called to her counsels Margery Jourdain, commonly called the Witch of Eye, Roger Bolingbroke, an astrologer and supposed magician, Thomas Southwel, Canon of St Stephen's, and one John Hume, or Hun, a priest. These persons frequently met the duchess in secret cabal. They were accused of calling up spirits from the infernal world; and they made an image of wax, which they slowly consumed before a fire, expecting that, as the image gradually wasted away, so the constitution and life of the poor king would decay and finally perish.

Hume, or Hun, is supposed to have turned informer, and upon his information several of these persons were taken into custody. After previous examination, on the 25th of July 1441, Bolingbroke was placed upon a scaffold before the cross of St Paul's, with a chair curiously painted, which was supposed to be one of his implements of necromancy, and dressed in mystical attire, and there, before the Archbishop of Canterbury, the Cardinal of Winchester, and several other bishops, made abjuration of all his unlawful arts.

A short time after, the Duchess of Gloucester having fled to the sanctuary at Westminster, her case was referred to the same high persons, and Bolingbroke was brought forth to give evidence against her. She was of consequence committed to custody in the castle of Leeds, near Maidstone, to take her trial in the month of October. A commission was directed to the lord treasurer, several noblemen, and certain judges of both benches, to inquire into all manner of treasons, sorceries, and other things that might be hurtful to the king's person, and Bolingbroke and Southwel as principals, and the Duchess of Gloucester as accessory, were brought before them. Margery Jourdain was arraigned at the same time; and she, as a witch and relapsed heretic, was condemned to be burned in Smithfield. The Duchess of Gloucester was sentenced to do penance on three several days, walking through the streets of London, with a lighted taper in her hand, attended by the lord mayor, the sheriffs, and a select body of the livery, and then to be banished for life to the Isle of Man. Thomas Southwel died in prison; and Bolingbroke was hanged at Tyburn on the 18th of November.